NIGHT SHADE

THE ROSENHOLM TRILOGY
VOLUME 3

GRY KAPPEL JENSEN

NIGHT SHADE

THE ROSENHOLM TRILOGY
VOLUME 3

translated from the Danish
by Jennifer Alexander

Arctis

This is a work of fiction. Names, characters, places, and incidents are from the author's imagination or are used fictitiously.

This translation has been published with the financial support of The Danish Arts Foundation.

Danish Arts Foundation

W1-Media, Inc.
Arctis Books USA
Stamford, CT, USA

Copyright © 2025 by W1-Media Inc. for this edition
NATSKYGGE © Gry Kappel Jensen og Turbine, 2021
Published by agreement with Babel-Bridge Literary Agency
First hardcover English edition published by W1-Media Inc. /
Arctis Books USA 2025

All rights reserved. The publisher prohibits the use of this work for text and data mining without express written consent. No part of this publication may be reproduced, stored in a retrieval system, or transmitted, in any form or by any means, electronic, mechanical, photocopying, or otherwise, without the prior permission of the publisher and copyright owner.

Visit our website at www.arctis-books.com

10 9 8 7 6 5 4 3 2 1

The Library of Congress Control Number: 2024953137

ISBN 978-1-64690-014-5
eBook ISBN 978-1-64690-614-7

English translation copyright © Jennifer Alexander, 2025

Printed in Germany

PROLOGUE

You took everything from me. You took my future. You took my life. But I still have revenge. Revenge is mine.

I want people to know my story. I want you to say my name. The world must hear it. They must see me and my nameless, forgotten sisters. They must see us and they must feel our anger when we rise. When we come.

PART 1
SUMMER

A kiss, one more, and then they must part
A thrush serenades with loving heart
The hawthorn in full glory, drips with bitter fruit;
Dewdrops fall like tears into the brook.

From the poem "Little Kirsten and Prince Buris"
by Hans Christian Andersen, 1869

JUNE 19TH
4:23 A.M.

Victoria

Victoria woke feeling chilled to the bone. Her light summer duvet had slipped to the floor, and as she reached down for it, she was struck by how cold her room felt. A crunching sound like footsteps in the frost made her shiver.

"Is somebody there?"

Victoria's voice was nothing but a whisper. No answer came. She lay back down and pulled the duvet over her. This could not be happening. She must be imagining things. Victoria was so used to having the spirit present in her life. Maybe that was why she kept sensing it, although it was no longer there. That weak, flowery scent of violets, the flicker of a white shadow in the mirror, a hoarse whisper in the darkness . . . It was all in her imagination. They had kept their promise to Trine, after all. They had found her killer, the man who murdered her, last year at Rosenholm boarding school.

Trine is at peace; you're hearing things. It's over now.

Still, she was shivering with cold, and sleep was impossible. Suddenly, the duvet was whipped off her.

"Trine!"

The white shadowy form stood at the end of her bed. A young

woman. She held both hands at her throat, and her chest rose and fell as if she couldn't breathe.

Victoria's heart was pounding, and her chest hurt. "It was Jens," she whispered. "Jens killed you. We know that now."

Trine did not answer. Her eyes were wide with fear, as if she was locked in a time loop, again and again forced to relive the horror she had been put through by the man who was now the school principal.

"Calm down," Victoria said. "Try to calm down, Trine."

"*Afraid . . .*"

Trine's voice was weak, the words barely passing her lips.

"Are you scared? He can't get to you now. You're safe here."

"*He is afraid . . . Don't forget that . . .*"

"I don't understand . . ."

The white figure shuddered as her head dropped back, and Victoria could only sit, powerless, on her bed and watch. She could not help her. She could not save her life because she had already been dead for many years.

"What can I do?" Victoria whispered.

"*My name . . .*"

"Your name? Your name is Trine," Victoria said.

The shadowy form hissed and shook her head from side to side as she continued to sputter out words. "*My name, my sisters . . . He is . . . afraid.*"

"Trine, stop, that's enough." Victoria could hear in her own voice that she was crying, though she hadn't noticed her tears until now.

"*Don't forget . . .*"

At that, she finally disappeared, leaving Victoria sobbing in her ice-cold bed. It wasn't over after all. Not yet.

10

We're coming tonight. Meet us in the castle gardens at 4

JUNE 25TH
3:25 A.M.

Chamomile

Some nights, it can seem like it never gets completely dark. That the warmth of the sun never leaves the stones and house walls but rather radiates from them during the night so that, placing your hand there, you'd find them still warm. And the night air smells of beach roses and jasmine while the stars pierce through like tiny, glowing knife pricks, uncompromising and endless, leaving you dizzy if you look at them too long. On a night like this, you ought to be leaving some party, high on laughter and dancing, hand in hand with your loved one.

But that was not what Chamomile was doing on this summer night. There was no dancing nor laughter. And no loved one ... Although, she wasn't alone either.

Chamomile peeked out from the hood of the robe she had pulled on over her white dress. Victoria walked alongside her, and her pretty, dark eyes glanced back at her as if to say, *Yeah, I'm here.*

Chamomile turned toward Kirstine. The tall, serious girl with long, sandy-colored hair was walking behind them, deep in concentration, uttering rune incantations in a whisper as the grass swished underfoot in the still of the night.

The three young women continued along the path. A horse stood in its field watching them as they passed, and shortly after, they turned into the avenue of old chestnut trees. Soon, they could make out Rosenholm as a dark silhouette against the sparkling carpet of stars. They all knew that Jens got up early, and they wanted to be there before him. Chamomile felt her stomach churn. There was no knowing how he might react.

Even though the night was quiet and there was no wind, the huge chestnut trees still shook their branches ominously as they neared the castle.

"*Eoh*," Kirstine commanded in a low voice, and the sound of the rustling leaves around them subsided. Kirstine's hair crackled with static, and Chamomile saw how the deep scar that twisted around her wrist glowed in the dark.

They continued through the open expanse of the park, crossing the footbridge over the moat and entering the castle courtyard with its lumpy cobblestones. Fallen petals from the great climbing rose lay like a carpet over the steps up to the school's entrance. There was nobody around.

Chamomile checked her phone. It was two minutes to four. "We'll wait a bit," she whispered.

When she looked up at the castle, she saw it. A faint light, visible in one window, and a shadow that looked like a silhouette. It was just a glimpse and then was gone, but Chamomile was certain.

"Malou! She was standing at the window looking at us. She's coming."

"Don't you think it was just a shadow?" Victoria asked, looking up at the school's whitewashed walls.

"It was her," Chamomile said.

They stood waiting awhile in silence. Kirstine shifted her weight impatiently from one foot to the other. Victoria checked the time. The stars were fading in the sky above them; it would soon be sunrise.

"She's not coming," Victoria eventually whispered. "We can't stand around here any longer."

"But she did see us . . ." She sighed. Malou hadn't answered any of the messages Chamomile had sent since she left Rosenholm a month earlier, so why would she suddenly come now? But the thought that Malou was there, somewhere in the castle, was almost too much to bear. And Chamomile was certain that it had been her at the window. She felt the tears welling in her eyes and reminded herself that she was lucky. She didn't have to do this alone; there were three of them. *But there should have been four.*

It was dark and quiet as they climbed the great steps. Rosenholm was normally empty of students during summer vacation, but members of the Crows' Club, Zlavko's student association, had remained in school while the others were home. Luckily, they didn't run into any of them now. Chamomile was the only one who had been to Jens's office before, so she led the way along the empty halls and up to the principal's large corner suite. They came to the door and snuck quickly inside. Victoria turned on the desk lamp, and Kirstine pulled the curtains back so they could see the sky, which was lit pink by the sunrise. Now, they just had to wait.

At half past six, the door opened. It was him, of course, the man they were waiting for, yet she was still startled when she laid eyes on him. Jens, as always, was dressed completely in black. A solid, athletic man in his fifties. Not especially tall and with short, steel-gray hair. His eyes narrowed for an instant when he spotted them, but in the next second, his face slipped back to relaxed and impassive as if he had expected to find them standing there. His intense, intelligent look pierced her like an electric shock.

"Good morning," he said. "What can I do for you all, so early in the morning and during vacation time, no less?"

Suddenly, Chamomile couldn't remember a single one of the things she had prepared to say. Instead, she stuck her hand in her pocket and pulled out a slip of paper. Her hands were shaking as she unfolded it. It was a copy of a photograph, which had been pieced together from two separate parts. One half was in black and white and showed a smiling young woman. The other half was in color and showed a younger version of the man standing before them. Jens Andersen. Their Spirit Magic teacher, principal of Rosenholm boarding school—and Chamomile's father. The latter part was something only three people in the world knew. Chamomile's mother, Jens, and Chamomile herself. And that was how it needed to stay.

"What's going on?" Jens asked. She held out the photograph to him.

"She was called Trine," Victoria said, her voice calm and controlled. "You were a couple."

Jens raised his eyebrows. "Fascinating," he said with a little smile on his lips. "But I'm pretty sure I would remember if I'd been together with such a beautiful girl. You said her name was Trine?"

"You were her teacher. Back in the late eighties," Victoria said.

"I've taught so many young girls over the years," Jens said, holding the photo up in front of him to look at it closely. "No, I can't remember her at all." He crossed his arms, looking at them. "This

15

Trine must have fed you a right bunch of lies," he said. "It's possible I did teach her at one time, although I don't remember it, but we were most certainly not a couple."

"Besides this photo, we also have the letters Trine wrote to her sister back when she was a student at this school. In them, she writes about your relationship," Victoria said. "How do you explain that?"

Jens shrugged. "Perhaps it's just a case of a student who fell in love with her teacher and wrote some romantic stories to send home to her little sister. What would I know?" He smiled at them, tired. "I'm sorry to disappoint you. You've not scooped some great scandal, girls. Was that the only reason for your visit?"

Chamomile felt dry-mouthed and tongue-tied, and her mind had gone blank. What had she imagined was going to happen? That he'd be shocked or get nervous? Angry, maybe? But instead, he seemed not in the least affected by what they had said.

"How do you know that?" Kirstine asked quietly. "That it was her little sister? You say you don't remember Trine, and we only said it was her sister."

Jens looked at her and slowly shook his head. "No, now this is getting ridiculous. Listen, I have work that I need to do. I don't have time for this."

"That was why Leah tried to kill you," Chamomile whispered. "Leah was Trine's little sister. It wasn't an attack on mages or on Rosenholm. It was an attack on you."

Chamomile could picture her: crazy, unhappy Leah, who had tried to avenge her sister's death and who took her own life when it all went wrong.

"I really don't know what you're talking about," Jens said. Clearly, his patience had run out.

"You have to confess," Victoria said.

16

"What did you say?" He frowned, and for the first time, Chamomile sensed anger in his voice. "I should confess to going out with a girl who I cannot even remember?"

"You need to confess that you killed her," Victoria said.

"What?"

"You killed Trine. I've seen it myself; she showed me." Victoria's voice trembled ever so slightly, but she didn't lower her gaze. "You were together. You made her believe that you were going to run away with her, but instead, you knocked her unconscious and hid her down in the castle's cellars. And after that, you carried her down to the brook, and you strangled her. I've seen it all."

Jens narrowed his eyes and looked at her. A tremor ran through Victoria's body, as if she were fighting against something they couldn't see.

"It's madness, what you are saying, Victoria," he whispered.

"Trine is dead, but she hasn't yet found peace," Victoria said. "She'll only have peace when you confess to killing her."

"And why should I confess to something I haven't done?" His eyes were on Victoria alone, his voice was calm, but his threatening tone made Chamomile a lot more afraid than if he had been shouting at them.

"If you don't confess publicly and resign from your post immediately, then we will leak all the evidence that we have," Victoria whispered. "It's your choice."

"And what evidence are you talking about? This here? An old photograph?" He snorted and threw the photo on the floor so that it landed at his feet. "You don't seriously think that the police would accuse me on the basis of that? Or perhaps you're going to tell them that you can talk with the dead?"

"We'll go to the Council of Mages," Victoria said.

Jens took one step closer and pointed a finger up in her face. "I strongly advise you not to go making these kinds of false accusations about me!"

"Come on," Kirstine said. "Let's go. He's made his choice."

They went toward the door. Chamomile's legs were trembling underneath her.

"Chamomile?" His voice was suddenly gentle. She didn't want to, but her body obeyed of its own accord. She turned in the doorway. He took a deep breath in. The anger had gone from his eyes.

"You need to know that I don't blame any of you for this. Somebody has used you all to try and pull one over on me. But I need to warn you. If you go any further with this, I won't be responsible for the consequences. I won't be able to protect you."

Chamomile felt a rush in her ears. Victoria grabbed her hand and pulled her away, and the door slammed after them, echoing down the empty hallway.

18

I saw you. I know you saw us.

What's going on, Malou?

JULY 2ND
3:10 P.M.

Kirstine

"I'm still not sure this is the best thing to do," Kirstine said, looking at Victoria, who stood in the middle of her bedroom.

"Try to imagine the impact it will have," Victoria said urgently. "No one will be able to act like they don't know because they were all sat there, hearing it at the same time. They can't just go ignoring it or denying it."

"But..."

"And I will be the one to answer for it. Just don't worry."

Victoria was interrupted by the sound of the doorbell ringing below. "Boys, get that, will you?" Victoria stuck her head out the door and yelled to her little brothers, but there was no answer. As the doorbell went on again, she sighed and turned to Kristine.

"Hang on. It must be Chamomile."

Kirstine waited in the bedroom, letting her fingers trace across the bright blue bed throw as she looked out at the summer sky, almost the same in color. It was a lovely, large room. Everything in Victoria's house was beautiful, but Kirstine didn't like being there.

"It's for you." Victoria sounded a bit out of breath, having run up the stairs. "It's Jakob..." She raised her eyebrows and gave Kirstine a knowing look.

Kirstine frowned. "Jakob? Why?"

"I'm guessing that he wants to see you, seeing as he's standing outside the front door asking for you," Victoria said, looking like she was quite enjoying herself.

"Chamomile will be here soon . . ."

"We'll just wait for you to get back."

"But . . ." Kirstine couldn't think what to say.

Victoria smiled. "Go on down and see what he wants. Do you want to brush your hair first?"

"What?" Kirstine reached up to her ponytail.

"Forget it. You look great. Hurry up before he starts to gather dust down there."

Kirstine sighed and got up. She went down the curved staircase and through the hall.

"Hey." Jakob was standing at the foot of the steps to the big main door. He smiled shyly and ran his fingers through his strawberry-blond hair, the way he always did when he was nervous. "It's good to see you."

"Hey." Kirstine looked down at his shoes. There was a foot, at least, between them, but she immediately felt how a faint buzz filled the air between their bodies.

"So, this is where you live," he said, smiling.

"It's Victoria's house," Kirstine said, even though he knew perfectly well, of course. "It's just for a while."

"Okay," he said.

It was hot, and he was wearing a white T-shirt. She tried to stop staring at it. She tried to stop startng at *him*.

"Uh, can we go inside, or . . ." He smiled again.

Of course, she should have invited him in and offered him something to drink. That's what normal people did. But then this was not her house, and she also didn't know why he was there.

"We could always go for a walk? Or maybe you could show me the garden? I bet a house like this has a beautiful garden."

Kirstine nodded, relieved. The garden would be fine. Better than going indoors and risking a run-in with Victoria's parents, who might be home soon.

"We can go this way." She considered going inside to find her sandals but dropped the idea and went out the front door in her bare feet. Jakob followed behind her, and she noticed he was walking too close. It hurt to walk on the gravel barefoot, but when she stepped onto the lawn, things only got worse. There was a sizzling beneath her feat. She frowned.

"You don't seem too excited to see me?" he said, trying to meet her eyes.

"It's just that . . . Chamomile is on her way, and—"

"I won't be long . . . I just wanted to . . . Kirstine?"

"What?" She stared down at the well-trimmed lawn.

"Happy birthday."

Now, at last, she looked up. He smiled reassuringly and held out a small box toward her.

His smile made her heart race. She was sure she had never told him when her birthday was. She hadn't told anyone, but, of course, in his role as teacher, he could find it in the school records if he wanted to.

"Let's go down to the orchard," she whispered. They carried on past the English roses and bedding plants and went in among the old apple trees, where they were less easily seen from the house. It crossed her mind that most of their meetings had, in fact, been this way. Secretive.

22

He held out the box to her again, and she hesitantly reached out and took it. Her fingertips brushed briefly against the palm of his hand, and immediately she felt a shooting pain run up her whole arm, as if she had touched an electric fence. It hurt Jakob, too.

Kirstine's cheeks burned. Things were going much better, but clearly all it took for her to lose control again was having Jakob standing close. Why couldn't she get on top of this? Jakob didn't mention it. Instead, he smiled at her expectantly. "Are you not going to look at what's inside?" It was a jewelry box. Kirstine sensed that she was blushing. It felt awkward and somehow too intimate. She wasn't the type, in any case, for celebrating birthdays, and she wasn't someone people bought jewelry for.

"It doesn't bite," he said, laughing softly.

She opened the lid. A silver figure lay on a cushion of cotton wool. It was little more than a half-inch high and depicted a small woman with a sword and shield.

"It's a Valkyrie," Jakob said. "Replica Viking jewelery. Look, you can wear it as a necklace . . ." He reached his hand out to take the figure but stopped short and made do with pointing. Kirstine could see it right away. Between the little Valkyrie's neck and her long plait, there was a loop so it could be used as a pendant. At least it hadn't been a ring; that would have been so much worse.

"Thanks," she whispered, closing the box. "Would you mind not telling the others? That it's my birthday?"

She looked up toward the big white house, where the windows lay open in the summer heat.

"I don't know anyone else quite like you." He was smiling, but his eyes looked sad.

Kirstine tucked the box into her pocket. "I think Chamomile must be on her way, so . . ."

"I'll get going, but I was wondering if you'd like to meet up one of these days? I've got the summer off, so I've got plenty of time. We could just go out for a walk. I know I said it myself that it was a bad idea, but Thorbjørn told me that things are much better now, right?"

Kirstine had no idea what to say. Yes, things were better. She had her powers under control now. But that control all dissipated when he looked at her that way. There was a ringing in her ears. She felt the scars on her arms and legs smarting, and, for a moment, she imagined the glistening tree roots breaking through the grass beneath her feet. Giving him a kiss or even holding his hand was out of the question.

"I don't think it'll work," she whispered.

He nodded and took a deep breath in. Then he turned his face up toward the green of the fruit trees and the blue sky above them before slowly sighing the breath out again.

Kirstine wished she could find the right words to explain to him how it felt to be in this situation. To have powers that she was afraid of, powers that she had never asked for or wished for. Powers that meant that falling in love put her life in danger. Instead, they just stood without talking until Jakob finally turned his gaze away from the treetops and gave her a sad smile.

"It was great to see you again," he said, and then he turned and walked away. Kirstine stood watching until he had disappeared from sight. *Maybe it's better this way, given we can't be together anyway.* She sighed and headed up to the house.

"Hi!" Chamomile was sitting cross-legged on Victoria's bed in the process of braiding her hair when Kirstine entered the room.

"What did Jakob want?" Victoria asked.

"Nothing," Kirstine mumbled.

"Did you invite him for Saturday?" Chamomile asked.

"I forgot," Kirstine said.

"Never mind, I'll write to him," Victoria said, pulling out a list of names. She ran her eyes down the list. "Thorbjørn and Lisa are coming to represent the school. And Benjamin is coming."

Chamomile raised one eyebrow and threw Kirstine a look from the bed but said nothing. Victoria and Benjamin had broken up before the summer vacation, and Kirstine could see no immediate reason why he should also be invited to the event.

"Benjamin knows a lot of the old families," Victoria said quickly as if she could read their minds. And maybe she could; it certainly felt that way at times.

"Is there anyone else we can invite?" Chamomile asked. "I don't know any 'powerful people,'" she said, dropping the braid to make air quotes with her fingers. "Besides the teachers, and they're already coming."

"Hmm." Victoria consulted the list. "My mom has invited the most important people from the old mage families. And, of course, all the ones that sit on the Council of Mages. A few have RSVP'd no, but they'll still hear about it. The news will travel super fast." She looked up from her list. "She's put me as the first speaker."

"Isn't it a bit weird to have speeches at a party?" Chamomile asked.

"That's how it's done in these circles," Victoria said, shrugging. "It's a kind of excuse to get drunk, I think. First, there is a boring talk on history or politics or world affairs, and then everyone gets drunk and talks about the people who aren't there. But this time, at the very least, I don't think it's going to be boring."

"What did you say you'll be giving a talk about?" Kirstine asked.

"The rights and responsibilities of a young mage," Victoria said.

"My mom didn't ask anymore about it; she was just happy I'm finally showing an interest in joining one of their dreadful cocktail parties with all their creepy friends. She even let me add people to the guest list without splitting any hairs."

Kirstine looked at Victoria. She navigated "these circles," as she called them, with complete ease. The rich and powerful mage families. Victoria had been born into that world. Kirstine, however, had not, and neither had Chamomile. "How do you actually get to sit on the Council of Mages?" Kirstine asked.

"It's certainly not that easy," Victoria said. "I just know that there are ten or twelve members and that once you're in, you're in for life. They have to be voted in by the current members."

"What do they actually do in that Council?" Chamomile said.

"They work on guidelines for mages and also give advice to those who break them. In the last instance, they can hand them over to the authorities."

"And these are the people who come to your parents' parties?" Chamomile asked.

"Not only ours," Victoria answered. "My parents are part of a lodge, and the members take turns holding those parties a few times every year."

"It sounds like a pretty scary gathering," Chamomile said. "Are you sure you've got the nerve?"

"If I can say it to Jens, then I can also say it to a gathering of my parents' friends," Victoria said. "It'll be okay."

"You're a tough cookie," Chamomile said. "Should we practice it one more time?"

26

It's great that you can come

Okay, but what's this about?

You'll see. Can't say more just now

See you Saturday!

See you . . .

JULY 4ᵀᴴ
5:46 P.M.

Victoria

"Come in!" Victoria said with a big grin. A little too big, perhaps, judging by the frown that appeared on Benjamin's face. His blue eyes fixed on hers, and a muscle in his jaw twitched. "It's great you could come a little earlier," she said, with a touch more reserve this time, and gave him a hug, which he half returned. His energy confused her; it felt both discouraging and overwhelming at the same time.

"Why, exactly, did you want me here so early?" he asked, and Victoria felt herself blushing. *So I can convince you that you've made a mistake.*

"My mom said she could do with some help getting everything all set up," she lied.

At that moment, her mother came out into the hall with a huge vase filled with white lilies. "It's so typical. The florist only delivered them just now," she said, setting the vase down in front of the huge mirror in the hall as she blew a lock of her dark, shiny hair away from her face. The scent of the flowers was already reaching Victoria so by the time the guests arrived, the whole room would be filled with it. Behind her mother came Niels, one of Victoria's younger brothers. He scrunched his nose and looked skeptically at the flowers and then at Benjamin.

"What's he doing here?"

Victoria's mother turned, neatly ignoring Benjamin altogether. "The forecast is for rain. I was hoping we could have had welcome drinks out in the garden." Her high heels clicked off the parquet flooring as she headed back toward the kitchen. They could hear her asking someone or another to distribute the rest of the flowers in the lounge.

"I thought you two broke up?" Harald had joined his brother and both twins now stood scowling at Benjamin. If the situation hadn't been so tense, Victoria might have been quite amused by the two soldiers coming to her defense.

"Benjamin is just visiting," Victoria said. "Go on now."

"Victoria cried her head off," Niels said. "Because of you breaking up."

"Mom says she falls in love too easily," Harald added. "And that you're not worth it."

"Enough now!" Victoria said. "Go on out to the garden."

"We're not allowed out there," Niels said sulkily. "We're not allowed anywhere."

After a few more grumbles and moans, the twins disappeared upstairs to their rooms.

"Did you tell them it was me who broke up with you?" Benjamin asked as they went through to the kitchen.

"Is that not what happened?" Victoria replied without looking at him.

"It was you who decided it."

"You gave me an ultimatum. I had no other choice," she said, trying to keep her tone light. "It didn't have to be like that. It didn't need to be an either-or."

29

"Well, that's where we'll have to disagree," he muttered.

Victoria's courage faltered. It was not the answer she'd been hoping for, but she straightened up and smiled when her mother stepped into the kitchen from the garden. If nothing else, she wasn't going to let her mother have the pleasure of being right; of course, she had thought it a big mistake to invite Benjamin.

"The weather's still nice for now," her mother said. "Will we take our chances on it staying dry? Though, that would mean getting the garden tables set out."

"Benjamin will be happy to help, I'm sure . . ." Victoria said, but her mother acted as if she hadn't heard.

"No, tell you what, we'll have welcome drinks in the library instead." She turned toward the two young women who were going to be serving drinks and started giving instructions on setting out the glasses.

"Sorry," Victoria whispered.

Benjamin shrugged. "Your mom has never been one of my greatest fans," he muttered under his breath. "And it certainly doesn't seem like she needs any help from me?" He raised his eyebrows and looked at her.

Victoria lowered her gaze from his. She had missed him so much, and she had hoped that after spending some time together today, he might start feeling like he missed her too. Feeling like splitting up had been a mistake. She had also been holding onto a faint hope he'd discover her parents weren't quite as bad as he thought.

"I just thought this was a good opportunity for you to get to know them a bit better," she mumbled.

He sighed. "Your parents aren't the slightest bit interested in getting to know me better, and I have to admit, the feeling is mutual. So, if my help isn't needed, I'd like to go up and play FIFA with the little rugrats instead."

"Of course." Victoria nodded and tried to force her mouth into a smile. "Just go ahead."

"Are you okay?" Kirstine asked, pulling down on the dark top Victoria had loaned her, which was still a touch too small, though Victoria had assured her it wasn't.

Victoria took a large gulp from the glass of chilled white wine Chamomile had brought her. She nodded. "We can't stand and threaten him with outing him in public and then not dare to go through with it."

"Dare to go through with what?" asked Benjamin, who had crept back up on them.

"Nothing," she muttered.

"Thorbjørn, Jakob, and Lisa have arrived," Chamomile said. "Kirstine and I are going over to say hi. Are you coming?"

Victoria shook her head. "I'll just stay here," she said while Chamomile and Kirstine edged toward the hall, where they could make out Thorbjørn's bulky form among the other guests. With his great beard and his long hair, he was far from the type of guest her parents normally invited.

"Are you nervous?" Benjamin asked.

"A bit," she answered, that being the understatement of the year. Mortally terrified would be closer to the right term, and she had absolutely no desire to greet all her parents' friends right now. She preferred to stand where she was in this dark corner.

"But look, is it Victoria?"

Clearly, it was not dark enough. A woman wearing a low-cut, cherry-red dress was smiling at her. "Well, look how grown up you are now." She clinked her glass against Victoria's and then Benjamin's, observing them openly. "And who do we have here?"

"Benjamin Brahe," he said, offering her his hand.

"Brahe . . ." the woman said, surprised, clasping his hand in hers and leaning toward him. "Then I guess I know your parents."

"I'm sorry to hear that," Benjamin said and slipped his hand gently, yet decisively, out of hers.

The woman's face betrayed her surprise, but she quickly gave a broad smile, exposing the gums around her unnaturally white teeth.

"Let's talk later, Benjamin. It's so lovely that young people have started coming as well." She gave his arm a complicit squeeze before turning around to greet some other guests.

"She was flirting with you," Victoria said, and it occurred to her that this must be something that happened to him frequently, judging by the almost professional way he had handled it, which should hardly come as a surprise to her. Benjamin's handsome looks were no less striking now, dressed as he was in a neatly fitted suit.

"Not interested," Benjamin said.

They looked up at the sound of a glass falling to the ground and shattering. A tall, dark-haired man with a meticulous mustache looked down for a moment at the waiter, who was doubled over picking up the pieces, before reaching out for a new glass and continuing toward them.

"Now it's all kicking off," Benjamin said, and Victoria realized it was this man he was alluding to. She vaguely recognized him as someone who had been here before to her parents' lodge parties. But he wasn't someone they otherwise met with privately, and Victoria couldn't recall having been introduced to him before.

32

He was wearing a tailored suit and wore thin glasses with a gold frame. "The prodigal son," he said as he came nearer. He raised his glass to Benjamin.

"Victoria, this is my father," Benjamin said. "Vilhelm Brahe."

"Hello," she said, surprised, offering him her hand.

"Ah, you're in the company of a young lady." The man brushed her palm lightly with the very tip of his fingers without looking at her. "A pretty girl," he said, still turned to Benjamin. "I suppose it was . . ." He gestured toward her but stopped. "I'm sorry, the name escapes me?"

"Victoria."

"Victoria, yes. I suppose it was Victoria who persuaded you to come this evening?"

"In a way. Victoria will be giving a talk on a mysterious topic she refuses to tell me any more about."

"Aha, another mysterious speaker," said the man.

"Sorry, I don't think I quite understand," Victoria said.

"I'm sorry," said Vilhelm, "but I don't want to spoil our hosts' surprise."

"It's Victoria who is the surprise," Benjamin said. "Her parents are the hosts."

"Hans is your father?" Vilhelm looked her over, unsmiling.

"Yes, he has been angling for a place on the Council for a few years. But there are many others in the running, of course."

At this point, it was clear to Victoria that Benjamin's father was a member of the Council of Mages, which was why he would have been at her parents' parties previously.

"I can perhaps tell your mother that you have come to your senses? That you've started mixing with the right kind of people again?" Vilhelm asked, looking at his son.

"Absolutely not," Benjamin said. "I'm only here for Victoria's sake."

Victoria felt a wave of gratitude wash over her, but her smile stiffened on seeing the contemptuous grimace on Vilhelm's face.

"No, well, that was, of course, too much to expect," he said, nodding to them both. "Good luck with your speech, Victoria."

"Did you know he was coming?" she whispered once Benjamin's father had turned away.

"I figured there was a risk of it," he said.

"How long has it been since you last saw him?" she asked.

"Two years," Benjamin answered. His voice was calm and emotionless, but she could sense the anger radiating from him, making her nervous about saying something that would make him snap at her. They stood for a while without talking until a voice suddenly cut loudly across all the others. Victoria checked the time. Now, already?

"Welcome, everybody!" Victoria's mother sounded a little strained, but perhaps it was only Victoria who noticed the quivering nervousness that hung around her in the form of a purple aura. Outwardly, she seemed like the perfect host in her black cocktail dress, high stilettos, and discrete jewelry. The guests gathered in a circle around her.

"The wait is over because, in a moment, it'll be time for this evening's speech. My husband and I . . ." She held out her hand, and a tall, elegant man with silvery-gray hair took it and let himself be led out into the middle of the floor. "Yes, I know you would rather keep yourself in the background, Hans, but you're not getting to escape," she said, and people laughed and even broke briefly into applause.

Victoria automatically forced a smile without feeling any kind of happiness. They were an attractive pair. Her father was a little older than her mother, but he was still a handsome man, while her mother's beauty was commented on wherever she went. Victoria only wished that the sight of them, surrounded by all their friends, could have sparked a sense of pride and happiness in her rather than the simmering unease she was now feeling.

"My husband and I are delighted to welcome you all to yet another lovely evening together at our little lodge," her mother continued once quiet had resumed. "As you may have noticed, we have more guests than usual here with us tonight. These are some friends of our beautiful, talented daughter Victoria, who is going to talk to us about her views on young mages' rights and responsibilities."

People clapped politely, and Victoria took a deep breath and tried to keep a handle on her nerves.

"But, first, I have a little surprise," her mother added with a wry smile.

Victoria felt her stomach lurch. She twisted her prompt cards in her hands. What kind of surprise?

"Before Victoria steps up, Jens Andersen, principal of Rosenholm Academy, will tell us about his vision for the school and for the future of magic in general terms. Please, give a hand to Jens!"

"What?" Victoria whispered. A surge of panic took hold of her, and she struggled to breathe.

Her parents slipped aside, both still clapping, and Jens stepped up instead in the midst of the crowd. As ever, Victoria was struck by his intense charisma that drew everyone's attention. Just as it did now. Everyone there was looking intently at Jens. Dressed in his usual black and at least a head shorter than her father, he still seemed to fill the room in an entirely different way. Jens nodded warmly and scanned the guests, but when his gaze reached her, he held it there. Victoria felt his energy. It was like being run over by a bus in slow motion. It pushed her back and pressed her down, but she refused to look away. She wasn't going to let herself be intimidated.

JULY 4TH
9:07 P.M.

Chamomile

"Thank you all so much for coming this evening," Jens said. The guests had gathered now in the large side room. Jens was the only one still standing, while the rest had sat down in the chairs that had been set out.

Chamomile would have preferred to sit in the back, as far away from Jens as possible, but she, Kirstine, and Victoria had sat in the front row. It had been her own idea. She had asked herself what Malou would have done, and the answer came to her right away. *Let's sit right under his nose so he can see we're not messing around!* Chamomile could almost hear her saying it.

"I know you will all be interested to hear what young Victoria has to say, but as the saying goes: *Age before beauty,*" Jens said, and people laughed. "I hope you will bear with me. I'll keep it as short as I can, but I do have, in my humble view, important things to tell you."

Chamomile felt annoyed at how quickly Jens was stealing the show. Suddenly, it was he who was showing people to their places, thanking their hosts, and greeting guests. Suddenly, it was he who had important things to say.

He began his speech, and Chamomile's irritation grew. Jens's voice was warm, and he spoke with insight and humor about his experiences as the school principal, as well as his own time as a student at Rosenholm. It was easy to see why people found him charming and inspirational. But all that was only a shell, a cloak he pulled on. Underneath, something entirely different was lurking. An ice-cold manipulator. A murderer. *Nobody can know. Nobody can ever find out.* Shame burned inside her, knowing that this man now holding everyone's attention was her father.

"They're swallowing it completely!" Kirstine whispered in frustration.

Chamomile looked at Victoria. Beautiful as always, in a simple, dark blue mini-dress, she brought to mind some French film star. She sat, looking down at her hands, which concealed the keywords she had noted down. Her lips were moving as if she was muttering something to herself.

"And that brings us to what I came here to talk to you about this evening," Jens said, bringing his hands together in front of him. "I know that many of you agree with me that we have been bowing our heads and hiding away in the shadows for far too long. We have forgotten what we once were. My dream is of a bright future for mages. A future in which we can lift our heads again with pride. But to find the way forward, sometimes you have to look to the past."

Some of the guests started to clap, and Chamomile cursed. *This is not what was meant to happen.* There were also some in the audience who were more skeptical.

"And what kind of past is it that you want to go back to?" Chamomile turned around. The question came from an older man in a shabby suit.

"Of course, I don't want to return to the past," Jens said, smiling. "But it's not so many generations ago that we mages were at the heart of power. Always behind the scenes, tucked away, but nevertheless there, where decisions were being made. There, where we were able to make use of our special talents and knowledge. I will strive for us to be empowered once more so that we can influence those who legislate and govern, and to our own advantage. A kind of lobby group, so to speak. But of a very particular sort."

A tall woman with a bald head cleared her throat.

"Yes, Gertrud?" Jens asked.

"I would quite like to know how, exactly, you intend to get mages a place at the seat of power again?"

"I'm glad you're asking that," Jens said. "First and foremost, I see it as my job, as the leader of a new generation of mages, to make sure our students develop their skills in a way that they can reach their full potential. We need to understand that there is variety in our ranks. The talents of some are greater than others. If we dare to put our faith in the strongest, cleverest, and most capable among us, then we will all reap the benefits. We must stop being afraid of supporting those students who show talent that we don't immediately understand. That childish fear of what some call 'dark magic' should be cast aside, and blood mages and spirit mages should no longer be discriminated against."

"Since when have they been?" Kirstine whispered loudly so that a man in the row behind them shushed her.

"Secondly, I will make the students aware of the great responsibility that mages have always had but which older generations—including my own—have, unfortunately, neglected," Jens continued. "We must put an end to that, and I believe this new generation will be the springboard for us mages making our comeback."

"And what about the rest of the magic community?" an elderly man asked. "Everyone over twenty. You have no use for them, or what?"

"Experienced mages will remain an important part of this next step toward the society I want to work toward," Jens said. "There's the establishment of the lobby group I mentioned before. Or, to be more precise, the resurrection of the Magicus Comité. The Committee for Magic."

A murmur of chat broke out among the guests. Some seemed agitated, outraged even, but many others were clapping or giving some other signal that they endorsed Jens's viewpoint.

Chamomile turned to Kirstine, who simply shrugged as if to say she didn't understand what they were talking about either. Victoria was still sitting with her card twisted in her hands without appearing to have heard a word of what Jens had said. Chamomile reached across Kirstine to take Victoria's hand and give it a squeeze. She looked up.

"Let's do this," she said softly.

Chamomile nodded. "Let's do it."

JULY 4ᵀᴴ
9:39 P.M.

Kirstine

The majority of guests applauded when Jens finally finished his speech. Some even rose into a standing ovation, and Jens placed his hands modestly at his heart and bowed slightly before slipping aside to leave the floor to Victoria's mother, who thanked him warmly and then introduced her daughter. But Kirstine didn't look at Victoria's mother. She was looking at Jens. He sat down, composing himself calmly with his arms crossed, and studied Victoria as she nodded to the audience with a slight smile. Kirstine was in awe of her. She stood there calmly in front of all these powerful people. That took a huge amount of courage.

Victoria took a deep breath. "I also have something important that I'd like to share with you this evening." Her voice had a slight quiver, and she took another deep breath before continuing. "And it may be even more important that you know it now, after what we have just heard." She paused as if to prepare herself to say the next part. "It is difficult to talk about, so I hope you will be patient with me. If . . ." Victoria paused again, and Kirstine looked around the audience, who nodded in a friendly and tolerant way.

"I . . ." Victoria's voice cracked, and she turned her face down as if she was overcome with emotion.

"My daughter is obviously a bit nervous," said Victoria's mom with a soothing little laugh from her place in the front row. "It's to be expected with so many people here tonight. Just take your time, Victoria. We're not monsters."

People laughed politely, and some of the guests started to clap to give Victoria some support. But she still said nothing.

"Should I go up to her, do you think?" Chamomile whispered.

Kirstine looked at Victoria's face. She was facing down so much that she couldn't make out her expression, but she could see a muscle in her cheek was twitching. *Something was wrong.*

"Victoria!" Chamomile shouted.

"She's having a seizure," Victoria's mother screamed. "Do something!"

Suddenly, Victoria physically collapsed and fell to the ground.

"Out of the way!" shouted a small woman with long, dark hair.

Lisa roughly pushed aside the guests who had gotten up to see what was happening.

Kirstine tore her eyes away from Victoria's pale, agonized face and the froth around her clenched teeth and looked up. At Jens. His eyes were locked on Victoria, and his lips were moving lightly. Kirstine slowly got up. *"Naudiz!"*

The Naud rune flew across the room toward its target, but rather than breaking Jens's covert attack on Victoria, it only made him teeter.

"What's happening?" screamed Victoria's father, who stood bewildered, looking from his daughter twitching on the floor to Kirstine, still standing with her arms outstretched toward Jens.

"It's her! Grab her!" the bald-headed woman screamed, and Kirstine was just able to lower her head as the rune spell came flying at her head.

42

"Duck!" Thorbjørn's voice made them all jump. Despite the fact he'd been sitting up the back, he was down beside Kirstine in no time and put his great arm around her. "You're coming with me!"

"No!" Kirstine pulled herself free, her hair sparking with electricity around her face, and Thorbjørn looked at her alarm as he realized he was unable to keep hold of her. "It's Jens! We need to get Victoria away from Jens!"

His blue eyes narrowed for a second, and he studied her. Then he nodded and let her go. "You stay here! Jakob?" Thorbjørn indicated to Jakob that he should take over by Kirstine's side, but she didn't know whether it was for him to guard her or protect her. With two steps, Thorbjørn plowed through the guests huddled around Victoria. Kirstine couldn't see what was happening, but she could hear Victoria's mother's hysterical sobs and Lisa speaking gently to her until, shortly after, she fell quiet.

"Make way; we need to get her out of here!" It was Lisa's voice.

The guests stepped aside and let Thorbjørn pass, Victoria in his arms. Her eyes were closed, her arms and legs hung limply, and her head was dropped back.

Behind him, Lisa followed with Victoria's parents. "She needs to receive treatment immediately," Lisa said to them.

"Will it be the same place as the last time?" Victoria's mother asked, but Kirstine couldn't hear Lisa's answer.

"Come on," Jakob said.

Kirstine had completely forgotten he was standing there. She shook her head and stayed where she was.

Jens was still standing up against the wall at the opposite end of the room. Nobody was looking at him anymore, but he was looking at her. His hand rested on his shirt collar. And a little smile played on his lips.

I have the power to harm you, Victoria. Can you feel that? And not only you but everyone you care about and everyone you tell your lies to. Do you hear me?

44

JULY 5TH
12:25 A.M.

Victoria

Victoria opened her eyes and blinked up at the roof beams above her. She was no longer in her own house, but where was she?

"Here, drink this. It'll help you regain your strength," said a woman who seemed like an older version of Chamomile, except for the eyes, which were brown. She passed Victoria a small glass containing a deep purple liquid. "Iris and carnation," she said. "The taste isn't so great, but the effects really are."

Victoria's hand was shaking as she lifted the glass to her lips. It did taste awful, so she was quick to knock the bitter liquid back.

"Well done," said the woman, smiling at her. "I'm Beate. This is my house, and you're safe here. Does it hurt anywhere?"

"My head," Victoria whispered.

"Chamomile, take over here, and I'll go make some peppermint tea."

Victoria hadn't even noticed that Chamomile was sitting on a stool by the side of the sofa. As Chamomile placed her hands at her temples, Victoria lay back and closed her eyes. The pain was instantly relieved a little, but she still ached all over. Despite the fire blazing in the stove in the low-ceilinged living room, her entire body was still shivering.

"Is she awake?"

At the sound of Lisa's voice, Victoria opened her eyes again, but Chamomile softly whispered, "Relax. Rest a bit longer."

"She's coming around," Chamomile's mother said.

Victoria lay for another few minutes, then opened her eyes. "I'm okay to sit up now," she whispered, and Chamomile lifted her hands away.

Beate held out a steaming cup of tea. "I'll tell the others that you're better. I threw them out so they weren't getting in the way."

"My parents—"

"Lisa is calling them to tell them you'll stay the night here."

"Thanks." Victoria sipped her hot tea.

Beate smiled and went back to the kitchen.

Victoria and Chamomile looked up as the old stable door gave a creak and Kirstine stepped inside. Her hair was drenched with rain. She sat down beside them.

"What happened, Victoria?" Kirstine whispered. "Was it Jens?"

Victoria nodded. "I don't understand it. It was like I couldn't do anything. He was so strong . . . Before, I've always been able to shut him out or at least control what he could see, but suddenly, he was just right inside my head. He . . . he was talking to me . . . he threatened me . . ."

"And then you weren't able to talk, or what?" Chamomile asked.

"I couldn't speak or move, but that wasn't even the worst part . . ." Victoria could feel tears running down her cheeks. "He saw everything . . . Not just the stuff about Trine, but absolutely everything. My parents, Benjamin . . . Even that thing with Louis." Victoria hid her face in her hands and sobbed. She felt she had been invaded. Violated. Jens had seen all her most pitiful thoughts, everything she was most ashamed of, all the pain and hurt, all her hopeless romantic daydreams, her desires, her fantasies. Nothing had stayed hidden from him.

"Oh, Victoria." Chamomile put her arm around her but did nothing other than let her cry. They sat that way for a while, to the sounds of Beate puttering in the kitchen and talking quietly with Lisa. The crackling of the fire in the stove, footsteps on the floor, the murmur of low conversation, and the soothing sound of summer rain on the windowpanes slowly lulled Victoria back to sleep. When she eventually lifted her head again, she found them all sitting around her in the little living room—Lisa, Beate, Thorbjørn, Jakob, Benjamin, Chamomile, and Kirstine.

"We've told them," Kirstine said. "We've told them about Trine."

Victoria nodded. She rubbed her eyes and propped herself up.

"Who else knows about this?" Lisa asked. Her dark eyes looked at them with concern.

"No one else," Chamomile said. "The idea was that we would tell everyone gathered tonight about who Jens really is."

"So, besides Jens and us, no one else knows about it?" Jakob asked.

"No . . . well, yes. Malou, of course," Chamomile said.

"And where is Malou?" Lisa asked.

"She's still at Rosenholm," Chamomile said. "Together with the rest of the Crows . . ."

"But, Miley, have you not told her it was Jens who killed Trine?" Beate asked.

"Yes, we have!" Chamomile exclaimed in frustration. "She was the first person I told. But she . . . She won't reply to my messages . . ."

"We haven't gotten a hold of her since the start of the summer vacation," Kirstine said.

"I can see she's reading my messages, but she never answers them," Chamomile whispered. "I don't know why."

Victoria saw how Thorbjørn and Lisa looked at each other but said nothing. Benjamin did speak, though.

"It's possible that Malou has just chosen her side, have you thought about that? Maybe she thinks Jens is innocent. Or maybe she doesn't care because she'd rather be a part of Jens's project."

"What are you talking about?" Chamomile said. "Of course, she cares. Victoria, say something!"

Benjamin shrugged and looked at her questioningly. Victoria's headache pounded at her temples. She had been thinking along the very same lines herself. How far would Malou be prepared to go to fulfill her ambitions?

"I don't believe that she doesn't care," she said, looking away from Benjamin and over to Chamomile. "But Jens can be very convincing . . ."

"Quite. And he is obviously planning to start a minor revolution," Benjamin said. "You heard it yourselves what he was saying about the Committee of Mages?"

"Yes," Chamomile said, "but what is that?"

"Magicus Comité was a forerunner to the Council of Mages we have today," Jakob explained. "But the Committee was far more powerful than the Council is. It was more a kind of secret, powerful elite, hidden from ordinary people but tightly linked to the royal court. And it was rotten to the core with corruption. They say that some kings were merely puppets who were manipulated by those powerful mages, who busied themselves practicing dubious magic and getting their hands on land and privilege. Many Committee members also had honors bestowed upon them by the king. But after democracy was introduced and the monarchy lost some of its power, the Committee was also weakened, and at the beginning of the 1900s, it was dissolved and replaced with the Council of Mages."

"And Jens is just thinking of resurrecting the Committee, or what?" Beate said. "That sounds like madness. How did people react to that?"

"I'm not completely sure," Chamomile replied. "Most of them clapped. But then all that stuff happened with Victoria, and we marched out of there. Have you ever heard Jens talk about that before?"

Thorbjørn and Lisa looked at each other. "We've barely heard anything from him. The year-planning for the next school session should have been started a long time ago," Lisa said. "We have wondered if he is trying to freeze us out. And after what we've heard here tonight, I'm almost certain that he won't want us interfering."

"There's something I don't understand," Thorbjørn said, who until now had been sitting deep in his own thoughts. "Kirstine's rune incantation. There's no doubt that it was very powerful," he continued, "and Kirstine is a rune mage with unusually strong powers. I'd hazard a guess that any other person hit by that would have been knocked instantly off their feet. But Jens wasn't even affected by it, and it didn't stop his attack on Victoria in any way."

"What do you mean?" It was Chamomile's mother who spoke.

Thorbjørn frowned. "Jens is a talented mage, but that should simply not have happened. There's something going on here that we are not seeing."

"I agree," Lisa said. "You'll need to keep quiet about all this until we have a better idea what Jens is up to and what his plans are. And I'm afraid that he was right with what he said to you all. If he

49

won't confess himself, then you have no evidence strong enough to put him before a judge."

"Then we have to force him to," Chamomile said.

Victoria closed her eyes. The pain in her head was so strong it was making her feel sick, but she knew that Chamomile was right. They needed to find a way to force Jens to confess to Trine's murder. He would never do it of his own free will.

50

JULY 5TH
4:30 A.M.

Chamomile

"There you go." Chamomile's mother passed her a mug steaming with spicy, herbal aromas of chamomile flower and citrus balm. She carried a mug for herself in her other hand and had a crocheted throw tucked under her arm. They sat down together on the old bench at the east side of the house, and Chamomile's mom spread the throw over them both. The night's rain had stopped, and the birds' morning chorus gathered force as the sun rose up over the horizon. They sat in silence, drinking their tea as they looked out over the still mist-covered fields where the dewdrops caught the first morning rays, making the long grass sparkle like crystal.

"Don't you want to go in and take a nap?" her mother said.

"I don't think I can," Chamomile answered.

"Did you make the bed up for Kirstine?"

Chamomile nodded. Kirstine was on a mattress on the floor of her bedroom, while Victoria slept on the sofa in the living room. But she, herself, couldn't settle at all. And she knew perfectly well why.

"I need to tell you something," she whispered. Her mother found her hand without looking at her. "I'm not sure I can cope with many more revelations right now," she said quietly.

"I know," Chamomile said, "but you need to hear this. I want you to know before I say it to the others. It's about how Jens has suddenly gotten so strong. How he was able to take control of Victoria in that way, and why Kirstine's rune spell didn't do him any harm . . ."

"What's going on?"

"He's got your amulet." Chamomile felt her voice quivering. It was hard to force the words out. "The victory stone."

"My victory stone?" Her mother instinctively dropped Chamomile's hand and reached for the leather pouch she always wore around her neck, where the victory stone had always been kept until the day she passed it down to Chamomile. "How come?"

"I'm so sorry," whispered Chamomile. "He must have taken it while I was sleeping."

Now her mother turned to her and looked at her wide-eyed. The morning sunlight highlighted traces of silvery white in her auburn hair.

"Don't hate me," whispered Chamomile.

"How did he get it?"

"He tricked me. I think that was his plan all along, but I only understood afterward." Now she was crying, her voice breaking. "I'm so sorry . . ."

"Chamomile . . ." Her mother put an arm around her and pulled her in close. "Tell me how it happened."

Chamomile buried her face in her mother's wool cardigan. It smelled of wool and wood smoke. *Of home.*

"We were talking about Victoria. Jens was really worried about her, or at least that's what it sounded like. It was him, too, who told me you should never make any promise to a spirit. But we had already done that by then. We had promised Trine that we would

52

find her killer. Of course, I didn't tell him that part, but I think he guessed it. He said that the only thing that could help was a victory stone. And that they are very rare. But then I remembered—"

"That I had one," her mother finished off her sentence. "So, at Christmas, when you asked about my amulets, when you wanted to see my purse . . . you were just out to get a hold of it?"

Chamomile could feel herself burning with shame. She had tricked her own mother. In a way, she had stolen the stone from her so that Jens could get it. *It's my fault.*

"Sorry."

"But, Chamomile, why didn't you just tell me that you needed the stone? Why didn't you tell me about the promise?"

"I don't know. I was angry with you. Because you waited so long to tell me that Jens was my father. I thought he would help me, that he was concerned about me. But in reality, I did exactly what he wanted. I got a hold of your stone and took it to Rosenholm. And he stole it from me there. I take it he knew that you owned one?"

Her mother nodded. "Yes, I told him that, back when we were . . . an item. But then he wasn't particularly interested in it. Not at that point in time, in any case."

Chamomile dried her eyes on her sleeve. "What was he like back then?" she asked, holding her breath. She wanted to hear it, and she didn't want to hear it. Thinking about her father was like having a scab you couldn't stop picking at, even though you knew that would only make it hurt more.

Her mother took a deep breath. "He was . . . charming. Intelligent, funny. Everyone loved Jens's classes. Including me. And when he started to take an interest in me, of course I was incredibly flattered. I found him handsome and clever and exciting. And for whatever reason, he saw a spark in me. I didn't understand why, but after what you told us tonight, it occurred to me. It was, quite simply, because I looked like her. Trine."

"Why did you tell him about the victory stone?" Chamomile asked.

"I so wanted to impress him. But he was almost indifferent. I told him it was a very rare and powerful amulet that helped in cases of difficult births. He just said, *You're not pregnant, are you?* I thought about that later. And that was one of the reasons I didn't tell him when I found out I was expecting you."

"Why did you split up?" Chamomile asked. Her thoughts were a swirling labyrinth full of anger at her mother for being taken in by Jens and shame at having done the same herself. Why hadn't they seen it? Seen who he really was?

"At some point, though, I finally started to think for myself," she said. "I started to challenge his views. And as soon as I started getting difficult, he lost interest in me. He said I had let him down. After I left Rosenholm, I never heard from him again. Except one time."

"When?"

"It was shortly after you were born. I hadn't heard from him in many months, but one day, he rang and asked if we could meet up and talk. He didn't know anything about you, but I decided to tell him when we met. I thought he maybe regretted the way he had treated me, but there was a completely different reason for him coming."

"The stone ..." whispered Chamomile. "The victory stone!"

"Yes." Her mother nodded. "We met in the woods near Rosenholm and went for a walk, just like we had done so many times before. First, he asked how I was. But it wasn't long before he started asking about the victory stone. He wanted to know if

54

I carried it on me, what I used it for, and where I'd gotten it from. Once I realized he wasn't the least bit interested in me, I focused on trying to get away. Then he dropped the false niceties and suddenly offered me a large sum for the stone. When I also said no to that, he got angry."

"What did he do?" whispered Chamomile.

Her mother took a mouthful of tea and frowned as if weighing up her words. "Nothing. He quickly got it under control. But still, it must have set alarm bells ringing for me because I got a new phone number and a secret address so he wouldn't be able to track me down again. Thinking back to that day now, I think he was close, in that moment, to revealing his true self to me. But maybe he knew he couldn't take the stone from me."

"Why not?"

"A victory stone has a connection with its owner and would be difficult to take by force. It can be done through deception or trickery, but in a straight-up confrontation, it's hard because it will protect its owner."

"In the same way, it's now protecting Jens," whispered Chamomile bitterly. "I . . . I haven't told the others. About him. That he's—"

"Your father?" her mother asked.

"I don't want them to know. "I don't want *anyone* to know. I don't want people thinking of him every time they look at me." Chamomile cried again. Quietly, at first, but the tears kept flowing. She couldn't stop it, and she howled like a little child. "How can you love someone who is the child of a monster?" she sobbed.

"Hey, little Miley," her mother said, pulling her close again. "Of course, your friends will love you, even if they find out."

"But you kept it secret, too," Chamomile said. "For years. Can you please not tell anyone now? For my sake?"

"I won't tell anyone, darling," her mom said, kissing her on top of her head. "That's up to you to do whenever you're ready."

Chamomile said nothing, but she had already made up her mind. Nobody would ever find out. She hid her tear-streaked face in her mother's wool cardigan again.

"We need to get the stone from him," Chamomile muttered. "But how? Jens knows what it is worth to him. He won't let himself be tricked the way I did."

"Perhaps there is a way to weaken the stone's power," her mother said, looking thoughtful.

Chamomile sat up. "Do you know something about that?" she asked.

"Afraid not. I think we should talk to Thorbjørn about it. He knows a lot about amulets." She smiled at her daughter and stroked her cheek. "And now you should go in and go to bed, Chamomile."

"Are you angry with me?" Chamomile asked.

"No, I'm not angry, but I need to sit here a while and think it all over."

"Okay." Chamomile kissed her forehead. Before entering the little cottage, she turned and looked at her mother, sitting alone on the bench in the early morning. She wasn't making a sound, but her whole body shook with her sobs.

They're saying that I can't trust you anymore. Is that true?

Is that true, Malou?

JULY 10ᵀᴴ
2:07 P.M.

Kirstine

Ouch! Kirstine bashed her head on the door frame. She'd forgotten to duck. *Again.* She was not built for the low, timber-framed house Chamomile and her mother lived in.

"Are you okay?" Chamomile asked.

Kirstine rubbed her head and nodded. "Can I help clean up?" She picked up a dish towel that was hanging on the back of a chair at the stove. Chamomile and her mother didn't have a dishwasher. No problem, though; Kirstine liked washing dishes. She took a cup with a chipped handle that Chamomile had just finished washing and put it on the drainer. Kirstine carefully dried the cup and put it away in the cupboard, but no more freshly washed cups followed. The red-haired girl by her side seemed to have ground to a halt despite the huge quantity of dirty dishes stacked on the kitchen table. She stood staring out of the small panes of the kitchen window, pushing the sponge aimlessly around the sink among floating cups and cutlery.

"Is that him arriving?" Kirstine asked.

"No, it was probably just the cat passing outside," Chamomile said, looking down again at the dishes.

Kirstine glanced at her. Chamomile had been checking for

Thorbjørn every five minutes for the last hour, but she still hadn't explained why they were gathered there to wait for him.

"Is Malou coming, too?" Kirstine regretted the words as soon as she had said them. Chamomile looked at her. She wore a smile, but it looked frozen.

"Sorry," Kirstine said.

"It's not your fault," Chamomile said, getting on with the breakfast plates. "No, she's not coming. She still won't answer my messages."

They finished the rest of the dishes in silence, and when Chamomile finally drained the sink of water and said thanks for the help, there was a knock on the old stable door.

It was a tentative knock, as if the person on the other side was worried they might be interrupting something.

"That's him now," Chamomile said, going to open the door.

"Hello," Thorbjørn greeted them, stepping inside. If Kirstine had problems being in the little farmhouse, they were nothing compared to Thorbjørn's. The tall, broad, bearded man simply looked comical inside that low-ceilinged living room. It looked like someone had tried to can him. He clumsily tried to get free of a sprig of rosemary that Chamomile's mother had hung up to dry but which was now tangled in his long hair.

"Hi, Thorbjørn," Beate said, coming in from the yard. She went on her tiptoes and, to Kirstine's surprise, gave Thorbjørn a hug.

"They're old school friends," Chamomile said in response to Kirstine's gaping expression.

"We have something important to tell you," Beate said. "Let's sit out in the garden. Kirstine, can you make sure Beate uses the glasses from the cupboard next to the sink?"

Chamomile went inside to wake Victoria, who was sleeping in Chamomile's room. She had arrived a few hours earlier but had gone to lie down, not yet having made a full recovery.

Kirstine found the glasses and set them on a tray while Beate plopped some lemon slices, fresh mint, and ice cubes into a large pitcher of iced tea. She took hold of the tray handles but then sat it down again with a light groan.

"Shall I take it?" Kirstine asked.

"Yes, could you? I'm a little arthritic in my right arm," Beate said, giving a quick smile before heading outside.

Kirstine watched her go, then lifted the tray and went out the back door. They were sitting in the shade under an old apple tree at a round garden table and five mismatching garden chairs in various stages of disrepair.

"My mom likes to buy pre-loved," Chamomile said by way of explanation as Thorbjørn winced nervously at the chair's loud creaking when he sat down.

Beate brushed the hair from her face and leaned over the table to pour their drinks. "Thanks for coming, Thorbjørn. We want to talk about why Kirstine's rune spell didn't harm Jens. And why he was able to do what he did to Victoria."

Chamomile glanced nervously at the dark-haired girl sitting quietly on the edge of her seat, saying nothing.

Beate turned to Thorbjørn. "Do you know what a victory stone is?"

"Well, yes. It's an amulet," he answered, somewhat surprised. "A very powerful and legendary amulet. They say that whoever owns a victory stone will always win, no matter what struggle they are fighting for. They're very rare."

Beate took a sip from her glass. "I had one," she said.

"A victory stone?" Thorbjørn asked.

"Yes. But Jens has stolen it."

"What?" Victoria looked at Chamomile, shocked.

Kirstine frowned. She could picture them all sitting in their dorm kitchen at Rosenholm looking at the dull black, oval stone Chamomile was showing them.

"Stolen? But Beate . . . if it was your stone, then . . ." Thorbjørn looked at her. "How?"

"It doesn't really matter how he did it," she said, giving Thorbjørn a look that made him bite his tongue. "The main thing is, he's gotten his hands on it, and I'm afraid that the victory stone is the reason his powers are so strong."

"A victory stone . . ." Thorbjørn rubbed his beard. "Yes, that would certainly be a dangerous weapon in the hands of someone like Jens."

"As long has he has the stone, he is a danger to everyone who stands in his way. And especially to anyone who knows the truth about Trine's death," Chamomile said. "We need to get it back."

Thorbjørn frowned and nodded gravely. "That won't be easy. Jens is a careful man. And as far as I know, a victory stone cannot be taken by force."

"Have you ever heard of any way to weaken the stone's power?" Beate asked.

"Unfortunately not," Thorbjørn said.

"I thought you knew all about amulets?" Chamomile said, looking expectantly at Thorbjørn and then at her mother.

"Viking amulets, yes," Thorbjørn said as little beads of sweat appeared on his forehead. "But not victory stones. I've actually never seen one."

Chamomile leaned back in her chair, disappointed.

"I'd like to try and ask my grandmother," Victoria said. "She collects magical artifacts and amulets."

"Does she have a stone?" Beate asked.

"I don't think so, but she might know something about them."

"That's great, Victoria," Chamomile said. "But the best thing would still be to find some kind of victory stone expert."

"Ah, well, now speaking of that . . ." Thorbjørn said, "Beate, do you remember Sigsten Juul?"

"Our old Blood Magic teacher?" Beate said. "The world's grumpiest teacher."

"Exactly. Wasn't there some rumor that he owned a victory stone?"

"Yes, that's absolutely right," Beate said.

"Sigsten Juul may not be a pleasant man, but he has a great deal of knowledge. About both the good and the darker sides of magic. I think if you really want to know about victory stones, you should pay a visit to Sigsten," Thorbjørn continued.

"Hmm . . . Sigsten Juul switched between despising me or ignoring me," Beate said. "I don't think he'd be especially interested in helping if I were to ask."

"Could *you* not go to him, Thorbjørn?" Chamomile asked.

"Well, he wasn't especially interested in me either," he said, looking quite horrified at the mere memory of his old teacher.

"I think Chamomile's got something there," Beate said, looking at that moment so exactly like her daughter that it was hard to see any difference, aside from some wrinkles and the gray streaks in her hair. "You do teach at Rosenholm, just as he did in those days. He'll respect that," she continued.

Thorbjørn frowned and shifted in his chair. "I'm not quite so sure about that," he said. "But maybe we can draw him in, if we can get his attention first."

Kirstine felt his focus suddenly on her. "What?" she said.

"I think old Sigsten will find you quite exciting," Thorbjørn said, facing her. "He always liked the extraordinary."

Kirstine grimaced. She didn't want to be spoken of as extraordinary.

"Well, that explains why he hated me," Beate said. "I was an entirely ordinary student."

"As I said, he wasn't a big fan of mine either," Thorbjørn admitted. "But if I can take Kirstine with me, I can certainly try paying him a visit."

"What do you think, Kirstine?" Chamomile said anxiously.

Kirstine hesitated for an instant. She couldn't help feeling she was being used like some kind of hostage here. But if she could help by going with Thorbjørn, of course she would do it. She nodded.

"Good, then let's go up there. It might be nice for you, too, to make a visit home," Thorbjørn said.

"What do you mean?" Kirstine asked, horrified.

"Sigsten lives in Thy," Thorbjørn said, getting up. "Didn't I mention that?"

JULY 15TH
2:55 P.M.

Kirstine

Kirstine let the car door thud behind her and followed Thorbjørn up the road. White, fluffy clouds scudded across the sky, and the wind rustled the rowan trees that stood guard on either side of the narrow gravel track, long since overgrown with grass and weeds. The battered treetops were a sign that the harsh westerly wind had taken its toll. Here and there one of the older trees had blown clean over, but nobody had taken the trouble to plant new ones to fill the rows.

"Have you been here before?" Thorbjørn asked.

"No," Kirstine said. She passed it on her regular bus route down the main road but had never given this little avenue a second thought. From the road, it was impossible to see what it led up to, but once they had put a few hundred feet more behind them, they finally came to the house. It was big, more of a manor house. Kirstine had lived her entire childhood only twenty-five miles away without ever having heard of this place.

The main building itself seemed to be made up of several sections, and one wing in particular stood out. She stopped in her tracks to take in the unusual construction, and that was when she noticed half of the manor house lay in ruins. The window frames were gapingly empty, there was no roof, and a tangle of lush, climbing vegetation had spread itself up the blackened walls so that it looked as if the building might, before long, disappear under all the greenery.

"The West Wing burned down in '96," a nasal voice from behind them said.

Kirstine whirled around. The shock had set her heart racing, and she noticed her hair starting to crackle with electricity. *Take it easy.*

"Sigsten, thank you for seeing us," Thorbjørn said politely, extending his hand to the tall, elderly man, who was dressed in a dark green wool suit, a tie, and high boots. His hair was white and both cheeks and his nose were a flushed red.

"My pleasure," he said slowly and took Thorbjørn's hand, though without looking at him. Instead, he studied Kirstine unabashedly.

"It's good to see you again, sir," Thorbjørn said. "This is Kirstine." Sigsten took her hand and held it in his while curiously taking her in with his eyes, assessing her as if she were some kind of rare bird.

"Let's go inside where it's warm," he said eventually, turning around, propped up by his walking stick. "I'm always cold these days. It's my age." Despite using a stick, he walked tall and moved quickly. He took them to the opposite wing and opened the door, signaling for them to go inside. "This part of the main building was actually where my paternal grandmother lived in her last years after she was widowed," he explained. "Now this is the only part of the house I keep heated."

Despite Sigsten's words, the narrow, high-ceilinged hallway they now stepped into was not especially warm, and although the sun was shining outside, Kirstine shivered. Sigsten closed the door behind them and fumbled for the light switch. A chandelier lit up above them, but only a few bulbs in it still worked.

A strong smell of earthy dampness filled Kirstine's nostrils. The walls were covered in a gold-colored wallpaper that might once have been pretty but now was stained, with large damp blotches in several places. Patches of mildew grew along the skirting boards, and the floor was dark with rot in the corners.

"The family coat-of-arms," Sigsten said, pointing above the door at the end of the hall.

Kirstine strained her eyes in the dim light. A knight's helmet with some kind of plant wound around it.

"I am the last one left." He pronounced his a's in a dramatic way, like something from an old movie. *Laaast.* Sigsten opened a door leading into a lounge filled with sofas and armchairs, set around an open hearth where a fire was burning. The wallpaper in here was dark red, and Kirstine suddenly felt hot.

"Take a seat," Sigsten said, sitting himself down on an oversized armchair nearest to the blazing fire.

Kirstine and Thorbjørn sat on a small sofa opposite him. Its floral upholstery was faded and, in one place, ripped so the filling poked through.

"A lovely picture," Thorbjørn said, nodding up toward a large painting above the hearth. A tall man posed with a rifle on his shoulder and a hunting dog by his side. A brace of pheasants lay at the man's feet.

"My father," Sigsten said with a short, gruff laugh. "Frederik Juul. He couldn't have hit a cow from two yards away. He still had his portrait painted as a great hunter. My father was a charlatan, and he squandered the entire family fortune." Sigsten sat looking at the portrait, then shook his head and turned his gaze on them. "What is it that you want?"

Thorbjørn jumped a little as if he suddenly remembered how it used to feel sitting on a school bench under Sigsten Juul's piercing gaze. "We've come because we'd like to know more about victory stones," he said directly.

Sigsten raised his white, bushy eyebrows. "Interesting . . ." he said slowly. "And you think I can tell you about that?"

"Back when you were a teacher, there were rumors that you owned a stone," Thorbjørn said.

"Hrm," he growled, bending forward to pick up the poker so he could push a piece of firewood deeper into the flames. "Yes, so I've heard. But I must have inherited that rumor from my father. So, I did get something from him after all."

"It was perhaps your father who owned a victory stone?" Thorbjørn asked.

"My father was very interested in anything that could be an easy path to wealth and success. At some point, he became interested in victory stones. He studied them for years, and right up to his death, he was almost obsessed with finding one. When I was a child, it was a classic from his repertoire of tall stories—the one about how he had gotten hold of King Nidung's victory stone. Have you heard of King Nidung?" Sigsten looked directly at Kirstine.

She shook her head.

"But you do know the Saga of Didrik of Bern?"

Kirstine shook her head again.

"They really ought to teach the students that," Sigsten said, turning to Thorbjørn. "They do teach history, don't they? Being ignorant of history—it's unforgivable in my view." Sigsten gripped the arms of his chair and stood up. He went over to a bookcase by the window at the other end of the room. Soon after, he turned back with an old book that looked so well-thumbed that it might fall apart completely at any moment.

"This is in gothic script," Sigsten said once he had sat down again. "I imagine you students don't learn to read this anymore either."

Kirstine didn't say anything, but she had a feeling that Sigsten, despite his grumbling, was enjoying having an audience to lecture and educate.

"In *The Saga of Didrik of Bern*, you can read about King Nidung. He was King of Thjode," he began. "*Thjode* means 'Thy,' which is, of course, the reason this precise story grabbed my father's attention in the first place." Sigsten flicked slowly through the pages of the book until he found the part he was looking for. Then he began to read.

"*There was a king called Nidung, who ruled over Thjode and Jutland. As the king sat to dine one day, some men came to report to him that a great enemy army had crossed into his realm and was causing much damage. The king gathered his army and rode out, but toward evening, once they had set up camp, it occurred to him he had left his victory stone behind. This stone had been passed down from father to son for generations of his family, and whoever was in possession of it would never lose in battle.*"

Sigsten closed the book. "King Nidung sends a man back to retrieve the stone. After that, a lot of other things happen that are irrelevant to this matter, but Nidung gets his stone and wins the battle. My father solidly believed that the king's victory stone was still here somewhere in Thy. And that he could find it if he just looked long enough."

"When was King Nidung alive?" Thorbjørn asked thoughtfully.

"If he ever lived at all, then it would be over a thousand years ago. Maybe fifteen hundred."

"*If* he ever lived?"

"Yes, as I said, it's just a tall story. Entertaining, though."

"Do you mean to say," Thorbjørn said, "that your father never found a victory stone?"

"Yes and no," Sigsten answered. "He never got his hands on King Nidung's magical amulet. But he did get something else." Sigsten casually lifted one white, long-fingered hand to direct their gaze toward a smaller portrait hanging on the wall behind them. Kirstine turned on the sofa. It was a portrait of a small boy with blue eyes and blond hair.

"Is that you?" she asked.

"Yes, it is. *Sigsten* means 'victory stone.' My father named me after a tasteless, hopeless fixation. So, no. I do not have any stone that you can buy or steal from me. Are you disappointed?"

"What we're most interested to know is what such a stone is capable of," Thorbjørn said. "And how it can be either conquered or weakened."

"Aha," Sigsten said. "All that was my father's specialist subject. I've never been interested in chasing the pot of gold at the end of the rainbow. But clearly, there are lots of people who are."

"What do you mean?" Kirstine asked.

"*What do I mean?*" Sigsten retorted a little irritably.

"Do you mean that others have been here before us?" she tried.

"Yes. That's the interesting thing," Sigsten said slowly, interlacing his long fingers. "Not so long ago, I received a visit from your principal, Jens Andersen."

"Jens?" Thorbjørn blurted out. "Did he want to know if you had a stone?"

"No, because he already knew that I didn't. It's been fifteen years since Jens started coming into my office to see me. Back when we were both teachers at Rosenholm. It took him a good while to come out with what it was he really wanted. And he was very cautious. But when he first revealed his business, I could only disappoint him. He took it very badly when he found out the truth. That I had never had such a stone. I retired shortly after that, and since then, I never heard from him again. Until one month ago."

"What did he want?"

"He came here because he wanted access to my father's research. My father had collected a wealth of more or less fatuous texts in the style of those he hoped could lead him to the victory stone. But Jens must have thought there was something in them that he could use."

"Do you know if he found anything?"

"He did not. I turned him away at the door. I never really liked him that much. I won't forget how he tried to curry favor with me that time. Just because he'd been made principal, he shouldn't imagine he can come around here after not even calling or visiting once in fifteen years. Does he really think that any Tom, Dick, or Harry can turn up and get access to my father's papers? Is that not quite wrong?"

"Well, I . . ." Thorbjørn said.

"And I don't forgive him either for supporting the appointment of that scoundrel they employed in my place," Sigsten continued bitterly. "Imagine that such a thing should happen at an old, dignified school like Rosenholm. It would have been unthinkable just a few years ago. To let in riff-raff like that as a student was bad enough, but then to go and employ him as a teacher . . ."

"Jens has recently come into possession of a victory stone," Thorbjørn said, letting Sigsten's other comments pass unacknowledged.

"I guessed as much," Sigsten said. "When he last came to visit, he seemed less interested in finding a stone but more in learning about how one can make use of its power."

They sat in silence, listening to the crackling of the open fire. Kirstine looked at the old man, who, despite his years, sat brightly in his chair as if he could spring up out of it again at any moment. Sigsten had taught at Rosenholm for many years. Of course, he knew Jens. But did he also know . . .

"Does the name Rose Kathrine Severinsen mean anything to you?" Kirstine asked. "She was also known as Trine, and she was a student at Rosenholm at the end of the eighties."

"I don't remember all the students I've taught. Luckily enough. Most of them were hopeless," Sigsten replied without lifting his eyes from the flames.

"Trine was Jens's girlfriend," Kirstine said.

He turned slowly to look at her. "A student and a teacher. Against the rules, of course, but nonetheless something that you do hear about," he said, raising one eyebrow. "But that doesn't really ring any bells."

"Her sister was named Leah; she was a blood mage . . ."

"Tell me, has this got anything to do with your interest in victory stones?"

Kirstine looked at Thorbjørn. He gave an almost imperceptible shrug.

"Trine disappeared. We're trying to find out what happened to her," she said. "Are you sure you don't remember a girl who disappeared from the school?"

"I'm afraid I can't help you," Sigsten said, shrugging. "Young girls who vanish without a trace, it happens. They run away or get into trouble . . ."

"Or get murdered," Kirstine said. She felt her heart getting faster.

"That too, yes," Sigsten said, studying her with curiosity. "The Sagas have a lot of that. Just read what happened to King Nidung's daughter." He patted the tattered old book on his lap. "Terrible, but then she was spared her life."

Kirstine stood up, her hair crackling around her face.

"You're not a blood mage, are you?" Sigsten asked, but he didn't wait for an answer. "But you know about sacrifice. We humans do terrible things in order to feel powerful and untouchable, don't we?"

"I think we should probably go," Thorbjørn quickly interjected, following Kirstine off the little sofa, which gave out a sighing sound as the weight of this large man was lifted off. "But, as you've probably guessed, we would also be very interested to see your father's papers and research. It concerns not only that missing girl but also the safety of the current students."

"Hmm," Sigsten said, turning to face the fire. "Normally, I would say no. But you have piqued my curiosity, my dear Thorbjørn. And it need be no secret that it wouldn't upset me any to put a wrench in the works of Jens's plans. I assume that the victory stone you are so interested in conquering or weakening is the self-same stone that has come into Jens's possession?"

Thorbjørn nodded. "Exactly."

"Hmm, I must admit I've thought about it, and not just a little, since Jens was here," Sigsten said, looking to the fire again. "About

72

what he plans to use the stone for. And now you arrive, too, looking for answers." He slowly shook his head. "No, I don't want to let
you see my father's papers . . ."

"You don't?" Thorbjørn asked, disappointed.

"No. But I will go through them myself. My father was always
keen to share his discoveries with me when he was alive. But I de-
clined. Perhaps the time has come for me to see what it was he
busied himself with for all these years." The old man leaned back
in his chair and looked thoughtfully into the flicker of the flames.
"I will get in touch with you if I find anything interesting."

"Thank you, we're very—" Thorbjørn began, but Sigsten interrupted impatiently.

"Yes, yes, fine," he grumbled. "Close the door behind you, please.
Such a cold draft in here."

JULY 15TH
5:05 P.M.

Victoria

Victoria peered out the window. She had taken this train ride so many times as a child that she could almost conjure up each of the houses and stations with her eyes closed. She tucked her legs in toward her. The man opposite had his legs stretched out, so it was hard to avoid their feet touching. He gave off an aggressive, repellent energy. But she'd given up trying to find another spot as she'd be getting off soon anyway.

Victoria hadn't told her parents where she was going. Generally, she hadn't told them anything. Jens's words had lodged themselves in her mind. He could harm her. And he could harm them. If she told her parents anything, they might confront Jens, and then he would let them pay the price. Victoria's mother had taken her to be examined by their own doctor, who had concluded she was in need of rest and quiet, and Victoria had explained Kirstine's rune spell away by saying Kirstine was unstable. She hadn't said anything to Kirstine about how easily she convinced her parents of that.

Once off the train, she carried on along mundane streets with their broad sidewalks. The rows of pretty, old houses were baking in the afternoon sun. Reaching the front door, she rang the bell.

"Victoria! It's been such a long time!" Victoria's grandma waved her into her apartment, closing the latch behind her and rattling the many lock chains. She had always been afraid of her home being broken into. "How are you? I heard you had a bit of a funny turn?"

"It was nothing," Victoria said.

"You look quite pale."

"I just didn't sleep well last night."

"Well, that's nothing a bit of blush can't sort out. Go sit in the living room, and I'll get us some coffee and cookies," her grandma said.

Victoria went on through the apartment while her grandma could be heard clattering around the kitchen with something. It was peaceful here with the apartment being situated on a quiet road and her grandma living here alone. Nothing had changed. The paintings on the wall were the same, the vases on the windowsills, the large display case where her grandma kept all her many treasures. Victoria went through the dining room and into the living room. The rooms were big and filled with furniture and items her grandma had either collected throughout her long life or inherited from her own parents. She considered sitting on the flowery sofa but stopped in the middle of the room, where she stood breathing in its particular smell, one that reminded her of her childhood.

"Come over and sit by the window," Victoria's grandma said, coming in carrying a tray with two black coffees and a plate of cookies.

Her grandma always sat at the little table over by the window. From there, you could look down the street and keep an eye on who was going by. Victoria pulled the curtain aside to have a better look. Sunlight streamed lazily into the room.

"So, what could be the reason for this lovely visit today?" her grandma asked.

Victoria felt the guilt rise up in her as she knew she hadn't visited her grandma often enough since starting at Rosenholm. Her grandma looked at her with her brown eyes and a half smile dancing on her lips. She was a tall, slim woman who was always well-dressed and wore lots of jewelry that jangled at her wrists when she gesticulated with her hands. Today, she wore a gold blouse tied at the neck and a tight black skirt that stopped just below the knee. She wore red lipstick, and her hair was dyed dark and blow-dried to sit in loose waves around her face. A few years before, she had fallen and broken her wrist. But she hadn't called Victoria's father to take her to the hospital without doing her hair and makeup first.

"I have to ask you something about an amulet," Victoria said seriously.

"Ah, that's something you know I can't resist!" her grandma said. "I've actually just got my hands on a very rare Egyptian scarab. Would you like to see it?"

"Yes," Victoria said, wondering to herself how to formulate her question without giving too much away. Her grandma stood up and went over to a large display cabinet with glass doors. She opened it and carefully took out a small, greenish stone, handing it over to Victoria. It was in the form of a beetle, very finely crafted, and you could even see the outline of tiny antennae.

"This is around four thousand years old," her grandma said, looking at the amulet. "The scarab was the animal of the god Khepris. Khepris was the god of the sunrise, the day's beginning and rebirth. And an amulet like this is said to give courage and strength and work against depression. It's very rare. I was really lucky to get the chance to buy it," she said, smiling. "But, let's not mention it to your dad. He thinks I have too many things already. I think he'd prefer me to keep his inheritance in mind!" She chuckled.

"No worries, I won't say anything," Victoria said, "but shouldn't something like this be in a museum?" She had heard tales of grave robbers who sold Egyptian findings on the black market.

"Museums have plenty of this kind of thing lying in storage. They don't even have the space to display it all. It's better that this has come to a place where it is appreciated," her grandma said, snatching the scarab up again. Her long, red nail grazed Victoria's palm, and the gold rings on her fingers glinted in the light of the sun.

"Well then, what was the amulet you wanted to ask about?" she asked after placing the Egyptian stone back in the cabinet.

"A victory stone," Victoria said, and her grandma's eyebrows immediately shot up.

"A victory stone? Well, now. That's not for the faint-hearted," she said, looking at Victoria meaningfully.

"What do you mean?"

"Recently, when I bought the scarab, I was warned about all the curses that ancient Egyptians placed on their crypts. It's the usual load of nonsense and, in any case, nothing a capable mage couldn't handle. But I'd think very carefully before getting myself a victory stone."

"Why?" asked Victoria.

"A victory stone bonds with its owner," she explained. "And the longer you have had it, the closer a bond it will have with you."

"But, is that a bad thing?" Victoria asked.

"Only if you lose it," her grandma said. "If you pass it on, the stone will generally accept that as its master's wish. But if you lose it, it will take a little of your strength with it. Perhaps you will manage without it, perhaps not. I'm an old woman—I can't risk losing any of my strength if I happened to be robbed."

Victoria frowned. "But can a young person tolerate it better, having lost a victory stone?"

Her grandma closed her eyes momentarily. "I think that's the case. But it also depends on how long the person has owned the stone and if it has been in the family for a long time. That's often the case with victory stones. They are passed down." She looked at Victoria questioningly. "Where does this sudden interest come from?" she asked.

"It's a school assignment," Victoria said, but her grandma's smile told her she wasn't fooling anyone.

"That's a little tough, giving you assignments to do in recess," she said with a wink. "But whatever the reason is, I'm still just happy to see you. You know what, we should have a little liquor." She stood up again and took two small green glasses and a bottle from yet another cabinet in the living room. "Everyone likes this one here."

Victoria took a taste of the sweet, strong liquid and tried not to grimace. Her grandma emptied her glass and poured herself another before putting the bottle down on the table. Beside it, she laid down a pack of cards. "How about I tell your fortune, like in the old days?"

Victoria smiled. When she was a little kid, she had always loved looking at her grandma's hand-painted tarot cards. Like everything else her grandma owned, they were rare and expensive and she was never allowed to touch them, but every now and then she had persuaded her grandma to read them for her. Victoria hesitated. She had always thought of the tarot cards as a kind of game, and the things that concerned her at the moment seemed too serious, somehow, to feel like playing around with them now.

"What about your love life?" her grandma said, smiling cheekily as she lifted her glass in a toast. "Isn't there a young man with a special place in your heart?"

Victoria gave in. "Yeah, there is, actually. Can you . . . can you read the cards for him?"

"Well, normally you read for the person present, but if you'd rather it was for him, we can at least try it. What is his name?"

"Benjamin."

"Good, so we'll read for Benjamin." Her grandma shuffled the old cards carefully. Then she placed four of them face down on the lace tablecloth in front of her. "Let's see what Benjamin has to tell us," she said, turning the first card. The Emperor. "Uh-huh," she said and turned over the next one. The High Priestess. Victoria's grandma frowned. Then she turned the remaining two cards. The Empress. The Magician.

She leaned back in her seat and folded her arms, looking at the cards with a raised eyebrow. "Tell me, are you getting anything from these?" she asked Victoria.

"Erm . . ." Victoria leaned over the beautiful, old cards. She had never read the cards herself. "The Magician makes sense because Benjamin *is* a mage—"

"No, no," her grandma said, shaking her head. "Something's quite wrong. I don't think these are telling us about your young friend at all. These are four character cards. Four people. Does that say anything to you?"

Victoria looked at the cards lying between them. It was so obvious. "So, I have three friends . . ."

"So, four young women. Yes, that makes more sense. And you are one of them yourself. But which? Do you remember what the cards stand for?"

"Not quite," Victoria admitted.

"Look here. The Magician." Her grandma placed her finger on the young man with a red cape. "On the table before him, there are four magical objects. Those symbolize the things he needs. When the Magician has the things he needs, then he can fulfill his task, and he will have the strength and the will to do it. And next, we have the High Priestess." She pointed to a woman dressed in a sky-blue robe, sitting between two columns, one black and one white. "The High Priestess sits between two columns from the fabled Solomon's temple. They symbolize dark and light, and the High Priestess is wavering between these two poles. Her strength is her intuition and wisdom."

Victoria's grandma pointed at the third card, which showed a woman with yellow-blond hair sitting with a golden cornfield in front of her and a green forest behind. She is wearing a white dress patterned with red fruits. "The Empress is the great mother, a symbol of creativity, abundance, and care. She has a strong connection to nature. And then we have the Emperor." She pointed to the last card. It showed a man sitting on a white throne with a crown on his head. "He represents all those things we have traditionally seen as masculine traits. Strength, ambition, control, dominance, drive."

Victoria studied the four figures. She had an instinct for which card represented each one of them. Her grandma's description of the Emperor made her think immediately of Malou, and she was also certain that the Empress, who symbolized care and connection with nature, had to be Chamomile. She herself felt most

80

drawn to the High Priestess. She even looked a little like her. The woman in the blue robe had dark hair and dark eyes, just like Victoria. Her expression was inscrutable. Serious yet soft at the same time. If Victoria was the High Priestess, that had to mean Kirstine was the Magician.

"Now, I'll turn a fate card for each of you. That will show something that awaits you in the future. But I'm afraid I can't say which one belongs to which person. Normally, you'd only do one at a time, but the cards obviously want something different today." Victoria's grandma laid out another four cards face down. "This time, you turn them," she said, looking at Victoria.

Victoria slowly reached out to the first card. The moon.

"The first will go into the darkness," her grandma said.

The lovers.

"The second must choose between those she loves," she said.

The Hanged Man.

"The third will make a sacrifice."

The Judge.

And the fourth will pass judgment."

She slowly took yet another card and laid it out on its own underneath the eight already on the table. "And at the end of the journey, there lies . . ." She turned over an illustration of a skeleton on horseback.

"Death?" Victoria looked up, horrified at the sight of the disturbing drawing.

"Stay calm," her grandma said. "Death rarely heralds death itself. It can be a good card to turn. It represents change. Something ends while something else is beginning.

"But it can also mean . . . death?"

"It can," her grandma answered slowly. "But, as I say, that's rare."

Victoria nodded. She looked at the cards in front of her. The colors seemed even brighter in the afternoon sun, but although it was warm in the apartment, she noticed she was freezing cold.

"Could I maybe borrow your cards?" she asked. "I'll take really good care of them."

Victoria's grandma looked quite alarmed for an instant. She was happiest with all her things close by her, Victoria knew that well. But then she relaxed a little.

"Of course you can, darling."

82

JULY 16TH
10:17 A.M.

Kirstine

The sea crashed in between the partly subsided concrete structures. An extra-large wave thundered in between two bunkers and rolled on up the beach, the sound reverberating right through her.

The Germans had built these bunkers on the west coast during the war, but now they were being reclaimed by the sea and stood some feet out in the frothy waves. Another huge wave pushed between two bunkers and exploded in a rush of salt water, casting its spray several feet high in the air so some drops splashed her cheeks. The wind wasn't even that strong today. She loved it. She had missed it.

The sea along the west coast of Zealand wasn't anything like this. She had taken the bus from Rosenholm to the beach one weekend when they had leave to go home, but she had been really disappointed. The sea was the almost flat calm of an estuary. It was low tide as far as she could be bothered wading out, and inland, there were heaps of foul-smelling seaweed. It wasn't like this here. Here, the air was fresh.

"Kirstine!"

The yell reached her, though it sounded like it was coming from far away. Her ears were filled with the noise of the wind, and she had no desire to listen to anything other than the crashing waves. Here, she wasn't aware of the buzzing sensation in her body, and she couldn't hear any humming sounds from the ground beneath her. He called again, and she reluctantly turned around. Thorbjørn was standing at the top of the dunes, waving his arms. She sighed before turning back to cross the wide beach. He had tried to convince her they should visit her parents while they were in the area anyway, but she had refused. The sea, however, was something she wanted to visit now she was finally back home.

"What is it?" she asked once she'd finally located Thorbjørn in the parking lot, where he was sheltering behind his van.

"Sigsten is on the phone. He only wants to talk to you. Here, get inside," he said, and opened the car door for her before handing her his phone.

"Hello?"

"Is that the young Kirstine?"

"Yes, it's me."

"I've had a think about it, and I decided to call and tell you that I lied to you."

"Lied?"

"Well, maybe it was more like lying by omission. I didn't remember the girl, Trine, who you spoke about. But I did remember the other one you named. That girl, I remember her so distinctly."

"Leah?"

"Precisely. I was involved myself when she was expelled in her day. For improper behavior. Sadly, I didn't manage to convince the principal that the young Mr. Kovacevic should also have been thrown out with the same."

"Leah died by suicide a few months ago," Kirstine said. "When she failed to avenge the murder of her sister."

84

"Hmm, yes, it is very tragic, of course, in all its banality. But listen, I found something interesting in my father's diary."

"About the victory stone?"

"Yes. He made a significant discovery. But, as far as I can see, he committed an error. In any case, I'd like you hear your opinion on it."

"When can we come?" Kirstine asked.

"Let's say at tea time. That's five o'clock if you weren't aware."

This time, they drove all the way up the long avenue and parked in the courtyard. The sky was overcast, and it looked like rain. There was an open view from the main building out across all the surrounding fields, and Kirstine could see that it was raining in the west, with dark clouds almost meeting the ground. They went over to the door they had entered by last time, and Thorbjørn knocked. They stood and waited a little before knocking again, louder this time.

"Perhaps he doesn't hear so well," grumbled Thorbjørn, trying the door. It was locked.

Kirstine found the window of the red sitting room and looked inside. The large armchair was there by the hearth, but no fire was lit. The room was empty.

"Come on," Thorbjørn said. "There might be another place we can knock."

They continued around to the other side of the building. A gust shook an old windbreak made of lilac shrubs, which sheltered the garden from the fields on the other side, and the first raindrops were beginning to fall. There was an old, dried-up fountain surrounded by the remains of what must once have been some elegant rose bushes.

"Look!" Thorbjørn pointed to a double glass door leading from a hallway out into the garden. That, too, was locked, but the door was missing several panes, and Kirstine could easily put a hand through to open up for them.

"Hello? Sigsten?" Thorbjørn shouted, his voice echoing around them. This had to be a part of the mansion Sigsten didn't use. Kirstine looked down, feeling something crunch underfoot. A fine layer of sand covered the floor, blown in through the broken panes. It smelled faintly of cats, and climbing ivy had found its way in somewhere and was growing up across the ceiling above them. Kirstine could also make out several swallows' nests.

"Sigsten?" Thorbjørn called again. There was no answer. "Shall we try upstairs?" he asked, nodding toward the broad staircase leading to the floors above. The wide stairs were covered in worn, red carpet patterned with gold motifs. The only sound was that of the rain, which drummed insistently against the windows now, and the drip-dripping from a leaking tile onto the hall floor.

At the top of the stairs, they followed a long hallway with several doors along it. Most of them were locked, but one door opened up, revealing a room of heavy furniture covered with white sheets. On the walls hung portraits of women in grand dresses with their hair pinned high. All the women had the surname Juul and must have been Sigsten's ancestors.

"Kirstine!" Thorbjørn's voice boomed from a distance.

She tore herself away from the portraits and went back into the hall. On the other side, another door lay open.

"I found him," Thorbjørn said.

Kirstine entered the room. It was an office. There was a large mahogany desk by the window, and in a chair at the desk sat Sigsten. His head was tipped back, his eyes were wide open, and his mouth gaped. He was dead. Kirstine had no doubt. She had worked in care homes, and it wasn't her first time seeing an elderly person who had passed away.

Thorbjørn placed two fingers on his neck to check Sigsten's pulse and gently shook his head. "It can't be more than a few hours since he died. How did he sound? On the phone?"

"Like he did yesterday."

"Not unwell? Was he struggling for breath?"

"No."

"Sigsten was old," Thorbjørn said. "But he wasn't a man who was at death's door. He seemed pretty spry when we saw him—"

"Have a look . . ." Kirstine took hold of his wrist. Carefully, she pulled up his right shirt sleeve a little. Around his wrist, a large bruise was clearly visible.

"He was tied up!" Thorbjørn exclaimed.

"The killer removed the ropes," Kirstine said. "But after he died, for sure."

Thorbjørn reached up to Sigsten's neck and carefully unbuttoned his shirt.

"What is that?" Kirstine whispered. A dark pattern covered Sigsten's sunken chest as if his veins had suddenly started running with dark ink. The pattern formed an X.

"Dark magic," Thorbjørn whipsered. "He was murdered."

"It's Jens." Kirstine looked at Sigsten's face. His gaping mouth, his wide eyes. He had been in pain before he died. She had a sudden urge to run from that room and get as far away as possible.

"We can't hang around here too long," Thorbjørn said as if he, too, shared her thoughts. He started manically rummaging through the piles of paper that were spread out over the desk. "See if you can find that diary Sigsten wanted to show us."

Kirstine had only paid attention to Sigsten's dead body at first, but now she noticed how messy the place was. Someone had rummaged through all the papers. They were all over the desk and the floor around it. How would they find anything in that chaos?

Her eyes fell on a book lying on the floor. She bent down to get it, but it wasn't a diary. The title was *Orpheus and Eurydice*, and something was sticking out from under the book, something Kirstine took to be a walkie-talkie at first. She lifted the book. It was an old-fashioned Nokia cell phone. She put it into her pocket, stood up, and just then noticed something else. Sigsten's left hand lay clutching the chair's armrest. But his right hand was clenched. She gathered the courage and reached out for his hand. Rigor mortis had not set in yet, and his long fingers allowed themselves to be unfolded, one by one. In the palm of his hand, he had a ball of scrunched-up paper. She could picture it. He had been surprised by his killer, but, at the last minute, he had grabbed this piece of paper on which he had been writing his notes, scrunched it up, and hidden it in his fist. Kirstine slowly smoothed out the piece of paper.

He is afraid
of the shades!
SIGSTEN
Little Kirsten?

JULY 16TH
6:15 P.M.

Chamomile

The upper branches of the old linden tree rustled in the wind as Chamomile crossed the courtyard. Summer lilac had taken root between the bumpy cobblestones, and its long, purple tendrils swayed in the breeze. A tabby cat trotted out of the old stables. It stopped and had a long stretch without giving her a glance, though she was sure it had seen her.

"Mismis!" Chamomile called, and after first ignoring her a little longer, the cat finally sidled over and allowed her to be pet for a while until a watering can toppled in the wind, causing it to jump up in fright and run away.

Chamomile went to the kitchen door but stopped short at the small living room windows. Her mother was lying on the sofa, and beside her sat a woman with long, dark hair and tanned skin. *Lisa.* She was holding a droplet-shaped crystal on a cord over her mother's chest, the crystal swinging back and forth. Chamomile realized that Lisa was dowsing. She knew the technique well. It was an ancient method of getting an answer to things you were worrying about. By studying the movements of the pendulum, you could get either an affirmative or negative answer to your question. Chamomile watched how Lisa concentrated on shifting the pendulum from her mother's chest to her forehead and how it slowly started to oscillate. Chamomile took one step closer to the window to see better, and suddenly, Lisa looked up. At the same point, she grabbed the pendulum as if its oscillations were revealing something. Chamomile waved and went inside.

"Hi. What are you doing?" she asked, coming into the kitchen and slipping out of her sandals.

"Hi, darling," her mother said, sitting up. "I've not been feeling quite myself lately, and Lisa was kind enough to come and take a look at me. It might be that I'm just going into early menopause." She got up from the sofa. "Won't you have something to eat with us, Lisa? Chamomile dug some potatoes up from the garden, and a neighbor came by with some flounder he caught this morning."

Chamomile threw herself into an armchair while her mother tipped the potatoes into a basin in the kitchen and started peeling them.

"Thanks, but I can't stay, Beate," Lisa said, packing the pendulum away in her old leather bag. "I'll come back in a few days with an herbal infusion for you. I should maybe swing by Rosenholm this evening. All my supplies are at the school. Your own blend of herbs is effective, of course, but I think there are some rare plants that might benefit you, too. Marsh orchids are in bloom just now, though I'm afraid they don't grow in New Zealand. But I do have some in dried form . . ." Lisa took a little pad out of her bag and made some notes, still muttering to herself. Chamomile caught the words *royal fern* and *spleenwort*.

Chamomile's phone vibrated in her pocket, so she pulled it out. At first, she didn't understand what she was seeing. Kirstine had sent a photograph of something that looked, more than anything, like a receipt. But the words were strange.

"He's afraid of the shades . . ." Chamomile read.

"What did you say?" her mother said.

"I don't know," she answered. "Kirstine sent me a weird text." She could see that Kirstine was typing something else, but it could take a moment. Kirstine was severely dyslexic, and even a short message could be tricky for her. Finally, the phone vibrated again.

> Sigsten is dead. J murdered him.

"He's dead," Chamomile whispered.

"Who is dead?" her mother asked, leaving her place at the kitchen table. "Chamomile?"

"Him, your old school teacher. Sigsten."

"Oh, well, he must have been really quite old," she said. "Was it recently?"

"You don't understand," Chamomile said. "Kirstine and Thorbjørn visited him yesterday. Kirstine wrote me last night. But now, he's dead. She wrote that 'J murdered him.'"

"Who?" asked Lisa. "She can't mean . . . Jens?"

"I think so," Chamomile said.

"That's dreadful!" her mother said, letting herself sink into a chair.

"I don't understand it," Lisa said. "He's killed him . . ."

"You can't go to Rosenholm tonight," Chamomile said.

"No," her mother said quietly. "I'm afraid none of you should go back to Rosenholm as long as he is in charge there."

"But, the students. We can't desert them," Lisa said. "And what about the school? Are we just to abandon Rosenholm without a fight?"

"You'll need to find a different way to fight for Rosenholm. It's far too dangerous to go back," Beate said. "If we didn't know that for sure before, we certainly do now. Jens will go to any lengths to keep us quiet."

"And we know one other thing," Chamomile said. "There has to be something he is very afraid of us finding out. Otherwise, he wouldn't kill some old man who was already nearing the end of his life." Suddenly, another thought came to her. "Should we be worried about him coming here?"

Her mother lifted her face and looked at her. "You needn't be afraid, Miley. Jens doesn't know where I live, and even if he did, he couldn't risk his reputation by having people hear he'd turned up to threaten a pupil in her own home."

"A *former* pupil," Chamomile said. Her mother was right. She couldn't go back to Rosenholm now.

September 23, 2003

Was visited by J. Andersen, teacher at Rosenholm Academy. Very committed and friendly. Showed great interest in victory stones but was noticeably disappointed at not finding an example of one here. Possible research partner? Shared with him the latest interpretation of the prophecy, including the ending, over which he became quite animated. Have agreed to write to him with any new discoveries.

JULY 16TH
7:00 P.M.

Kirstine

"Why kill him?" Thorbjørn rubbed his beard and looked out at the rain, which was beating down on the windshield and over the gas station they were driving into.

"To stop us from finding out what Sigsten had discovered?" Kirstine thought out loud. "Or maybe Jens was trying to force Sigsten to tell him about it. And when he refused, he killed him."

"Yes, Sigsten certainly was a stubborn old fellow," Thorbjørn said. "But how did Jens know? That Sigsten wanted to tell us something?" He shook his head and sighed. "I'll get some coffee. Would you like anything to eat?"

"No, thanks." She was still in too much shock to think about food. While Thorbjørn put gas in the tank and fetched coffee, she remembered the old Nokia and pulled it from her pocket. It still had some charge. Kirstine went to the menu and opened the list of most recent calls. The very first number was one she recognized. It was Thorbjørn's number, and the time matched up with Sigsten calling them in the afternoon. But earlier in the day, Sigsten had called a different number. Thorbjørn returned with a bag of pastries and two cups of coffee. He handed her the coffee and treats and sat down in the driver's seat.

"Do you recognize this number?" Kirstine asked, showing him the phone.

"That's Jens," he said, looking shocked. "Sigsten simply called him himself."

"Why would he?" Kirstine asked.

Thorbjørn took a sip of his coffee and let out a sigh. "Maybe the old guy just couldn't contain himself from calling and crowing over how he'd found out something Jens didn't know."

"And it was the death of him," Kirstine said. "Jens killed him. What does the X that Sigsten had on his chest mean?"

"I don't know. Perhaps it was some form of torture? To get Sigsten to talk."

"I wonder if Jens found out the thing he wanted to know," Kirstine said.

"We can't tell. But he didn't find the note, in any case. What do you think it means?" Thorbjørn asked, indicating the crumpled note sitting on the dash. "Sigsten was his own name. Why write that? We knew fine well what he was called." Thorbjørn took the paper and read Sigsten's other notes. "*He's afraid of the shades!* Does he mean Jens there? And what does it mean that Jens is afraid of shadows? Sunglasses? Window blinds? And then we have this Little Kirsten—I don't know what that's about—"

"I know," Kirstine said, sipping her coffee. "We learned about it in school. Little Kirsten and Prince Buris. They're buried at Vestervig Church. It's not so far from here."

"That doesn't mean anything to me," Thorbjørn said.

"Little Kirsten was the king's sister, and she fell in love with a prince called Buris," Kirstine explained. "When the king found out she was pregnant, he killed her and locked Prince Buris in a tower with a chain around his ankle. A chain just long enough for him to reach her grave."

"The king's sister," Thorbjørn mumbled. "But is it anything to do with the king Sigsten spoke about?" The King of Thy . . . what was he called . . . Nidung?"

"I don't think so," Kirstine said. "I'd never heard of King Nidung before."

"Hmm," Thorbjørn said, typing into his phone. "No, it says here that Little Kirsten's brother was Valdemar the Great. He lived later, in the 1100s. So, what's the connection with the victory stone?"

Kirstine shrugged.

Thorbjørn drained his cup and popped half a custard pastry in his mouth. "Let's go out and look at that grave. Where did you say it was?"

The rain was easing off as they reached Vestervig Church, and a flock of sparrows had alighted on the pathways between the little graves. They rose up as one when Thorbjørn swung open the little black iron gate into the churchyard. He let Kirstine enter first. It was a large church. The tower itself was white, but the rest was plain stone. They both looked around carefully. Kirstine couldn't quite escape the thought that Jens might be here somewhere, watching them.

"It's over there," she pointed. An old gravestone was marked with a small plaque. LITTLE KIRSTEN AND PRINCE BURIS was all that it said. The grave itself consisted of a strange, oblong flagstone with two crumbling headstones—one at each end. The two lovers had been buried alongside one another.

"Couples who get married in the church still leave bouquets of flowers on the grave," Kirstine said.

Thorbjørn was standing with his face buried in his phone. "It says that many folk ballads were written about Little Kirsten and Prince Buris. And a poem by Hans Christian Andersen. It says that the king made her dance to death. That doesn't sound at all pleasant."

Kirstine turned her back on the grave and walked a little along the cemetery paths. She had never really liked going to church, but for some reason or another, she had always liked churchyards. In this one, there were an unusual number of old graves with sunken headstones and inscriptions that were hard to decipher. She stopped at one of them, where the writing was still legible, although peculiar and a little eroded.

WITHOUT MERCY FOR BEAUTY'S RADIANCE AND CRUEL AGAINST THE BLOSSOMING OF YOUTH IS THE DAY THAT REGRETS NOTHING HERE, ALAS, MAY YOU, THE CITY SUN, UNMARRIED MAIDEN, CHRISTINE, BE MARRIED TO THE EARTH.

Kirstine spelled out each of the strange words. Poor Christine. Yet another young woman, dead before her time.

The evening sun broke through the clouds, and she felt it instantly warming her back. The birds had settled in some bushes beside her, where they hopped around from branch to branch, chirping cheerily. She turned and walked back to Thorbjørn, who was still standing reading on his phone.

"Is there anything about the headstone?" Kirstine asked.

"Yes, that's just what I'm reading about," he said. "The inscription has never been fully understood. It's thought that the word *sister* can be seen on the single stone, and some researchers take that as an indication the grave really contains a pair of siblings and not two lovers from ancient history."

Kirstine examined the single gravestone, but it seemed to be completely flat. She knelt down at the other end of the grave and let her fingers run over its surface. Her fingertips tingled, and the buzzing sensation spread up her arm and beyond, making her feel dizzy. The birds' twittering faded away, and an unusual whistling sound filled her ears instead.

"Perthro," she whispered. The name of the rock rune, the rune of stones and the earth. The rune connected with all things hidden and repressed to knowledge that has been forgotten over many generations. *"Perthro,"* she commanded again, this time louder, letting herself be consumed by the tingling sensation, letting her vision change. Colors began to fade, but she saw everything to the tiniest detail. The stone before her became a landscape of hills and valleys, thousands of small elevations and hollows that contained a message that she couldn't see.

"Reveal your secret!" she asked, and after she blinked once more, something began to take shape before her very eyes. The gray jumble of tracks in the stone began shifting. Some of them disappeared, while others became more distinct. And now she could see what was on the ancient headstone.

SLEEP, MY SISTER, BENEATH THIS STONE.

Kirstine blinked again, and another word appeared. The letters were completely different; they were rough and uneven, as if they had been carved hastily underneath the first inscription.

SIGSTEN

> **Something has happened.**
> **I need you to call me back!**

JULY 18ᵀᴴ
10:00 A.M.

Victoria

Victoria was keeping an eye out along the road for the two big elm trees appearing. Chamomile had promised her she'd wait there at the bus stop, and now Victoria spotted her. Her red hair was pulled into a tousled-looking braid, and she was wearing a sun-yellow summer dress in the heat. She waved cheerily to the driver as he pulled over. Victoria gave a sigh of relief on seeing her. She looked just like herself.

"Hi!" Chamomile gave her a hug, and Victoria made a conscious effort to feel it. She let her barriers drop and instead allowed the sensory impressions to flood over her as Chamomile pulled her close in her arms. Victoria sensed Chamomile's mood. She was happy, but Victoria also sensed an underlying current of worry and fear. And . . . shame? But there was no feeling of weakness, no signal that any of Chamomile's life strength had been stolen away when Jens took the victory stone from her. Feeling better about her friend's mental state, Chamomile let her go. Those blue eyes and her rosy cheeks flushed in the summer heat. She looked well and healthy, and Victoria was relieved, even though her grandma's words remained with her as a nagging worry she couldn't put to rest.

"Are you all right?" Chamomile asked. "You look so serious. Is it because of Sigsten?"

"Yeah, I guess," she answered.

"It's SO horrible, isn't it? Poor Kirstine, finding him like that."

"How is she?"

"Hmm, she's acting like she's taking it all okay," Chamomile said. "But you know Kirstine. She doesn't say much."

"How about your mom?"

"She's scared. She's forbidden me from going back to Rosenholm as long as Jens is principal."

"Yeah, that's out of the question now," Victoria said.

"It's weird, isn't it? I'd never have thought that we wouldn't do all three years at the school. Who knows if we'll even get to be there for our exams? My mom has agreed with Lisa and Thorbjørn that they'll arrange some lessons for us. I don't understand why she thinks it's so important right now. Have you told your parents you're not starting back at school in September?"

"Not yet," mumbled Victoria. "Have you heard from Malou? Is she thinking she'll stay after the school year starts?"

"I don't know, I haven't tried calling, but . . . I just don't think I'd tell her that stuff about Sigsten in a message," Chamomile said. "What did your grandma say? She didn't happen to have a victory stone in her stash?"

"Sadly not," Victoria said. "But she read all our fortunes in her tarot cards."

"Are we going to be rich and happy?" Chamomile asked.

Victoria looked at her. "I don't know. It actually seemed pretty ominous to me, to be completely honest. She pulled Death . . ."

Chamomile stopped in her tracks. "Maybe she predicted Sigsten's death!"

Victoria thought it over. "It's possible. But she also said that it more often stands for change."

They carried on down the drive to the farmhouse without saying any more about Jens, Sigsten, Malou, or the victory stone. Instead, Chamomile enjoyed interrogating her about types of grain and flowers. She laughed when Victoria couldn't tell wheat from oats and then pointed out across the undulating, golden fields to indicate cornflower, poppies, and ox-eye daisies growing in among the corn.

Once they got there, they wandered around the garden. The grass was long and tickled Victoria's bare legs and ankles. Beate was resting in a hammock hung between two fruit trees.

"Victoria's here now, so you might wanna get up, Mom."

Kirstine came outside from the living room. She had to duck her head to pass under the low doorway. Victoria gave her a hug. Swallows were swooping elegantly back and forth from the surrounding fields to the old farm buildings where they had built their nests.

"Show Victoria the note," Chamomile said once they had sat down at the garden table. Kirstine took the note from her pocket. Victoria studied the cryptic notes Sigsten had made just before his death.

"I think he meant Jens with what he wrote there," Chamomile said. *"He's afraid of the shades!* What do you think it means?"

Victoria had spent the last few evenings reading everything she could find about shade and shadow and about Little Kirsten. "I don't know. Perhaps it's just that Jens fears being in the shadow? But that seems unlikely. I found lots of old folk songs featuring Little Kirsten, but there was nothing about shade. I can't quite find any greater meaning in it all."

102

"And what about the X they saw on Sigsten's chest?" Chamomile asked. "Does that mean anything to anyone?"

Victoria frowned. "An *X* is a letter, obviously. It could also be a cross. A mark, like you place on a ballot paper. *X* also stands for *Gebo*—the gift rune. And, if you're using Roman numerals, X equals ten. But none of that says much to me."

Chamomile sighed. "Maybe we could use a ritual to give us a clue. A truth ritual. That's a thing, right?" She looked at her mother. "What about that thing with the pendulum Lisa had?"

Beate shook her head. "The pendulum can only be used if you have a very matter-of-fact, yes-or-no question you want answered. And it needs to be swung over the object or person the question concerns. And we don't have an exact idea of how to understand this. But there are other rituals . . ."

"Do you know of one?" Chamomile asked.

"Yes, though I've never performed it myself. But time is on our side," Beate said.

"What do you mean?" Victoria asked.

"The ritual I'm thinking of needs to be performed on Lughnasadh. August first. It's not so far away."

Victoria tried to remember everything she knew about Lughnasadh, which was a date midway between the summer solstice and the autumn equinox. Where *Imbolc* marked the arrival of spring, Lughnasadh marked the arrival of autumn. Victoria remembered their Imbolc celebration in February when Lisa had dragged them out into the freezing cold forest to let them walk over red-hot bonfire embers in their bare feet. It now seemed like an eternity ago.

"Why does it need to be performed exactly then?" Chamomile asked.

"Do you remember what the god Lugh stands for?" asked Beate.

"Something to do with war?" Chamomile guessed.

"Yes, but also for truth. And if you perform a ritual in his honor on this particular day, he may reveal to you a truth that has otherwise been hidden."

"That's perfect," Chamomile said. "Is it difficult to perform?"

"No, it's not difficult, but it needs four women, all from Growth. I'm sure Lisa will want to do it, but then we'll still need one more."

"It needs to be somebody we can trust," Victoria said. "Someone we dare tell the whole story to."

"That's the issue," Beate said. "Do we know any such person?"

"Yes, actually, I think we do," Chamomile said, smiling.

Can you help me, please?

Do you understand what you're asking of me?

Who else can I ask?

SEPTEMBER 23ʳᴅ
2:00 P.M.

Victoria

He was angry with her. Angry at what she was getting him to do now. Benjamin didn't need to say anything; Victoria could tell as soon as they met up at the train station. It was only once they'd gotten off the train and were walking when he finally spoke.

"What was it that gave you this fantastic idea?" he asked.

"It was something Jakob said. About the Committee of Mages," Victoria said, relieved that he was finally talking to her. "He said that the members often had honors bestowed on them by the king. I had never thought about that. That the aristocracy was almost just magic's elite. And then I got to thinking—"

"About what my last name was," he finished.

"Yup," Victoria said as they continued walking past Kronborg Castle, which looked like a perfect fairy-tale castle, basking in the summer sun. It was almost like it wanted to remind them of the mages and their prestigious past. "And as I understand it from your father, he was a member of the Council of Mages," she continued. "We may need their support if we want Jens removed as principal of Rosenholm."

They continued until they reached a large sixties-style villa in yellow-colored stone, discretely set back from the road.

"This is it," Benjamin said. "Let's go in the back. I arranged with him that we'd meet down by the summerhouse. It's better if my mother doesn't find out." He took her down along a high hedge and showed her where they could squeeze through. It was a luxurious house, and on emerging through the hedge, they were met with an open outlook onto the white sands of the beach, the blue sea, and the Swedish coast opposite.

"What a view," Victoria said.

"Let's get this over with," he replied, pointing. At the end of the garden was a small, octagonal, wooden summer house. When they went in, they were immediately immersed in a rush of classical music streaming out from speakers under the rafters. Sitting there in a wicker chair was Vilhelm Brahe, Benjamin's father. This time, he was not dressed in a suit but still wore smartly pressed trousers and a crisp, white shirt.

"Welcome," he said, turning down the music.

"Thank you," Victoria said, sitting in a basket chair across from him. Benjamin remained standing with his back to them, looking out toward the sea. He didn't greet his father.

"It was kind of you to have us here," Victoria said.

"Not at all. I have some business to attend to later, though, so I'd appreciate it if this doesn't take too long," Vilhelm said.

"It's about the speech Jens gave," Victoria said. "Back at my parents' house."

"Yes, it was quite a memorable evening," Vilhelm said. "I hope you are better. That was a serious bout of stage fright you had."

"Yes, thanks. I'm fine," Victoria said curtly. "We're here because I would like to hear your views on Jens's plans for Rosenholm. And his thoughts on reinstating the Committee of Mages."

He peered at her through his glasses. He seemed to be sizing her up, almost assessing her in some way. She felt as if he was considering how much she was really worth spending any time on.

"Yes, it's an interesting idea," he said, eventually. "As Benjamin has perhaps told you, both his grandfather and great-grandfather were members of the Council of Mages, as am I. And before that, several of his ancestors sat on the Committee of Mages. The Brahe family has a long tradition of being positioned close to power."

"We've always shown up as yes-men for those in power, as long as we could see some advantage in it," Benjamin said without turning. "Isn't that what you're trying to say?"

"We are opportunists," Vilhelm said. "And for that reason, we've enjoyed a position of privilege, and we are also in possession of a small fortune, which you too have benefited nicely from, Benjamin. Your mother and I have made sure that you've never wanted for anything."

Benjamin snorted but didn't say any more.

"In our family, we grab opportunities wherever they appear," Vilhelm continued. "And Jens is also a man for opportunities, that much, I am sure of. As I say, our family has hundreds of years' experience of acknowledging and understanding nobles and kings and ministers of state."

"What do you think Jens's project is all about?" Victoria asked. "What is it that he wants from Rosenholm?"

He lowered his gaze for a moment and smoothed out a crease in his trousers. "I rather doubt, in any case, that he is particularly concerned about the young people and their education."

"So, why does he want to be principal?" asked Victoria.

"Jens wants power," Vilhelm said, shifting his gaze to the sea outside, unless it was his son he was looking at.

"And power lies at Rosenholm?"

"Perhaps not in the first instance. But if it was me who wanted to take over power and needed a large troop of easily influenced young mages who I could turn into my loyal followers, I know exactly where I would start."

"Rosenholm," Victoria said.

"Precisely. But that alone is not enough. Jens needs to have the elite on his side, too. And he's well on the way. Several members of the Council are willing to vote for the discontinuation of that self-same council. In return for getting a place on the Committee, you understand."

"And you are one of them," Benjamin said.

"As I said, we have always been opportunists in this family," he said.

"And why is it so important to have a committee rather than a council?" Victoria asked.

"The Council is a democratic institution subject to the laws of society," Vilhelm explained. "If a mage has committed a sufficiently serious offense against the Council's values, they will be handed over to the authorities. To the police and the justice system. But that's not how it was when the Committee was the mages' highest authority. The Committee operated independently of society, which meant, in real terms, that mages were above the law. They could not be held accountable for things that ordinary people considered to be a crime."

Victoria frowned. "Jens wants to absolve mages from punishment?"

"As far as I can assess, that seems to be one of his goals, yes. To reinstate mages to the status they previously held. Above everyone else, close to power, and not subject to the petty laws and rules that might prevent them practicing magic that is no longer permitted."

Victoria frowned. If Jens managed to do this, he could never be brought to justice for Trine's murder. And he might also be able to go around as he pleases committing new crimes.

"But surely you can't let him do that?" Victoria said. "The Council needs to stop him!"

"I don't think you should count on the support of the Council." Benjamin's father clasped his hands together and turned to face her. "Jens is a dangerous man. I wouldn't cross him if I were you. And if you are planning on trying to stop him, I would be very careful to keep that hidden from him."

"It's too late," Benjamin said, turning for the first time to look at his father. "He already knows that we're against him."

"In that case," Vilhelm said, "I would advise you to keep an extra careful eye over your shoulder."

At that moment, he didn't seem like the cynical, calculating man Victoria had been introduced to. He seemed like any worried father.

110

AUGUST 1ˢᵀ
4:08 P.M.

Chamomile

Chamomile had just come in from the garden when there was a knock on the old stable door. Before she could answer it, though, the door opened, and Molly stepped in. It had been over a year since Chamomile had seen her, and their tutor from their first year at Rosenholm looked somehow different. Her hair had changed, her usual dark makeup was gone, she was suntanned, and she wore a top fashioned from a gaudy scarf she had wound around her body. But the most striking thing was the enormous backpack she was carrying. It looked as if it weighed about as much as Molly herself.

"Hey!" she yelled, seeing Chamomile. "Is this where the party's at?"

Chamomile rushed to meet her, and Molly pulled her into an embrace, the backpack still on her shoulders.

"Jeez, you've got so much stuff with you!" Chamomile laughed as Molly finally clicked the backpack loose and let it fall to the floor with a thump.

"Straight outta Goa. I came directly from the airport."

"It's so good to see you!" Chamomile said. "Thanks SO much for coming."

Molly shrugged. "I had to come home at some point, and now was the time. I felt it as soon as you called. I just wasn't sure if I would make it in time."

"Your timing is completely perfect," Chamomile said. "The ritual is tonight."

"It's so cool here!" Molly said, looking around the little house.

"I don't know about that," Chamomile said. "My mom did all the decor."

"I think your mom and I have the same taste." Molly smiled.

"You need to say hi," Chamomile said. "Mom! Molly's here!"

Chamomile's shout caused the other guests to start popping out from the garden or from Chamomile's room. Until now, it had always been just Chamomile and her mother in the little farmhouse. That was fine, but Chamomile always wanted siblings or a larger family. Right now, the house felt full of life, and she loved it. Lisa had arrived the day before, and Kirstine was living here now.

"Hey, are you running some kind of women's commune here?" Molly asked after greeting the others. "I've always wanted to live in something like that."

"You're very welcome," Chamomile said's mother, smiling. "I'm just making a pot of tea, and Chamomile has baked a cake for the occasion. After that, I'll go through everything you need to know about the ritual with you."

"Mom, what is it, exactly, that we should be looking out for?" Chamomile was keeping watch over the yellow fields, which bathed in the evening sunlight.

"A natural spring," her mother said. "The Maiden's Well."

"Yes, okay, but how are you supposed to look out for a spring?" Chamomile asked. "Is it marked with a sign?

"No," said her mother. "There's no sign."

"But, it can be found?"

"Yes, I'd say so. I've been there once when I was little. With my grandma. I'm almost certain it's somewhere near here."

Chamomile sighed and rolled her eyes at Molly, who was trudging alongside with her tanned legs shoved into big, dark boots. They had taken the train toward Copenhagen and gotten off at Knabstrup Station, which was little more than a skinny platform, and now they were continuing out of town on foot. Chamomile turned and looked behind them. Their shadows on the paved road had become long as the sun sank toward the horizon. Lisa followed not far behind them, barefoot, wearing a long, dark cotton dress. Now and then, she stopped to pluck a flower from the verge.

"Beate?" Molly called from a deep ditch running along the road edge. "It's very damp down here. Could this be water from the spring?"

"No," said Chamomile's mother. Her broad hips swayed with her stride and her long skirt swung at her ankles, as she continued down the road without looking any closer at Molly's find. "We have to find a kind of low well. It's probably quite overgrown by now. See if you can spot any red moss."

"Red moss? Is that a thing?" Molly asked, jumping up out of the ditch again, her muddy boots leaving wet footprints on the warm asphalt.

"Red moss grows around the spring. They say that the water came through on the spot where a young girl was murdered. Her blood colored the moss red, and it has been red ever since," her mother explained. "For hundreds of years, people have been coming to the Maiden's Well to leave offerings of the year's first fruit in the hope of receiving good health or some luck and happiness in return. And this wasn't the only place people came. There are sacred springs all over Denmark, many of them now forgotten. But, in the olden days, people gathered at the springs on Walpurgis Night or Midsummer Eve to drink the healing water.

"Can you still drink the spring water?" Molly asked.

"Maybe. But we'll be using the water for something else. Tonight, we will not be asking for either good health or fortune, but for clarity." Her mother stopped and looked out across the golden fields. "I think that cluster of trees looks familiar. Let's see what's hidden down there."

The sun had gone down by the time they finally found the spring, but the sky was still light enough for them to see. The spring itself was nothing special to look at. Long grass and wiry milfoil plants had completely covered the little hole, edged by rough stones. Once her mother had pulled all the plants aside, Chamomile caught sight of a reddish moss around the edge of the spring.

"Is there still water in there?" Molly asked.

"We'll soon see," her mother said, lifting a large silver cup from the bundle she carried over her shoulder. She tied a length of twine to its fragile handle and carefully lowered the cup down into the narrow hole. When she pulled it up again, it was full of water.

"Good." Lisa nodded approvingly and knelt down beside Chamomile's mother. "Come and sit yourselves here. Then we'll make an offering of the year's first fruit in the hope that the spring might bring us some clarity."

They each got out the items they had brought. Chamomile had picked the first wild apples from their hedgerow, while Molly had brought some bright red rosehips from the garden. Her mother had tied a little sheaf of corn from the field, and Lisa had picked a bouquet of different herbs. Chamomile recognized St John's wort, wormwood, and scentless chamomile. One at a time, they cast their gifts into the little well.

Her mother set the cup of spring water down between them. "Let's join hands."

Chamomile reached her right hand out to Molly, and her mother took her left. As soon as the little circle was closed, she felt the power they contained between them. All four of them were Growth mages, and their combined energy was a much greater force than she had imagined. Suddenly, it was as if she was aware of every single living thing present that summer evening—the heartbeat of every little bird, the potential for growth in every root. In that instant, it felt like nature was holding its breath and waiting to see what the four women wanted.

"We call on Lugh and ask him to reveal the truth to us this evening," her mother said ceremoniously. "Help us. Show us what it is Jens is afraid of."

She leaned over the cup, and the others did the same. The surface of the water reflected four different faces, some younger and some older, but the look in their eyes was the same. Alert and concentrated. Then the reflection disappeared, and instead, Chamomile saw something that caught her breath.

A young woman. Her hair was dark, pulled into a bun at her neck, and she wore a dress with an apron over it. Her clothes were old-fashioned; this had to be from long ago. The young woman opened her mouth in a silent scream, and now they saw how strong hands took hold of her by the shoulders. She was forced backward, down into a brook. The woman struggled, but more hands appeared. More hands held her down, and her face disappeared under the water.

"No," Molly whispered. "No!"

The image changed; it moved faster now—hands around a throat, a figure who was thrown into a dark hole, a ripped dress. New faces. All young women. Chamomile felt bile rising in her throat. She didn't want to see any more. A knife, a rope. It went so quickly now that she was only seeing little glimpses, and then, suddenly, the stream of images stopped. A single face was left in the water's mirror. Her eyes were closed, the red hair spread out across the blooming violets. She was dead.

Chamomile tried to get control of her own breathing, which was shallow and too fast.

"It's Trine," she whispered.

Suddenly, the girl opened her eyes and looked straight at them as if the surface of the water was a window she could see through. Her lips formed words, which came to them from far away.

"Find the Nightshades!"

The voice echoed around them, but the vision in the silver cup slowly faded away.

116

SIGRSTEINN DAUØI VILL VERJA

He gets up and reads over the prophecy. It calms him. Even if they should find it, they don't know the ending. The old man and his nonsense about a diary mean nothing now.

Sigrsteinn dauøi vill verja. Sigrsteinn dauøi vill verja. He reads the last line again and again. The proof that he's untouchable. It's what he clings to in these nights when he cannot sleep. When he has dreamed again of those blue bodies that wander at the edge of dawn.

PART 2
AUTUMN

Everything flashes red
Cross my fingers, tell a lie but hope
For a collision
The pressure comes in waves, like curves we follow
Nature is fantastic and it turns me on

From Bittersweet Nightshades *by Peter Sommer from the album*
Loved to dream, dreams on loving, *2018*

I'm not coming back to school after vacation. You know why. What about you? Are you staying?

I've decided to believe there's a reason for you doing what you're doing. I have to.

If you don't want me writing anymore, say so now.

SEPTEMBER 2ᴺᴰ
4:20 A.M.

Malou

They had no need for sleep. They had forgotten to eat. The moon's silvery-white light through the window made Malou's naked skin look like marble. But inside, she was burning. She could feel it all rising up inside her. Engulfing her like a wave, one she was no longer fighting. She let the wave rise and rise, and there was nothing to be done. All that she longed for was to let it flow out over everything, to break down the walls, to see it all burn. She wanted to let go, to set it free. *It's happening. It's too late now to stop it.*

"Malou..."

The way he moaned her name almost hurt. His tongue burned against her skin. She reached for him and pulled his mouth to hers. She could feel his pulse. She would have liked it to last as long as possible, but she was just carried by it, like being on a train with no brakes. She relinquished control; she let go.

Afterward, he lay sleeping on his stomach, his face turned toward her, but she still couldn't sleep. The fire kept burning inside her; the waves kept rolling. She felt broken. Like a wounded animal, only alive at another's mercy. How had she let this happen? She had always been so good at looking after herself, and now here she lay, vulnerable and helpless in someone else's bed. Why had she not stopped it? Had she thought they wouldn't go this far? Had she thought she had it under control? Or had she just been lying to herself?

Malou looked at his face as he slept. It would soon be getting light again.

This is going to end badly.

Dear Malou,

You are invited to attend an individual tutorial session in the drying loft on September 2, at 7 p.m., where we can work together on developing your unique abilities.

With kind regards,

Zlavko Kovacevic
Vice Principal of Rosenholm Academy

SEPTEMBER 2ᴺᴰ
5:30 A.M.

Malou

Malou snuck out of the room without waking Zlavko. She wanted to fit in a run around the park before class. Maybe it would help her chill out a little. She took a deep breath as the heavy door closed behind her. The air was cool and crisp, and the sky was clear. She normally greeted autumn with a wistful sense of acceptance. Summer came with such expectations, so much to experience and achieve before the lighter nights were over. When September set in, it was as if people finally gave up all their unrealistic dreams and hopes and began to live more normally again. But, even though the sunrise was creating long, pretty shadows and the tall grass was covered in dew, the blades glistening in shades of gold, Malou could not find peace. The autumn didn't help her now, never mind how beautiful it was.

She started to run once she'd crossed the little suspension bridge. The white castle with its four small turrets and red-tiled roof lay behind her. The gravel crunched underfoot. It was the perfect morning for a run, but she couldn't quite find her rhythm, and her thoughts batted endlessly around like thousands of butterflies constantly fluttering in her head, never giving her a minute's peace. *Damn it!* She upped her pace, the gravel spraying up from under her feet, a stabbing in her lungs, but she kept on going until she felt almost sick. Once she'd gotten all the way down to the road, she stopped and doubled over with her hands on her knees, gasping for breath.

Why is it that all the films and books are about how wonderful it is to be in love? It was the biggest lie in the world. Malou had never felt so terrible before.

She walked slowly back to the school. She still had an hour to kill before classes began, but she also really wanted a shower. Her thoughts crept back to what time she could let herself wake Louis . . . and then she spotted him. He was sitting on a bench under the courtyard's impressive climbing rose. She was certain he was waiting for her. He must have seen her head out for her run. Malou had a feeling that Zlavko didn't sleep so well at night either.

"An early start?" Her Blood Magic teacher stood up slowly. Unlike her, he was smartly dressed in a pressed khaki shirt, with his long hair pulled into a top knot. He looked at her with that same slight, mocking smile that seemed to sit permanently on his lips. "What about starting our tutoring right now, as we're both awake? Or maybe you'd like breakfast first?"

Malou shook her head. Her stomach turned at the very thought of food. "I just need to go change, then I'll be ready."

"Meet me in the loft in fifteen minutes." He pulled at one of his sleeves so that it covered his right hand. It was a habit he had developed ever since his hand was wounded and hadn't healed up neatly.

Malou nodded and made as if to do some stretches so she didn't have to follow him directly into school. Once she was sure he had gone, she hurried up to the room she shared with Louis. It was actually his room that she had moved into. He wasn't there, and she resented the feeling of disappointment that discovery immediately caused in her. *Seriously. Get a grip over yourself!* It was an hour at most since she'd seen him, and still, the sight of that empty bed felt like Christmas being canceled. He'd made the bed neatly before he'd left—he was almost certainly in the shower or down at breakfast. Malou had no time to shower now. She grabbed some deodorant and hung her sweaty running clothes over the fancy chair with the curved armrests that Louis had brought from home when he moved in.

Then she found a clean set of clothes in her closet. Since being accepted into the Crows' Club, she always wore black. It wasn't an actual rule, but most of the others did it, too. For now, the Crows were the only students at the school, but when the others started after vacation, the black clothes would also make it easier to tell them apart from ordinary Rosenholm students.

She checked her reflection, giving up the idea of makeup and settling for a quick brush of her hair. Then she fastened the little silver crow feather to her black shirt. The pin was another mark of being part of the Crows' Club. After that, she buckled the belt Louis had given her around her waist. She had started carrying her athame, the ceremonial knife of all blood mages. Usually, it was exclusively blood mages who had their own athame, and she was proud of it, even though it also left her feeling strangely unsettled.

Malou let her fingers slide over the handle. The knife had belonged to Leah, Trine's little sister and the great love of Zlavko's life. The woman who had ruined one of his hands and thrown herself to her death just a few months earlier. Afterward, Zlavko had presented Malou with the knife, and now it hung at her side as a symbol of the new privileges and power that she had been

126

entrusted with. But it also was a reminder of the responsibility that followed and the price to be paid.

Malou shut the door of the room and hurried along the empty corridor. She found her way to the drying loft stairs. When she opened the door, she thought she was alone at first. The large, open room up in the roof lay silent before her. The sun had found its way in through the roof tiles and was creating little streaks of light in which dust particles danced. At one end, there were some small rooms where, a long time ago, the maids had lived. Malou avoided looking that way. The drying loft had become one of the places the Crows hung out, and she actually enjoyed coming here but didn't like the maids' rooms. She shook her head to chase away the mental image, but it played out in her mind's eye in any case. *Zlavko, bent over Louis, Zlavko, licking blood from his neck . . .*

The door to one of the rooms opened. It was that room where she had found them. *Lying on a mattress, both bare-chested, Zlavko's dark hair hanging down over his face, Louis's white-blond hair spread out on the mattress . . .*

Had Zlavko done that deliberately, waiting in there for her? Did he want to remind her of it? Of course, he was probably trying to mess with her head. Malou did her best not to give anything away. She had told Louis she understood. That it was okay. He let Zlavko drink his blood every now and then. To help him. But it was a lie. She didn't understand, and it wasn't okay. It was anything but okay.

The blood rushed in her ears, and she was suddenly overwhelmed with hate for the man calmly walking toward her. She couldn't escape the thought that there was something between them. That Zlavko was using Louis for his own sick desires. She felt like screaming at him to keep away from Louis. Instead, she simply returned his silent stare as he walked over the dusty floorboards until he was standing in front of her. Far too close, as always.

"Ready?"

She shrugged. "You haven't told me what's going to happen?"

"We're here to work on your abilities." He took yet another step toward her. She felt she could almost feel his breath on her face.

"Why here? Why now? Without the others?"

"You're in need of some special attention," he said softly. "From now on, you'll have individual classes with me alongside your ordinary training with the Crows. I expect to see it reflected in your performance. Now, are you ready?"

She nodded.

"Close your eyes."

More than anything, Malou would have liked to knee him in the crotch and run, but she obeyed and closed her eyes.

"Good," he drawled.

She felt him place both hands on her shoulders. "Hey!" she exclaimed, opening her eyes and taking a step backward.

"Stop being skittish," he said, irritated. "Bodily contact is necessary at the beginning, as long as you still haven't mastered it. Close your eyes again."

She did as he said and let him place his hands on her shoulders. One was slender and strong, the other gnarled and deformed. Her face was up against his throat. She could smell his deodorant and sense the movements of his chest, rising and falling with his breath.

"Now you need to find your way into my blood."

She tried to concentrate, but every cell in her body resisted. She wanted to get away from there. She had no desire whatsoever to look into Zlavko's inner depths, into him, where his blood flowed and his heartbeat pulsed. All her muscles tightened, and she started to sweat. She took a deep breath in but couldn't seem to get the air down into her lungs. *Come on!*

"Use your willpower, Malou. Focus on your goal."

Her head was spinning lightly, and she couldn't concentrate at all. The completely irrational thought popped into her head that she should have told Louis she wouldn't be in the dining hall for breakfast. Was he sitting there waiting for her?

"Malou, what's going on with you? Draw your thoughts to what is important to you. What is it that you really want? Visualize it!"

She knew what it was he meant, but her instincts were much stronger than the rational side of her brain. She couldn't control her thoughts. Perhaps they weren't even thoughts but sensations. *Shit!* There was so much she needed to do, so much she ought to do, but right now there was only one thing that she wanted. *His skin, his eyes, his body, his voice . . .*

"You're thinking about him!" The words came as a snarl, and he tightened his grip on her shoulders until it hurt. Malou kept her eyes closed. She couldn't look at him. She tried to concentrate on the pain in her shoulders, on the anger, but the only words in her mind were: *I'm losing it.*

"This isn't working." He let go and stepped back from her, exasperated, running his hands over his glossy hair. "You need to pull yourself together. Your blood is all focused down between your legs! You need to use it up here." He tapped his temple.

"Sorry," she whispered, staring at the floor.

"You can't let your feelings get in the way."

"I'm not!" she said forcefully.

"If you don't get a handle on this, Malou, I'll need to split you two up. Do you understand?"

She nodded. "I've got this. Let's try again."

He sighed and seemed to be thinking it over for a moment. "No. It's a waste of my time if you're not focused. But next time it'll go better. *Much better.* Am I right?"

"You're right. Next time, it'll be better," she said.

"Okay," he said. "I look forward to seeing that. There's training this afternoon. It's possible you could impress me there instead. It would be a good idea, at least, to give it a try."

She nodded and bit herself hard on the cheek so that the words pushing themselves forward would not blurt out her mouth.

"I'm assuming I don't have to remind you why this is important, right?"

She shook her head. "No, there's no need."

"You made the choice yourself, Malou. And you made no secret about what it was that was most important to you. I think you said it was the most important thing in the world from now on?"

She nodded. "That's what I said."

"And you know that if you want to succeed in the task you've taken on, you'll have to make an effort."

"It would be a bit easier if I knew more," she said, her voice trembling with anger.

"I'm sorry. You'll simply have to trust me."

He shook his head disapprovingly as he walked slowly toward the door, slamming it behind him in his wake.

SEPTEMBER 2ND
3:00 P.M.

Malou

The Crows had already taken their places when Malou arrived at the Great Hall. She found a spot in the row and straightened to stand tall. The little troop consisted mainly of students who, like Malou, were starting their third and final year at Rosenholm. But there were also a handful who had taken their exams and actually left school already. Jens had offered them the chance to stay, where they would be paid a wage in return for fulfilling certain duties.

Malou tightened her ponytail. Like the others, she was in her training gear and barefoot. Combat training. It was one of Jens's initiatives, introduced already before summer vacation after Leah had forced her way into the school and almost succeeded in killing him. The Crows were to act as a so-called security reassurance unit whose members could defend not only themselves but the rest of the students at the school should the need arise.

Malou enjoyed the physical training, and she was good at it. She checked out the different stations Zlavko had prepared for them. Dumbbells, skipping ropes, floor mats, a punching bag.

"Here we are. You know what to do!" Zlavko commanded them, starting his stopwatch. Five minutes per station at high intensity, then on to the next. Malou sparred with Amalie. The tall girl, who'd now left school, was as strong as a bear, but Malou enjoyed being challenged. Her morning run had ended up a fiasco, but now she was finally managing to focus. She battered the punching bag until she started to see stars, and sweat dripped off her. When Zlavko's alarm signaled for her and Amalie to move on to the weights, she kept going. She didn't want to stop.

"Hey," Amalie said. She was holding the punching bag to stop it from swinging too much. "Stop, that's the timer."

Malou finally stopped and tore the boxing gloves off impatiently.

"Don't you think you should chill out a little?" Amalie said. "This is just a warm-up."

Malou shook her head. "Come on," she mumbled, grabbing one of the weights.

When they finally finished the last station, the little troop of students were all flushed and sweating.

"We'll continue our combat training," Zlavko said. "I expect you, by now, to have mastered the basic combat techniques we've practiced recently. I've decided, together with Jens, that combat training will be compulsory for all students from the start of this semester. As I'll still have my teaching to do, soon I'll be selecting one of you to be my assistant. That person will have the task of training the rest of the students. A very trusted and important position. So, let's see your best today! First on the floor, Amalie and Albert."

It was an unfair match, as anyone could see. Amalie was tall, broad, and strong. Her abilities as a blood mage also meant she could draw on some very potent powers if it came to that. Albert was almost as tall as her and, like Amalie, had finished school that summer, but he was lanky and thin. In a physical fight like this, it wouldn't be much use to him that he had an exceptional ability to contact spirits. If he wanted, he could easily call on his dead friends to protect him from Amalie's fists, but sadly for him, Zlavko insisted they all learn to fight and that such things were not allowed.

Albert approached the floor slowly. He was blinking and grimacing; his tics always got worse when he got nervous.

"Remember, you must follow your punches through. And no hits to the private parts. Off you go!"

Amalie quickly got herself into an attack position, her arms up, ready to swing for Albert, her feet dancing closer. Amalie was heavy, which was her weakness, but Malou knew Albert didn't have the guts to exploit it. Instead of trying to surprise her, he stepped hesitantly backward while trying to keep his defenses up. Suddenly, Amalie attacked. She feigned one way, her body turned to one side, but her blow fell to the opposite side just as soon as Albert left himself open. Her clenched fist hit his jaw, the sound of her knuckles on his jawbone made Malou wish she could let herself close her eyes or look away. Albert fell flat onto the mat, and Zlavko heaved him back on his feet.

"You shouldn't stand and wait for her to attack. Come on, Albert!" Malou knew Zlavko was right. An offensive strategy was all that would work. Amalie was a good fighter as long as she was the one deciding what would happen. If she was taken by surprise, though, she had trouble thinking fast enough to adjust, and that gave the attacker a good chance. Malou knew she could beat Amalie. And she knew that Albert could not. Again, she forced herself to watch as Albert threw himself into a clumsy kamikaze attack, easily evaded by Amalie, after which she rammed him in the shoulder with a well-calculated round kick, knocking him face down onto the mat.

"That's it—we've seen enough, I think," groaned Zlavko. "Albert, you're not using any of the techniques we've been practicing for weeks now. You're one of the most experienced in this group. You need to show me something better than this. Understood?"

"Yes," Albert said, drying the blood from his nose.

"And Amalie. You're not challenging yourself enough. You're taking the easy options. Do you follow? If you don't stretch yourself, you'll never get better, and then sooner or later, you'll be outdone by someone who wants it more than you do."

"Okay," Amalie said with a little smile on her lips, betraying the fact she was more focused on her victory over Albert than she was on Zlavko's criticism. Malou almost wished Zlavko would choose her as Amalie's next opponent, but she knew that wasn't what he had in mind today. That fight would be too fair and hardly dramatic enough for Zlavko's taste. No. If she knew him as well as she thought, she already knew what he was planning.

"The next pair today is Malou . . . and Louis."

Damn it! He was so predictable. She stepped onto the floor without hesitation. She had prepared herself. *You can do this.*

Louis stepped up to face her and gave a very slight bow. His face showed no expression, but there was a smile in his bright gray eyes under those dark, arched eyebrows. His white-blond hair was gathered at his neck. Malou returned his bow.

"Remember: I expect you to give it your all," Zlavko warned.

They circled each other. His face was open, his movements flowing like a dancer. It wasn't the first time they'd been up against each other, but it was the first time since they had begun to share a room, a bed, and nights without sleep. Malou pushed her thoughts back to the fight. Louis was an excellent fighter. He had been coached since he was little in various martial arts forms, and none of the others could touch him when it came to lightning-fast attacks and elegant countermoves. And every time, he managed to make it look so playful. It was only by the skin of her teeth that Malou dodged his first move, which just grazed her shoulder. She spun around and tried to take advantage of the shift in his balance and get a hit in, but he was already out of her reach.

He smiled a little as they made eye contact again. This was so easy for him. He could keep going for an eternity in this way; it was just like a game to him. But it wasn't for her. And Malou knew deep inside that he lacked the decisive conviction needed if you wanted to win.

He lunged, and she was ready for it. Still, the force of the blow surprised her, and she tumbled over and rolled along the mat but was up on her feet again superfast and ready for his next move. Louis held back at his end of the mat and only came forward again when she had regained her balance. He raised his eyebrows and nodded to her, but she just shook her head almost imperceptibly.

"Louis, that's the last time I want to see that. We're not here to be nice—we're here to learn. And Malou won't learn anything if you handle her like a delicate vase you're afraid you might smash into pieces."

Malou laughed to herself. *Too late.* She'd already been smashed into thousands of pieces.

They continued circling each other. Zlavko sighed with frustration. This was no good. She forced herself to do it. She had it in her. *You can do this.*

The scream that came out of her mouth seemed to come from

another place entirely. The distance between her and Louis disappeared in a fraction of a second. Their bodies collided, and they were rolling around on the floor. Her simple attack had taken him by surprise. Suddenly, he couldn't get himself free or get the chance to dodge, jump, or kick, which is what he most wanted. Malou locked her long, strong legs around his body like a clamp and squeezed one arm around his neck while giving him a hard punch in the kidney.

"*Oof!*"

She heard in the sound he made that she had hit the right spot, and she struck again. And again. This was far from the elegant combat techniques he had perfected. This was a simple fistfight, but it was effective. He flexed all the muscles in his body and wrenched himself free of her arm that had him in a headlock. They rolled a half turn so he was on top now, and his blow hit her right on the nose with a nasty, cracking noise. But she welcomed the pain. Without it, she wasn't sure that she could have gone ahead. Malou snarled, her legs still locked around him. She refused to let go, and as he swung for her again, she twisted her upper body to the side so his punch landed on the mat and then smashed her elbow into his temple. He collapsed, and she straddled him now, hitting him, blood flowing, her knuckles numb as they met with his cheekbone. His jaw. His nose. Someone pulled her off, someone dragged her along the mat, someone threw her onto the floor.

"Stop now, Malou. If that's how you treat the people you care about, then—" Zlavko smiled, his eyes gleaming.

She screamed at him. She could feel it so clearly. She could kill him if she wanted to.

"Malou!"

His heart was beating fast, *too* fast, she noticed. His eyes were wide with alarm.

"Malou, stop!"

She saw him saying the words, but the sound came out slower than his lips moved. The voice was deep and distorted, and his teeth were red with blood.

She didn't know where the blood had come from.

She was completely out of her depth.

Dear Malou,

I am pleased to inform you that I will be placing you in charge of combat training for our students. I'm sure you're aware of the honor and responsibility this carries. Don't let me down!

With kind regards,

Zlavko Kovacavic
Vice Principal of Rosenholm Academy

SEPTEMBER 11TH
9:05 A.M.

Malou

The Crows stood outside in the little courtyard that separated the castle's wings. Malou glanced up at the sky. It was gray, and a soft drizzle of rain landed on her face and glistened like miniature pearls on her sweater. She had deliberately not worn a jacket on top, but she regretted it now, with the wind cutting right through the thin, dark wool fabric. Louis stood beside her. As much as she tried not to look at him, her eyes were drawn to him the whole time. The swelling had gone down, and the purple-blue marks had faded to a sickly yellow green. His jaw was clenched, and he did not look at her. Yet even the sight of his profile caused her insides to knot. They hadn't talked about it. But that night, she had heard him crying when he thought she was asleep.

The clock above them started to chime just as the first students came into view up the path through the park. There were two girls. They had to be second-year students because even though Malou didn't know their names, she had seen them before. They were walking and chatting, dragging their huge suitcases, which couldn't be rolled over the gravel. One girl laughed at something the other was saying. They seemed relaxed and happy. Second-years knew Rosenholm already and thought of it as another home.

This was quite unlike the first-years, who the Crows had welcomed there one week ago. For them, everything was new and strange, and Malou could've sworn she hadn't been so young and innocent herself when she started at Rosenholm two years before. At least, she hadn't been as nervous and pathetic as the students they'd spent the last week helping settle into the castle.

The girls had reached the suspension bridge now, which led over the little moat and into the courtyard where the Crows stood, legs slightly apart and hands behind their backs. When the girls saw them, they stopped short.

"Oh, hey . . ." one said uncertainly, and the other one giggled.

"Welcome to Rosenholm," Malou said formally. "You should go into the Great Hall. Once you're all here, we'll tell you where you'll be living."

The girl who had said hey lifted one eyebrow mistrustfully. "Well, we know where our dorms are already. We don't need anyone to take us up."

"All students are getting new rooms this year," Louis said. "If you'd read the letter from Jens, you'd know we're grouping the students in a whole new way. You'll find out more once everyone has arrived."

"What, so we're not living together in dorms anymore?" the other girl asked. They started dragging their cases into the hall, all while discussing what the new room arrangements could mean.

In the next hour, more and more students arrived, all met by the silent troop that had taken up position in the courtyard. Some of the arrivals greeted them cheerily, some quite warmly, but still others ignored them and tried to go in and find their old rooms. The sisters Sara and Sofie gave her a friendly wave as they arrived, but Malou's formal tone quickly threw them off course, and the smiles stiffened on their faces as they joined the other students. Malou noticed that many of the other Crows' friends were also surprised or offended at their classmates' sudden insistence on cool distance. But these were new times at the school, and they might as well get used to it from the start. It was important the Crows made themselves noticed from day one. All the new first-year students would learn to respect them, and more or less, all of them had already seemed rattled. But the second and third years were less easy to impress. They had known the Crows beforehand, and Malou knew it would be hard for them to accept the student members of Zlavko's club now having more power and privileges than they did themselves.

When the time came, the Crows followed into the hall where the students were waiting. Malou discretely dabbed under one eye, hoping the rain hadn't made her mascara run. As instructed, they arranged themselves along the little stage that Jens had had built in the hall. They knew no more than any of the other students about what was to happen next. Malou let her gaze run over them all. The students sat in long rows of chairs, with all their luggage stacked along the walls of the hall. Normally, they'd have been split into boys and girls. But today, they were mixed. It was one of Jens's new rules that the school would no longer be divided by gender. He trusted that students could handle their magic abilities. Even though the new students and the second and third years were all gathered, it was quiet in the hall. Unnaturally quiet. It was a good sign. A sign of respect. Malou lifted her chin and looked back at the many faces turned to her and the other Crows. Above them, enormous chandeliers hung from the high ceiling, and the walls sported four impressive paintings, each one symbolizing one of the four branches of magic. A young, beautiful woman.

Growth. A strong, young man. *Earth.* A mystical woman with a skull. *Death.* And a strange, thin man, cutting himself in the palm of his hand. *Blood.*

Malou had always seen them as four paintings hung opposite one another. But now, it occurred to her that there might be meaning in the way they were placed. Two on one wall, two on the other. Growth and Earth opposite Blood and Death. Light opposite dark. Malou had been beside herself when she discovered she belonged to the Blood branch. But now she was proud to carry the blood mage's athame at her side.

The great double doors at the end of the hall opened up, and Jens stepped in, dressed in black. Malou hadn't seen him often since the start of recess. Jens hadn't involved himself in Zlavko's training with the Crows during vacation. Malou wasn't sure what she had expected, but Jens looked the same as always. Charismatic, friendly, and calm. His blue eyes looked carefully around the hall, and he nodded to students he recognized as he walked up toward the stage. But his eyes never fell on her. Behind him came Zlavko, dressed in tight black trousers and a red shirt. He, on the other hand, stared at her demonstratively, as if to make her aware he was watching her, but Malou ignored his superior expression. She didn't want to witness his obvious pleasure at walking through the hall as the school's vice principal. Instead, she focused on the two other people who walked in behind Zlavko. One was a small, older woman wearing some sort of brown cloak. Malou would have guessed she weighed less than 100 pounds, and once she'd got up— with some difficulty—the two steps to the stage, it was clear she was about half Zlavko's height. She smiled at the students, and her face was all wrinkled. She was like an old apple somebody had forgotten on top of a radiator. The second person was also a woman.

She was much younger, perhaps in her early thirties. She had long, dark hair, high cheekbones, and a broad chin that gave her an uncompromising look. Four thick, dark lines ran from under her lip to her chin. They looked tattooed, and when Malou looked closer at her hands, she saw they were also covered in dark graphic lines and patterns.

Unlike the older woman, this one did not smile at the students as she positioned herself by the others.

The last person to enter the hall was Ingrid, the school doctor and counselor. Though she didn't follow onto the stage with the others, she found an empty seat among the students instead.

"Welcome to a new year at Rosenholm Academy," Jens said, reaching both arms in front of him as if he wanted to embrace them all. "And welcome to a whole new Rosenholm. Those of you who are starting their second or third year here will discover that many things have changed. You will all be getting new rooms. Our students will no longer be separated by gender. That old-fashioned way of seeing the world should have been abandoned long ago."

The students burst out in spontaneous applause. Malou fell to thinking of her first days at school. How, at first, she had been irritated that she'd have to live in a dorm with three other girls she didn't know. But they had ended up friends, and she would never have believed if someone had told her that she'd be standing here in her third year without them. They had their reasons for staying away, and she had her reasons for staying. Their paths had diverged, and she knew that there was no other way it could be.

Jens smiled at the students' applause before quietening them down again.

"You will have a lot more freedom in some ways," he continued. "Freedom to each develop your own abilities, without facing any mistrust or judgment. No forms of magic or mage will be judged unacceptable." Jens looked up at the paintings on the walls. "There will be no more turning up our noses at magic's dark branches, no more oppression of those powers that make us mages something special. And so, we will have classes with a focus on practicing abilities that were previously unwelcome, and we will revive old and powerful rituals that have unfortunately been rejected and forgotten." He took a deep breath. "But greater freedom also brings greater responsibility. As mages, we have a responsibility to use our powers for the good of all and to fight for the place mages hold in society—a place that, over the years, has been increasingly under threat."

Jens looked earnestly out over the students, who listened carefully. "I hoped I would only have positive news to share with you today, but sadly, I must also warn you that we face a difficult time. As much as I'd like to give you freedom in all different ways, I am unable to do so when it comes to your safety. As you all know, the school was attacked last year. There are powers in our society that seek to destroy Rosenholm, and we have reason to believe that was not the last attack of this kind we can expect from these criminals. For that reason, some restrictions are needed for security purposes. At the front of the stage here, we have some current and former students who all make up the Crows' Club. Together with the teachers, they will be making sure you're all able to feel safe here in the school."

Jens smiled reassuringly at them all. "This year, all students will also be trained in self-defense, a task that the Crows have also agreed to take responsibility for. We will soon be needing more young people with the courage to defend our proud school, and before long, Zlavko"—Jens gestured toward Zlavko by his side—"will let you know about entrance tests to the Crows for second- and third-year students. I would recommend all of you who are willing and able to sign up."

Malou noticed how many of the students started whispering excitedly to one another, no doubt talking about how much they wanted, or didn't want, to sign up to be a Crow.

Jens cleared his throat, and the sound of the whispers dissipated. "As you can see," he continued, "I have been joined by some new faces here at Rosenholm. Thorbjørn and Lisa, who previously taught Norse Studies and Nature Magic, have sadly left the school. Instead, I am proud to present two very talented mages in their respective fields. From now on, Dagny Halvorsen will be our teacher in Norse Studies." Jens looked over at the short, elderly woman. "While Ivalo Jaspersen"—he indicated the dark-haired woman with the facial tattoos—"will be teaching you Nature Magic."

Jens paused, and it took a moment for Malou to realize he expected applause. The Crows clapped enthusiastically to bid the new teachers welcome, and the rest of the hall joined in a little hesitantly after. Jens interrupted the applause to request that the third years take more classes than just their compulsory main subject, and then he finally let them go.

"Now, I hand you over to the Crows to help you find your new rooms so you can all go up and unpack. I wish you a very good evening and a good school year. Thank you."

The students clapped again briefly while Amalie and Iris took up positions at the very back of the hall. Both wore black clothing with a shining silver crow feather pinned on their fronts, and it was their job to help the confused students who were trying to find out from big noticeboards at the back of the hall where exactly they were going to live. The rest of the Crows waited around the little stage as the hall gradually emptied. Malou had a feeling of being watched, but she tried to suppress the desire to look around her. When she did look anyway, she got a surprise. She had expected to see Zlavko's mocking smile, but he was deep in serious conversation with Jens. Instead, it was the new teacher Ivalo who watched her with an expression Malou couldn't decipher. She didn't avert her gaze when Malou made eye contact with her but just continued staring, and every part of Malou reacted as if the new teacher was challenging her to a fight. Then she felt a hand in hers and forced herself to look away.

"This is going to be good," Louis whispered to her and smiled. She couldn't manage to smile back.

I think about you a lot.
What's it like at school now?

Are you okay?

Do you even wonder at all how we're doing?

You know what? Just forget it!

SEPTEMBER 15TH
2:48 P.M.

Malou

Malou sat at one of the library's study tables and tried to focus on the book titled *Primeval Transition Rituals*. She had taken it out in a somewhat optimistic attempt to make a good start to the school year. Zlavko always managed to set his curriculum in a way that would totally make any student nervous from the very start, but she wasn't going to go down without a fight.

"Malou, do you have a moment?"

She lifted her head, surprised. Jens stood before her, holding an old, leather-bound book in his hands.

"Um," Malou hesitated, checking the time on her phone, "I actually have a class here in a little while." Besides their normal timetable, the Crows' extracurricular lessons seemed to be ever increasing.

"It will only take a moment." Jens took a step closer and leaned over the desk. "It's about your former roommates. Chamomile, Victoria, and Kirstine," he said softly. "As you'll have seen, they've chosen not to come back to school. Of course, that means they won't be able to graduate either, and I'm concerned that they are being led astray. Are you in contact with them?"

"No, I'm afraid not," Malou said. "We don't talk anymore."

"I rather had the impression you were friends?" Jens said.

"We were," Malou said, "but we . . . grew apart, I suppose you could say. They couldn't accept me being a member of the Crows."

"I see." Jens nodded amicably. "I'm sorry to hear that, but if it's any comfort, I'm certain you've made the right choice."

She looked at him for a moment without speaking. He had no idea how hard it had been to make that choice, but she was in no doubt either. She had made the right one.

Jens straightened up again. "I don't want to keep you any longer. You'd better get on with your reading."

Malou nodded, quickly packed up her things, and left the library.

"You're late, Malou," Zlavko snapped, as she shut the door to the drying loft behind her. Malou ignored him and her compulsion to point out that she was, at most, one or two minutes late. Instead, she focused on Ivalo, who was standing by Zlavko's side. She was dressed in a loose white shirt, and her long black hair hung down on either side of her face. She wore a silver leaf pendant—the symbol for Growth magic—but she also had a bunch of other necklaces and colored beads hanging around her neck, including some kind of animal tooth on a string of leather.

"What's she doing here?" Malou whispered to Amalie, who just shrugged.

"As you can see, we have Ivalo with us today, as we will be dealing with what we call hybrid ability. Does anyone here know what that means?" Zlavko asked.

None of the Crows moved to respond, not even Louis, who usually knew all there was to know about the world of magic.

"Hybrid ability refers to those instances when a mage is gifted within two or more branches of magic."

"But that doesn't exist," Amalie protested. "A mage always just has one branch of magic." She instinctively reached for the silver droplet she wore around her neck.

"That's where you're wrong," Zlavko said. "Understandably, as what you just repeated is exactly what the school has taught you. But that's not quite how it is. There are mages who master several branches of magic. They are rare, but not as rare as you might think."

Malou cracked her knuckles. This was nothing new to her. In her first year of school, she had met someone exactly like that, a student with abilities in all four branches of magic. But it hadn't been a particularly pleasant encounter.

"Until now, hybrid ability was something held in low regard here at Rosenholm," Zlavko continued. "Those students who demonstrate signs of hybrid ability were asked to suppress them—despite the fact that hybrid ability can often lead to very potent powers. For that reason, in the course of this year, we want to see if we can identify any students with abilities in more than one branch and instead, encourage them to cultivate these abilities."

"And how do you all feel it went, the last time the school experimented with students with hybrid abilities?" Malou asked.

Zlavko looked at her. "Ah, you're thinking of Vitus?" he said mildly.

"Yes," Malou said. "I'm thinking of Vitus!" She noticed the anger rising inside her. Zlavko's tone was condescending, as if she were a child getting herself worried over silly ideas. But Vitus was no silly idea. First, he had assaulted Anne, and then he had

150

targeted Chamomile, who would have died by his hand had it not been for Victoria, Kirstine, and Malou stopping him.

"Vitus was a former student here at the school," Zlavko explained to Ivalo, "who was highly capable and talented. Unfortunately, he was also completely unhinged, and he assaulted some of the students. The school's Headmaster at the time wasn't up to handling it in a satisfactory way. But with the current administration, we won't have any problems," he said with a broad, toothy smile.

"And what has Ivalo got to do with hybrid ability, if we may ask?" Louis nodded amicably toward the new teacher, who looked at him closely without returning his smile.

"Good question!" Zlavko said. "Ivalo is—besides being a capable nature mage—able to draw on another branch of magic, namely Death. Ivalo will be assisting me in the classes where we focus on hybrid ability. We are starting with you Crows first, but during the course of the year, the plan is to include all students who show signs of hybrid ability in the classes with Ivalo."

"That's cool," Amalie declared. "So, what things can you do? I mean, what can you use your hybrid ability for?"

"Lots of things," Ivalo replied, and Malou realized it was the first time they had heard her speak. She had a slight accent that suggested she hadn't been born in Denmark.

"Are you from Greenland?" Amalie asked.

"Aasiaat," she answered.

"Are you a shapeshifter, maybe?" Malou asked.

Their new teacher turned toward her and stared without blinking. Something in her jaw twitched.

"Where did you get that from?" she asked.

"Vitus was as well," Malou said, holding her stare.

"As Malou has so clumsily pointed out—it is thought that shape-shifters, besides Growth, often possess one or two other branches of magic," Zlavko interrupted. "That is what gives them the powers to do something so extraordinary."

"Wow!" Amalie blurted out. "What animal can you change into? Can we see?"

"My abilities are not a trick I use to entertain people whenever they want, like some circus animal," Ivalo hissed, and the impressed smiles dropped from the students' faces.

But Zlavko gave a low chuckle. "I invited Ivalo here because she may get a feel for which of you might have an aptitude for hybrid ability. Don't lose heart if there are no immediate results. It may be that you have suppressed your abilities for a long while," he said. "And for the same reason, I strongly recommend that you take classes in all branches of magic and not just in your main subject. But let's get started. Over to you, Ivalo, please."

Ivalo asked them all to lie down on the floor with plenty space between them and their attention focused inward. Meanwhile, she crept silently among them, and through half-closed eyes, Malou saw how she bent down over Louis and laid both hands around his head. Malou recognized the gesture. She had seen other nature mages doing it, and she had also felt the impact of their healing powers. A hug from Chamomile could feel like you were being bathed in warm, soothing water. *As if everything would be okay.* The thought took her unawares; she hadn't seen it coming, hadn't been ready, and, to her horror, she felt tears pricking at her eyes. Malou bit her inside lip and forced herself to empty her mind. She did not want Ivalo to get the impression she was completely unbalanced. She managed to get a grip on herself before their new teacher leaned over her and placed her hands around Malou's forehead. Malou tried to relax, to turn her focus inward as they had been told they should, but she could feel her muscles tightening. Having Ivalo's hands on her head did not produce any comforting feeling in her body. Instead, it felt the same as when a stranger stands too close to you on the bus or when a doctor pricks or pokes you with some cold instrument. Malou suddenly heard a humming in her inner ears. It grew louder then became a whisper that seemed to come from inside her own head.

Taartap ... terianniaq ...

Malou heard a new voice inside her, one that was much deeper and clearer. It was Ivalo's voice, but Malou couldn't understand the words.

Terianniaq ...

The whispering voice seemed to answer Ivalo before suddenly disappearing. An icy-cold feeling took over Malou's body and held her in its grip. It felt like a huge weight was pressing on her chest, and her lungs ached. Malou opened her eyes. The drying loft and Ivalo's face above her had disappeared. She saw only a mysterious, swirling darkness around her. Then she heard a voice, which sounded very far away. It was fuzzy and distorted, but it was clearly singing. A plaintive, chanting song that spoke of great sorrow and pain. Malou turned her head in the empty darkness to see if she could get a glimpse of whoever was singing, but she could still see nothing. Instead, she felt a pain in her right wrist, as if someone was tying a rope tight on her arm. Malou tried to pull her arm away, but her limbs would not obey. What had Ivalo done to her?

Arnaqquassaaq ...?

This was Ivalo's voice, and suddenly, Malou could feel her hands around her head again. At first, her grip just felt firm, but then a burning pain began to spread out from where Ivalo's hands were placed. At the same time, the grip on Malou's wrist tightened. It felt like she was being pulled at. *Downward.* Malou opened her mouth to scream, but no sound came out. And then it was over. The pain on her wrist vanished, the pressing feeling on her chest lifted, and the darkness pulled away. Malou blinked her eyes in confusion. Ivalo was sitting over her, gasping for air as if she had been running, and her nose was covered in small beads of sweat. Her brown eyes looked intently at Malou, and a deep crease in the middle of her brow showed she wasn't too happy with what she saw.

"What happened there?" Malou whispered.

"Asukiaq," Ivalo answered, shaking her head. "I don't know." Then she let Malou go and stood up to go on to the next student.

OCTOBER 3ʳᴰ
7:50 A.M.

Malou

"Are you coming?"

"No, and you're not going anywhere either." Malou tugged at Louis's arm to pull him back into bed. He gave a low laugh and pushed her away.

"Come on, you haven't been to a single one of her classes yet, have you?"

He looked surprisingly fresh, although she knew he hadn't slept all that much. They'd first gotten to sleep a good while after midnight, and when she woke at one point in the night, she found he wasn't there.

"I've been to Ivalo's deathly-dull lessons—is that not enough?" Malou muttered and pulled the duvet up over her face.

"You can't mean that," Louis said, getting out of bed and pulling a T-shirt over his head. "Ivalo is really good, much better than Lisa was. Don't you think?"

Malou thought about Ivalo's stiff hands on her head, her eyes boring into her, and the swirling darkness that she had called up. "To be quite honest, I can't see what everyone thinks is so great about her," she said. "Is it because of the shapeshifting thing? None of us have seen if she can actually do it."

"Come on, you have to admit it's pretty cool."

"Nah. I don't get why you're so mad keen on her."

"Are you jealous?" He whipped the duvet off her and held it above his head with outstretched arms.

She narrowed her eyes. "It's freezing. Give that back."

"Not if you don't answer. Are you maybe a little jealous of the mysterious Ivalo?"

"Certainly not," Malou said, snatching the duvet back from him.

"That's good," he said, bending to brush a strand of hair from her face. "Because the thing with Ivalo is nothing compared to the flirting I've got going with Dagny. Just wait and see!"

"I'm not coming," Malou said. "I've got no abilities in Earth, trust me. On the other hand, I've got homework for blood magic and a dumb exercise for nature magic, and I still have to prepare a whole training session for the first-years. I don't want to waste time taking a totally pointless class on the Vikings' coil technique."

"Coil technique, what's that?"

"It's the way they made those crappy clay pots. By rolling coils. Last year, Thorbjørn gave an hour-long lesson on it that I was forced to endure. Now I don't have to, and isn't that the whole advantage of being a third-year, that you don't have to take all those subjects that are totally irrelevant?" She pulled the duvet over herself again as a signal that the conversation was over.

"Malou?" His voice sounded half instructional, half teasing. "Do you remember what Zlavko said?"

Malou sighed under the duvet. "He says so many things."

"It's important that the Crows lead with a good example. And Zlavko thinks that we should give the new teacher a chance and take part in at least one of their classes."

"Argh!" Malou groaned, feeling that all her good arguments

were fizzling away. "And just think how great it'll be when Zlavko asks if you've been to a Norse Studies class and you can say yes. He'll definitely not be expecting that."

"Okay, you win," Malou said, kicking the duvet off. "How long have I got?"

"Three minutes," Louis said with a glance at his phone.

"Damn it, I can't go like this."

"Well, you could put some clothes on," he said, bending down to tie his laces.

Malou cursed as she pulled on some things. This was so unlike her. She didn't show up late, she didn't turn up to class with a messy bedhead, and she was never unprepared.

Five minutes later, when they walked into Dagny's teaching room, they were met by a strange humming noise that came from the gathered students. Most of them were Earth, which made sense because, for them, Norse Studies was a compulsory class. Malou nodded to Sara and Sofie, but there were also a few others there who had taken on their guidance counselors' suggestion to attend classes other than their main subjects.

The strange humming continued while Louis and Malou found a couple of spare seats in the row behind the two sisters. Unlike Thorbjørn, who taught in an ordinary classroom, Dagny had chosen to teach in one of the old auditoriums, rarely used nowadays. For that reason, there was plenty of space in the large room, with its fixed rows of chairs. On the board, she had written a rune. It looked like a *B* but with triangles instead of arches. Malou realized that the humming came from all the students repeating the name of this rune over and over: *"Berkanan."*

Malou wracked her brains. Runes were not her strong point, to put it mildly, but as far as she remembered, the rune had something to do with femininity. Down in front of the board, Dagny, their short, curious teacher, stood swaying back and forth to the sound of the students' peculiar humming. Finally, she raised both her hands in the air, and the students stopped.

"Can you feel it?" She chuckled as if she had just said something funny. "The feminine power, Mother Earth's voice. It works every time."

Malou leaned forward to Sofie in the row in front and whispered, "Does she always start class this way?"

Sofie nodded. "Yes."

"A new rune every time?"

"No, always the same one."

Malou leaned back in her seat and watched the old woman, who was smiling from ear to ear, her eyes almost disappearing in the deep wrinkles.

"And what is this rune called?" she asked.

Sara's hand shot into the air. "Berkanan, or the birch rune. It is linked to Frigg because the birch is Frigg's tree," she answered.

"Correct!" Dagny laughed, clapping her hands. "Fantastic! Absolutely excellent, well done."

Malou leaned toward Louis. "Tell me, is she senile or what?"

"Dagny gets excited pretty easy," he said, smiling. "Isn't it lovely, a teacher that's easy to impress for a change?"

Malou looked at him and sighed. Why had she let herself be talked into this?

"And is there anyone who can tell us who Frigg is?" Dagny asked when she eventually stopped clapping.

Another hand in the air: a tall, thin boy with tousled hair, who Malou vaguely recognized as one of Louis's friends. "Frigg is Odin's wife."

"That's right!" crowed Dagny, clapping again. "Very, very good! Frigg is Odin's wife, and she is one of the most important Norse gods."

"What does she mean?" Malou whispered to Louis. "I've never heard of Frigg being one of the most important gods before."

"Is there something you want to ask, my friend?" Dagny smiled up at her from the auditorium floor.

"Um..." Malou hesitated. She was surprised the old woman had even noticed her talking to Louis. "It just sounded like you were saying Frigg was one of the most important gods?"

"Precisely. One of the most important of all," Dagny answered, nodding eagerly.

"Okay, so I know she is important, but Odin is surely the most important. Together with Thor," Malou said.

"Aha, but you're wrong!" Dagny said, pointing at Malou with a little, crooked finger. "You're wrong about that, my friend. Absolutely. Frigg and Freya are the most important. And Idun and Hel. And Sif."

"Ah, so all the female goddesses?" Malou said.

"Precisely!" Dagny replied. "All of them very, very important. But, today, we will deal with Frigg." She turned and shuffled unbearably slowly to the great board, where she started to write something with a shaky hand.

Louis leaned over to Malou. "Maybe I should have said Dagny only teaches everything women: the lives of the goddesses, Viking women's lives, myths and legends on women."

"Seriously?"

"Yup. She seems to think everything else is immaterial."

At the board, Dagny was finally finished writing. The script was difficult to read, but it seemed to say *Baldrs draumer*.

"Frigg is the goddess of marriage. She protects mothers giving birth and the mothers whose sons are at war," Dagny explained. "We hear about her in the poem 'Balder's Dream,' which you have read for today. She tapped the board. "Who can tell the story of Balder? You, my friend, tell us about Balder."

"Me?" Malou sat up. "Well, Balder . . . He was the son of Odin . . . and Frigg, yes, of course. He was shot with an arrow . . . made of mistletoe, I think it was?"

"Correct!" Dagny exclaimed, despite Malou's rather unimpressive surface knowledge of the god Balder. "But the story of his tragic fate begins already long before that treacherous arrow of mistletoe hit him." Dagny closed her eyes as if a vision was forming in her inner mind. "Balder suffered from nightmares," she began slowly. "He saw his death in dreams. Balder's father, Odin, rode to Hel to find the seeress's grave. Odin woke the seeress from the dead to ask her who would kill Balder. The seeress divined that it was Balder's brother Høder who would kill him. After that, Frigg, their mother, got all the gods, giants, animals, plants, and things to swear that they would not harm Balder. But Frigg had forgotten to include the little mistletoe in the oath, and the scoundrel Loki found out. He cut an arrow from it and enticed Balder's brother, the blind Høder, to shoot it. And, boom! Balder was dead. So tragic, so tragic." Dagny bowed her head to the floor and stood for a moment as if overwhelmed by her feelings. Then she suddenly clapped her hands again and smiled. "But we have much to learn from this story, and that's what's so good about it! Tell me, what did you learn from Frigg's struggle to save her son?" Dagny nodded encouragingly at them.

Sofie had a try, her hand cautiously raised. "Maybe that it's not possible to escape your own fate?"

160

"Excellent!" Dagny declared. "In spite of Frigg's attempts, it was Balder's fate to die by his brother's hand, and that's what happened. Anyone else?"

"That mothers are pretty cool?" suggested a boy in the front row.

"A good insight! The story tells how a mother's love is the strongest in the world, and no being can deny a mother what she asks if she is trying to save her child," Dagny said. "Anyone else? What about you?" Her narrowed eyes found Malou again in the crowd.

Malou sighed. "Oh, okay. That if you have a job to do, you should do it properly?"

Dagny nodded thoughtfully. "Do the job properly," she muttered as if she had suddenly forgotten altogether that she was in the middle of a class. Then she turned and started to slowly write what Malou had said on the board.

"I gave you one chance with this, okay?" Malou whispered to Louis.

"Dagny's not for you?" he asked with a smile.

"Nope," Malou said, folding her arms. "Definitely not."

OCTOBER 10TH
3:00 P.M.

Malou

"Right, let's get started, please!" Malou said, her voice sounding much more confident and calmer than she actually felt. As she had expected, the first-years were by far the easiest to deal with. Malou had already been training them over several weeks, and they were easy to impress and hard to wear out. They listened wide-eyed and then went off and flung themselves at the punching bags and sandbags until their knuckles bled, eager to get some praise or recognition from the teacher on their combat techniques. Of course, there were a few who wanted to show off and tried to goof around, but after one round on the mat with Malou, they soon put their tails between their legs and did what they were told. She had started the second-years the previous week, and that had also gone fine, besides two boys who had started to have a fight for real and needed some patching up afterward. But Malou had waited to call the third-years in for combat training, which was now mandatory for all students. She had made an excuse to herself that it was hard to fit any training in with the year three timetable, but the truth was, she had put it off this long because she was scared of how the students would be. It was crucial that she came out of it well. The role of combat training teacher could end up being very important.

Malou shook her head to clear it and concentrate on the lesson.

"Try to get a bit more force in that punch," she ordered as she passed a group of three girls who were taking turns around a sandbag.

"Yes, boss," one of the girls mocked, and the others laughed. Malou had already passed them and was on her way toward four boys who had obviously watched too much mixed martial arts, but she stopped in her tracks. She might as well deal with this now; it wasn't going to get any easier.

"You think this is funny?" Malou turned and stared down the little group of her peers. She had already had a brief clash with one of them last year, the red-headed Asta. Malou had overheard her bad-mouthing Kirstine in one of the girls' bathrooms. Asta was also one of the students Zlavko had invited to an entrance test for the Crows, but she had been far from impressive with her spirit magic abilities and had not been accepted to the club. All that made it extra hard for Asta to accept Malou as her new coach. But then, she would just have to learn. *And there is no better teacher than bitter experience.*

"But it *is* for fun, isn't it?" Asta said, returning Malou's stare with a false smile. "We're at a boarding school for magic. We're supposed to be getting trained to be mages. So, it must also be a joke that we're expected to stand here and fight each other like some brain-dead lumps brawling in the street."

Malou ignored her scornful tone. "As Jens said in his welcome speech, it's important that all students learn to defend themselves."

"But why isn't there a proper teacher in charge of the training? Why is it you teaching us to fight?"

"Because I'm really good at it," Malou said. "If you have a problem with that, talk to Zlavko. He is the one who decided."

"It's not Zlavko I have a problem with," Asta said, the smile still frozen on her face. "It's you."

Malou took a breath. The worst thing was that Malou would have had exactly the same attitude if the situation was reversed and Asta had been appointed trainer. But that's not how things were.

"Come on!" Malou ordered.

"Come where?" Asta snorted.

"Up here, on the mat. Let's go a round." Malou unfastened her belt with the athame and let it all fall to the ground.

"What do you mean? That we're going to fight?"

"Yup."

"What? Are you nuts?"

"No."

"Forget it—go to hell."

"Training is compulsory. If students are not complying with the lessons, they can be expelled from the school effective immediately."

"You can't do that."

"Yes, I can. And I think I will if you refuse to follow my instructions. Come up onto the mat."

"This is crazy." Asta rolled her eyes and followed Malou with a look that more than suggested she was above this kind of nonsense. But Malou could see a red rash spreading on her chest, and she could sense an ever-faster rhythm deep inside her. It was a pulse, but not her own.

"So, just give it your best shot, and there's no need to hold back. I can take it." She waved Asta closer and lifted her hands into a block position.

"Seriously?" Asta turned to the rest of the group, who had long since stopped their training and stood quietly watching them.

164

"Come on!" Malou yelled, so it echoed around.

"All right!" Asta grumbled. And suddenly, she threw herself forward. Malou dodged her effortlessly and instead swept Asta's leg from under her, sending her flying to the floor.

"Again!" she ordered.

Asta was red in the face now. She was furious, and she snarled with frustration as she set about Malou. Malou blocked her blows and tripped her to the floor again. And then again. Now, the tears were running down Asta's cheeks. Malou knew she should stop at this point. A good teacher never humiliates their student. Teaching a lesson was one thing, but completely destroying someone was another.

"You're a goddammed loser, Malou. Did you know that?"

Asta hit the mat face first and had to shake her head before she could stand again.

"Be careful." Malou's voice was calm, but inside, she was raging. Unfortunately, Asta had long stopped being careful.

"Is this what you learned in your first trash school, huh?" she sneered. "To hit people? Wow, that's so great. I'll bet it's something that can get you respect in that hole you crawled out of. But what exactly are your magical abilities? Have we ever seen them?"

"Stop," Malou warned her.

"Zlavko must be really relieved he found a useful lackey who can do his dirty work for him. But if you think he can use you for anything else, you'll be sorely disappointed!"

Malou tried to concentrate on her breath, to breathe right down into her stomach, to focus on something else . . .

Asta laughed triumphantly. Her hair was tousled, and tears ran down her red cheeks. But her eyes gleamed at Malou. "You might well get to be Zlavko's minion here in school. But as soon as you finish here, you'll be done. You know that, don't you?"

Malou looked down at the floor. "You should shut up now." Her voice was low; she could hardly hear it herself because of the heartbeat. Her own and Asta's.

"Aww, is Malou getting sad?" she jeered.

Malou lifted her head. Asta's eyes were red, and the thin veins in the whites of her eyes had become clearer from her crying. It took so little for delicate blood vessels to burst.

"You're a loser and always will be, Malou. That's never gonna change!" She laughed, thinking she had won.

It's too late now to stop. Asta needed to learn to keep her mouth shut. Malou blinked, and then it happened. She made it happen.

"Argh!" Asta screamed and hid her face in her hands as blood suddenly started filling her eyes and running down her cheeks. "I can't see!"

"Asta, what's going on?" Her two friends ran to her across the mat but then drew back in shock when they saw the blood.

"Make it stop!" a boy's voice yelled.

Slowly, Malou realized it was her he was shouting at. She needed to get control of herself.

"Step away from her. I'll take her up to Ingrid!" Malou ordered and went to pull the girl up, but Asta screamed and collapsed as she reached out to her. Blood dripped down onto the light blue mat, and Asta was slipping in it as she tried to get on her feet. Malou didn't know what to do. The look of disbelief on the other students' faces sickened her. She wanted them to respect her, but that wasn't respect she could see in their faces. It was disgust.

"What's going on?"

Malou closed her eyes.

"Malou!"

She couldn't speak. She couldn't make herself open her eyes.

"I can't see!" Asta wailed.

"What happened here?"

"They were fighting, and then—then her eyes suddenly started bleeding," somebody said.

"It was her!"

Malou recognized Asta's voice but still didn't open her eyes.

"Did you see how she was looking at me? She made it happen! She's blinded me!"

"Stop all that screaming and come with me" came Zlavko's voice. "It's just a few burst blood vessels. It'll stop bleeding shortly. The rest of you can go, class is finished."

Malou felt a burning under her eyelids. *Nothing is how it should have been.* She felt a figure leaning over her.

"The idea was that you'd practice that in the sessions with me," Zlavko snarled in her ear. "Not experiment on your classmates. Get the mess cleared up, and meet me in my office."

Malou nodded without speaking. She collapsed onto the mat and left her eyes closed until the room was completely quiet and everyone had left. Then she opened them. There's no color that's as fascinating, terrifying, and alluring all at the same time as the color of fresh blood. She touched the blood lightly with her fingertips, lifted her hand up to her face, and looked at it closely. She had to go get something to clean up the mess.

OCTOBER 10ᵀᴴ
5:11 P.M.

Malou

Malou sat down in the chair opposite Zlavko without asking permission. His desk between them was neat. That was one thing they had in common. Malou also liked to keep her things organized.

"How is she . . . is she okay?" she asked.

"Well, no lasting damage."

"And it's stopped . . . bleeding?"

"Yes, it stopped. Although her eyes will be red for quite some time." Zlavko raised one eyebrow before continuing. "I don't suppose it will come as a surprise to you that I need to remove you from your teaching role?"

Malou shook her head.

"I'm handing the job to Amalie. I also considered Louis. I understand you're rooming together now?"

"Yes, we are." Malou saw no reason to deny it.

"Well. Maybe he can be substitute should there be any need for it. But Amalie will be a good instructor. I should have chosen her from the beginning, but I thought the job would give you a chance to prove you could be trusted."

"I'll find another way to prove it," she said.

"I very much hope so."

"Was that all?"

"No," Zlavko said. "That was not all."

Malou sighed. Of course, that was not all. She had caused a student to bleed from the eyeballs, and now she had to find a way to explain it.

"I don't know how it happened, it . . . "

"Yes, you do know. Stop lying. Especially to yourself. It's so tiresome."

She bit her lip. Was she lying? Did she know full well what had happened?

"I made Asta bleed so that she'd shut her mouth," she said. "I didn't mean for that to happen. I wanted to teach her a lesson, but then she started saying all kinds of crap . . ."

"You got angry, you wanted to harm her, and you took control of her blood. Is that not right?" He stared at her.

"Yes, that's right," she said, avoiding his eyes. Instead, she looked at her own nails, bitten to the quick, still red with Asta's blood despite having scrubbed them at the sink. "I don't know what's wrong with me."

"You're not listening to what your teacher tells you. That's what's wrong!" Zlavko said, slapping his hand down on the table so that she jumped. "You train your special abilities in the private lessons. And not anywhere else!"

"But I don't know how to do it!" Now it was Malou who was raising her voice.

"That's not true at all," Zlavko said. "You've just done it. And you did it to me that day you were up against Louis. When you get angry enough, then it doesn't seem to be any problem for you. It's actually easy for you, isn't it?"

Malou shrugged. "I suppose . . ."

"So, the only thing you need to do now is learn to control it. Why can't you do it in the private lessons?"

"Because . . . because I don't want to!"

"Want to? What's wanting got to do with it? Malou, you have a task to fulfill, and everything depends on you being in full control of your abilities in time."

"But I don't want to, I don't understand it, and you won't tell me anything. Why can't you just do it yourself? You're a blood mage. You're much more capable than me—why can't it be you?"

"I know you can do this. I saw it in you. And you can do it better than I can. Yes, I have the ability, but not to the same degree you do. You have a greater talent than anyone I've met before. Except one."

"Leah?"

"Yes, Leah. And that is why it should be you, Malou, and not me. It *must* be you. Do you understand?"

She lowered her head and stared at the floor. "And if I can't learn to control it?"

"You said it yourself. It's not a question of how far you are able to go. It's a question of how far you are willing to go. How much you *want* it. But perhaps I have one more idea of how we can resolve this. Let's have a look at it after the fall vacation. Am I right in saying you've signed up to stay at school during the break? Together with Louis?"

Malou nodded.

"Good. Use the time sensibly. You can go now."

He nodded at her, and without understanding fully how, she had a feeling she wasn't quite escaping punishment. It was just being postponed to an unknown time in the future.

OCTOBER 16ᵀᴴ
10:30 P.M.

Malou

Malou started typing but had second thoughts and deleted it. She sat with her phone in her hand. Darkness had fallen, and the day was nearly over. However you looked at it, it was far too late to be sending a Happy Birthday message. Now, she'd have to introduce it with something along the lines of: *Whoa, I was about to miss your big day.* But Malou wasn't forgetting anything at all. Last year, they'd celebrated Chamomile's birthday at the little farmhouse where she lived with her mother. She wondered if the other girls would be there this year. Were they having a party?

The screen had gone to standby, and Malou tapped it to bring up the text box again.

She hadn't seen Chamomile since this past summer when she'd been standing down in the castle courtyard with Kirstine and Victoria at sunrise. Malou had come so close to going down to them. But she didn't dare.

"Hey, is something up?"

The sound of Louis's voice startled her. She hadn't heard him approaching.

"No, it's . . . it's nothing . . . Listen, where have you been?" She had been sitting and waiting for him the last few hours, though she'd never have admitted that. She had seen him at lunch, where he'd only given her a passing kiss on the cheek and said, "See you tonight." She had taken that to mean they would eat together. Sometimes, they took dinner up to the room rather than sit with the others in the dining hall. But Malou had been forced to go down at the last minute and fill her plate with the sad-looking scraps left before the kitchen staff started cleaning up.

"Did you miss me?" he teased.

"Nope," she mumbled, looking back at her phone. He hadn't actually promised they would eat together. But she still couldn't help feeling angry at him for only arriving now.

"There was something I had to do," he said, sitting down on the bed beside her. "It took a while. Tell me what you're sitting here brooding about."

"It's just . . . It's Chamomile's birthday today. She's eighteen. I don't know . . . maybe I should text her? What do you think?"

He stroked her back and kissed the top of her head. "I think that's sweet. But I also think you should leave it. Chamomile will just get confused and might spend the rest of her birthday thinking about it. If you're not really planning on being in touch again, then that's not going to be good for her."

Malou looked at her phone. Maybe she could write tomorrow: *Sorry, I forgot your birthday . . .* Although it was more like: *Sorry I've ghosted you and ignored all your texts for several months.*

She shook her head. "You're right. It's best not to bring it all up again."

He put his arm around her and gave her a hug. "I'm going to do a last patrol. Want to come?"

"A patrol?"

"Yup." He stood up and held out his hand. Only the silvery feather at his chest and his almost white hair were visible in the room's half-darkness.

Malou looked over at her assignment on the Indigenous Maya and their blood magic. She had taken it out quite optimistically but had not even looked at it once yet. Zlavko always gave them homework that was to be submitted after the weekend or vacation. That way, he could be sure to also ruin the students' free time, not just their time in school.

"Is that necessary?" She couldn't help but smile a little at the sight of him standing there so eager to do his duties.

"We signed up for it ourselves. A quick patrol just to check everything's as it should be. Before bedtime."

He smiled at her innocently, but she noticed a sly undertone to his voice when he added *before bedtime*.

"Okay," she said, getting up. "Let's go."

Malou had been the first to sign up to stay at school over vacation, but that was quite simply because she had nowhere else to be. That's how it always was, every vacation and weekend, but now the Crows had given her a good reason to be in school. Now she seemed like an ambitious student and not just a loser. It was Zlavko's idea, of course. He said it would be a good exercise for the Crows, taking over responsibilities from the teachers during weekends and holidays. Of course, it was just an excuse so that he himself could have a little time off.

When Louis heard she was staying at school, he had canceled his autumn vacation. And she knew it wasn't because he loved the idea of policing the school. He had done it for her sake.

They went down the hallways together. Outside, the wind had picked up and was shaking the trees and rattling in through the old window frames. Most students were on vacation with their families, so they hardly met anyone else on their way through the castle. They checked the library but found no students there, sitting in the deep armchairs or in the small study spaces between tall bookcases. The fire in the hearth had gone out.

"Nothing here," Louis said, switching off the light. "Shall we go up and check the first-years' floor?"

"There's no need. We haven't heard anything from up there."

"We're supposed to check the whole school. So, that's what we'll do. Unless you're very tired? Desperate to get to bed?"

That mocking tone again. He was playing with her. It was the same when he was fighting her. It was always one big game. What they had between them made her sick with longing, but for him, it just amused him. Why should she have to feel like this when he didn't? Did it mean their relationship was less important to him than she feared it was becoming to her?

She ignored his comments and followed him up the stairs to the first-years' floor, where they now stayed in mixed dorms.

"Do you always do what you're told?" Malou asked once they'd established that all the rooms on this floor too, was quiet and in order.

"Only when I know that it's right," he answered. "Do you never do what you are told? Even when you know yourself that it's the right thing to do?"

She glowered at him. "Hey, I—"

Right then, they were interrupted by a scream from the floor above.

They ran up the stairs two at a time.

"This way!" Louis shouted as they ran down the hall. The floor was flooded, and water splashed up onto their pants. A voice screamed again. Then came another, yelling, "Come back and fight, Emilie!"

A fair-haired boy stuck his head out from one of the doorways. He was carrying a bucket filled with water. "Chicken," he yelled as he kept watch down the hallway, his back to Malou and Louis.

They stopped.

"Water fight," Malou muttered. She'd seen with her own eyes that nothing dangerous was going on, that it was just a few students carrying on. But her heart was still racing.

"What's going on?" Louis had run straight into the boy, who got such a shock that he dropped the bucket. Malou held back a giggle.

"Hell, you gave me a fright!" The boy hurried to pick up the pail.

"What are you doing?" Louis's voice was cold, the playful tone long gone.

"But . . . it was Emilie and Elinor. They were flinging water balloons at my bed!"

"And you're getting them back by chucking water all over the place? Who's going to pay for the water damage? Who's going to dry this all up? You do know you're not at some kind of holiday camp here, right? You're at Rosenholm, and you should behave respectably, not run around like some toddler in preschool."

"Okay, okay. Relax. I'll clean it up."

"Damn right, you will. And you can take breakfast duties tomorrow as well. Report to the kitchen at six a.m. Then I'll not bother to report this. You got it?"

The boy nodded, his eyes wide with alarm.

"Good, then get this cleaned up!" Louis said, turning away.

They continued down the hallway in silence.

"Was that really necessary?" Malou asked once they were out of earshot. "They were only having a water fight."

176

"Yeah, which is not allowed," Louis said. The cold edge to his voice had gone. "They need to know that. Or they'll never learn to behave themselves properly here at school. A good telling off now and then can be more effective than hundreds of words of praise—that's what my dad always says."

"And the breakfast duties? Wasn't that supposed to be your turn?"

"Yeah, something like that." He smiled at her and winked. "But now we can sleep in! We need to just swing by the drying loft. There's something I've forgotten."

She gave him a look but followed all the same. There were no students up here either, and he pulled her with him down into the farthest room, where long ago a maid would have had her quarters.

"What did you forget?" Malou asked.

"I forgot to look at the stars. Look, there's a completely clear sky tonight." He looked up through the little loft window. He was right. It was a new moon, so the stars glittered even brighter against the dark sky. Louis found a rug in one corner and spread it out on the floor. It was his own rug; he must have planned this.

"There's going to be a meteor shower tonight," he said, as if reading her thoughts. "I thought we should watch it."

They lay on the rug and looked up through the window. Malou rested her head on his chest, and he put his arm around her.

"It's supposed to begin in half an hour," he said.

"How do you know when something is right?" Malou asked.

"What do you mean?"

"You said that you do what you're told if you know that it's right. But how do you know that?"

"Hmm . . . I think you can sense it. And also, it depends if you trust that person who is telling you what to do."

"Like your dad?"

"My dad?"

"Yeah, you said your dad says a good telling-off is better than praise. Do you think that's true?"

Louis laughed. "It's not *always* best, of course. But every now and then, it's good to know when you've messed up. Most people just look away and pretend nothing happened but think to themselves, *What an idiot.* I'd rather have someone tell me what I've done wrong and what I should have done instead. Someone who gives a damn, instead of turning their back and not caring."

"Like your dad?"

"Yeah, like my dad."

"Was he strict with you when you were a kid?"

"Well, maybe he was. He was never horrible or hit us or anything, but it was clear what he thought was right and wrong. And if you broke a rule, you knew about it. But he's decent, my dad. I think you'd like him. He doesn't have much time for bullshit or sugar-coating things."

"What did your family say, about you not going home for vacation?"

"It was fine. I mean, it's not like they can decide for me. I'm an adult. But they didn't get angry or anything. My mom was a bit disappointed, for sure, but my dad understood when I said you were also staying at school."

She sat up and looked down at him. "You told them about me?"

He laughed again. "Yeah, I have. Or are we a secret?"

Malou ran her fingers over the surface of the rug. "Nah, of course we're not. I was just a bit surprised. What did they say?"

He shrugged, a smile on his lips. "They were happy for me, I think. They're looking forward to meeting you."

Malou lay down again with her head on his chest.

"Have *you* told *your* family about me?" he asked. She could feel him holding his breath, his chest not rising and falling as it did before. He'd have picked up on the fact she didn't like to talk about it.

"I don't have any family," she said, sitting up again.

"Malou?" He looked up at her.

"What?"

"I'm not bothered. It doesn't matter."

She turned her head and looked into his bright, gray eyes. "What do you mean?"

"I just want to say it, in case you were thinking it mattered to me. Who your family is, or if you even have one at all. I'm not bothered. It doesn't mean anything to me. The only thing that means anything is the two of us."

Her eyes blurred over, and a tear, burning hot, trickled from the corner of her eye. He saw it but didn't say anything; he just pulled her back down to lying and leaned in over her. His lips brushed hers. She kissed him, slowly at first, then faster and faster. She buried her hands in his hair and pressed herself into him. His body felt warm and strong against hers, and she became dizzy as everything around them melted away, even the stars.

"Argh!" He pulled away from her and touched his tongue to his lips. She mirrored his movement and tasted blood. Was it his?

"I'm sorry, I didn't mean to . . ."

"It's okay," he said, leaning over her and kissing her on the brow. "It's okay. I just got a bit of a fright. Go ahead."

"But I . . . No, it's just—"

"It's okay, Malou." He sat up and pulled off his shirt. Then he lay himself down on the rug and turned his face slightly away from her so his neck was bare. She stared at his pale skin in the darkness. She had never tried it before. Not properly, and not on another person. This was her first time. With Louis, everything was the first time.

Malou felt the artery pulsating more than she could see it. She wanted him; she wanted to own him and possess him. When she leaned over him, she heard him whisper it, the thing she so longed to hear.

I love you, Malou.

OCTOBER 22ND
2:15 P.M.

Malou

Ivalo walked quickly and silently, her dark hair flicking around her face. Malou could tell from the rising wind that they were nearing the sea, but they were still passing through the high fir trees, the greenery forming a ceiling above them. They were old trees, gnarled and lopsided; they tilted away from the wind and the water.

Now they could see the sea, with its white-topped waves. Bildsø Beach was not so far from Slagelse, where Malou had grown up, and she had been here once for camp. She remembered bunk beds and sunshine, milk in orange plastic cups, and friendly adults coming in to say goodnight. Some of the kids cried when it was time to sleep. They missed home. Malou never suffered from homesickness.

They left the trees and continued over the soft, short grass down to the beach. Only once they were a few feet from the churning water did the grass stop and become sand instead.

"Even by the sea there are trees growing," Ivalo said, scowling at the tall spruces.

"Don't you like the forest?" asked Iris, who was at least a head shorter than all the others and looked more like a middle school student than a senior. Her fair hair stood out in frizzy tufts around her face in the strong wind.

"I like to be able to see into the distance," Ivalo said, turning her back as if trying to ignore an unwelcome guest. At the same time, she signaled to the black-clad Crows to gather around her so they could hear better in the wind.

"The Inuits say that everything has an *inua*," she began, gesturing with her hands to indicate the sea, the sky, and the forest behind them. "Everything is alive, and everything has a soul. Animals, plants, the sea, the sun, and the moon—each has their own inua. All people have an inua, too, but theirs is of no greater value than an animal's. People are not considered to be above nature, and if people create an imbalance or disturb nature, that can be fatal." She paused and took a moment to look at them one by one. Malou avoided directly meeting her eyes. Instead, she looked for a moment at Ivalo's black face tattoos, which were unlike anything she'd seen before.

"People depend on nature," Ivalo continued. "It's easy for people like you to forget that. But, if you forget it for too long, nature will find a way of reminding you again."

The wind howled and whipped at their jackets and hair as if to emphasize Ivalo's point.

"Are you saying that nature is dangerous?" Magnus asked. He was one of the new members recently admitted to the Crows. Malou only knew him very superficially because he had shared a dorm with Louis last year.

"Nature is everything," Ivalo answered. "It is food and survival. It is hunger and death."

Malou looked around her. On the way there, they had passed both a playground and a closed ice-cream kiosk. The bus continued along the road, but farther down toward the beach was the holiday camp she'd been to as a child. It was a little hard to see how the place they found themselves in could be a source of both survival and death.

"It all sounds very dramatic," she commented, and Ivalo frowned.

"As I said, it's easy to forget. But even here, nature will catch up with you sooner or later."

"Isn't there something you can do so it doesn't catch up with you?" Iris asked.

"The Inuit have many different ways of protecting themselves," Ivalo replied. "They use amulets to protect against sickness and death. A polar bear's tooth, for example, imparts to its wearer a little of the polar bear's inua, of its strength and courage, but also some of its weaknesses. Amulets are not something to be played with." Ivalo looked sternly at Iris, who looked back with wide, alarmed eyes, and certainly not with the appearance of someone thinking of playing with amulets.

"But, let's get started," Ivalo continued. "You will spend the next hour by the sea or in the forest. Preferably alone. If you should sense that an animal, plant, or particular place speaks to you, then go with that feeling. Let it happen. Perhaps it is an inua that wants to connect with you." She signaled with her hands that they should spread out.

Malou gave Louis a quick smile but shook her head when he lifted one eyebrow in a question. It was no good; she wouldn't be able to concentrate if he was near. She had trouble enough gathering her thoughts when he wasn't even around. Images of his bare torso, his bright eyes, his veins pulsing under his skin—they plagued her thoughts almost constantly. He smiled and blew her an almost imperceptible kiss before she turned away.

Most of the students went closer to the sea, but Malou sought out some shelter in the trees. She followed a narrow path and, without thinking, walked in the direction of the holiday camp. Would she remember where it was? There was a large, grassy area surrounded by rosehip shrubs. The girls had always picked the pink petals and pressed them between their fingers, calling it perfume. At this time of year, the rosehip would not be in bloom, but as she reached the camp, she saw that the shrubs were still laden with bloodred berries. It was nowhere near as big as she remembered. Malou made a circuit of the dark green wooden buildings and decided to start back toward the sea, but on the way back, she came across a simple bench between two large firs. From here, there was an open view of the sea, and the wind had blown the clouds away so she could feel the autumn sun on her skin. She closed her eyes and concentrated on the sensation of her own pulse. The blood ran warm and strong through her body. She felt in control. That's how she had been feeling since that night in the drying loft. Calm, strong, and in control. It gave her the belief that she could manage it. That she would still fulfill her task. It was an incredible feeling, and she let it wash over her. The breeze rushed in her ears, the wind rustled the treetops, and then there was quiet . . .

The noises were all gone or far away, and there was only a distant whisper. Her movements were slow and calm. She was flying. Or floating. There was nothing here, nothing above or below, no pain or joy, just a blue-black darkness. A vacuum. Emptiness. Then she heard the song again. The mournful song. And she sensed something in the darkness. She wasn't alone. Something rose up around her, pressing around her body. Gently, at first. But when Malou

184

tried to move her arms, she understood that she was trapped, entangled in something she couldn't see. The more she fought against it, the tighter it held her. All around her, it was dark and icy cold as she was pressed farther and farther down. Toward the bottom.

"Arnaqquassaaq!"

Malou opened her eyes. The first thing she saw was the distinctive black tattoos on the hands that were clasped over her heart. Shocked, Malou threw them off as if she had woken to find a tarantula crawling on her chest. Ivalo squatted beside her, her eyes wide, gasping for breath.

"What are you doing?" Malou gasped. The wind chilled her skin, as if she were lying on the grass fully naked. She looked down at herself, horrified. She was fully dressed but dripping wet. "Ivalo? Why am I wet? What have you done to me?"

Ivalo rocked back onto her heels and let herself fall down to a sitting position. She propped herself up on the trunk of one of the large trees, and a drop of sweat dripped from her hairline and over her temple. "You must have fallen into the water when you lost consciousness," she said without meeting Malou's eyes. She was still out of breath.

Malou looked around. She was lying beside the little bench where she had sat down in the sun. "No, I haven't been anywhere near the sea. I've been up here the whole time. Why am I wet?"

Ivalo shook her head. "Asukiaq. I don't know." She stood up, still supporting herself on the tree trunk. "Come on, we need to find the others and get ourselves home."

Ivalo's legs shook as she walked. She didn't turn to check if Malou was following her.

OCTOBER 22ND
8:17 P.M.

Malou

"Are you going now?" Louis looked up from his phone.

"Yeah. I want to talk to her about what she's up to."

"I thought it could wait until tomorrow."

Malou shook her head. "No, it can't."

He looked at her with concern but then gave her a little smile anyway. "Okay. I'm meeting Magnus at the library soon, so I'll be gone when you get back."

"Will you be out late?" she asked, hoping it sounded suitably casual.

"For sure. I promised to help him with an assignment, and he hasn't even started it yet. Zlavko's breathing down his neck, and he wants to make a good impression now that he's in the Crows, too."

"Okay, well, say hi."

Malou let herself out of the room and headed to the teacher's hallway. She hadn't been able to settle down since they'd gotten back to the school. It wasn't because of the cold water or the feeling of her soaked clothes that had stayed with her. Malou had long ago mastered using her powers to warm herself from the inside if she needed to. Blood mages were able to survive for a long time in the cold and without food. But up against what she faced in that still darkness, she had felt defenseless. That was the part she couldn't forget.

It was getting late, and she didn't come across anyone else. The teachers' corridor was not a place students usually came to, but Malou assumed Ivalo had her own apartment beside the other teachers. She found the name on a door, and she realized Ivalo had taken Zlavko's old digs since he had become vice principal and been given a different, bigger place. Malou knocked. Nobody came, and she tried again, louder this time. No answer. Ivalo wasn't there, or perhaps she had visitors. Malou gave an exasperated sigh.

This had happened twice now. Ivalo had somehow conjured up a darkness that pulled Malou down without her being able to do anything to stop it. If she had gained herself an enemy, she wasn't planning on sitting and waiting until Ivalo struck again. Attack was the best form of defense. Malou knocked one more time before giving up and turning from the door. A sudden impulse made her continue along the teachers' corridor instead of returning to the stairs. She glanced at Zlavko's name on the door before knocking.

"Yes?" Zlavko opened the door straight away as if he had been expecting someone.

"Is Ivalo here?"

He raised one eyebrow and waved her inside without answering. Ivalo was sitting on the living room couch. Her face gave no indication of how surprised she was to see Malou. She neither smiled nor greeted her, but her expression was guarded, watchful.

"Good evening," Malou said. Two wine glasses were sitting on the table. They had been sitting and talking together. Had they talked about her?

"What do you want?" Zlavko asked impatiently.

"I want an explanation. What happened today, out by the beach? What happened up in the drying loft?

"I don't know what you mean," Ivalo said, looking away.

"Well, that's not true," Malou said. "What is it, that darkness?"

Ivalo kept her face turned away, overtly ignoring Malou's presence.

"Hello? I have a right to know what it is you're putting me through! Is that what you two were sitting talking about?" Malou turned to Zlavko, who stood with his arms crossed. "Has Ivalo told you about what happened?"

"As always, you think everything is about you. But that is not, in fact, the case," he answered.

Malou ignored Zlavko's attempt to derail the conversation and provoke her temper. "I was soaked. You can't act as if it's something I've just imagined," Malou said, this time facing Ivalo, who still refused to look at her. Her profile was still as if she were carved in stone.

"You fell in the water," she said.

"That's a lie. She's lying! I'm not taking part in any more of Ivalo's classes until I find out what exactly is going on!" Malou exclaimed.

At last, Ivalo turned to face her. "You needn't bother anyway. I would have told you, I feel quite certain anyway that you don't have any hybrid ability. So there's no reason for you to attend my classes."

"You're just saying that because you want to get rid of me!"

"Malou?" Zlavko said in a menacing tone. "I expect you to treat all the teachers at this school with respect. And as far as I remember, you weren't even interested in joining Ivalo's lessons. Forget whatever it is that's bothering you and concentrate on your own business. You don't have time to let yourself get distracted."

There was a knock on the door, making them all turn their heads to look at the same time.

"Would you be so kind as to answer that?" Zlavko said, getting up to fetch another wine glass from a dark wooden cabinet. They were obviously expecting one more.

"Am I your butler now or something?" Malou spat out as she turned anyway, took the door handle, and yanked it open.

"It's you . . . ?"

For a moment, she thought he was there for her sake. To back her up, maybe. Or because he was worried about her. But then she realized that was wrong. The third wine glass was for him. Zlavko was expecting him. "I thought you were going to the library."

Louis blushed a little, but his smile was convincing and betrayed nothing of his state of mind. "Yeah, I almost forgot that I had another arrangement."

"Come inside then, Louis. Malou was just leaving." Zlavko gave her a commanding nod. "Close the door behind you if you don't mind."

She stood, momentarily frozen, as Louis edged past her into the living room without meeting her eyes. He reached out and took the glass Zlavko was offering him.

Malou turned and closed the door behind her without another word. She went slowly up to the room. Why had Louis said he was meeting Magnus? Had he really forgotten he had an arrangement with Zlavko? No, he had lied to her. She felt sick. She knew already. He had secrets he kept from her. He snuck out in the night when he thought she was sleeping; he turned up late to see her. He wasn't in the places he said he was going to be. The question was, what was he hiding?

To all members of the Crows' Club,

You are hereby invited to the annual Samhain ritual, to be held in the drying loft on October 31 at 11 p.m.

Until then!

Best wishes,

Jens Andersen

Jens Andersen
Principal of Rosenholm Academy

OCTOBER 31ST
11:00 P.M.

Malou

"Welcome, on this All Hallows Eve," Jens said, clapping his hands together. The murmur of chatter around him immediately ceased. "Tonight, we will perform a ritual that is new to you, but is, in fact, one of the most ancient of its kind. Rituals have always played an important part in the work of mages. It is how we come into contact with our powers. Sadly, many powerful rituals have been forgotten or banned out of fear of the powers that can be released. But now is not the time for fear but rather for courage and action. And that's why we will be reviving this ancient ritual tonight, a ritual for calling on the spirits who are hidden from most of you."

Jens walked out onto the floor, where he had space all around him. "Draw it, Iris. The pentagram. Just here on the floor." He held out a piece of chalk to Iris, who took it, bent down on one knee on the drying loft floor, and, with trembling hands, began to draw.

Malou looked around the circle. New students had come along. Opposite her stood a tall, broad boy with short hair and dark eyelashes. His name was Elias, and he was one of those who joined the Crows because Ivalo believed he had hybrid abilities.

"As you all know, tonight is very special," Jens said. "It is on Samhain that we are the closest we can be to the spirits of the dead. Tonight, they walk among us, and those who have the ability will be able to see them, talk to them, and ask them about past events, as well as future events."

They stood in a circle around Iris, who was laboriously drawing a five-pointed star. All the Crows were there, and Zlavko and Ivalo were also taking part in the ritual.

"Good." Jens nodded as Iris finally finished the star. "Stand in a circle, all of you. But first, we need to choose a medium. All of our powers will be united this evening and channeled into the same person, and so it will be the medium only who will be able to see the spirits. And the stronger the medium is, the stronger our connection to the spirits will be. Ivalo, I have heard about your hybrid abilities. That would mean that you are a very capable spirit mage?"

Ivalo turned to him, surprised. She looked at him for a while without speaking.

"Or have I misunderstood?" Jens said.

"No," she said. "But this evening, I will only be observing. This ritual is for the students. So, the medium should be one of the students."

"Okay." Jens turned to the Crows. If he was disappointed or offended by Ivalo's blunt refusal, he didn't show it. "Albert?"

Albert blinked and twisted his mouth in a strange expression when his name was spoken aloud. "I can, but . . . Iris is the best spirit mage here."

Malou looked at him. It was a brave move. Both his going against Jens and his nominating someone else who was better than him. Brave, but maybe not particularly clever. Despite the fact he had actually already graduated, he found it hard to impress Zlavko. This could have been his chance.

192

"It's true that Iris is a good spirit mage, but she is not necessarily the strongest. But, okay, Iris, you can have the opportunity if you think you can perform the ritual without passing out." Jens's voice was stern. He didn't manage to hide his irritation or had perhaps made no attempt to. He tugged at his shirt collar with one hand as if it was choking him.

Iris looked at the floor. "It's been a long time since I fainted. I'd like to try."

Malou wasn't too sure what they were talking about, but she did remember the Crows, entrance test. Iris had impressed them all by embodying and giving voice to a spirit so that they could all hear it. But she had lost control of the spirit and fainted. It had obviously happened to her more than once. "Well, let's go with that. Iris, you stand in the middle of the pentagram. Now, I'll go around to each of you in the circle with this cup." Jens bent down to pick up an old, long-stemmed chalice that had been sitting on the floor. In this, you must offer up a little of yourself. Literally, it can be anything at all, but it must be something that means something to you. If you feel quite proud of your hair, then pull a strand off and throw it in. If you have long nails . . . well, you see where I'm going."

Malou looked at the others in the circle. If this had happened in first year, the students would have complained or wrinkled their noses, but the third-years had experienced many a thing already, and members of the Crows were used to, in any case, following Zlavko's orders without question.

Jens approached the first person in the circle, Amalie, who pricked her finger with her athame and offered a few drops of her blood into the chalice. Louis, smiling slightly, pulled at a strand of his shoulder-length blond hair and dropped that; others spat into the cup, bit off a nail, or pulled out an eyelash. Malou opted for

Amalie's method but didn't need to use her knife. By concentrating, she could get her blood to quietly run from her elbow crease down her lower arm and fingers, from where it finally dropped into the chalice.

"Many thanks to you all," Jens said when they were done. None of Jens, Zlavko, or Ivalo offered up anything into the cup. He set the cup in front of Iris and sprinkled some powder over it.

"In a moment, Iris will set the contents of the chalice alight. The rest of us will remain outside the lines of the pentagram, but as we join hands with one another, our powers will be magnified. We will direct the force toward you, Iris. Prepare yourself, as it can feel overwhelming."

Without giving Iris time to change her mind or have second thoughts, he nodded to her in the middle of the pentagram. Then he reached both hands out, taking Louis's on one side and Amalie's on the other. Malou had Amalie on her left and Albert on her right. His hand was ice cold when she took it in hers.

Iris, with shaking hands, struck the match Jens had given her. As it fell into the chalice, a hissing, crackling flame flared up, and white smoke rose up around her.

A shiver ran through Iris's body, which was half-hidden now behind the smoke, and she let out a hoarse, rasping sound. Malou almost expected Iris to faint, but she held herself steady on two feet, and after a moment, she straightened up and the smoke slowly spread out. Iris's light blue eyes had disappeared, and she stared at them with an empty white glare.

"Tell us—have the spirits joined us, Iris?" Jens said.

His voice was deep and calm.

"Yes," Iris whispered, the voice her own. She had not been possessed by a spirit, as Malou had seen happen with Victoria the first time they contacted Trine's spirit on All Hallows Eve. "They are here."

"Who? What are their names?" Jens asked.

"What are your names?" Iris repeated. She shook her head, then started suddenly as if someone had given her a push. "I can't . . . there are so many . . ." she whispered.

"How many are there?" Jens asked.

"I don't know," Iris replied. "Lots more than usual."

"Have you seen them before?"

"Some of them. They live here in the school. But not all of them. There are a lot of new ones. And they're not . . . spirits."

"What do you mean, they're not spirits?"

"They are dead . . . But they're not spirits," Iris maintained.

"Try to choose one and ask their name."

Iris closed her whitened eyes for a while as she focused on listening. Then she nodded.

"Have you got one?" Jens asked. "Describe what you see."

"A young woman," Iris whispered. "She looks like a person, but her feet . . . they're wrong."

"Wrong, how?" Jens asked.

"They're turned the wrong way. The toes point backward. And she's . . . blue."

"What?" Jens shifted his weight from one foot to the other. "What do you mean? Is it a vision, Iris? What do you see?"

Iris's lips were moving, but she wasn't saying anything.

"Focus!" Jens said, and his voice was no longer calm. He was openly impatient. One hand reached again to his shirt collar. "What is it saying?"

Iris shook her head; her slight form quivered as if an electric current was going through her.

"*Tassa*," Ivalo said, "we should stop now."

"No, wait," Jens commanded. "You mustn't break the circle! Iris, is the spirit talking to you?"

Iris gasped for air. "She is only saying one thing," she said, and her voice was so weak they could barely hear it. Then, suddenly, her head tipped back, and a terrifying, deep, hoarse voice came out of her mouth.

"SAY MY NAME!"

Iris fell to the floor as if every joint in her body had given in all at once. Ivalo went to her, leaned over her, and placed two fingers on her neck.

"She's just fainted," she confirmed.

"Elias!" Zlavko snapped. "Take Iris down to Ingrid so she can keep an eye on her overnight."

Elias bent down, scooped Iris up, and disappeared downstairs with her.

"Well, we'd better stop for this evening," Jens said crisply. "It might be an idea to train some strength and stamina with your Crows, Zlavko. Talent alone isn't everything."

Zlavko bowed his head slightly. "That's true," he said, and although his voice was calm, Malou knew him well enough to know he was furious at being called out in that way.

Once Jens had gone, Zlavko turned to Albert. "Next time you are asked to do a task, you say thanks instead of passing it up for someone else to do, do you understand?"

Albert gave a quick nod without looking at Zlavko. Then he turned and left, blushing.

Sigrsteinn dauøi vill verja. Sigrsteinn dauøi vill verja. He reminds himself of it. They cannot touch him; he is untouchable. *Sigrsteinn dauøi vill verja.*

He has the stone, and he has the white light to protect him. But it's not enough. He is still afraid, and he hates himself for it. He is not strong enough yet.

But there are other ways.

NOVEMBER 7ᵀᴴ
8:15 A.M.

Malou

It was frosty. They were only one week into November, but it had turned suddenly cold and snow had fallen overnight. It was no more than a couple inches, but it lay in a white, sparkly layer, the sun now shining, and the world was clean and pretty and white. November was usually brown. Brown, fallen leaves, brown mud, bare brown branches. And then suddenly—a white day. Like a diamond in rough ground. Malou took a deep breath of the cold air and crouched to tighten her sneaker laces again, although they hadn't come undone. She had woken early but had lain in bed watching the sunrise color the sky with pink, feeling his breath on her neck. She felt light with a bubble of hope fizzing inside. He had said it to her again that night.

First, they'd had a fight. He'd been away again. This time, they'd had a clear arrangement to meet, but he'd kept her waiting for hours. She wasn't the type to sit wringing her hands, sighing, and staring out the window while she waited for some boy or other, and she hated him for turning her into exactly that. But it wasn't just the times he'd stood her up and the fact that she'd discovered, several times, that he wasn't in the bed beside her when she'd woken at night. It was the intimacy he shared with Zlavko. The wine glass that was handed to him as he was asked to close the door behind him. What were they up to?

She had prepared herself, but when he finally arrived, it didn't go anything like she had planned. She should have kept her head high and stayed strong. Ice cold. That's how she should have confronted him. Instead, her voice had trembled, and tears had started to prick at her eyes. Thankfully, he hadn't denied it. Louis had said it like it was—or at least, he'd told her as much as he could. That, yes, he had something going on, and that, yes, it was Zlavko who was involved. Some kind of task. And he couldn't tell her any more about it, not yet, but soon, he said. Malou had almost started to tell him that she had a task of her own as well. A task that *she* couldn't tell him about. But she had a hunch he knew that already.

He had been afraid. Afraid that she would break up with him. And he had said it to her again. *I love you, Malou. You just have to trust me. Because I love you.*

She wanted to believe it. She wanted to live in a white day forever. It worked out for some people. Why not for her, too? If she just managed to do what she had to do? Was it possible, then?

Malou started to run. She was like an animal, a deer streaking through the woods. She was light on her feet, running faster and faster, but feeling like she would never tire, as if she could go on forever over the white carpet of frosty snow.

She caught sight of the first drop but didn't stop. Maybe she didn't want to see it. The next bloodstain was clearer, impossible to ignore. She came to a standstill. The snow was no longer just white. It was also red. But still completely undisturbed. Where had the blood come from?

Malou spotted further red stains in the snow up ahead. There were no tracks, either human or animal. She carried on, this time following the trail of blood. It led her along the forest's edge, but before she reached the dark trees, the mystery was solved in front of her eyes. There was a disturbed patch of snow and blood where some animal had attacked another. There were dark feathers. The blood came from a bird. It must have been attacked at some other spot and had gotten itself free. It had been injured, and the blood had dripped down onto the snow as it tried to fly away. That's why she hadn't seen any tracks. Finally, it had sat here, probably too weak to fly any farther, and its killer had caught up with it.

Malou looked up again. A movement had caught her eye. With its white fur against the white snow, the animal was almost invisible. It was a dog. It appeared not to be scared of her. Black eyes, a black nose, white fur. Its ears were pricked up attentively. It was beautiful. Malou liked dogs. When she was little, she had always wanted a dog. She pursed her lips and made a little kissing sound. The dog was startled but didn't run away. Instead, it sat down, watching her. Malou went slowly toward it.

She almost reached it. It was still sitting motionless, and she could sense how all its muscles were tensed. She doubled over a bit to not frighten it, and was suddenly overcome by the desire to feel its soft fur between her fingers. Carefully, she crouched on the snow and reached out her hand.

The dog flattened its ears and growled at her. It bared its teeth, still red with the bird's blood. Malou got such a fright that she sat down on the snow. At that, it turned around and ran back into the woods.

She watched it go, but her vision grew blurry. She realized she was crying. The tears streamed down her cheeks. She cried like a kid, not holding back, and she didn't understand why.

It was just a bird, after all.

New rules

Regrettably, the school management team has received further information regarding another planned attack on the school. In order to ensure students' safety, the following new rules will be in force at Rosenholm Academy as of today:

- No students are permitted in the outdoor grounds of the school after 10 p.m.
- After 10 p.m., all students should be in their own rooms.
- Weekend trips home and for vacation must be approved by the school principal.

Members of the Crows' Club are exempt from these rules and will patrol the hallways to ensure they are being upheld in order to guarantee student safety.

With best wishes,

Jens Andersen

Jens Andersen
Principal of Rosenholm Academy

NOVEMBER 11TH
3:00 P.M.

Malou

Malou couldn't put it off any longer. The last three times Zlavko had called her to one of these hellish private lessons, she had made up an excuse. But it was no use hiding anymore. She had to master this, and she risked running out of time if she didn't face up to it.

Jens had introduced his new rules after Samhain, so now only the Crows were free to go where they wanted. Amalie and Elias had started accompanying Jens around the school as some form of private bodyguard, which meant they were skipping nearly all of their lessons. Malou had asked Amalie if she knew anything about threats made against the school, but she hadn't heard.

There was an uneasy mood among the students because of the new rules, and that didn't make Malou's task any easier. There was no way out of it.

She took a deep breath and turned the door handle. She had steeled herself to see him there, but nevertheless, it gave her a little start. Louis was standing talking casually with Zlavko, and they didn't even look up as she came in.

"Here I am," she said.

Louis gave her a big smile. "Surprised?" he asked.

"Well, we've managed it," Zlavko said. "At long last. You'd think there would be nothing more important than this, but still, it's clearly very difficult to pin you down. As I said, I've been working on a solution to your little issue with 'wanting' this enough. For that reason, today, you'll practice on Louis. I imagine he'll be able to get you motivated, shall we say."

Malou looked down at her feet.

"I came of my own free will—don't worry," she heard Louis say. He still seemed relaxed, almost cheery, but she was afraid he didn't know what he was getting into.

"Stand close together. Physical contact is important at the beginning, but I'm assuming you two have a little experience in that area?" Zlavko was clearly amused, but Malou stood nailed to the floor still, her eyes fixed on her feet.

She sensed him coming nearer. The tips of his shoes entered her visual range, and she felt him placing his arms around her and bending his head lightly forward to touch his forehead against hers. Her body reacted right away. Despite the unnatural situation, despite Zlavko being there, her heart started to race, purely because he was so near she could smell him. Before, when Zlavko had laid his hands on her shoulders, her only thought had been to fight him off and get as far away from him as possible. But with Louis, it was the opposite. She couldn't get close enough. Malou had no doubt that she could do what Zlavko wanted her to. But she was scared of what would happen if she permitted it. If she let this brewing feeling boil up and take over and just went with it. From her. Into him.

"I don't want to . . . hurt you," she whispered.

"I know what you're training to do. *Impero Spiritus.* Zlavko explained it all. It's okay, Malou. I trust you. Just do it." He closed his eyes. The feeling was so overwhelming that she had difficulty holding it in. Impero Spiritus was dangerous, and besides, practicing it was wholly prohibited, even when the victim took part voluntarily.

"It's okay," he whispered.

She let out a sob as she gave in. Her blood was simmering in her veins. She was reacting to him, to his blood. They were forever bound to each other. She had taken in some of his life's force, and he was letting her in—he opened himself to her. She was everywhere—in his minor and major arteries, in the deepest veins, the capillaries, and microscopic venules, in the whole network running through his body. Malou breathed in deeply. It felt like a cold rush of desire running through her whole body, going on and on. An ice-cold, neverending high. At that moment, she knew she could control him. Not just freezing his movements or tripping him off his feet, but she could control him completely. She could get him to jump out of a window or kill another person. He was completely in her power. And she had never experienced anything that felt even half as amazing.

"Good," Zlavko whispered in her ear. "That's good, Malou."

NOVEMBER 12ᵀᴴ
4:30 A.M.

Malou

She slept restlessly that night. The sensation of floating in an empty darkness blended itself with the intoxicating feeling of pushing into Louis, a mixture of fear and rapture kept her pulse throbbing in her ears. Each time she dozed off, she woke again with a start. At 4 a.m., she got up. She was on early watch with Iris. Jens insisted that the Crows patrol all night long now, and the shifts were divided among them.

Malou glanced at her reflection in the bathroom mirror. Her face was pale, and she had dark circles under her eyes. She could do it. It was frightening, but at the same time, it made her feel calmer. The task she had ahead of her no longer seemed insurmountable.

Malou met Iris at the bottom of the great stairs. She was standing quietly in the dark.

"I was scared you weren't coming," she said.

"Why would I not come?" Malou asked, slightly annoyed, shining her pocket flashlight into Iris's face. Her large, wide eyes stared back at her, but Malou realized she still couldn't see anything with the beam of light stuck up in her face like that so she lowered the light.

"Last week, I was supposed to be on watch with Magnus, but he slept in."

"Oh, well no danger of that for me," Malou said. "I couldn't sleep. Shall we do a round?" They set off slowly to the great hall, then continued up toward the classrooms.

"I can't sleep either," Iris whispered.

"Is that quite common with spirit mages?" Malou asked, without any real interest in the answer. "Victoria could never sleep either. You know, the one I shared a dorm with before?"

Iris nodded. "The dark-haired girl? I do remember her, actually, she was really pretty. Why isn't she at school anymore?"

"Who knows?" Malou said, wishing she'd kept her mouth shut. "Maybe her parents got her into a school abroad. They're super rich."

"It's gotten worse since Samhain. I dream about them."

"Who?"

"The ones I saw."

"That's just your subconscious working through something that scared you," Malou said.

Iris frowned. "In my dreams, they're here. At the school. They're in the corridors."

"That's how the brain works. It jumbles all the things we experience," Malou said as she checked the large auditorium where Dagny taught to make sure all was quiet. "You should be more concerned about the fact you're always fainting. Have you got a better handle on it?"

"I hope so," Iris said. "I'd like to be stronger. Jens needs strong fighters, he said." Iris lay her hand on Malou's shoulder. "I'd like to be like you, Malou. Can't you tell me what I need to do to get strong?"

206

Malou shone the flashlight at Iris again as she resisted the urge to shrug off her hand. Iris hadn't done her any harm. There was no need to be unfriendly.

"Never give up," Malou said. "You just have to stick with it. People think it's difficult, but it's actually very simple. Tough? Yes. Painful? Maybe. But it's not difficult. You just have to keep going."

Iris stared with even wider eyes, if that was possible, nodding seriously. "Can you teach me how?" she whispered. "Would you coach me? I promise I'll work hard."

Malou cleared her throat. "Eh, maybe," she said. "If I've got time."

"Thanks, that'd really be a great help!" Iris smiled gratefully, making Malou immediately regret that she hadn't answered honestly upfront. She had no intention of using her scarce free time together with the peculiar Iris.

"Hey, there's a light on in there," Iris said, pointing to a classroom door that stood ajar. A narrow slit of light from the door drew a line across the floor.

"It's probably just someone who forgot to turn it off. You wait here, and I'll go check," Malou said, relieved to slip away from Iris's overpowering gratitude.

Malou took out her set of keys. Before, all the doors in the castle had been unlocked, but since the start of this year, they were all now locked at 6:00 p.m. It was only as she walked in that she realized this was Lisa's old classroom. The walls were decorated with hand-colored posters of various herbs, and at either end of the old, worn, wooden table, there was a small stove. Students used it to cook their different mixtures in the small black cooking pots hanging on the farthest wall beside a huge enamel sink.

On the opposite side, a huge apothecary cabinet almost filled the length of the wall, with hundreds of drawers for all the herbs that were used in class. On top of the cabinet, there was a small reading lamp that was switched on. Malou went over to switch it off but something caught her eye—she noticed that a number of the drawers had been left pulled out, and the contents looked disturbed, as if someone had been rummaging through them. There was a light crunching underfoot as she stepped on some dried leaves she didn't recognize. Had someone been in here, searching for something? Or was it just some students who hadn't cleaned up properly after class?

She straightened up and shone her flashlight into the corners of the room, but she couldn't see or hear anything. Still, something there did catch her attention. One of her cheeks felt cooler than the other. She turned toward the windows. One of them was open. Malou went over to shut it. As she closed the latch, she realized something else. She could sense a pulse. It was very close by. Malou cast the beam over the floor-length curtains, which had been pulled aside. Slowly, she took hold of the fabric and pulled it back.

Only a very slim man could hide himself behind the curtain. And that's what he was. "Do me a favor and open the window up again, Malou." The flashlight illuminated the pale face and blue eyes of Benjamin.

Malou gasped. Her heart was absolutely pounding. But Benjamin looked at her very calmly as if they had arranged to meet there behind the curtain.

"What are you doing here?" she asked.

"You don't need to worry about that," he said coldly. "Just get out of here, and nobody needs to get hurt."

"Get hurt? What are you talking about? You're the one who's broken in. Did you steal anything?" She looked him up and down, but his hands hung empty by his sides.

"You can only steal something if you haven't been given permission to take it," he said. "And now you should get out of the way. I have somewhere else to be." He took a step toward her and the closed window.

"Malou, what—"

They both turned around. Iris stood at the door, staring at them. In the same instant, Malou took a rough shove in the chest, fell backward, and bashed her tailbone on the floor so hard the pain shot up her spine.

"Help me, help me, stop him!" Iris screamed, both shrill and commanding at the same time. Malou got onto her feet, groaning in pain. Benjamin fumbled with the latches and threw the window open, but suddenly, he was hit on the back of the head by a black object that came flying at high speed. Malou just managed to duck behind a table before she, too, was hit by a similar black object as it whistled through the air like a cannonball.

"Stop him!" Iris yelled, and Malou realized Iris wasn't talking to her. It must be the spirits. Malou looked up and met Benjamin's eyes as he, too, sheltered behind a table a few feet away. His eyes flicked between her and the window as a black cauldron rolled past him along the floor. Malou ventured a look up and saw how the black pots that had been hanging on the wall seemed to be ripping themselves free of their hooks and shooting toward them like lethal projectiles.

Benjamin cursed, and Malou knew what he was thinking. The noise would have long since alerted the teachers, who slept in rooms above. With a deep growl, he grabbed the huge oak table and carried it as a shield as he half ran, half staggered toward Iris, who ceased screaming at the spirits to stop him.

"No!" Malou yelled, but it was too late.

With a roar, Benjamin threw the table down on Iris's fragile figure, after which he turned, ran to the window, and jumped out.

They have stolen something from a classroom. Nothing important, but a strange thing to run such a risk for. He shouldn't really give a damn, but he does. Because he's certain that's not what they came for. He presses it in his hand. He has realized it's possible he could lose it. Perhaps the old man's threats weren't so empty after all. And that horrifies him. Killing him wasn't enough, and he has started to think about the ritual. The ultimate ritual ... If only he had known about it back then. Then none of this would have been necessary.

NOVEMBER 13ᵀᴴ
2:16 P.M.

Malou

The others were angry. Malou could tell from the beat of their hearts and the blood that rushed faster through them. The Crows stood quietly with their hands tucked behind their backs and their legs slightly apart, under the stage from which Jens was addressing them from the lectern. Inside, they were fuming. Jens explained that Iris was laid up in bed. She had broken her collarbone and several ribs on her left side.

"Iris is the latest victim of evil people who are trying to destroy Rosenholm and stop you young people from getting an education." Jens's voice rang out, indignant, over the students gathered in the great hall. "Iris is a talented and loyal student who looks after her school and is active in the Crows. She has done no harm, and still, these people wish to hurt her. Why? I will tell you why. Because although you are young, you deserve to hear the truth." Jens took a sip of water from a glass that stood on the lectern before continuing. "Iris is a spirit mage. Benjamin Brahe and the people he is in cahoots with want to ban all the magic that they themselves don't practice, that they don't understand—it's the magic they call dark magic, just because it is different. And they are prepared to turn against their own. But I promise you that I will not be intimidated. I will continue to fight for freedom and progress for all mages, Blood as well as Growth. Death as well as Earth. And I will fight for our beloved school, Rosenholm. But I cannot do that alone. I need your help. I need your courage. We must all be prepared to show the same courage Iris showed if it becomes necessary. I'm sorry to have to ask it of you, but this is becoming your fight. I promise you, you will be the victors!"

Jens paused as applause broke out, led first and foremost by the Crows. Malou looked out over the students. Some clapped enthusiastically, others frowned suspiciously, and many had their heads put together, whispering to the person beside them.

Jens continued his speech, calling on more students to sign up for the next entrance tests for the Crows, as well as introducing extra classes in combat training and a further tightening of the school rules. As soon as Jens had stepped down, the students broke out into a buzzing of different conversations, all of them about what had happened with Iris and what exactly Jens had just told them.

The Crows remained standing until everyone had left the hall. Then, they, too, broke into chatter.

"Jens is right," Louis noted. "It's not without risks, the job we do. Are you scared he'll come back again?"

"Benjamin?" Malou asked absentmindedly. "No, I'm not scared of him."

"Okay, but you just need to say if you want me to go with you when you're on duty."

"I'm fine, thanks."

"Are you not coming?" he asked when she didn't follow him up the stairs.

"I'll be up soon," Malou replied. "There's something I need to go check."

Jens's speech had cut the school day short, and the students were using their free afternoon to relax, go to the library, or get some fresh air before the sun went down and they had to stay in their rooms as required. For that reason, the hallways on the way down to the classrooms were empty, and Malou didn't meet another soul. The door to Lisa's old class was ajar, and Malou pushed it open. A figure with long, dark hair stood bent over the big cabinet. She stood up as Malou came in.

"Malou," Ivalo said. "What are you doing here?"

Malou glanced over the floor. The cooking pots were no longer lying all over the place but hung once again on the wall, and the dried herbs she had trodden on had been swept up. It must have been Ivalo who had done it, and Malou realized that this, of course, was her classroom now.

"I just wanted to see . . ." Malou said. "Do you know what it was he took?"

Ivalo turned to the cabinet again. "I think it was something from one of these drawers here. They contain the most toxic herbs, and they are locked up so students don't end up using them by mistake. But the guy who broke in must have had the key because the drawers haven't been broken into." Ivalo pulled out a drawer and went through its contents before closing it and opening another. "It seems like they've taken the school's entire stock of banewort."

Malou frowned. She was certainly no herb expert, but the name seemed familiar. "That rings a bell somehow."

"Banewort is of the nightshade family," Ivalo said. "You might have heard of the Vikings using it in their berserker's drinks."

Now Malou remembered it. "Ah, yeah, they drank it to get into some kind of frenzy. What would Benjamin want with banewort?"

Ivalo closed the drawers and locked them. "No idea," she replied.

Dear Malou,

You are hereby invited to a reception for patrons of Rosenholm Academy, on November 20, 8 p. m., at the apartment of the undersigned.

With best wishes,
Jens Andersen
Principal of Rosenholm Academy

NOVEMBER 20ᵀᴴ
7:41 P.M.

Malou

Malou checked herself in the mirror. Her dress was new, but she'd used all of her savings on it. It hadn't been particularly expensive, but for her, it was a lot of money. She twirled to see herself from the side. Yeah, it was sitting as it should. She had almost chosen a black dress like she always ended up doing, but at the last minute she had gone for a white one instead. It was full length, with an elegant cut and a long slit. The upper body had sequins and pearls sewn in, right around the back, too, and they caught the light when she moved. The thin spaghetti straps and the low cut on both the back and front accentuated her strong physique and toned upper arms. She thought for a moment about wearing something on top of the dress, but then decided against it. She liked that people could see how strong she was, even when she was wearing an evening dress and heels.

Malou checked her makeup again. Black eyeliner and a light pink eyeshadow. Her hair was pulled back in a tight knot. She wanted to look sophisticated. Like somebody who belonged there. She thought she'd pulled it off, even though it would be possible to tell—for those who understood those things—that the dress wasn't one of those expensive designer brands.

"You look so beautiful." Louis stepped up behind her, so she was looking at them both in the reflection. With the heels, she stood only a couple inches shorter than him. They were an attractive couple. He was in evening wear—of course, he had such things hanging in his wardrobe, and he wore a white carnation in his buttonhole. He'd had his white-blond hair cut to his jawline, and he wore it tucked behind his ears. He held out his arm.

"Are you ready?"

They went down the school's long hallways, her arm tucked under his and her letting him lead. He set a pace that was a little slower than normal for him, and she guessed it was so she didn't have trouble keeping up in high heels.

"Who's actually coming tonight?" she asked casually.

"In the first place, the people who pay," Louis said. "Rosenholm Academy's patrons are former students who help the school financially every year. And the more you give, the more important you are, of course. A few times a year, you get to drink champagne with the principal and certain promising students."

"You've been before?" Malou asked.

"Yeah, my parents contribute, so that's definitely why."

"And so why am I here?"

"You, my lovely, have earned it. You scared Benjamin off."

"It was Iris who did that," Malou objected. "And she's certainly not coming." Iris was still not well enough, suffering from her painful broken ribs.

"I'm sure Iris couldn't have done it on her own." Louis blinked. "So, here we are."

Malou had never been in the principal's office before and had wondered why the party would be held there. As they entered through the open oak doors, she understood better. Despite the many well-dressed guests who stood around in groups chatting, they weren't short on space. Jens's office was enormous and seemed to consist of several interconnecting rooms. High-ceilinged sitting rooms with paintings on the walls, bookcases, ceramic sculptures placed on windowsills, thick carpets on the floors, and heavy furniture in gilded wood. This was how she imagined rich people lived.

"I'd no idea Jens's office was so huge!" she whispered to Louis, taking care to hold tight to his arm so she wasn't suddenly left standing alone in the midst of all these strange guests.

Louis laughed. "It's not all his office. Just this room here. But he has opened up his private rooms. The principal's apartment is an extension of the office." He pointed down toward the adjacent sitting rooms, which were clearly Jens's private residence.

"What the hell, Louis! I wondered if you'd be here this evening." A broad-shouldered, young man with a prominent jawline slapped Louis firmly on his right shoulder before pulling him in for a bear hug.

"Of course." Louis smiled, letting the slightly unusual greeting pass. "Malou, this is August. My tormentor from the old days."

Malou reached out her hand to the man, who had cropped hair and was a little shorter than her but had hands as big as spades.

"Hello, Malou," he said, pressing her hand. "You shouldn't believe that tormentor thing. A little light teasing never did anyone any harm." August gave a hoarse laugh, and Malou thought he seemed more like an apprentice mechanic who'd been popped into a suit than a progeny of the elite.

"August's parents are friends of my parents. We've known each other since we were kids. What do you do now? Was it law you were studying?"

August nodded and sighed. "Daddy wanted me in the family firm, but I don't know . . ."

"Are they here tonight, your parents?" Louis asked, looking around.

"Yeah, yeah, they're here, too. And big bro. He already finished up studying a while ago and has gotten himself a fancy job in the Ministry of Justice. Good that it's worked out for one of us."

Louis smiled. "I'm sure you'll get there too, August. You normally land on your feet, as far as I remember."

August gave another low laugh. "Well, it was Hans who got my brother in. Maybe he can help me too when the time comes. You know who Hans is, right?"

"I do," Louis nodded.

"Well, of course, you know that, don't you? There was that little thing with his daughter." He raised one eyebrow and looked knowingly at Louis. "Well, I should carry on. You know how it is. Mingle first and get drunk after. My mom did teach me something after all. Good to meet you, Malou!" He gave them a wave before disappearing among the evening dresses and smoking jackets.

"Shall we get something to drink before we find the host and say hello?" Louis asked, looking around for one of the waiters circulating with tall-stemmed glasses on silver trays. Malou watched how Louis drew a waiter's attention to the fact they needed drinks. He did it with a look that was confident and insistent but at the same time still friendly. Seconds later, they were being offered a glass from one of the trays.

"Champagne, sir?"

Louis took two glasses and handed her one. "There are oysters, too. Would you like some?" He nodded to another waiter who was going around with a vast platter, complete with ice and tongs, that held some large, mother-of-pearl colored seashells.

"No, thanks," Malou said as she watched how August stopped the waiter and greedily poured the contents of a shell into his mouth, slurping contentedly as he reached out for another.

"You don't like oysters?" Louis asked.

"Oh, yeah, I just got sick of them. I used to get them every day in my lunch bag at my old school," she said, turning her face away from him.

He laughed. "Ah, sorry, if I sounded like an asshole. I didn't mean to. I've no idea anyway why those are always served at these things. Oysters actually used to be something poor people ate the most of."

"Like me?"

"Malou . . ." He took hold of her shoulders and tried to get her to look at him.

"It's fine," she said, pulling herself free. "Forget it." She took a gulp from her glass. "That was Victoria's dad August was talking about, right?"

"How do you know that?" Louis asked.

"The name, Victoria has said it before. And also the way he said it."

"Yeah, I'm sure August thought he was being very discreet," Louis said, making a face that was somewhere between a smile and a painful wince.

Malou felt her stomach lurch, and an ice-cold feeling of unrestrained jealousy gripped her. Victoria and Louis had been together. It was before they started at Rosenholm, and it was Victoria who had been in love with him, but he had turned her down. Still, it hurt to think about it. And also, why had he turned her down? It didn't make any sense. Victoria was the most beautiful girl Malou had ever met. She was clever and elegant and would be completely at home in company such as this. *Stop it!* She tried to turn her thoughts to something else, but the taut feeling in her stomach remained.

"Are they here?" Malou asked, immediately regretting it.

"Victoria's parents? Yes," Louis said. "They're standing over there with Jens." He pointed discretely over to one of the large windows facing the park. Jens stood together with a tall, beautiful woman wearing a midnight-blue evening dress and an elegant-looking man. Both were listening intently to whatever Jens was telling them.

"Benjamin's parents are usually here as well, but they won't be able to turn up here after what their son has done."

A thought came to Malou. "Your parents, are they here, too?"

"I was just wondering when you were going to ask." He smiled. "No, they're not coming. I would have said so if they were. They had something else going on. I'm sure my mum is crying bitter tears that she had to turn this down. She loves this kind of thing."

"I thought you did, too?"

"But not to the same degree as my mom. I'm not interested in who is the wealthiest or who can trace their ancestry right back to Sweyn Forkbeard, the king of Denmark, or whatever else. Yeah, there are plenty of these people who just sit twiddling their thumbs, living off the family fortune until it's gone. But there are also so many talented and ambitious people who I admire. For example, the beautiful young woman in the white dress right here." He took her hand and lifted it to his lips.

"Also like Jens? And Zlavko?" she asked.

"Yes. Precisely. We're lucky, Malou. To get to experience this."

She narrowed her eyes and took him in. "Do you mean that?"

"One hundred percent. We're entering a whole new era. And the two of us are getting to be a part of that. The spearhead of the Movement."

"The Movement?"

"That's something we've started to call it. The Movement, to restore the mages." He squeezed her hand. "Come on, now we need to go over and greet our host."

NOVEMBER 20TH
10:55 P.M.

Malou

Malou looked despondently at the clock over Jens's enormous desk. A gang of Louis's old friends had dragged him off, and now she'd been left on her own. For the last fifteen minutes, she'd been standing with a couple of middle-aged men who had been polite enough to say hello to her, and she was trying to follow their conversation, appear interested enough, and nod in the right places. But Malou had long lost the thread of what they were talking about.

She made it look as if she'd spotted someone she knew at the other end of the room, although she could have saved herself the trouble. The two men paid no attention to her leaving the conversation.

Malou edged through the room and took another full glass from one of the trays. She shouldn't really drink any more now, but having the glass in her hand gave her something to do. She scanned the room for Louis and couldn't help feeling a little angry that he'd obviously dropped her for more exciting company.

As a child, she'd dreamed of this. Champagne, parties, beautiful dresses, and rich, powerful people. Now here she was. It had happened. And it only made her feel like even more of an outsider. It didn't matter how much you rose through the ranks; there was always a door you couldn't get through and a party you weren't invited to.

Malou observed the people in all their finery. Louis was familiar with all of this. She couldn't lay her eyes on anyone she recognized, besides Zlavko, who stood holding court in one corner. He was hard to overlook, tall and elegantly dressed in a suit, with his glossy, dark hair swept back. Beside him, a fair-haired woman in a provocative powder-blue silk dress leaned in toward him and laughing at whatever he was saying. She also spotted Amalie, who was barely recognizable in her black, frilled dress.

For a moment, Malou was so desperate she thought about going over there, but she couldn't face Zlavko. Instead, she emptied her glass and decided to go to the bathroom. That would kill some time. On the way there, she bumped into a tall woman with cropped hair wearing a green dress, who stared her down angrily. Malou apologized and took a step back.

"There you are!"

She gave a sigh of relief at the sight of Louis. "Where have you been?"

"I'm just about to explain. Some of us have decided to get the party started upstairs instead. And let the oldies carry on down here."

"In the drying loft?"

"Exactly, the bar up there is open. Come on!"

They wove their way through the guests. The atmosphere had become a bit more relaxed in the meantime, as well as becoming much noisier, but once they were out in the hall, it was cool and quiet. Malou briefly wondered if she could entice Louis to bed instead, but he was chatting freely about all the improvements he'd made to the DIY bar, so she quickly dropped the idea. Up in the drying loft, a heavy bass was pounding, and lots of people had started to dance.

"Ah, we have customers in the bar!" Louis said, hurrying over to the corner where people were lining up at the counter, while a pretty, young girl she didn't know was already mixing drinks.

Malou stayed where she was standing and watched the dance floor, where August was making a seriously ridiculous attempt at breakdancing. Despite his lack of talent though, people laughed and clapped as he polished the floor with his attempt to do the worm.

The door of the drying loft opened, and Zlavko came in together with Amalie and the woman in the powder-blue dress, who immediately reeled over to the bar.

"Pleased to see me?" Zlavko asked, coming to stand beside her.

"As always," she said without looking at him.

"You hide it well."

"I thought up here was only for the young ones," Malou said, watching the woman in the blue dress, who, despite her very smooth forehead, must have been around Zlavko's age.

"Don't worry. Her husband will come looking for her soon. He usually does," he said, turning to look at her. "Marriage can really be an unsuitable fit, can't it?" He gave her a look, which she cared for even less than his usual scornful sneer. "Petty people trying to control things that cannot be controlled. It's rarely a pretty sight." He waved at her nonchalantly with his bad hand. "See you later, Malou," he said before sauntering off across the room. Malou couldn't help but wonder what he had meant, although she knew that would also have been his intention.

The music switched gear, and the people on the dance floor did, too. August tumbled into a group of spectators and caught sight of her. She noticed it too late, as he was already giving her a big smile, and it wasn't possible to escape.

"Are you a girl who dances, Malou?" he asked as he wiped his sweaty brow dry.

"No," she answered bluntly.

"Do you smoke then? You look like a girl who smokes. Want to come out for a cigarette?"

She shook her head. "Only losers smoke."

"Ouch!" He lifted his hand as if she had rapped him on the knuckles.

"Tell me, what's a wildcat like you actually doing with a weed like Louis? Aren't you in need of a real man, instead?" he asked, demonstratively stepping up.

"You're a walking goddamned cliché, August," she said, tired. "Get the hell away and go screw yourself."

He laughed hoarsely. "Will do, my lady, will do," he said, bowing fancifully before her, then walking away, still laughing.

She sighed and went over to the bar.

Malou perched on the edge of an old armchair, empty glass in hand. She had drunk a glass of white wine, though she didn't even like wine. She looked down over her own shins and ankles and down to the high stilettos. They were pretty, but now she was dying to take them off and crawl into bed. She got up to find Louis, but he was no longer at the bar.

The guests had begun to thin out. The lady in the blue dress had been fetched by her husband long ago as Zlavko predicted, and there were only a few people on the dance floor now. She'd held out quite a while, even though she hadn't particularly enjoyed herself. Louis had, though. She caught sight of him over in a corner. Louis and Zlavko were standing close together. It looked like they were talking about something private, a joke only they would understand. They were smiling. Zlavko lifted his hand to his face and ran his hand through his recently cut hair.

Malou closed her eyes. Was that what Zlavko had been hinting at? That she should behave "suitably" while he stole her boyfriend? Not try to control things that couldn't be controlled. Not come running after Louis, the way the blonde woman's husband had ...

Malou crossed the room, her insides churning. "Louis?"

He smiled at her and held out his hand to pull her nearer, but she didn't take it.

"I'd like to go home now." It sounded pitiful and not casual and indifferent as she had thought it would.

"No, stay a bit, Malou. The night is young." He laughed. He was drunk.

"I'm tired ..." *Why are you still standing so close to him?*

"Malou wants to go to bed now, Louis. Let her go," Zlavko said.

"Okay, one moment," he said to Zlavko, and finally stepped away from him. But not to go with her or even walk her down to the room. Just to give her a quick kiss on the cheek and send her on her way.

"I'm going to stay here a bit with Zlavko, right?" he said.

"But ..." She looked up at him. His pupils were dilated in the darkness. "You're not going with him ... you know?"

"Malou—"

"Can you just not?"

"You could also stay."

"What ... ?" She looked at him, amazed. "Are you asking if I want to be there while you two ... ?"

228

He shrugged. "If you want to? Why not?"

She pulled away from him. "No! Why . . . why would I want to do that? With him! Why do *you?*"

"I don't judge him. Just like I don't judge you. Why should there be any difference?"

She felt as if her heart would stop beating. *There it was.* What they had together was nothing special for him. It was something he could have with anybody else. With Zlavko. For him, there was no difference. For her, there was only him.

"Louis, are you coming?" Zlavko stood at the open door of the room with the large mattress.

"I thought you understood," Louis said. "I thought you, of all people, would understand . . ."

"Louis, you mustn't do it!" she whispered.

"You can't tell me what I should and shouldn't do," he said mildly. Then he turned and walked away across the room. Zlavko held the door for him and let it slam behind them.

NOVEMBER 21ST
2:43 A.M.

Malou

To hell with him. He wasn't worth it. But it didn't help that she didn't even believe that herself. Malou felt the tears streaming down her face. Why had she let him get so close? The answer was that she thought he felt the same way that she did. But that was obviously not the case. Why else would he have gone with Zlavko? Even though she had asked him not to?

She needed to end it with him. Otherwise, she'd be reduced to being one of those pathetic women there seemed to be so many of, the kind she had always despised. But deep inside, she felt the anxiety bubbling up to the surface. What if she couldn't do it?

She sank onto the bed. It was still unmade, for once, and the duvet was rolled up at the foot, revealing a formation of blood droplets on the white sheet. *His blood.*

Malou swallowed a sob and got up to tear the dirty sheet off. The movement was so violent that the whole mattress topper shifted to the side. When she leaned over the bed to push it back into place, something caught her eye. Something that had no place being there. A black, shriveled leather cord. She froze. Slowly, she lifted the mattress topper aside. It was surprisingly heavy. As she let it fall to the ground, she saw that on the mattress itself, there was a bird's head.

Malou stood, staring. Her brain couldn't connect what she saw with anything that made any sense. It was a black bird, a raven. The head was dried out, and through the empty eye sockets, someone had pushed a leather cord, which was black with hardened blood. The cord was tied together under the beak, and when she looked closer, she saw that the bird's claws were bound tightly to the head with the same leather cord.

Malou felt herself pulling back from the bird head in disgust. Someone had done this. Cut off the head and claws, poked out the eyes, and tied the cord around. And someone had hidden the bird head in their bed. She had no idea what it meant, but someone had caught and killed a raven with exactly this purpose in mind. Could it have been Louis? Who else had access to the room? Her eyes flicked from the dried bird head with its empty eyes to the blood drops on the white sheet. And at that moment, she realized she knew full well who it must have been.

Drops of blood in the snow, the black feathers. And the white dog . . . But it hadn't been a dog. Why hadn't she realized it then? What she had seen that day in the snow was an arctic fox. An arctic fox that normally lived a long way from Rosenholm. It belonged in Greenland. It suddenly seemed so obvious. Ivalo had even said it herself. She was a shapeshifter. She wore an animal tooth around her neck, a tooth that could well be from an arctic fox. It had gifted her a part of its inua so she was able to transform herself when she wanted to. The question was just why? Why was Ivalo going to all that trouble? Malou leaned over the bed. Slowly, she picked up the bird head and lay it in her palm. It was almost weightless. The empty eye sockets glared at her. Was that it? Was the bird head some kind of curse? Was Ivalo trying to prevent her from seeing? Was there something she didn't want Malou to find out about? Was that why she had tried, several times, to pull her down into that darkness?

She stood still for a moment, the bird head in her hand. If Chamomile, Victoria, or Kirstine had still been at school, they would no doubt have talked her into investigating first, maybe going to the library or reading up on amulets, before doing anything rash. But they weren't here. Malou was alone. And she had already decided what she had to do.

Malou didn't bother to knock. She pulled the handle down, opened the door, and entered in one fluid motion. Then she stopped. It was dark in the room. Ivalo hadn't been at the party, so Malou imagined she had been home and would have gone to bed. But then why hadn't she locked the door? Malou turned in the darkness. There was a full moon, and despite the pulled curtains, a little light was pushing into the small apartment. She could make out a door at the other end of the room. It was open, but Malou couldn't see in. Something was blocking her view. She slowly crept closer. When she got to the open doorway, she reached her hand carefully in front of her into the dark room on the other side. There was a dry rustling sound, which startled her. Something was hanging in the doorway. It felt like dried leather, perhaps an animal skin. Malou pushed it aside and went in.

"Terianniaq..."

Ivalo was sitting on the floor just inside the door, lit up only by a single live flame in front of her. She was kneeling, her hair was pulled back from her face, and she had a strap of leather bound tightly around her head. She was otherwise naked. She rocked

232

slowly backward and forward, whispering words Malou didn't understand.

Malou froze. Ivalo must have heard her come in when the door opened, but she still didn't react, just continued with the uncanny rocking. She was perspiring. Her skin looked yellow in the candlelight, and it was only now Malou noticed that both hands were tied behind her back. Who had tied her?

"Ivalo! Ivalo are you okay?" Malou's voice sounded louder than she would have wanted, but the bound woman in front of her still made no reaction. "Ivalo!" She leaned over her and took hold of her shoulder. Her skin was burning hot. With a scream, Ivalo fell to the side, her head thrown back as if she was having a spasm. Malou fumbled for the light switch. By the time she found one, Ivalo had gone still. Little tremors still ran through her naked body, but the unpleasant hissing from her throat had stopped. Malou leaned down to loosen the cord on her wrists and realized that it was made of two loops Ivalo had stuck her hands through. Had she wanted to, she could easily have wriggled them free.

"Angakok," Ivalo mumbled.

"What?" Malou asked,

"Angakok, do you know what that is?"

"No," Malou said, uncertain what she should do with herself.

"An angakok is a Greenlandic shaman," said Ivalo, her voice still hoarse and weak.

"And that's what you were doing? A shamanic ritual?" Malou asked.

"Yes. I've been having difficulty connecting with my spirit guide. I hoped this would work." She slowly sat up while slipping her hands free. "I should have locked the door. So nobody could interrupt me. Now it's all wasted."

233

"Terribly sorry," Malou said pointedly.

"He wasn't coming anyway," Ivalo said, loosening the band on her head. "My spirit guide."

"The arctic fox?" Malou asked.

"Yes," Ivalo nodded. "Terianniaq. He's hiding from me. It was only that day of the snow that he came."

"That day you were making this thing?" Malou threw the raven's head down in front of them.

"Yes, that was the same day," Ivalo answered. If she was surprised at being exposed in that way, she hid it well. "My powers were strong that day. But since then, they've gone again."

"And you also used those powers to put some hex on me?"

Ivalo laughed aloud and shook her head. Then she picked up a mug from the floor beside her and drank from it thirstily. A drip of water ran out the corner of her mouth and continued down her neck and between her breasts. Malou looked away and tried to ignore the utter inappropriateness inherent in her standing in her teacher's bedroom in her long white evening dress and high heels while her teacher sat stark naked on the floor at her feet.

"Tell me what it is," Malou insisted.

"It's an amulet," Ivalo replied. "I made it to protect you."

"Against what?"

"Arnaqquassaaq, the Sea Mother."

Malou mouthed the word silently.

"That's who you met in the darkness," Ivalo said.

Malou recalled the mournful song, the feeling of something tightening around her wrists and pulling her down, and Ivalo's firm hands on her head.

"She's the one who wants to bring me down to the depths. Who is she?"

Ivalo pulled her knees up toward her and wrapped her arms around them. "She is the inua of the sea. Mother of the Deep, they also call her. If you offend her, she keeps all the sea creatures entrapped in her long hair. Only a powerful angakok can venture down into the depths to appease her and to cleanse her hair so that the animals can swim free."

"What has that got to do with me?" Malou asked. "Sea Mother, inua . . . none of that stuff belongs to my world. You're the one who brought it here!"

"You're right, but also wrong," Ivalo said. "I didn't want to bring it here with me, but it happened all the same. Sometimes, fates can become intertwined, and two people have an influence on each other's life paths for a time. Our lives have become entwined. But, as yet, I don't know why."

"You have to get it to stop!"

Ivalo shook her head slowly and rested her head on her knees. "I can't," she whispered. "I thought I could. Twice, I've already pulled you free of the Sea Mother's embrace. But she's too strong. At some point, she'll succeed."

"Succeed in what? What is it that she wants with me?"

Ivalo's voice was soft and slow as if what she was saying took some effort. "The Sea Mother will come again, and she will pull you down to the ocean floor. Then she will show you what she wants you to see."

"And what after that?"

"After that, she'll set you free. If you're lucky."

NOVEMBER 25TH
1:35 A.M.

Malou

The fire in the hearth had gone out, but the embers still gave the room a warm glow. She ought to lie down to sleep. Malou had pushed two of the big armchairs together. It wasn't perfect, but it was better than sleeping on the floor. She had told Louis she couldn't share a room with him anymore and that she needed a break. First, he had been shocked, and then angry. In the end, his eyes had welled up as Malou packed her things. But there was no other way.

Her old room had been taken by someone else, and for the last few days, she had to pretend she was behind on her assignments and needing to stay in the library in the evenings to study. Once the last students had gone, she locked up, with the keys she had for her duties with the Crows. It worked because it had to. But she needed to find a more permanent solution soon.

Malou closed her eyes and laid her head down on the armrest. She had almost nodded off when she was suddenly woken by someone trying to open the door. She opened her eyes. Who could want into the library at this time? The students didn't have keys. She jumped to her feet but hadn't managed to separate the armchairs forming her too-small bed before the door opened up.

"Ah, so this is where you're to be found?" Zlavko looked her up and down. "I saw your things in the cellar, but it didn't seem like you were sleeping down there."

"Where I sleep is none of your business."

"Of course it is. Students can't go lying around the school, sleeping like homeless people. Either you find a place to sleep, or you'll be allocated a room by me."

"Can I get a single room?"

"There are very few vacant ones left. Louis has one. It's actually one of the school's best rooms, I should think. But that wasn't good enough for you?"

"No, as you clearly know, I'm not living there anymore. So, there should be plenty of room for you there in the double bed. Was that what you came to ask about?"

He laughed. "Ah, ever the drama queen, Malou. You're acting like a child. A little jealous child, stamping her foot on the ground because somebody took her teddy bear. Can I give you some good advice?"

"No."

"You're getting it anyway. Grow up. I am not trying to steal Louis from you. He helps me now and then, and that's all. Just like he helps you. But apart from that, there is nothing between us." Zlavko looked at her, judging. "So, dry your eyes and pull yourself together. You're getting your baptism of fire tonight."

"What . . . What do you mean?"

"I'm sure you've discovered that Louis has been busy with things he hasn't been able to tell you about, right?"

"Just like I've been busy with things I can't tell him about," Malou answered.

"Precisely," Zlavko smiled. "It's like this: Louis and some of the others have been keeping an eye on a little group they call the traitors. Besides Benjamin, the group also includes two former teachers from Rosenholm. And your former friends."

Malou stared. *Is that what Louis had been doing when he wasn't in his bed at night and didn't stick to their plans? Has he been out chasing after Chamomile, Victoria, and Kirstine?*

"Since the break-in to the school, Louis and the others have intensified their efforts to find out what that little group is up to. And tonight, they finally found their hiding place. I think you can perhaps guess where it is if you think about it?"

Malou felt suddenly chilled.

"Jens would like you all to recover what Benjamin stole from the school. It's a wooden box."

"A wooden box?" Malou said. "According to Ivalo, it was only a bunch of old, dried herbs Benjamin ran off with. And what do you mean by *recover it*? In the middle of the night? That sounds more like an ambush."

"You could call it that, yes."

"You seriously want them to go and attack them?"

"I want *you all* to go and attack them. You're going, too. You now have such great control over your abilities that it has been decided that you should join them."

"You can't ask that of me," she whispered. "You can't!"

"I'm not asking. It's an order. And it comes from Jens himself. He asked if I thought you were ready. And I truly hope that you are, Malou. There's a lot depending on this."

"You promised!" she objected.

"I intend to keep my promise, but that requires you to keep yours. As you are perhaps aware, Jens has started to use bodyguards. That would be a suitable role for you."

238

She hid her face in her hands. "When?"

"Now. The others are already ready and have been briefed. It took me a little while to find you. But maybe that's a good thing. You won't have the chance to have second thoughts or run off."

She stood up. "Nobody will be killed, right?"

Zlavko regarded her seriously for a moment before answering. "I truly hope not. Get your stuff and get down to the main entrance. We're leaving in ten minutes."

...

Get away from there!
They're going to ambush the house!

Malou?!?!?

NOVEMBER 26ᵀᴴ
5:57 A.M.

Malou

They crossed the field in the darkness, with the jagged stubs of wheat, long since harvested, crunching underfoot. Malou's cheeks glowed under the mask despite the icy wind, which whipped at the bare trees. Louis walked beside her. Despite the black mask covering his face and the darkness, she could tell it was him just by the way he moved. And maybe she could also sense him, even with her eyes closed. Sense his pulse beside her own, which was racing. They hadn't said a word, but Malou was sure he knew where they were headed. Just as she did. A tall figure waved them to the side of the field to walk on the muddy grass there instead. Amalie had been given responsibility for this "little excursion," as Zlavko called it, when he dropped them off. Amalie had led them away from the road and let them walk over the fields instead so that no one would see them coming.

They continued through the damp grass of the field edge, and Malou's pant legs were soaked through and freezing by the time they reached the little farmhouse. Although it was a year since she had last been here, she recognized it straight away. This was where Beate and Chamomile lived.

For an instant, they gathered around Amalie, who was nothing but a masked, dark silhouette. "We're heading into the courtyard now. Be completely quiet. Once we've broken in, I'll give you the signal. If we're lucky, we can take them from their beds and force them to hand over the box."

Malou felt Amalie's eyes boring into her from behind the mask. "You know the house, right?"

Malou nodded.

"Good, then come with me," Amalie whispered.

As they stepped into the courtyard, Malou and Amalie continued toward the house while the other Crows held back behind them. The wind rustled the hedgerow windbreak nearby. "Are you ready?" Amalie whispered.

Malou nodded but didn't speak. A loud noise made them jump. The front door was open and was banging in the wind. A steely whistling noise made her turn to Amalie.

"What? You're armed?"

"Shh," Amalie scolded her, adding: "It's my athame. I always have it on me."

"But you're not thinking about using it? Or are you planning on stabbing them while they sleep?"

"Be quiet." Amalie pushed the door open carefully so they could step over the threshold and into the little kitchen. The Crows crept after them.

The dishes were still sitting in the drying rack on the counter. It was dark and quiet in the house. Amalie went over to the stove. "It's warm," she whispered. "Where are the bedrooms?"

"That way," Malou whispered, pointing.

They passed through the living room, where the sofa was made up for somebody, but the duvet was piled at one end. The room was empty. They carried on toward the bedrooms. There were only two, one for Chamomile and one for her mother. Malou stopped outside the door to Beate's room.

"Get ready!" Amalie whispered and took a step back. Then she kicked at the door so it slammed open with a bang, and the Crows scurried into the little room. Malou took her flashlight and shone it over the beds and into the corners of the room. There was nobody here. Amalie turned on the main light, and Malou was trying to still her racing heart when they heard yet another door being kicked open.

"Empty here!" Elias shouted from inside Chamomile's room.

"They're gone," Amalie said. "Where the hell can they be?" Malou pulled her mask aside and looked at the room. A mattress lay on the floor, and clothes were spread all over. They had been in a hurry to get away.

"Look for the box!" Amalie yelled. "They might have hidden it somewhere before they left."

The others came out of the bedroom, but Malou remained where she was while the farmhouse was filled with the sounds of cupboard doors being flung open, drawers being emptied, and furniture being shoved around. It felt like an assault. Can you commit assault on a house? On a home, maybe. She jumped as something in the kitchen fell to the floor and shattered.

Elias stuck his head into Beate's room. "Have you searched it all?"

"Yes. It's not here."

"But you haven't even looked in the dresser? And what about the bed?" He bent over Beate's white-painted double bed and looked under the mattress. After that, he started systematically emptying all the dresser drawers out onto the bed. Beate's underwear landed in a heap in the middle of the mattress. For some reason or other, it made Malou's stomach lurch.

"Search everywhere!" Amalie's voice yelled.

"I need to do something," Malou said, leaving the room. Opposite, the door to Chamomile's room lay open. Malou saw her yellow sundress lying at the top of a pile of clothes dumped on the floor. Amalie was going through the drawers in the sky-blue dresser. On the mirror over the dresser, there was a photograph of two girls smiling goofily as they took a selfie. Only half of Malou's face showed in it.

"Don't you think they'd have taken the box with them when they left the house?" Malou asked.

"Maybe, but we need to be completely sure we've looked through everything. Have you seen if there's any way up to the attic anywhere?"

Malou shook her head and looked out the window. Chamomile's room overlooked the fields. The sky had turned a light pink along the edge of the horizon. A sudden crash startled her.

"What the hell are they doing?"

It sounded like some of the Crows had started to throw furniture out the windows in the living room.

"THAT'S ENOUGH!"

A sharp voice came from outside in the courtyard. Amalie looked up. Her eyes were wide. "They're here!" she said, pulling her mask back in place and grabbing her knife, which she had put back in its sheath. "Come on!"

Amalie pushed her way through the chaos in the living room, Malou just behind her. They spilled out the door. In the middle of the courtyard, a small, round figure stood under the orange sky. It was Beate. Malou closed her eyes for an instant. She was suddenly so grateful her face was covered by the mask.

"That's enough now! Whatever it is you're looking for, you're

244

not going to find it here!" Beate's voice caused a flock of black-birds in a nearby tree to take to their wings. They swooped over the thatched roof, and their curved outlines against the red sunrise looked like a kid's drawing.

"Maybe the others took it with them?" Amalie shouted, nodding a signal to the Crows, who had now all come out of the house. Silently, they spread themselves around Beate. "Or are they hiding somewhere?" Amalie looked sharply over to the old stable buildings.

"There's nobody here but me," Beate said, ignoring the rest of the black figures. She focused purely on Amalie. "And now you need to leave." She took a step toward the door.

"We're not leaving until we have the box Benjamin stole! It belongs to the school. Where is it?"

Malou could hear the panic in Amalie's voice, and she was surprised to find that she felt sorry for her. Amalie had been given the responsibility of getting the box, and now she couldn't return empty handed.

"I don't know what you're talking about," Beate said. "Benjamin collected some of Lisa's herbs, which she needed for a mixture. Lisa foraged for them herself—they belonged to her!"

"She's lying!" said a voice, which Malou recognized as Elias.

Beate took another step toward Amalie, who was standing across the doorway. "This is my house, and I will not allow a little gang of troublemakers like you lot scare me away from it!"

"So, hand over the box!" Amalie yelled, still with her athame in her hand.

"There is no box," Beate said angrily, taking yet another step nearer. "Go back home to wherever you came from." She laid a hand on Amalie's arm, but the tall girl shrugged it off.

"Don't touch me!" she yelled and pushed Beate so that she stumbled back a step. In that split second, Malou heard only her own pulse beating in her body. Then Beate tumbled and fell backward.

"LEAVE HER ALONE!"

Footsteps thudded across the cobbled courtyard, and Malou barely had time to see what was happening before a huge figure threw itself in front of Beate, who sat where she'd fallen on the ground. It was Thorbjørn. He was perspiring and breathless as if he had been running, and his upper body was bare so the black dragon tattoos that covered his back were visible in the dawn glow. He didn't stop to think but grabbed Amalie's hand and twisted it so she dropped the knife. Keeping his tight grip on her arm, he forced her down to the ground, and she cried out in pain when, with a horrible loud crunch, her arm broke.

"Let her go!" The voice came from behind Thorbjørn.

"Louis!" Malou gasped. She saw him now, with the mask covering his face and his blond hair. And she saw the knife in his hand.

No . . . don't . . .

Malou felt as if the air had stilled around them. She no longer heard the wind whistling through the hedge.

Then he jumped, the knife raised above his head. Thorbjørn threw the sobbing Amalie from him and dodged, but not in time. Malou had seen it before—Louis seemed to be able to change direction in the air, and he jumped further than should be possible. Thorbjørn gasped as the knife plunged into his left shoulder.

"Argh!" Thorbjørn lunged after Louis with his right fist and hit his jaw, and Louis fell instantly to the ground without making a sound. Malou felt her throat tightening so that she couldn't breathe.

Blood was gushing down Thorbjørn's left arm; a fierce energy was released in their midst. Malou felt it like a crackling hum deep inside, while Thorbjørn himself seemed not to register his wound. In a movement resembling a bear lunging after an enemy, he swept the nearest Crow aside. "Beate!" he yelled.

A black-clad figure attacked him from behind but was bounced back by the rune spell Thorbjørn cast at him. Malou stepped back up along the wall of the house to get away from the shapeless mass of bodies and fists now fighting to get Thorbjørn away. Her eyes searched for Beate's red hair among the black-clad bodies. There she was.

Beate came crawling on all fours to avoid being hit by any of the punches or rune spells flying left, right, and center. Malou helped her sit in a safe spot by the house wall.

"Are you hurt?" Malou bent over her, but Chamomile's mom didn't acknowledge her. "Beate! Are you okay?"

Now she lifted her head. "Malou? Is that you?"

"Stay here!" Malou said and turned again toward the gang to find Louis among the legs and feet. *Where are you?* Malou bent down to see if she could see him anywhere. A boot came flying wildly through the air and hit her on the cheekbone, making her ears whistle, but finally, she found his long, slim figure lying lifeless on the ground. Malou grabbed Louis's ankles to pull him from the fight, and to her relief, she heard him groaning, but in that moment, Thorbjørn stumbled on a loose cobblestone. It was as if they were all holding their breath, and time slowed in a peculiar way as all eyes were frozen on the struggle in their midst. He didn't fall, but he lost his balance momentarily and had to put one knee down on the ground.

This is going to end badly.

Straight away, someone jumped onto Thorbjørn's back to force him to the ground. Their mask had slipped off, and Malou recognized Elias. His eyes were alight with a mixture of fear and brutal intent, and he plunged a short, broad-bladed knife into Thorbjørn's already injured shoulder so that blood came spurting out like a fountain. Thorbjørn screamed and reached up and over his shoulder. He got a hold of Elias' sweater and flung him to the ground, then landed a punch firmly in his face. Elias lay inert at his feet while Thorbjørn, with a strange, half-choked sob, straightened himself up to his full height. "Is this what you all wanted?" he screamed. "Is it?"

We need to get away. Malou let go of Louis and left him lying. She looked around her. Amalie was standing only a few feet away. Her arms hung strangely loose at her sides.

"We need to go now! Elias and Louis are seriously injured. Give the order. Thorbjørn won't come after us, I promise."

The black mask turned to her, but no sound came from it other than rapid, heaving breaths.

"Amalie!" Malou pulled her mask off and threw it to the ground. "It's over. We need to go home now."

Amalie stood as if frozen, and Malou gave up trying to get through to her. *Shit, shit, shit!*

"Thorbjørn!" she yelled, and took a few steps toward his broad back.

He turned slowly. The sun was rising over the roof edge. Blood ran down his shoulder and dripped from his elbow onto the unconscious Elias, who lay at his feet. Malou could sense Thorbjørn's deep pulse and smell the blood that was trickling out of his wound. She stepped right up to him. "This stops now. Let us take our injured with us, and we'll leave now."

248

He shook his head slowly. His deep-set eyes betrayed he was a person in great pain, but Malou had a feeling that had nothing to do with the bleeding wound on his torso.

"The injured stay here," he said quietly. "They're in no condition to travel such a distance. We'll look after them. Leave them and go.

"I can't do that," Malou said. "We're taking them with us. Step back!"

"You can't give me orders, Malou," he said. "That's—" His eyes widened as he felt it, and the words stuck in his throat.

Zlavko was right. It wasn't difficult for her. It was easy. Simple. It felt natural. Thorbjørn may well have been fighting it, but his blood wanted to obey. It longed to yield to her, and it swaddled his organs, muscle fibers, and lung tissue like a blanket around an infant. And she was the one controlling how tightly they were held. Thorbjørn sank to the ground with a stifled gasp.

"What's happening?" Beate screamed. "Malou, stop!"

"Is he dying?" a voice shouted from behind her.

"Help me!" Malou commanded, bending down to lift Elias. A wave of nausea rose in her when she looked at his face, but she forced herself to put her arm around him. Together with Albert, she began to walk him out of there.

"Amalie! Make sure everyone is with us!" she shouted over her shoulder, checking that someone was helping Louis up on his feet. He was staggering but was able to walk. "Come on!" she ordered, and they all set off, tramping toward the road, leaving Thorbjørn lying gasping in the courtyard, with Beate sobbing by his side.

NOVEMBER 27TH
9:05 P.M.

Malou

Malou knocked softly on the medical room door, but nobody answered. She knocked again, a little louder, then opened up and went in. It was quiet and dark. The mustard curtains were pulled across the tall windows, and Ingrid was standing at end of the room beside a tall, metal table, her back to the door.

"Ahem." Malou cleared her throat, but Ingrid seemed not to notice. "Ingrid?"

Malou went closer. She turned, slowly, and Malou noticed the dark circles under her eyes and how her hair seemed tousled and unkempt.

"I've come to see Louis. Zlavko said he woke up?"

Ingrid shook her head and looked at her sadly. "I shouldn't have stayed here. I should have left," she said.

"What do you mean?" Malou asked.

"But if I'm not here anymore, who is going to look after the students?"

"Ingrid, are you okay?" Malou asked.

"Are *you*?" she whispered.

"I'm fine. I'm here to see Louis," Malou said.

Ingrid smiled sadly. "By the window," she whispered, turning

250

back to the metal table, where she was sorting a selection of small bottles and glasses.

Malou went over to the bed. Louis was pale, but otherwise, there was only a slight discoloring on his cheek where Thorbjørn had hit him. He smiled when he saw her. Then the smile faded. "Are you injured? Did he hit you, too?"

Malou touched her cheek, where she knew a blue bruise had developed, and shook her head. "It's nothing. I got a boot to the face when I was trying to find you."

"You saved me." He smiled. "I heard about how you stopped Thorbjørn. The others didn't understand how you did it, but it worked, didn't it? Impero Spiritus?"

She nodded. He looked so happy, so proud. But she only felt completely cold inside.

"What are they saying? How bad is it?" she asked him.

"Just a little concussion," he said, taking her hand. Malou wanted to pull it back, but her hand lay in his, like a tiny, traitorous piece of proof of how hard it was for her to be away from him.

"I've got to take it easy and rest as much as I can. Ingrid says she'll know in a week or so if there's been any serious damage, but she doesn't expect any," he explained.

"And you're sure she's got the diagnosis right?" Malou asked. "She seems like she might be a bit . . . unwell."

"I think she's finding it hard to understand why things need to change. And why I'm willing to fight for that."

Malou looked at him. There was so much talk of fighting, but could it really be true that the enemies they should all be afraid of were Beate and Chamomile?

"When did you find out where they were?" she asked.

"That same afternoon. We've been looking for them for a while now. Jens knew Chamomile's mom had a house in that area, but he didn't know where. When we found the house, Jens wanted us to fetch the box straight away before they found somewhere else to stay."

"But you knew that I'd been there. You knew that I could take you to that house. Why did you never ask me where it was?"

Louis looked at her as if it were her who was sick and needed to be looked after. "Whatever's going on now, Malou, they were your friends. I wasn't going to ask you to betray them if I could avoid it. Right to the last minute, I was hoping that they wouldn't be there. For your sake."

"I wish you hadn't attacked Thorbjørn," she said. "Why did you stab him?"

"To defend myself, to defend us. And I'm glad I did it. He would have killed Amalie."

Malou shook her head. "If he had wanted to kill her, he could have done it."

He frowned. "We can't allow ourselves to be naive, Malou. You saw what Benjamin did to Iris. And you saw Elias. His face is completely smashed. He'll never look the same again."

"I'm only saying that Thorbjørn could have broken all of our necks if he had wanted to. He could have overpowered us so easily."

"The rest of us, maybe. But not you."

Finally, she pulled her hand away. She knew he was right.

"Malou, you are our secret weapon." He sat up in bed and stroked the hair from her face. "That is what Zlavko has been telling you all along. Unknown possibilities. If you just let him help you, then nothing can stop you."

"I don't want to be anybody's weapon. I fight for myself."

"But you're part of something bigger. This is our fight. Wherever there is change and progress, there will also be resistance, and we need to be prepared to fight for the Movement."

"Louis, you're talking as if we are on different sides. But Thorbjørn and Benjamin and the others are mages, too."

"Mages who refuse to acknowledge all types of magic as equally worthy. And who want to oppress blood mages like us. Mages who will attack their own. Now we know how far they are willing to go. And if people don't believe that, they just need to look at Elias's face, and then they'll see what a serious threat they are." Louis looked flushed, and his eyes were watery, as if he were feverish.

Malou shook her head. It was all so wrong.

"You're tired, you should rest, as Ingrid says."

Louis gave a little smile. "You're right. I *am* tired. I can't remember ever feeling this exhausted . . . Malou, will you stay until I've fallen asleep?"

She nodded and pulled the duvet up over him.

The school was quiet and dark as she left the ward and went up to her own room. After what happened with Thorbjørn, Malou had been given a single room. Jens had personally approved it. Single rooms were a privilege only the most trusted students enjoyed. She took it as a sign that both Jens and Zlavko were happy with her performance, but she found very little to be happy about.

She had done it because she had to. But she still couldn't stop seeing Thorbjørn's distended eyes and hearing Beate's scream. And now Ingrid's rambling comments muddled themselves in with the burning unease she felt inside. Had she also made a mistake, staying at school? Should she have left? She stopped at a window overlooking the little courtyard. *Stop yourself!* Doubt was the last thing she needed now.

Malou took a deep breath. She needed to pull herself together and think about what she had said to Iris. She needed to stick with it, even though it was hard and painful. Never give up.

She looked out. The moon was almost full, and the night was still. It might even be getting a little frosty. The best thing she could do for herself now was to sleep, but she wasn't sure sleep would come. The empty bed reminded her too much of what had happened between her and Louis and now of him lying there with a concussion. And when she finally gave in to sleep, she would only be haunted by dreams of the mythical woman trying to pull her to the depths of the sea. Sometimes it helped if she was physically exhausted, and then she'd manage to fall into a dreamless sleep. Malou stood for a moment, looking at the moon. Then she got her jacket and left Rosenholm by the main door.

It was cold and the air nipped her face, but if she just walked briskly, the cold didn't bother her. She went through the park but turned when she reached the forest's edge. She didn't want to go walking among the trees in the dark. Instead, she went back up toward the castle and into the kitchen garden, which had always been Lisa's domain before.

Malou thought about going to sit for a while in the warm greenhouse, where the more delicate plants were kept for the winter, but she became aware of a deep, grunting noise. It came a short distance from the small beds surrounded by box hedges. She carefully went nearer. A little away from the school's kitchen garden, a small fenced enclosure and a simple shed had been built. And in the enclosure, there was a pig. She breathed again. Okay, nothing to be scared of.

"Now then, let's see. I'm on my way."

Malou stepped quickly back from the path and watched the little figure toddling down from the school toward the fence. *Dagny.*

"I've got some tasty snacks with me—just wait."

Malou decided there was no reason to hide, so she stepped back onto the path. "Hello," she said.

"More like good night," she said. "Are you visiting the garden at this time?"

"Just getting a little fresh air before bed." Malou gave a sideways glance at the pail Dagny was carrying.

"Scraps," she said. "From the kitchen. The staff insist it should be thrown away, so you'd best not go telling anyone you saw me. It's completely crazy to throw out good food now that we have our piggy to plump up for the Yule celebration, wouldn't you say?"

"For sure," Malou answered tentatively, but Dagny's whole face lit with a sly smile as if she had now found a partner in crime.

The pig grunted to remind them it was still waiting for the contents of Dagny's pail, so she tipped the scraps over the fence, laughing and chatting.

"Good pig," she cooed as it polished off last night's fish lasagna. Malou wrinkled her nose. She didn't eat fish if she could avoid it.

"Did you know that in the olden days, they used to call November slaughter month?"

Malou shook her head and only half listened. "Winter was on its way, the weather turned cold, and people could then slaughter their animals without worrying about worms getting in the meat before it was dried or salted," Dagny eagerly explained. "But this pig has a little more time yet. Having trouble sleeping, are you, my friend?"

255

Malou looked at Dagny in surprise. "What? Yeah, I mean, sometimes. But everyone does."

"Oh yes, lots of us have monsters that come out when darkness falls and our heads hit the pillow," she said, cheerily, as if it was something to be pleased about. "With time, you get quite used to them. It can feel almost lonely if they leave you alone for a while. But as a rule, they do always come back." Dagny took the pail and went over toward the greenhouse, where there was an outdoor tap. Malou followed her.

"Monsters, you call them? What kind of monsters?" Malou asked.

Dagny bent over the hose and rolled up her sleeves to fill the pail. Her arms were thin and frail and her skin wrinkled and gray, but that was not what caught Malou's eye. From her wrists upward, she had obvious scars, which twisted around and up her arms and seemed to glow in the moonlight.

"The monsters vary from person to person. I have mine," she rolled her sleeves down again and blinked at Malou with her small, deep-set eyes, "and you have yours. Can I give you some advice, Malou?"

Malou raised her eyebrows a touch. Zlavko had asked her the same question, and she was partly bemused by her teachers' sudden desire to give her good advice. She was most surprised, though, by Dagny using her name. Malou had only been to one single class of hers. She nodded.

"Look your monster in the eyes. Find out what it wants from you. If you run from it, it will only get stronger."

To Ivalo,

I've decided I want to find out
what the Sea Mother wants with me.
Can you take me to her?
And back again would be
really great.

Regards,
Malou

NOVEMBER 28ᵀᴴ
11:09 P.M.

Malou

Ivalo tightened the leather cord, and Malou felt a touch of panic, making her heart rate quicken. *Get yourself out of here.* All her instincts were telling her this was a bad idea.

"Is it really necessary, all this? You weren't even properly tied yourself."

"I've done it many times before. I don't get second thoughts halfway, through," Ivalo said, straightening up. Her bare feet came into Malou's view. She was kneeling on Ivalo's floor, naked and with both hands tied behind her back.

"Is that why I'm tied? Because you're worried I'm going to back out?" Malou asked.

"It's a normal reaction to have. Your survival instinct will kick in. Normally, that's a good thing, but not for this. In this, your life is at the Sea Mother's mercy. The only way you can get to her is by surrendering yourself to your fate," Ivalo said, tying a new leather strap tightly around Malou's head. Then she took hold of the dark blue dress she was wearing and pulled it up over her head. She had nothing on underneath, and Malou averted her eyes to the candle on the floor before her. Animal skins hung from the ceiling all around them, so it felt more like they were in a tent than in Ivalo's room at Rosenholm. Ivalo knelt beside her. She slid her right arm under Malou's left and then twisted her hands into the noose she held behind her back. Now that they were linked, Malou could feel the warmth from Ivalo's bare arm where it rested on hers.

"Now, it's time," Ivalo whispered. "Call her."

Malou cleared her throat and concentrated on pronouncing the word as Ivalo had taught her, slowly, letter by letter. "Arnaqquassaaq."

It happened in a flash, and even though Malou was prepared for what was to come, she still gasped for air in a panic as the water enveloped her body. She found herself again in the dark, icy-cold, empty space, but this time she was not alone. Malou turned her head. Ivalo's skin glowed pale in the dark water. Her black hair floated around her face, and her eyes were open. She nodded to Malou. Ivalo knew where they should go, and Malou let herself be led. Downward.

Ivalo kicked through the water with her strong legs, and Malou lifted her head and looked up. Above them she could see the ice; it was a luminous sky blue. Perfect, untouched, with no holes or cracks. They wouldn't be able to break through it. They were trapped, but, strangely enough, she felt calm. There was a wonderful peace in giving in.

Malou felt an insistent tug on her arm, and she turned to look ahead. Downward. Into the endless dark beneath them. A school of fish slid silently past them. At one point, she sensed a huge shadow passing underneath them, perhaps a whale. The water pressed against her body as if it were trying to crush her flat, into nothing, and she started to hope it would succeed. Becoming nothing meant no pain. No mistakes. No betrayal . . .

Ivalo pulled at her arm, and Malou opened her eyes, not having realized she'd closed them. Ivalo was glaring at her angrily and pulled at her arm again, the one tied to her own arm. Malou blinked. She mustn't lose her focus. She was here for a reason. She nodded to Ivalo. Her pale face had almost completely disappeared in the black water, but Malou could still feel the warmth from Ivalo's body in the icy sea. They continued farther down. Malou's eyes felt so heavy that all she felt like doing was lying down to sleep, but Ivalo kept on, tirelessly kicking behind her and taking Malou deeper and deeper. She tugged at her arm again, and now Malou could see it. A cold, bluish light. Just one shade, a stripe of ice blue in the black.

Ivalo swam toward the light, and now they could also hear somebody singing. The Sea Mother. Arnaqquassaaq. They had to be near the ocean floor. The song got louder and louder and the blue light stronger and stronger. Malou could see the ocean floor beneath them. It was sky blue, like the sea ice. She could see Ivalo's face beside hers. She looked exhausted. Her long, toned legs hung limply from her like an octopus' tentacles, but they had no need to swim farther. The Sea Mother was pulling them to her, and they slid on through the water. Reddish seagrass enfolded them. It rippled around them, enveloping their bodies, twisting around their arms and legs and pulling them as if it had a will of its own. The light grew stronger, streaming out from someplace in the middle of the seaweed forest. As they drew nearer, they could see a column that rose from the sea floor like a yellowish stalagmite. The blue light seemed to be coming from that pillar, and the reddish seaweed grew on top of it. But it wasn't seaweed, Malou finally realized. It was hair, the Sea Mother's. She was enormous. A golden female form that was almost house height. She had her back to them. Her skin was covered in shells, faded with age. Her hair pulled them nearer and nearer to her. Only when they were close enough to almost touch her did she turn to them and reveal her face. Her eyes were the same blue as the sea ice. Malou opened her mouth in a silent scream. The Sea Mother had Chamomile's face.

"You came," she said, with Chamomile's voice, which Malou heard loudly and clearly. "You came." The Sea Mother reached out to her as if she wanted to pull her into her arms. Her fingers were short and stumpy and covered in seashells and molluscs.

Malou looked into her light blue eyes. "Chamomile?" She let herself be pulled closer.

Suddenly, she felt a violent tug on her arm, and the gurgling sound of an underwater scream reached her ears. Malou turned to see Ivalo, her eyes wide with fear, vigorously shaking her head. She pulled Malou back, away from the huge sea woman, and at once, Malou realized how empty her lungs were of air. She was gripped by the overwhelming urge to take a breath, but she knew that if she gave in to that urge, her lungs would simply fill with water and she would drown. The Sea Mother stretched her stubby hands out to grasp for them. Her expression was entreating, but Ivalo pulled at Malou and kicked with everything she had through the ice-cold water. At last, Malou understood why the Sea Mother must not get hold of them and began to kick her legs, but they were stiff and heavy, and a strange numbness was spreading through them.

At her side, Ivalo worked like crazy to get them free of Arnaqquassaaq's long red hair, and when she finally succeeded, the Sea Mother's plaintive scream filled the water all around them as they turned their faces to the surface, so endlessly far away.

Ivalo pulled her on, Malou's legs feeling like a dead weight, and her arms tied behind her back. Red dots started to dance before her *eyes, and she noticed Ivalo becoming quite limp by her side. The ice lay above them, and they didn't have too far to go, but Malou didn't know how they would break through it. She used her last drop of energy to kick and kick until she felt the rough ice scrape across her naked back. Malou bashed her back against the ice again and again. Ivalo's head flopped from side to side, her eyes closed. The water around them turned red. She remembered a school lesson from a long time ago. A drop of blood in a glass of water . . . Her blood was a part of the sea. The sea was a part of her. It would yield to her now.*

Suddenly, the sea ice broke, and a rush of water flung them high into the air.

262

NOVEMBER 29TH
5:10 A.M.

Malou

"Still sitting here, are you?" Ingrid sighed, tired at the sight of her. "Let me have a look at that."

Malou dropped the sheet she had wrapped around herself and let Ingrid see the bloody lacerations across her back.

"How's Ivalo doing?" Malou asked, giving a groan as Ingrid went about cleaning her wounds in a slightly rough-handed way.

"She's alive, but she needs rest. Whatever it was you two have gotten yourselves into, it has completely exhausted her." Ingrid found a bottle of liquid, which she dabbed onto a cloth and used to cleanse the gashes on Malou's back. "If I knew more, I'd be better able to help her."

Malou said nothing, just stared out the window. It was almost morning, but you couldn't tell. It was dark nearly all day long. The winter had only just begun, and she already felt worn out.

"Yeah, this certainly isn't pretty," Ingrid said, taking a step back to study her back. "But it will heal. You blood mages heal easily." She opened a drawer and took out a gauze dressing. "You need to recover your strength. Once I've put a dressing on, you should go down to the kitchen for some breakfast and then get your head down to sleep."

"Okay," Malou said. "Can I speak to Ivalo first?" She ignored the pain as Ingrid administered a tight dressing.

"A very short visit," Ingrid muttered, passing her a hospital gown and a laundered bathrobe from a closet. "And I mean short!"

Ivalo lay in the ward. The bedside light was on, but her eyes were closed.

"Ivalo?" Malou whispered.

"Just come in, I'm not sleeping."

Malou crept barefoot across the cold floor. She sat on a chair by the side of the bed. The same chair she had sat on a few days ago when it was Louis who lay here.

"What happened?" Malou whispered.

"I don't know," Ivalo whispered, looking at her gravely. "I've never seen the Sea Mother's face before. It's normally hidden by her hair, and she's also never tried to reach out for me like that."

"She had my friend's face," Malou said.

"What is her name?"

"Chamomile."

Ivalo's eyes were almost black in the darkness. "She must be the reason that the paths of our lives are connected. I think she is in danger."

"In danger? How?" Malou asked.

"The Sea Mother's magic is the ancient kind," Ivalo whispered. Her breathing was rough and labored. "As old as the hills and the ice and the sea. She doesn't concern herself with little ripples on the earth's surface. She can only be woken by a magic that is equally ancient and as powerful as she is herself."

"What magic?" Malou asked.

Ivalo closed her eyes again. "I don't know—" Her body started to tremble, and she gasped for air.

264

"You need to rest now," Malou said. She stayed sitting where she was and looked at Ivalo's face in the lamplight. Her chest rose and fell, and after a while her breath slowed, calmed, and deepened. Once she was sleeping, Malou switched off the light and left.

Her mind was racing with thoughts going in circles, and Ivalo's words had done nothing to settle them. Why was Chamomile in danger? And what kind of ancient magic had awakened the Sea Mother? She needed to talk to Zlavko. They had to warn Chamomile.

He wasn't sleeping. He didn't even look like someone who had been in bed, and he asked no questions as he let her inside. Malou sat on the low bed. She hadn't even stopped to get dressed properly but was still barefoot in the hospital gown and robe.

"What is it?" Zlavko asked.

She told him everything about the ritual, which had nearly gone all wrong. About the Sea Mother, who had Chamomile's face, and about Ivalo, who thought their life paths were intertwined.

"I wish that—" Zlavko broke off mid-sentence, and she could see that he wanted to yell at her. He rubbed his deformed hand and narrowed his eyes. "I really wish I could understand you, Malou. I thought I had made it clear to you how important this is. We are so close now, and then you go and fling yourself into something that could ruin everything. Why can't you just trust me?"

"You said if I trusted you and did what you said, then you'd make sure nothing happened to them!"

"And have I not kept that promise?"

"The Crows smashed up the house! If Beate hadn't stopped them, there would have been nothing left. And the Sea Mother had Chamomile's face . . . Ivalo says she's in danger. What does it mean?"

"Have you considered that it might mean the same thing I have been telling you from the beginning? That if you want to protect your friends, you need to do what I say?"

Malou closed her eyes. She pictured it. How she had been standing, on the last day of the summer holidays, packing her things into her big case, when Zlavko came into her room and closed the door behind him. He had spoken to her in a low and urgent voice. And he had asked for an answer immediately. Would she commit herself to protecting her friends? Whatever it took for her? Even if it meant trusting him? Even if it meant that, when the time came, she would be the one to disarm Jens? Stun him so that Zlavko would be able to kill him. She was the only one who was capable of it, Zlavko had said.

He sat down beside her. "You're ready, Malou. You have control of your abilities. You are almost strong enough to use Impero Spiritus on Jens. Think about everything we've worked toward and fought for. You can't ruin it now."

"But why can't I warn Chamomile?" Malou said. "If she is in danger, she needs to know about it!"

"Jens can sense betrayal better than anyone else I know. It's important he trusts you, and after the thing with Thorbjørn, he seriously sees you as someone he can have in his inner circle. I don't think it will be too long before he assigns you as a bodyguard. But if he finds out you are still in contact with Chamomile, everything will be lost. It's the only weak point in my plan: that you let something slip."

"Are you even worried about them at all?" Malou asked. "Or is it only to avenge Leah that you want to kill him?"

"Does it actually matter?" Zlavko fiddled with his damaged hand.

"I'd like to hear you say it."

"Leah jumped over the cliff herself. But it was Jens who killed her. She died already, back when he killed her sister. When I finally understood that, I swore to avenge her," he said. "That is my greatest wish, my only goal, my reason for doing it. That's your answer." Zlavko looked her in the eyes. "But I can't do it alone. I need you. Luckily, you also need me. If you want to keep your friends safe."

Zlavko stood up and opened the door to show her visit was over. "I will contact you soon so we can put the final details in place. Once Jens includes you in his team of bodyguards, you'll have the possibility to get fully close to him. Then, it can happen. I can trust that you won't destroy everything for us before then?"

"Yes," she whispered, getting to her feet.

Malou felt exhausted by the time she finally got to bed, but her thoughts continued to whirl around her head. The conversations with Ivalo and Zlavko merged with each other, and she went over them again and again. Something or other was wrong. It was like a bum note in a song. It nagged at her. Malou tried and tried to think of it, and at last, it became clear. *He was lying.* She had instinctively sensed how his pulse and heartbeat quickened when she asked him why the Sea Mother had Chamomile's face. *Have you considered that it might mean the same thing I have been telling you from the beginning? That if you want to protect your friends, you need to do what I say?* But that was a lie—or, in any case, it was not the whole truth.

She opened her eyes and looked into her dark room without actually seeing. Zlavko knew the real reason. He understood what it was Arnaqquassaaq wanted Malou to see. And if he wasn't telling her what it was. She would have to find out herself.

NOVEMBER 30TH
3:24 A.M.

Malou

Malou looked up from her book when a log she had just put on the fire crackled loudly as the fire took hold of it. She rubbed her eyes and pulled the band from her hair. She had a headache from staring at her books for so long. Nobody else was in the library at this time of night, and she had it all to herself. Malou got up to lock the door from the inside. Maybe it was the report she had just read that gave her a sudden urge to make sure she was really alone and that nobody could come into the Library without her knowing.

Ivalo's talk of ancient magic had given Malou the idea of looking back at the little booklet she once stole from the mysterious basement on Vester Voldgade, the library of the Society for Psychic Studies. The booklet contained a short roundup of all the forms of magic that were banned in the 1810 reform, and it was where she had first read about Impero Spiritus. Malou had read through the booklet, but many of the descriptions of banned magic were very specialized. But she had come across a footnote that referred to the Vikings' "blot" rituals, and unlike many of the other magic forms discussed in the booklet that you couldn't find information on in the school library, these Viking rituals were described in several of the history books there.

Malou turned reluctantly back to the book she had just been reading. In fact, it wasn't really a book but more of a report, or the records of an archaeological dig at Trelleborg, which happened fifteen years before. First, Malou had skimmed the countless records of post holes and pottery fragments that were found, but then she was grabbed by the description of a so-called *hørg*—a sacrificial altar—from around the year 980. The sacrificial site had been used in connection with blot, but the interesting thing, and what this excavation really was about, was that in the well beside the sacrificial site, people had uncovered the skeletons of five children between the ages of four and seven years old. The children had not died of natural causes; they were sacrificed to the gods. The children, whose parents were presumably enslaved, had been killed at the site, and afterward, their bodies were thrown into the well. Archaeologists believed the sacrifices reflected the story of Odin, who cast one of his eyes into Mimir's well in exchange for permission to drink the water and become all-knowing. If a single eye could make Odin so wise as to be all-knowing, what could five human children be worth?

Malou forced herself to read the section to the end, but the matter-of-fact tone of the report and the line drawings of the all-too-small skeletons left her quite uncomfortable. She knew it was generally accepted that the Vikings hadn't only sacrificed animals, but this was making it all a bit too real. Who killed little children and threw them into a well? She was just about to snap the report shut when her eye caught a comment that had been added in handwriting in the margin. *H Villumsen's paper on sacrificial sites, dark magic, and rituals.*

Malou studied the handwriting. It seemed somehow familiar, and she realized she had seen it last on the handwritten invitation she received from Jens a few weeks ago. Malou couldn't say when Jens had written these notes on the report, but now she knew that he had read it. She stood up and went to the dark corner where she had found the archaeology report. The paper, written by this Villumsen person, was on the bottom shelf but bound in dark brown leather, finely embossed in gold on the front, and had a much older look. Malou flicked through it and decided to take it with her to her room; then she glimpsed an illustration of a tree. It was a black line drawing of a large tree with a thick trunk and large crown. Black silhouettes hung from the tree's branches. They looked like people.

Malou read the text beside it. *Ritualistic human offerings have taken place since the Iron Age. A person was the most valuable offering to be made, and the reward given in return would be equally great. The bodies were hung in sacred trees or buried at the tree's roots. This custom continued into modern times.*

She studied the tree again. It was just a tree, like hundreds of others, but she couldn't escape the feeling it looked like one very particular tree. The old oak tree out in the forest. The tree that assigned new Rosenholm students their branch of magic. The tree that had taken Vitus' body into itself and, in exchange, had gifted Kirstine some potent powers. Malou read the sentence again. *A person was the most valuable offering to be made, and the reward given in return would be equally great.* Kirstine would never have wished for such powers. But there were others who would. *Jens.* Was that the real reason Zlavko was so intent on Malou learning to disarm him? Was this not only about Leah? Malou set the book at random on the shelf and pulled out her phone. She typed a few words in the search box. *Greenlandic myths.* A section on the Sea Mother was one of the first results.

Arnaqquassaaq is powerful and formidable, but she was once a young woman. Her father had found a husband for her, but she did not want to marry him. Her father was furious. He took her out in an open boat and sailed far out into the sea. There, he threw her to the waves. She tried to get back up into the boat, hanging tight to the gun whale, but her father chopped her fingers off. They say that the chopped-off fingers turned into the animals of the sea, while the young woman herself sank to the ocean floor and became Arnaqquassaaq, the Sea Mother.

Malou lowered her phone. She looked down at her hand, where her nails were bitten to the quick. She pictured the Sea Mother reaching out her hands to her. She hadn't had nails; her fingers were just short stumps. It was her own father who had cut them off. Her own father had taken her out to sea in a boat to kill her . . .

Malou felt like she was being hit by an icy wave that wanted to pull her down to the sea floor again. She saw those blue eyes before her. Suddenly, she knew who Chamomile had inherited her blue eyes from. Jens was Chamomile's dad. Jens had been Beate's boyfriend, just as he had been Trine's. And just like the Sea Mother's father, Jens was planning to sacrifice his own daughter. *The greater the sacrifice, the greater the reward.* No sacrifice could be greater than your own child. Malou struggled to breathe, feeling like the walls of the room were closing in on her. That was what she was supposed to see; that was what Zlavko hadn't told her. With shaking hands, she pulled her phone out once more. She had promised Zlavko she wouldn't contact Chamomile and had only broken her promise once before, but now she had to do it again. She didn't dare not. Malou typed a message.

> **We need to meet**

He will be remembered as the one who led the mages from the darkness out into the light. The future will be beautiful. The future will belong to the strong, the beautiful, and the intelligent. The future will belong to him. He is prepared to make the utmost sacrifice. His own flesh and blood. It feels as if that was what was meant to happen all along. That it is fate. And once it is done, he won't need to be afraid any longer.

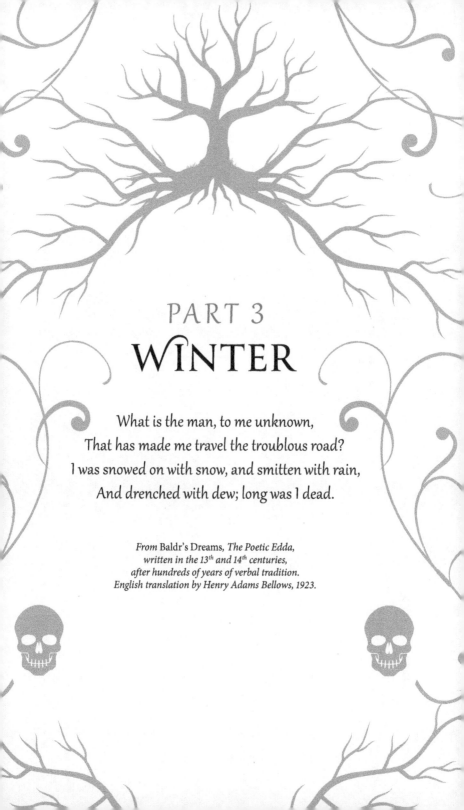

PART 3
WINTER

What is the man, to me unknown,
That has made me travel the troublous road?
I was snowed on with snow, and smitten with rain,
And drenched with dew; long was I dead.

From Baldr's Dreams, *The Poetic Edda,
written in the 13th and 14th centuries,
after hundreds of years of verbal tradition.
English translation by Henry Adams Bellows, 1923.*

DECEMBER 1ˢᵗ
6:07 A.M.

Chamomile

"It's really great you're happy to come along," Chamomile said, looking over at Molly, who was pulling on a sweater and then her knitted Nepalese pompom hat, which left her looking like some kind of elf with an undercut.

"Of course, I am. Can't wait to hear what we're actually doing, though."

"You'll see." Chamomile passed her the car keys. She didn't feel like telling Molly anything yet because she'd only start trying to dissuade her. She hadn't said anything to Victoria or Kirstine for that same reason.

They went out through the low front door, Chamomile closing it carefully behind them. There was a dim light on in her mother's bedroom, but otherwise, the little farmhouse was quiet and dark. After the Crows had smashed up their house and injured Thorbjørn, Beate had started sleeping with the light on. Besides that, she refused to behave any differently.

They went around the back of the old barn where Lisa's car was parked. Molly took the keys from her pocket, unlocked the car, and got behind the wheel.

"Right, so where are we going?" she asked, adjusting the mirror.

"To Rosenholm."

Molly turned to her, horrified. "To Rosenholm?"

"Not right up to it. There's a lay-by on the road there, a few miles before you reach the castle."

"And what are we doing at this lay-by?" Molly asked.

"Meeting someone."

Molly started the car, and they drove off in the darkness. Lisa's small red Citroën had become a communal car for them all, but Chamomile still felt unsure if this was okay, borrowing the car without asking.

"It's Malou you're meeting, right?" Molly briefly took her eyes off the road and turned to her.

"Yes. It's Malou," Chamomile said.

Molly nodded. "What makes you sure we can trust her? This could also be an ambush."

"I just know. I know her," Chamomile answered.

"And what about what happened with Thorbjørn?"

"There has to be an explanation. I mean, she was the one who warned us they were coming. I don't believe she consciously meant to harm him."

"But, aren't you worried you might be wrong about her? It happens that people turn out not to be what they seem . . ."

"You mean Vitus?" Chamomile said, sounding angry. She didn't mean to, but Molly had hit a raw nerve. Molly shrugged.

"Maybe." Her brown-green eyes fell on Chamomile, a hint of worry in them. When Chamomile first got to know Molly, she always used lots of eyeliner and mascara, but since coming back from India, she no longer used makeup.

"I didn't know Vitus. Not the way I know Malou. If I say we can trust her, then that's the truth."

"Okay," Molly said. "We can trust her then."

They drove farther in silence along the empty road. Chamomile looked out into the darkness. In someone's yard, back from the main road, a string of lights had been hoisted over the flagpole so it looked like a Christmas tree.

"I wasn't trying to put any blame on you when I said that about Vitus," Molly said.

"I know what people think. I should have realized that something wasn't right with him. But I didn't. Not before it was too late," Chamomile said.

"Nobody did. Not me either," Molly said. "We've got that much in common. Or did you maybe forget I also had a thing with Vitus at one point?"

Chamomile looked out the window, avoiding Molly's eyes. It was Molly who had first told her about Vitus, who she had obviously had a crush on since she'd started at school herself.

"I knew that," Chamomile said. "I don't know why I never asked about it."

"I could have said something, too," Molly said. "But maybe it's one of those things we don't like to talk about much. You know, having fallen for a murderous psycho type."

Chamomile smiled and sighed.

"No, you're right about that. You need to turn—the next right."

They continued through the countryside on narrow, paved roads and then dirt tracks that took them alongside fields and woodland.

"This is it," Chamomile said, showing Molly where she needed to turn. They rolled into the empty lay-by, and Molly cut the engine.

"What now?"

"Now we wait," Chamomile said.

The wind stirred the trees bordering the road. The temperature in the car began to fall as soon as the engine stopped, and there was no longer warm air being blown in on them.

"Somebody's coming," Molly said. Chamomile saw it, too. A light was bobbing and dancing its way toward them. A headlamp. Its beam darted across the car windshield for a second, then went out. They sat silently in the darkness, but then someone opened the back door. The car's inside light came on briefly.

A face became visible in that flash, its expression serious.

"Molly, do you mind leaving us alone?" Chamomile asked.

"Are you sure?" Molly whispered as if that would stop Malou from hearing her.

"Yeah, it's fine," Chamomile reassured her.

"Okay, but I'll stay close."

She let herself out, and the light went on again. Chamomile turned and looked at the girl sitting diagonally behind her. She was dressed in running gear, and her nose and ears were red with the cold. Chamomile felt the butterflies in her stomach.

"Why aren't you wearing a hat? It's bloody freezing . . ." Chamomile said.

Malou frowned, then smiled before the light went out again.

"Forget it. I don't know why I said that," Chamomile said in the dark.

"My hair," Malou said. "A hat totally messes with my hair."

Chamomile laughed. "It's so good to see you again." She wanted to give her a hug, but she still didn't know why she was there.

"I don't have much time," Malou whispered. "They think I'm out for a run. But you need to hear this."

"Okay," Chamomile said. "Tell me."

Chamomile listened as Malou told her all about Zlavko and the promise she had made him. Only a very slight tremble in her voice gave away how uncomfortable it was for her.

"But Zlavko . . . he's one of Jens's supporters. Why would he protect us from him?" Chamomile asked.

"Because Zlavko finally understood that Jens killed Trine, and he also blames him for Leah's death. Zlavko hates Jens. He is planning to kill him."

"But, Malou, why didn't you tell me any of this before? Why didn't you answer my messages?"

Malou took a deep breath in through her nose. "Zlavko says that Jens is uncannily good at sensing when people hide things from him. And it's important that I win his trust. Until the point that Jens is gone, Zlavko will protect you. That's what he promised, in any case, but I don't believe anymore that he can keep his promise."

"They smashed up our house. They attacked Thorbjørn." Chamomile couldn't make herself say it. *You smashed up our house. You attacked Thorbjørn.*

"I know," Malou whispered. "But that's not even the worst of it. "I don't know how to say this . . ."

"Come on," Chamomile said.

Malou nodded. "I think . . . I think that Jens is planning to perform an ancient, dark ritual, which will give him even stronger powers than those that Kirstine has. And, unlike Kirstine, Jens will not hesitate to use them."

"What ritual?"

"He will make a sacrifice of the most valuable thing he has. His own daughter."

Chamomile closed her eyes. The wind lifted and rustled the treetops, and the air was cold. *My own father is planning to kill me.*

"You know?" she whispered. "That I'm his daughter?"

"I worked it out . . . with a little help."

Chamomile was crying behind her closed eyes. The tears were warm against her cold cheeks.

"I didn't want anyone to know," she whispered. "I didn't want anyone to look at me and think of him."

"Do you remember what I said to you that time?" Malou asked. "It doesn't mean a damn thing who our parents are."

"You also said he must definitely be a total shit," Chamomile recalled.

"Yeah, well, at least I got that right."

Chamomile gave something between a sob and a laugh and dried her eyes. "Come back with me," she whispered.

"I can't do that," Malou said. "It all depends on me. But I needed to warn you. You need to get away. You should all go somewhere far from here until it's all over. The Crows are keeping watch of your house. None of you are safe there."

There was a buzzing in Malou's pocket, and she took her phone out and quickly typed an answer. "I need to get back," she said.

"Is it Louis?" Chamomile asked. Malou didn't answer.

"Are you together?"

"It's a bit complicated," she replied.

"Are you in love with him?"

The cell screen lit up Malou's face from below, and Chamomile saw, to her surprise, how her face crumpled and tears began to stream down her cheeks.

"I wish I wasn't," Malou whispered.

Chamomile nodded. It all hurt so much. "You don't get to choose who you fall in love with."

"Are you in love, too?" Malou asked.

280

"I have been for a good while. But the girl I fell for hasn't answered my messages in a long time. And she's in love with someone else, so . . ."

"Chamomile . . ."

Malou didn't say any more. Neither of them did. It was freezing in the car.

"You're my best friend," Malou finally said. "Maybe my only real friend when it comes down to it. I'd do anything for you. I do love you. But not in that way . . ."

"I know that. Maybe I just need to hear you say it," Chamomile said, looking out into the darkness surrounding them. "It's not looking so great for me, is it?"

The phone buzzed again. "I'll sort it out," Malou said, putting the phone in her pocket and zipping it shut.

"Malou, you can't do all this on your own," Chamomile protested.

"Yes, I can. That's what I want to tell you," Malou said.

"*I* am the solution. I'm the one who can overpower Jens. Impero Spiritus. Zlavko thinks I'm strong enough now to control him." She opened the door and swung her foot out onto the road. "Promise me you'll be careful. I'll write to you when it's all over."

Then she was gone, and the door slammed behind her. Only then did Chamomile understand what it was Malou had told her. She closed her eyes while the realization washed over her. That was how Malou had overpowered Thorbjørn. They should have worked that out. All that pain and to no avail. Malou's plan was not going to work. And Chamomile would need to tell her that.

Don't do anything until we've spoken!!

DECEMBER 10TH
6:17 P.M.

Kirstine

Kirstine walked between the tracks. She put her feet on the broad rails so she wouldn't tread on the loose, jaggy stones lying between them. They didn't quite fit with her strides. If she stepped on each rail, her steps became too short; if she skipped every second one, it made her take an extra-long stride. The winter sun was already setting behind the large silos of the abandoned factory behind her. She hopped up onto the platform. That, too, was abandoned. It was a long time since any train had run here, and the station building was a lonesome leftover of the decommissioned railway line. She looked inside. It looked as if someone was using the place to store a whole load of junk. Several of the window panes were shattered, and the abandoned station got her thinking of her visit to Thy with Thorbjørn and of Sigsten's ramshackle manor house. She hadn't particularly liked the man, but neither did she much like remembering how his life had ended.

She carried on down the run-down platform. An old train carriage still stood on the rails, as it must have done since the station was abandoned. Somebody had painted it over with graffiti and likely also tried to set it on fire because one side was blackened and singed.

Kirstine left the tracks and skirted the empty factory grounds, passing a car park behind a supermarket and down a path toward the spired tower, which was still just visible in the darkness quickly falling over the town. This place reminded her of where she herself had grown up. A little town where people kept to themselves and didn't ask too many questions. What went on behind closed doors was nobody else's business. Many of the houses stood empty, and large signs in the shop windows indicated properties that were up for lease. They had first looked at the back rooms of one of the empty shops, but it hadn't had enough space. Instead, they'd decided to move into a bigger building, which also lay empty and abandoned. An old church.

A tall, slim figure stood outside the porch, and she knew he was waiting for her.

"So, here you are," Jakob said, smiling at her. "And there you are," she answered, hiding a smile.

"I just wanted to get some fresh air," he said.

"I can look after myself, you know," she said.

"Believe me, I know that." He gave a gentle laugh. "But who's going to look after me while you're gone?"

She shook her head at him. "I hope we won't be living here for long," she said, taking in the strange building, once a meeting place for a small minority who had fallen out with the priest and built their own church.

"I think it's a good place to hide away," Jakob said. "There's enough room for everyone to be here, and the place is pretty deserted. And who would think to look for a little group of mages in a church?"

She watched him as he tipped his head back to look at the night's first stars. She wanted to run her fingers through his hair.

This wasn't any easier now that they had to live together and be in close proximity every single day.

"Is there any news from the Council of Mages?" Kirstine asked.

Jakob scowled. "They've decided to treat it as straightforward breaking and entering," he said. "As far as I understand it, they called Amalie to a meeting. She was obviously the one responsible for the attack."

"Jens was responsible!" Kirstine objected.

"I know that," Jakob said, "but Amalie is clearly willing to take the blame. She already confessed. Not that I imagine there will be any consequences."

"Benjamin's father said it to Victoria and Benjamin quite directly. We can't count on the Council of Mages," Kirstine sighed.

"Not in its current form, in any case," he said.

They stood awhile, looking at the stars. Kirstine's toes were freezing in her boots. "It will be strange seeing her again. Are you sure Thorbjørn is okay with it?"

"So he says," Jakob said. "Come on, let's go in." He opened the heavy door, and they entered the porch. As always, they made sure the outer door was properly closed and that they had given the agreed knock before opening the door into the church itself.

The church interior was high-ceilinged and painted white. It was not a traditional medieval church—the kind Kirstine had been in as a child—this church had been built just over 100 years ago. Besides the little tower, only the pulpit, chandeliers, and a plaque commemorating the church's founders were any indication that hundreds of church services had been held here. The others were sitting in a cluster around a lit gas stove, where a pot of soup was bubbling away.

"Can you go get Thorbjørn?" asked Beate, who, more than ever, looked quite witch-like stirring the soup.

"I'll do it," Jakob said. Shortly after, he came back, followed by Thorbjørn, who was still wearing a sling to protect his injured shoulder.

They ate in silence, nobody seeming to have much of an appetite. "I can't get my head around it, us doing this," Benjamin said, pushing his half-full bowl away.

"We talked it over," Lisa said. "And we need someone who can get close to Jens."

Benjamin sighed with frustration and crossed his arms, mumbling something Kirstine couldn't make out.

"Her bus arrives in ten minutes. I'll go down and get her," Chamomile said.

"Not on your own, Chamomile," Beate said.

"We'll go with her," Victoria said. "Kirstine and me."

They took the back path through the empty factory and didn't stand out by the road; rather, they waited behind an overgrown hedge where they could keep an eye out for the bus.

"Here it comes," Chamomile whispered.

The bus stopped at the bus stop, and a young blonde girl got off. She looked around her before crossing the road.

"Malou, over here!" Chamomile whispered.

Kirstine looked at her. Malou was wearing a long, elegant wool coat with a belt, black trousers, and leather boots, and her blond hair was pulled into a tight knot on top of her head.

She greeted them. Not unfriendly, but hardly heartfelt—more like how a teacher or bank assistant would greet you if you saw them at the supermarket. Professional was the closest word Kirstine came to, and she didn't really know if this black-clad, young woman with the reserved air was still her friend. Malou seemed so distant.

"Let's get out of sight," Victoria said, and they hurried into the deserted factory grounds.

"I wish you'd gone farther away," Malou said to Chamomile. "Haven't you told them what I said to you? It's best that you disappear completely until it's over and we've beaten Jens."

"Malou, there's something we need to tell you," Chamomile said, coming to a stop. She looked back and forth between them all. "Your plan . . ." she began. ". . . Zlavko's plan, it's not going to work."

"I did it to Thorbjørn," Malou said. "And I only need to disarm him long enough for Zlavko to kill him."

"Malou, listen to me now," Chamomile said. "Do you remember how you borrowed the victory stone so Leah couldn't use *Impero Spiritus* on you?"

"What do you mean?"

"Jens has stolen my stone. He has it now. You can't take control of him. The stone will protect him."

"But . . . what?" Malou's certainty crumbled right before their eyes and was replaced with disbelief.

"It's true," Victoria added.

Malou stood frozen, lit only by the streetlamp's yellowish glare. Kirstine had imagined that she would kick off and start shouting and scolding them, but she said nothing. They all waited for her to react, but she just stood and stared vacantly in front of her. "Malou?" Chamomile whispered.

"It's all been for nothing," she whispered.

"Not necessarily," Victoria said. "Jens trusts you because you stayed at school. Even if you can't overpower him, that gives us a big advantage. We also have a plan. But we need your help to carry it out."

Kirstine held her breath. The truth was, if Malou didn't help them, they'd have no plan.

"Come on," Chamomile said, taking her hand. "You need to at least hear what we have to tell you."

At last, Malou nodded slowly, and they continued toward the abandoned church.

DECEMBER 10ᵀᴴ
7:10 P.M.

Chamomile

Chamomile felt her heart racing as she opened the door and stepped into the church. She could barely imagine how Malou must be feeling right now. She looked at her pale face. The conviction she had shown as she got off the bus was all gone. Most of all, she was like someone standing on the edge of a precipice she would soon have to jump off.

"You'll be fine," Chamomile whispered.

Malou looked at her but didn't speak or even nod. The others were sitting around the gas stove when they came in. Benjamin stood up and stared Malou down as she crossed the floor. "Thanks for seeing me," she said flatly. "I'm sorry about what we did with your house, Beate. And what I did to you, Thorbjørn. I had to... or I thought I had to."

"Give us one reason to trust in you." It was Benjamin who spoke. He was still on his feet.

"Malou has risked her life for us. For me," Chamomile said.

"Has she? We only know that coming from her."

"Chamomile is in danger. I did it to protect her," Malou said quietly. It sounded as if she had given up, and it made Chamomile's heart ache.

Benjamin looked at her skeptically. "But now the dangerous plan you were going to risk your life with seems to have been dropped, isn't that right?"

"Benjamin!" Victoria said.

"Sorry, Malou, but I don't think your explanation sounds entirely trustworthy," he said. "If Jens wants to perform a ritual that will make him unbeatable, why doesn't he choose any other random victim? Why should it be Chamomile?"

Malou turned away from Benjamin and found Chamomile's eyes. Chamomile took a deep breath. Then she looked at her mother. Beate nodded. *There's no other way but to tell the truth.*

"Jens wants to kill me," Chamomile said, "because I'm his daughter. He wants to sacrifice his own flesh and blood."

The church fell completely silent.

"Is that true?" Thorbjørn whispered, but it was her mother he was looking at.

"Yes," Beate said. "Jens is Chamomile's father."

"Oh, Chamomile," Victoria said.

"Well done!" Molly hissed at Benjamin.

Benjamin sat down. "Sorry," he muttered.

"I hoped I wouldn't have to tell anyone about it. That my father is . . ." Chamomile's voice petered out, a lump in her throat and on the verge of tears.

"Chamomile was frightened that you would see her differently if you knew about it," Beate said.

Nobody spoke. Chamomile looked down at her feet. Then the sound of a chair being pushed back echoed around the high room.

It was Kirstine who had gotten up. They all looked at the tall girl with her serious expression.

"My parents don't want to see me," she said. "They think I'm possessed by the devil." She gave Chamomile a nod before sitting down again. Chamomile felt the tears pricking at her eyes.

There was the sound of another chair being pushed back. "My parents care more about their work than their children," Molly said.

"My parents belong to dark magic and are generally total assholes," Benjamin said quietly.

"My father left us when I was three years old," Thorbjørn said.

"My parents wear matching anoraks," Jakob said.

Chamomile smiled, with tears trickling down her cheeks.

"That's what I've been saying," Malou said quietly. "It doesn't matter one damn bit."

"Thanks," Chamomile whispered, sitting down beside her mother. Beate put her arm around her and pulled her close. "Now we know what Jens is planning, it's just even more important that we put a stop to him," Thorbjørn said.

"Sadly, Malou can't take control of him when he has the victory stone, but, Malou, we'd like to show you what we've found out," Victoria said, getting up and going over to the end wall. There, where the altar should have been, a huge corkboard hung, covered in scraps of paper, photos, handwritten notes, and newspaper clippings. Running between them, thick bands or thinly drawn lines connected various things in a mass of crisscrosses, so it looked more like a chaotic spider web than something that could give them any kind of overview. In the middle of a messy set of notes was the word *Nightshade.*

"Does that mean anything to you?" Victoria asked. "Have you ever heard Jens talk about nightshade?"

"No," Malou answered.

"I'm sure it's not something he goes around talking about, but we believe that nightshade is key to overpowering Jens." Victoria told Malou about the vision at the Maiden's Well, Trine, and how it led them on the trail of nightshade.

"But, what is it?" Malou asked.

"Nightshade is a family of plants," Lisa explained. "There are lots of different plants and flowers in that family. Potatoes and tomatoes, for example. But many of them are climbing plants that produce poisonous berries." She stood up and went over to the board and pointed to a drawing of a plant. "This one, for example. Black nightshade, it's called. Or this one." She pointed to another, which showed a pretty, creeping plant with small flowers. "Bittersweet nightshade. But this plant quickly got our attention." Lisa let her finger hover over a different drawing.

Malou stepped closer to study the illustration of a plant with green leaves and purple flowers. "But what has a climbing plant got to do with Jens?" she asked.

"We couldn't understand that at first, either, but the more we read about it, the more curious it became," Victoria said. "In Latin, it's called *Atropa bella-donna*. *Atropa* is from the Greek goddess of fate and destiny, Atropos, who cut the life threads of mortals. *Bella donna* means 'beautiful woman.' In ancient Rome, women used it as a beauty product, as it could be used to dilate pupils so that they got large, beautiful eyes."

"But is it poisonous?" Malou asked.

"Very poisonous," Chamomile said. "Not the cleverest thing to use just to make yourself look good. It's actually one of the most lethal plants in Denmark."

"And it's also called deadly nightshade," Victoria added. "It has lots of different names, like devil's breath, dwale, and death cherries."

"Before it was used as a treatment for cramps, as it paralyzes the nervous system," Lisa told them. "As its formidable names also suggest, it has also been used as a strong poison, and it can be used to lift certain curses and disarm certain magical spells. The Vikings used it as well. They called it banewort."

"Banewort . . ." Malou whispered. "The box! That was the box Benjamin broke in to steal, wasn't it? The one with banewort?"

"I got the banewort, yeah, but it was in an unlocked drawer," Benjamin said. "I just shoved the stuff in my pocket. There was no box."

"Of course." Malou snorted and shook her head.

"What do you mean?" Chamomile asked.

"Jens sent the Crows out to your house, demanding that they recover a box you had supposedly stolen from the school," Malou explained. "And when you weren't there, they ransacked the house looking for it. But there was never any box."

"Why would he do that?" Molly asked.

"To create conflict," Thorbjørn said quietly. "Nothing unites people like a common enemy. Jens has fabricated the story of a threat that doesn't exist. He is teaching the students that we want to attack and harm them."

"That's true," Malou added. "Jens used Benjamin's break-in as proof that you're all out to get everyone who supports him. He is making them believe you want to ban spirit magic and blood magic, and he's training the students to fight for his cause. They're calling it the Movement."

"Idiots," Benjamin sneered. "I don't understand how they don't see he's just manipulating them?"

"I can understand it," Beate said, looking directly at Benjamin. "Don't judge them. It's only human to believe that your teacher wants the best for you and is telling you the truth. It is Jens who is the idiot for exploiting that."

Benjamin lowered his gaze.

Chamomile squeezed her mother's hand.

"What's the connection between banewort and Jens?" Malou asked.

"It all has to do with the victory stone," Victoria said. "That is what's protecting him." She pointed to a little black-and-white picture they had found in Thorbjørn's old yearbook from his time at Rosenholm, which was now stuck up in the middle of all the other clippings on the pin board.

"Who is that?" Malou asked.

"That's Sigsten Juul," Kirstine said. "The previous Blood Magic teacher at Rosenholm. I visited him, together with Thorbjørn. He wanted to tell us something important about how the victory stone's powers could be reduced. But he didn't manage to tell us before Jens got hold of him first. He left this note."

*He is afraid
of the shades!
SIGSTEN
Little Kirsten?*

"*He is afraid of the shades,*" Malou read. "I don't understand that. We think it means shades, as in Nightshade. Banewort," Chamomile said.

"Banewort used to lift curses. We think Sigsten was trying to tell us that banewort can also neutralize the victory stone's power if the owner of the stone ingests the berries."

Malou looked at her. For the first time that evening, Chamomile could see her eyes brighten a little. "And you need someone who can smuggle it in to him?"

"It's a risky undertaking," Thorbjørn said. "I wish I could take it on myself, but it needs to be someone Jens trusts and who can get close to him. And that is certainly not a description that fits me."

They all looked at the Malou. Chamomile could feel that her mother's whole body was tense. But she, herself, had no doubt whatsoever what the answer would be.

"I'll do it," Malou said. "And I already know when I'll get the chance."

DECEMBER 15TH
1:30 A.M.

Victoria

It was freezing cold in the old church, and Victoria had put her legs down into her sleeping bag in a vain attempt to get warm. She ought to get to sleep now, but it was hard to find any peace. A church wasn't exactly the most optimal place for a spirit mage to spend the night. Victoria shone her pocket flashlight onto the cards she sat with in her hand and tried to ignore the white shape that kept pacing back and forward in agitation. It was an elderly woman who was wringing her hands in front of her. Her lips were moving, but Victoria only caught fragments of what she was saying.

She'll be home soon. She'll be home sometime soon...

The woman must have been a church regular; she had been here every single night. She never tried to contact Victoria, which gave her all the more reason to think that the woman had not come there because of her. Other night visitors to the church were much more demanding.

She spread the cards out before her. The same ones her grandmother had pulled out of the pack when she told their fortunes. *The first will go into the darkness.* What darkness? Could it be the ritual Jens was planning? That was a kind of darkness. Or was it a warning that Malou's attempt to sneak banewort to Jens was going to go wrong?

Victoria looked up when she heard the door softly close. Benjamin was talking with Lisa down below. She would have been attending to Beate, who had a really bad cold. A moment later, Benjamin came up the stairs to where Victoria was, the internal gallery that ran around the church walls about three feet above floor level. The staircase was old and worn and normally creaked loudly, but not when Benjamin stepped on it. His footsteps were light, like an animal stalking its prey.

"Not sleeping?" he asked when he saw the light of the flashlight.

"Is it calm outside?" she asked without answering his question.

"Yeah. There's not even a cat loose in this town. For now, it's the perfect hiding place. What are you doing?" he asked. "Are those tarot cards?" He sat down beside her and picked up the lovers. "I've always thought it was all a bit lame."

"They're my grandmother's," Victoria said, taking the card from his hand.

"What does this mean?" Benjamin asked, picking up a new card. "The Hanged Man. That sounds unpleasant."

"Yeah, I'd say so, too, but my grandma says it stands for sacrifice and letting go."

"But can it also not be unpleasant?" he asked. "Maybe." Victoria stacked the cards together and put them away. "Can I show you something else? I'd like to hear your opinion." She handed him a book, a worn paperback she had bought through a used bookstore online.

Benjamin studied the cover, which showed a black skull on a yellow background. The title was written in large, angular red type: *Historical Crime Mysteries*.

296

"Murder, Mystery, and Manslaughter," he read the subtitle. "Are murder and manslaughter not the same? Why are you reading this garbage?"

"I think it's exciting," Victoria said. "The case I'm reading about now is from 1885, and it happened near Rosenholm. That's why I bought the book. If the ritual continued right up until modern times, like it said in the old book Malou found in the library, then there must be some traces of it. Someone must have missed the people who disappeared."

"But did girls even go to the school back then?" Benjamin said, unzipping his jacket and peeling it off. "Wasn't Rosenholm a boys' school?"

"Yeah, it was a boys' school, but lots of young girls also lived there. They just weren't students." She looked at him, raising an eyebrow.

"The maids?" he asked.

"Exactly. And kitchen staff and so on," Victoria continued. "The unsolved crime case I'm reading now is called *The Maid Who Vanished*."

"It's really great with titles, that book," Benjamin said.

"Do you want to hear it?"

He shrugged and leaned back. The little bench they were sitting on stood against the wall near one of the church's arched windows. It had been a long time since they had sat so closely.

"*The Maid Who Vanished*," Victoria read. "*Thursday April thirtieth, 1885 was a special day for many young people all over the country. May first was changeover day for service staff, and it might be the last day for them at their workplace, when they had to say goodbye to those they had worked beside for the last year or six months. So the occasion was to be celebrated, and the last night of April was also Walpurgis Night, which was commemorated in many places with bonfires and dancing. A party was also held at Østergaard, Zealand. But some weeks later, landowner Heinrich August Lorenzen, overseer of Østergaard, received a message that a maid who was supposed to change posts and move to another estate had never shown up. The maid's name was Astrid Ebbesen. The people on the estate had last seen her at the Walpurgis Night celebration, but since then, she had vanished. The strange thing was that she hadn't taken her few possessions with her. The investigation that followed revealed nothing, and Astrid was never found. A search of nearby wetlands, however, did uncover the clothes she was last seen wearing."*

Benjamin narrowed his eyes. "And you think this has got do with Rosenholm because . . ."

"Because the estate was in that area."

"Have you . . . talked with her?"

"With her spirit? The maid? No, I haven't tried, and also, there's far too much traffic here. Even Trine is keeping far away."

"You mean . . ." Benjamin frowned and looked mistrustfully around them, which made Victoria smile. The old woman wringing her hands was passing them just at that moment without taking any notice of either her or Benjamin.

"Don't worry, there's nobody that wants anything to do with *you*," she said. "But what do you make of it, what I read aloud?"

"Really? Okay," he said, letting out his breath, "*if* we were to say the young woman was actually murdered and didn't just die in an accident, then it could hardly have been Jens murdering her back in 1800 and whatever. Or not?"

"No, of course it wasn't Jens."

"Is that not a weird thing to spend your time on?" he asked. "We should really concentrate on the crimes where the perpetrator is still alive."

"Maybe," Victoria said, annoyed with herself for how put out she suddenly sounded. "I should probably see if I can get some sleep." The sleeping bag slipped to the floor as she stood up, and she bent over to pick it up. At that moment, she heard a small, hollow sound. The kind of sound that happens when a carved wooden figurine hits the cold tiles of a church floor.

"Whoa, you've dropped—" He bent over to pick up the little wolf. The one he had whittled for her for last year's birthday.

"I didn't know you still kept that with you," he said, turning it over as if examining it.

"You said it would look out for me when you couldn't. Or *didn't want to*, I should maybe say . . ." She could have kicked herself. Why had she said that? Couldn't she just let things lie?

"Victoria, I will always happily look out for you. Just because we can't be together doesn't mean I don't care about you."

Something inside her crumbled, and she gave up playing it cool. "And why is it that we can't be together?"

He avoided her eyes. Instead, he took her hand and laid the wolf in her palm, closing her fingers around it. "Because you still hope you can be reunited with your parents and that we can all just be friends."

"Is that so terrible?"

He finally lifted his face and looked at her. "I don't see how you can keep your relationship with them and at the same time fight against Jens and everything he stands for. It's either-or."

"You're wrong. My parents will realize that we're right. They'll turn against Jens sooner or later." She put the wolf into her pocket and turned her face away so he couldn't see the tears in her eyes.

"You live in a fantasy world, Victoria. I know your family. I know what kind of people they are. If you don't distance yourself from them, it can't come to anything between us," he said. "I'm sorry if you can't see that, but that's how it has to be."

Victoria fell back onto the little bench and let her tears flow once Benjamin had crept back down the steps. She cupped the wolf in her hands. Why did she keep on getting herself hurt like that? She should have been more clever; she should know by now how to handle Benjamin. With a distant politeness and nothing else. And instead, she made herself vulnerable again and again, even though he kept on making it clear to her that he couldn't wasn't going to be there for her. She had to stop it. For her own sake.

She dried her eyes. Suddenly, she became aware of a pale light coming in through the window. She looked up. Lisa stood, a dark silhouette against the tall, narrow window, looking out at the moon.

"It hasn't been easy for Benjamin," Lisa said quietly. "What . . . Did you hear us?"

"No. I saw Benjamin come down, and when I got up here, you were crying. And although students think that us teachers know nothing at all about what goes on, I do know that you were a couple last year." She looked at her briefly. "And that you're not anymore."

"So, I guess you also know it wasn't my decision to split up," Victoria said.

"I guessed that part," Lisa said gently. "It wasn't so difficult. When you're young, you think nobody has ever felt the same or gone through the same things you're going through. But it seems just like yesterday that I was young myself. And in love. And unhappy. Sometimes, it feels like long ago. On a night like this, it feels like no time at all.

"Everything is so simple for Benjamin," Victoria said. "Either you are on the side of good or outright evil and not worth knowing."

"Perhaps it's the other way around?" Lisa said, sitting down beside her on the bench. "Perhaps it's actually incredibly complicated for Benjamin. And that's why he has had to make such strict life rules for himself so that he has something to help him navigate in the dark and the mess. But life is sometimes dark, and it is almost always messy."

"But, if it's like that, like you say . . . If Benjamin's life is also dark and messy, why does he judge me so harshly, just for still hoping that my parents will come to understand?"

"Maybe it's because the price he has paid to be able to look himself in the eye has been very high. And he has struggled really hard. The first year at Rosenholm was no picnic for Benjamin."

Victoria had actually never thought about how Lisa must have been Benjamin's closest teacher and guide at Rosenholm, given he was Growth. And since that was the time he cut contact with his family, maybe their bond had been even stronger.

"I wish I knew a bit more about what he went through," Victoria said, looking at Lisa with curiosity.

"I'm sorry, my friend," she said, patting Victoria's hand.

"It's not my job to tell you about that. That's up to Benjamin, when he's ready to share that with you one day."

"I'm afraid that day might never come," Victoria said, sighing.

"Let's just see," Lisa said. "Life is long and full of surprises." There was a smile behind her dark eyes.

Victoria gave a start at the sound of a loud cough filling the church. "Beate," Lisa whispered, frowning. "She's not doing so well living in such a cold, damp building."

"Has she not gotten better since you got the herbs from school?"

"It helped, but not as much as I had hoped."

Victoria could sense Lisa's concern, and it blended with her own so that it almost became one. At that moment, she could have sworn Lisa's thoughts also turned to the victory stone, which Beate had passed on to her daughter and Jens had stolen. What did the stone have to do with Beate's illness? Victoria wondered if she should try to read her thoughts, but Lisa stood up.

"I'll go down and check on her," she said. "You should get some sleep."

Victoria nodded. "I'll lie down in a moment."

But she didn't. The truth was, she didn't dare. Her dreams no longer felt like her own. Instead, Victoria stayed sitting by the window, looking out at the stars as they slowly faded until the sounds of the living in the old church began to supplant the sounds of the dead.

302

DECEMBER 21ˢᵀ
6:00 P.M.

Malou

Malou turned her face down to the ground to avoid the driving rain that went on and on, pouring down on the park. She did one last circuit of the huge tent to check all the ropes holding the canvas in place were pulled tight. Jens had entrusted the Crows with the job of setting up the Yule celebration this year. Normally, it was Thorbjørn who led the festivities, but this year would be different.

Malou entered the tent. Jens had allowed a small stage to be built in front of the bonfire, and it was already finished. Thorbjørn had never had a problem leading events from his ground-level position in the midst of a chaotic mass of dancing, sweaty students. But Jens liked a stage, Malou had noticed. He wasn't a tall man but didn't have any trouble keeping everyone's attention, so Malou had a feeling that Jens's fondness of stages had less to do with being seen than with being able to see. Seeing out over all of them and feeling elevated above them. Another thing Jens liked was order, and if there was one thing the Yule celebration at Rosenholm was not, that was orderly. Yule was celebrated Viking style. Both students and teachers drank loads of strong mead, and a pig was sacrificed and eaten, just as the Vikings did. Since reading about those small children who were sacrificed and thrown in a well, Rosenholm's Yule ritual suddenly seemed less innocent to Malou.

"What was the name of that pig in Valhalla?" Malou asked the young man who was putting bowls out on a table beside the stage. Elias turned to her, and Malou suppressed the urge to look away. Ingrid had sewn a mask for him, which would hide his face while the skull fractures healed. The dark brown leather covered everything but his mouth and chin, and his eyes, with their dark lashes, peered out through holes in the mask.

"Pig?"

"Yeah, the Vikings in Valhalla eat from it every night after they've been out fighting."

"It's called Særimner," he said, turning back to the bowls on the table.

"Exactly," Malou said, immediately forgetting the name again. She had always found it almost comical that the Vikings' wildest dream was a pig you could continually eat flesh from for eternity.

"Is everything ready?" Amalie came into the tent. Her right arm was still in a sling.

"Yes, Elias just needs to finish laying the last plates out," Malou said. "Then everything's done. I'm going up to change now."

Amalie nodded to her. Her broken arm wasn't healing easily, and she had lost both her duties as combat training coach and the honor of following Jens around wherever he went. To Zlavko's disappointment, Jens hadn't chosen Malou but rather Louis to replace Amalie as bodyguard.

Malou went out into the rain that was still falling as if it might never stop again, but although her shoes were soaked through and chilled, she wasn't feeling cold. She was trembling deep inside, and her cheeks burned. Tonight was the night. The riotous atmosphere of the Yule celebration was her best chance to slip some-thing into Jens's glass. After that, hidden by the crowd, she would see if she could get into him to control him. See if the poisonous banewort would weaken the victory stone's power. She knew it was risky, and she'd considered letting Zlavko in on the plan, but she wasn't sure if he would let her carry it out if he knew about it. Zlavko still didn't know anything about the victory stone, and Malou wanted to hold off telling him until she could hopefully present him with a solution.

A few hours later, when Malou headed back down to the tent wear-ing Louis's oilskin jacket and a black pantsuit with a low-cut back, the party was already in full swing. Some of the torches outside the tent were sputtering angrily in the rain, while others had just given up the fight and gone out. Inside the tent, the fire had been started, and the heat from it caused steam to rise from the damp ground and the student's wet jackets. Elias and Louis stood by the great vat of mead, serving it up in tin mugs, and soon, the sound of chatting loudly filled the whole tent. Malou kept to herself in the background, sipping at her own mug. She had no intention of getting drunk this evening. Instead, she kept an eye on Louis and Elias and saw how they exchanged a few words, after which Louis left the tent. Now was the time. Malou discretely let her mug tip, spilling the contents onto the floor. Then she edged closer. She made it look like she wanted her mug refilled and squeezed through the students until she was up close to Elias. He had his back to her and was in the middle of serving a second-year girl. Malou focused. She tried to block out all of the noise, all of the heartbeats beating around her, the sound of her own blood rush-ing too quickly in her ears. Then she found it. Elias' pulse. Maybe she was nervous, maybe it was the throng of people around her, or maybe Elias was stronger than she'd reckoned with, but she couldn't quite push into him. *Focus!*

Malou took a deep breath, and two laughing students bashed into her in their attempt to get to the vat of mead. She closed her eyes. She could still feel Elias' pulse. She let her consciousness slide toward it, vaguely aware of the sound of students talking and laughing. They sounded far away. Then, she was there. *Finally.*

Elias collapsed onto the floor, and little sounds of alarm broke out around her. Malou opened her eyes.

"Hey, are you okay?"

"What's happening?"

Several students stood around Elias, who clasped his chest and gasped for air.

"He needs to get out and get some air!" Malou ordered. "You two, help him out, and I'll take over here."

A couple of students grabbed hold of Elias and pulled him to his feet. He shook his head, but Malou insisted. "He can't get his breath in here with all these people. Hurry up and get him outside." Malou took up the big ladle and started filling the mugs being held out toward her while a couple of third-year students moved off with Elias. At the same time, the students began whispering, and Malou looked up. Applause broke out as Jens stepped onto the stage, followed by the dark shadow of Louis, who was acting as his bodyguard that night. Malou quickly turned her gaze back to the vat. She grabbed a mug from the stack and filled it with mead. Her hands trembled, and some of the sweet liquid ran down the side. The students clapped rhythmically, and Malou laid the ladle down as Jens smiled and thanked them. She put her hand in her pocket. Her fingers found the crushed berries.

She tried to visualize the amount Lisa had shown her she should use. The poison in the berries was concentrated, as they were in dried form, Lisa had said. Her hand shook as she grasped what she could in her fingers. Then she lifted her hand discretely from her pocket.

"Tonight, we are gathered to toast the beginning of Yule!" Jens said, and as the applause erupted again, Malou lifted her hand over the glass and sprinkled the pulverized berries in. They landed on the surface and lay there like tiny, wilted leaves.

"Let me lead you in a toast!" Jens shouted, and Malou looked up and caught the eye of Louis, who nodded to her urgently from the stage and held out his hand for the mug. Malou shook her head. She didn't want to risk the mug getting into the wrong hands; she wanted to hand it over herself. For someone not protected by a victory stone, the berries could perhaps be lethal.

"Let me through," she hissed hoarsely, and the students around her pulled back to let her through all the way to the stage. The contents of the mug sloshed around a little, and Malou saw, to her relief, that some of the crushed berries had started sinking to the bottom. However, some still lay on the surface, and if Jens looked, he'd see them. Malou held the mug out toward him but kept her eyes down on the tips of his toes, hoping he would interpret her respectfully lowered head as some sign of deference. The truth was, she was horrified by the thought of him being able to sense her betrayal if he looked her in the eyes.

Malou felt him taking the mug from her, and she backed off, head still bowed. Soon, she was lost again in the throng of students, who crowded eagerly around the stage with their drinks, impatient about getting the introductory part over so the real party could begin.

"This year, we will not toast the past and our ancestors," Jens announced. Malou didn't dare look up. She could barely breathe.

"This year, we toast the future. To the future of mages. To the passing from darkness into light."

The students clapped and cheered. Somebody in the back shouted cheers.

"If you are musical, people think it's fantastic to pay money to see you on stage. If you're good at running fast, you can win gold medals. But if you are a talented blood mage, then you are supposed to be ashamed of your abilities. But that is not how it should be!" Jens continued.

Malou noticed how his words connected with something in her. A deep anger and a fundamental feeling of injustice. If she didn't know the truth about him, would she also have stood with the others applauding him with real enthusiasm? She didn't want to admit it to herself, but if she was to be honest, there was no doubt about it. She was exactly the sort who would have let herself be taken in.

"I promise you all a future where you need not bow your head in shame but can lift it proudly!" Jens said from the stage, and people clapped and whooped. "Let's drink to a bright future for all mages. Let's raise a toast to Yule!"

Finally, his speech was over, and Malou couldn't help herself. She looked up. Jens smiled, lifted the mug to his lips, and downed it in one.

"Let the ritual begin!" he yelled, throwing the mug away across the stage.

He had drunk it all. Malou felt her knees buckling under her. The first part of her plan had worked, and now she just had to wait. But for how long? How long would it take for the berries to start to take effect? Would Jens collapse on stage? Would he get unwell or tired? Or could he get aggressive? After all, wasn't that one of the reasons the Vikings used banewort in their berserkers drinks?

Jens moved into the background a little but remained standing on the stage with Louis. Malou watched him closely without being too obvious. Now Dagny appeared, again together with the pig who followed her faithfully like a dog. Dagny made a smacking sound with her lips, and the pig, without hesitating, climbed the three steps up to the stage. The tent went quite silent, and the first-years, in particular, stared wide-eyed while Dagny happily took the long knife Zlavko respectfully presented her with. Normally, the pig would squeal and resist, but this animal was tame and seemed convinced that Dagny could only have brought it into the tent because an even bigger-than-usual bucket of left-over scraps was waiting there. The pig's calm state somehow made the scene all the more absurd, as Dagny chatted and scratched its back while also, in a flash, stuck the knife into its throat, cutting its jugular vein so that the students standing the closest got splattered with blood.

After this shocking sight, the students hit the mead even harder, and soon they were all dancing around to the pulsing beat of Zlavko's drum, accompanied by a lesser round, flat drum played by Ivalo. Malou watched her as she played the drum with her usual closed, impenetrable facial expression. They hadn't talked since that time in the medical room.

The rhythms from the two instruments blended into one another, even though Ivalo and Zlavko themselves were positioned at opposite ends of the tent and didn't appear to be playing together. The music caused a buzzing inside her, and her powers were strengthened by the blood of the sacrificed animal, which had been scattered over the students with birch sprigs. Malou cracked her knuckles and tried to ignore how clearly she could feel the others' pulses beating. She had to concentrate on Jens, who was standing in the shadows watching the students, and Dagny, who was carving the pig so that the meat could be roasted over the fire in the middle of the tent.

Malou felt the minutes ticking by. How long should she wait? Jens wasn't swaying or showing any sign of discomfort. Soon, he would maybe step back, and then she would have no way of knowing if the dried nightshade reduced the victory stone's power.

She made a decision and sought out the edge of the round tent. From here, she was able to get around behind the stage.

Jens and Louis were standing with their backs to her, looking out over the students. She was close, but she was also alone and unable to hide herself in the crowd as she had imagined she would. Malou took a deep breath. This may have been a really dumb idea, even by her standards. She needed to be very careful. The idea was not to take control of Jens now, and he mustn't discover her. She just needed to see if she could. Sense if she could penetrate his bodily boundaries of skin and muscle. She closed her eyes.

She focused on him alone. He was there, but far away, as if he was buried under a drift of snow, something white and freezing cold stopped her from pushing into him. Malou pushed closer; she let her guard drop just a little. All around her, it became white, like a barrier of light. She couldn't get past it. Not unless she dared use her powers to their full. Malou let the power from the slaughtered pig fill her, her ears filled with whistling sounds; she felt herself get dizzy as if she were in the vortex of a primitive force. She opened her eyes and looked at Jens from behind. Then, she tried again.

A white light burst in front of her eyes, and she collapsed.

DECEMBER 21ST
11:02 P.M.

Malou

Malou woke up with freezing cold raindrops hitting her face. She opened her eyes and looked up into a small, shriveled face under a large hood.

"Ah, it's good that you've come around. I nearly didn't manage to drag you out of the tent," Dagny said.

"What happened?" Malou asked. Her throat felt sore, and she was shivering with cold.

"That's what you'll have to tell me," Dagny said. "I found you behind the stage. You were completely out. It must have been the mead. Are you going to be sick?"

Malou shook her head but didn't tell Dagny that she had hardly touched a drop. It would be just fine if the rest of the school believed Malou had had too much mead.

Dagny helped her to sit up. Malou dried the rain from her face, and the music pumped out of the tent. She noticed that it wasn't only raindrops but also tears. It hadn't worked. The nightshade hadn't had enough of an effect on Jens.

"Are you sure? That you're not going to be sick? It often helps," Dagny said, patting her comfortingly on the shoulder. "No, don't start crying, my young friend."

Malou couldn't stop it. Her shoulders shook as she sobbed. Her whole body ached; she felt so exhausted. She had nothing left. She was tired of fighting. She felt like giving up. Like leaning back on the muddy ground and letting the earth swallow her up.

"It'll all be all right, you'll see," Dagny comforted her. "Is there perhaps something I can help you with?"

Malou lifted her face and looked at the old woman. "Do you know anything about nightshade?"

That gave Dagny a shock, and she looked back at Malou without her usual smile.

"Where have you heard about the Nightshades?" she asked.

"From a friend."

"*The Nightshades sleep in the hall of the dead; the Nightshades roam the valley of shadows,*" Dagny whispered.

"What? What are you talking about?"

"Malou!"

She wrested her eyes from Dagny's and looked toward the tent. Louis came racing from the tent door, where the torches had long since burned out. "I've been looking for you! Iris said you fainted. Did something happen?"

"She's just needing to get up to her bed," Dagny mumbled, sounding like herself again. "And probably so does an old woman like me. I trust that you'll get her safely and sensibly up to her room, Louis, am I right?"

"Of course. I'll take good care of her."

Dagny nodded and set off quickly toward the castle with her characteristic swaying walk while Louis pulled off his black sweater and placed it around Malou's shaking shoulders.

"Come on, you need to get inside, into the warmth. What happened?"

"I reckon I've just not had enough to eat," Malou mumbled.

"You push yourself too hard," Louis said, putting his arm around her. "I wish you'd let me look after you a bit."

"You're busy looking after Jens," Malou said, giving up on keeping herself balanced and leaning onto Louis. Her legs wobbled under her. "Where is he, by the way?"

"He went up to his room. Albert took over my duty when I was looking for you."

"How did he seem?" she asked.

"Albert? Fine enough."

"No. Jens."

"Same as usual. It was a good speech, don't you think?" Louis asked. They had finally reached the castle, and he opened the door with one hand and helped her in with the other.

Malou didn't answer; her legs were about to crumple under her. Louis looked first at her, then at the stairs, measuring the situation. Then he lifted her in his arms and carried her.

"Are you never scared that Jens is in the wrong?" she asked him, with her face buried in his shirt.

"Um . . . no, I believe in the Movement," he answered. "And I believe in Jens, but . . . sometimes I'm scared that I don't want it enough."

"What do you mean?" Malou asked, discovering they had reached her door. Louis opened it with his elbow and laid her carefully on the bed.

"I want Jens to succeed in what he has set out to do and want to be a part of that, but it's not the most important thing to me," he said slowly, as if he was carefully considering each word. "But you are. *We* are the most important thing. We're meant to be together. Ever since I had that vision a year ago at the Yule celebration, I've never doubted it. You stood there in the middle of it all; you saved me when everything around me was black and terrifying."

Malou wanted to protest, but Louis shook his head. "No, you need to hear this. I've always been scared. All my life, all my childhood. Scared of sleeping alone in my room, scared of the big boys in the school playground. Shit, I was scared of peeing my pants. But since that night, I haven't felt scared. Because I know you'll come and save me."

"You can't say things like that, Louis . . ."

"I just know it," he whispered, and leaned over her to dry her cheeks of tears.

That wave rose up inside her. It flushed the tiredness away, and she couldn't stop it. "This doesn't mean we're back together," she whispered. Then she took his head in her hands and pulled his mouth to hers.

314

The Nightshades sleep in the hall of the dead; the Nightshades roam in the valley of shadows.

He presses the stone in his hand. They cannot touch him. But still, the sickening verse rings in his ears. He hated it as a child, and he hates it now. And he dreams about it at night. The Nightshades.

"How did it go?"

Write back now! I'm so worried!

Malou—HAS SOMETHING HAPPENED TO YOU?!?!

I'm okay. But it didn't work.

I'm sorry . . .

DECEMBER 24ᵀᴴ
5:30 P.M.

Chamomile

Chamomile chopped the pistachio nuts finely and tipped them into a bowl, then started to slice open a pomegranate. "Where's the mint gone to?" She scanned the makeshift kitchen table they had built using pallets and the top of a garden table discarded at the abandoned railway station.

"Behind the potatoes," Chamomile's mother said. "There's parsley and coriander, too."

"Can I help with anything?" Molly asked.

"You could get the seeds out of this," Chamomile said, handing her the pomegranate and a spoon.

"Okay," Molly said, starting to scoop out the dissected fruit.

"Like this," Chamomile said, taking the pomegranate back, turning it over and hitting the outer shell with the spoon so the seeds started to sprinkle down onto the plate she'd set on the table.

"Aha. Clever!" Molly said, taking over again.

"Ho, ho, ho," said a voice from over by the door. Benjamin came into the church carrying a small, lopsided Christmas tree in a pot. He set it down in the middle of the floor. "Now, it's Christmas!"

"Where did you get that from?" Jakob asked, lifting an eyebrow doubtfully in a way that made him suddenly look like a teacher, which he was, of course.

"I got it cheap at the grocery store," Benjamin said, going over to hang up his jacket.

Chamomile didn't point out that the supermarket wouldn't be open yet, and Jakob said no more either, though he stood for a little while longer, looking at the pitiable tree with a distrustful expression. Chamomile was relieved that Jakob just let it go. They had no need for further conflicts inside the old church. The atmosphere had been very strained since it became apparent that the nightshade didn't work in the way they'd hoped.

"How lovely," Victoria said, smiling warmly at Benjamin. "That's such a nice idea to bring a tree."

Benjamin just nodded without saying anything further, and Chamomile sighed at the sight of Victoria bravely smiling while Benjamin swept by her and went upstairs.

"We don't have anything to decorate it with, do we?" Molly asked.

"Who cares? It's good as it is," Chamomile said.

"I can make a paper star," Victoria said. "For the top. It should have that, at least." She disappeared up the stairs to where she kept all her books, which also happened to be where Benjamin had gone. Chamomile shook her head.

"Is something wrong?" Molly smiled.

"Ah, you know, life is just complicated," Chamomile said, lifting the lid of the huge pot she had filled to the brim with a simmering stew of chickpeas, sweet potato, eggplant, tomatoes, dried apricots, ginger, and scallions.

"It smells of Arabian nights," Molly said. "You're so lucky your mom taught you to cook. I can't remember my mom ever actually cooking."

318

"What did you eat, then?" Chamomile asked.

"Coco Pops. Or she bought something on the way home from work. My friends were always jealous that I could get takeout nearly every day. But I'd rather have had a mom who had time to cook for me."

"You always want what you don't have," Chamomile said. "When I was a kid, I dreamed of eating chips with gravy on Christmas. I heard some classmates say that's what they did. Seriously, chips with gravy! I thought it sounded so wonderful," Chamomile said, replacing the lid. "But now, this looks good, too."

"So, it wasn't the stew you were talking about when you said life was complicated?" Molly asked, giving her a meaningful look. Her smile made a dimple on one of her cheeks.

Chamomile shrugged. "No, I just think that everybody seems to be falling in love with someone they can't have at the moment."

"Malou."

"What?" Chamomile looked up at her, horrified. She felt herself blushing. "What do you mean?"

"Malou," Molly said. "She's coming—I can see her from the window."

Chamomile looked out the tall, arched window. "Oh," she said, hoping her cheeks hadn't gone as completely red as they felt. "That's good. The food's nearly ready."

"Merry Christmas," Malou said as she walked in the door.

"You too," Chamomile said, giving Malou a hug. "Hey, is it snowing?"

"Yeah, but I don't think it's going to stick." She shook a few snowflakes from her hair.

One hour later, they were all sitting together around the tree on throws and cushions scattered on the ground. Victoria had, somehow or other, folded a perfect paper star from some old pages of a book, and it made the tree look like something you might find in some lifestyle magazine article "Quirky, Handmade Christmas Decorations." Lisa had found a box of altar candles, and the large, white candles over half a foot high now stood around them on the floor, illuminating the church, while outside, snow continued to fall. Beate served them all with bowls of the aromatic stew.

Chamomile felt herself warming up again from the inside. This was her family. Her strange, wonky, ill-fitting family was made up of underdogs and outcasts, but they were here for her. Maybe Malou was right. Maybe it didn't matter so much who her real father was. And if nothing else, it felt like a great relief that everybody knew her secret now.

"It's a bit basic, but it's all good, is it not?" her mother asked as she held out a coriander-topped bowl to Thorbjørn, who gave it a cautious sniff.

"If it was good enough for Jesus on Christmas Eve, then it's good enough for us," Chamomile said.

"What do you mean, honey?" Beate asked.

"Well, Jesus was born on Christmas Eve, right? In a church. So, in a way, he celebrated Christmas in a church. Like us," Chamomile said, reaching out for a bowl but then stopping when she realized there was still silence around the tree. "What?" she said, shrugging.

"He didn't though, you nut!" Malou said. "Jesus was born in a stable."

"Ah, well . . ." Chamomile said. "Is that what it was?"

"Church. Stable. I mean, what's the difference really?" Molly said, giggling, and Chamomile couldn't help but also laugh. "Oh dear, I'm afraid that's my fault," Beate said, laughing. "I was never very good at telling you all those Christian stories. What was it again? Something about how Jesus' mother and father had to travel . . ."

"Jesus's father is God, though," Benjamin interrupted. "That's the whole idea of it. The son of God and all that."

"Kirstine, can't you help us out here?" Beate asked. "We don't really know what we're talking about, as you can probably tell."

Everyone turned to Kirstine, who for a moment looked like she'd most like to jump up out the door, run, and never turn back.

"Would you tell us about the nativity story?" Jakob asked. "Don't worry, nobody here will even know if you mix things up or leave anything out." He smiled at her encouragingly, and at that moment, Chamomile was hit by a jolt of envy, which she tried to hide by taking a good slurp of sparkling wine from her enamel cup. If someone were ever to look at her in the same loving way Jakob was looking at Kirstine right now, then she'd never want for anything for Christmas ever again.

Kirstine nodded and give a short smile before starting her story. The rest of the group ate in silence while they listened to the tale of Mary and Joseph, who had to leave their home when she was very pregnant because some king or other wanted to do a count of the people living in his realm.

"Typical man," Molly mumbled. "Look at me—I've got the biggest population!"

Kirstine continued to tell of how Mary and Joseph, who had not found any room for them at the inn, which was a kind of hotel or hostel, were allowed to sleep in the stable instead. And that was where Jesus was born.

"Now I remember hearing about the stable before," Chamomile said when the story was over. "Did you get told that story at Christmas when you were a kid?" Chamomile asked her.

"Yeah," she nodded. "The priest read it in church at the Christmas service, but we also got it at home. My dad . . . He always read it before we went around the tree." A crease appeared between her eyebrows, and Chamomile regretted having asked.

"What about a Christmas song?" Beate asked once they'd finished eating. "Shall we sing a carol before we have dessert?"

They decided on "Silent Night," but given only Kirstine knew all the words, it was a bit of a mixed result.

Afterward, they scoffed down a sickeningly sweet round of baklava with rose water, which seemed to be even more of a challenge for Thorbjørn than the coriander had been. And then it was time for presents. Despite the circumstances, Chamomile had insisted. There should be a present for each of them on Christmas, and they had each been assigned a person to gift something to, something small and either cheap or homemade. Chamomile had gotten Thorbjørn, and she had bought a pair of secondhand thermal gloves. They were so big that a sea lion could have easily warmed its fins in them, and Thorbjørn seemed pleased with them once he'd checked they actually would fit him.

Molly had the job of getting Chamomile's present, and in the small parcel, she found a pretty bracelet woven in black leather and with a turquoise-colored bead.

"Wow, this is lovely, Molly. Did you make it yourself?"

"Yeah. I mean, the bead is from an old necklace, but I wove it myself."

Chamomile put the band on her arm straight away. "Mom, look what Molly made for me."

"It's really pretty. And well chosen. Turquoise is often worn by healers, as the stone helps heal wounds and illnesses."

"And people also say it gives the bearer strength to face the truth," Lisa commented. She was in the middle of putting on the sparkly scarf Victoria had found for her at the same secondhand shop as Chamomile.

"The truth and healing properties—that's something you can always use," Chamomile said, giving Molly a hug. "Thanks so much."

Chamomile's mother got up with a sigh to warm up her special Christmas mulled wine, which she made with spiced apple juice and a whole lot of rum, while Molly tried to explain to Chamomile how she had woven the little bracelet.

"Chamomile, I need to get going soon. Can we talk for a minute?" Malou indicated to Chamomile to follow her upstairs behind Victoria and Kirstine, who were already on their way.

"Oh . . ." Chamomile said, looking from Malou to Molly, who smiled.

"Just go. I'll help wash up in the meantime."

"But it's not because there's anything secret, I don't think."

"Great, then you can just tell me about it later, right?"

"If that's okay?"

Molly waved her off as if to say it was no problem at all, and Chamomile hurried after Malou.

"Molly is one of us now," she said softly, catching up with Malou on the stairs. "They all are."

"It was us four who started searching for Trine's killer," Malou whispered. "I think you should be a bit careful about who you trust."

Chamomile shook her head. "What do you mean?" She felt as if Malou had just given her a slap in the face.

"You're all getting a little too comfortable. Thorbjørn's car is sitting out there; you go shopping in the town. I bet it wasn't that easy getting hold of all the ingredients you've used to cook with. People remember that kind of thing. Unusual outsiders, asking for uncommon items. If the Crows hear about it . . ."

"They won't," Chamomile whispered. "We're being super careful."

"And what about those gloves for Thorbjørn? Did you go down to the shop yourself to buy them?"

"Yeah, but . . ."

"Chamomile, you have to stay here!"

"Don't worry. Nothing can happen to me. And we're moving again soon, in any case. Jakob has found a new place for us as a precaution. A holiday cottage that's up for sale. We're moving after Christmas. My mom also can't cope with the damp here in the church."

Malou looked at her gravely. "Is she sick? Your mom? She looks different . . . older . . ."

"What do you mean?" Chamomile asked. "She's just got asthma. What's wrong with you?"

"Hey, are you two coming?" Victoria asked from the top of the stairs.

Malou looked at Chamomile appraisingly. Then she turned to Victoria and began to climb the steps two at a time. "We're coming. I need to go soon, too, if I'm going to catch the last bus. I said I was spending Christmas with my mom."

Chamomile sighed and followed her up to the others, who stood by the window, looking out at the falling sleet.

"I just want to tell you something that Dagny said," Malou said once they were gathered. "I asked her about nightshade. It was a

324

little careless, but I had such a fuzzy head after what happened with Jens—"

"Do you think he didn't notice it at all?" Victoria interrupted.

"No," Malou said. "It was as if it didn't touch him. And when I tried to get into him, it was the same. Something was protecting him somehow. There was a white light all around him, and all my powers drained from me as if I'd been punctured somehow."

"The victory stone protected him," Chamomile said. "And it must be because of the stone that the poison didn't affect him either. He should have been killed outright by a dose of nightshade."

"Have you told Zlavko?" Kirstine asked.

"No," Malou said, pursing her lips into a thin line. "I'll do it after vacation. Maybe he'll have some idea of how we can get the stone from Jens."

In spite of their minor clash, Chamomile had a feeling of fondness welling up in her. Malou was always so brave, but to have to tell Zlavko that his plan would fail before it had even been put into practice, was no easy task.

"What did Dagny say about nightshade?" Victoria asked.

"I can't remember it exactly. I wasn't quite clear in the head," Malou said. "But it was something like nightshade wanders in a valley, I think. It sounded like some children's rhyme or poem? Maybe it doesn't mean anything, but I just wanted to tell you in case it makes anyone think of anything." She pulled out her cell phone from her pocket and checked the time. Chamomile saw that she had several unread messages.

"I need to go now if I'm going to get that bus."

Malou hurriedly said her goodbyes and thanked Beate for the food and Thorbjørn for the present (he had sewn a small leather pouch for her, which she'd held in the tips of her fingers like it was something toxic), and in the blink of an eye, she was away out the door.

Chamomile sighed as she heard it close. Something had changed between them. But maybe that was actually a good thing. In any case, she was glad to escape all the butterflies in her stomach. Now, she was left only with a simmering unease.

"I think my mom made mulled wine," she said, standing up. "Are you coming down for some? There are cookies, too."

DECEMBER 25ᵀᴴ
2:18 A.M.

Victoria

She sat in the dark. The little candle had burned out, but it didn't really matter. It was as if the dark helped her get nearer to that thing, which was slipping away from her the whole time. It was a memory, and Victoria could sense how it fluttered around in the outer edges of her consciousness like a little bird that couldn't be caught. If she tried too hard, she scared it away. Instead, she just sat in the dark and let it flutter. Here, it was quiet, besides the rustling and moaning of the spirits. Tonight, the old woman had the company of a younger man, who sat down somewhere in the church, crying with heartbreaking sobs. But Victoria wasn't going to let herself get distracted. What Dagny had said to Malou had rung a bell somewhere with her. She had heard the words before. It reminded her of something.

Victoria sat for another hour, but it didn't come to her. One of her legs had gone to sleep, and she stretched them out in front of her. If she couldn't think of it now, she might as well read one of the books she had dug up. She sensed that it wasn't a good night to lie down and sleep. Her dreams were filled with whispering voices and cryptic smells of damp and earth.

Victoria fumbled with the matches, struck one, and lit a new candle. And all at once, it came to her. It was the sound of the match that set it off, and suddenly she could smell it. Her grandma's perfume. Mixed with the smell of the filterless cigarettes she used to smoke when Victoria was a kid. She could hear the clink of her diamond bracelets as her grandma lifted her thin wrist. And her slightly gruff voice, whispering to Victoria, when it was time to sleep. "*The Nightshades sleep in the hall of the dead; the Nightshades roam in the valley of shadows.*"

Malou was right. It was a nursery rhyme. *The Nightshades roam* . . . A plant can't roam. They had gotten so fixed on that poisonous plant. Maybe there was another meaning that held the key here. She grabbed the book that lay on the top of her pile. *Dictionary of Symbols* was the title.

SHADE

Shade symbolizes the negative, the hidden, a shadow, but also the soul. There is a series of superstitions in connection with shade. Shade is linked with doppelgangers, spectres and death, with possession and demonization, and with the unconscious.

There is a widespread notion that the realm of death is a land of shadow, as in, for example, the Norse Hel and Greek Hades.

Victoria laid the book in her lap. The candlelight flickered, although there was no draught where she was sitting. She gave a start when she looked up and saw the white outline of that young man sitting right in front of her on his arms on his knees. He rocked back and forth, crying. She thought about chasing him away, but on the other hand, he wasn't doing her any harm. He must just need the company. And she could use that, too. There was still a long time to go before the first bus left.

The morning came gray and chilly, and it was drizzling rain as Victoria got off the S-train. Her grandma was not one for getting up early. She might also have come home late the night before if she'd spent Christmas with Victoria's family. She hadn't allowed herself to think about her family. About the enormous tree her mother decorated every year in a different theme color, about her twin brothers, who certainly wouldn't understand why she hadn't come home. But now, the thought made her eyes well with warm tears, which spilled out and ran down her cold cheeks. It was no use torturing oneself with these things. It was just a phase, after all, and they'd soon be together again.

Victoria stood in front of her grandma's green front door. She wouldn't be too pleased with someone visiting so early, but Victoria was freezing and felt vulnerable and a little strung out. She longed to come inside to the warmth.

She had to ring several times before a gruff voice answered the intercom.

"Yes?"

"It's Victoria."

"Who?"

"Victoria!"

The door opened with a buzz, and Victoria hurried into the stairway. When she got up to the door, she could hear the rattling of all her grandma's locks until, eventually, the door opened.

"Well, well," she said when Victoria fell sobbing around her neck. "I'm sure it's not as bad as all that," she mumbled gruffly and patted her on the back while Victoria carried on crying, her face pressed into her thin shoulder.

"Dry your eyes, now. You're much prettier when you smile." Her grandma stepped back to look at her. Victoria shook her head resignedly. Outbursts of emotion were not really done in her family. It wasn't dignified to let yourself be overcome by tears and helplessness. In Victoria's family, adversity was to be was faced with complete calm.

"So," her grandma said with relief, "go on into the living room and sit down, and I'll make us some coffee. Nobody is quite themselves at this time of day."

Victoria took off her jacket and hung it on a hook in the entrance hall while her grandma put some coffee on in the kitchen. Then she took her bag and went into the dark living room. Her grandma came shortly after, carrying a tray. She was wearing a colorful silk kimono and turquoise-heeled slippers, and her hair was wrapped in a towel, turban-style. Her face had no makeup, and Victoria realized she hadn't seen her grandma like that since she was a little kid and had slept here when her parents went to the theater or a party.

"I don't have any bread," she said, filling their cups. "I don't eat breakfast. Are you hungry?"

"Coffee is just fine," Victoria assured her.

"Tell me, then, what's happened. Is it love again? Your parents say it's that Brahe boy who has messed with your head and persuaded you to drop out of school and run away from home."

"He hasn't messed with my head," Victoria said. "It has nothing to do with him."

"But you're still in love with him?"

"Yes," she admitted. "I am. But he's not in love with me."

"Sweetheart. Forget him. Men come and go, and it doesn't pay to get attached to them. Is it him you are living with? No, wait, I don't want to know"—she cut herself off and waved dismissively with her coral red nails—"then I don't need to lie to your father if he asks. But you look like someone who is not getting enough sleep at night . . ."

"Maybe," she said. "But that's got nothing to do with Benjamin. And that's also not why I dropped out of Rosenholm."

"You can imagine your parents were furious when they heard. But I said to them if you don't rebel at your age, when exactly are you going to do it? Are you short of money?"

Victoria shook her head. "No, but I need your help with something. I remembered a rhyme you always used to whisper to me when I was little. About the Nightshades."

"Ah, yes. My great-grandma taught me that when I was a little girl." She looked at her curiously, her eyebrows raised.

"What are nightshades?" Victoria asked.

"The Nightshades," her grandma said, sitting up straight on the sofa. "As a child, I was both frightened and fascinated by my great-gran's stories of them. In the olden days, when my great-gran, your great-great-gran, was a child, the world was full of beings who couldn't be seen. Trolls and elves and spirits are things most people have heard of. But there were many others. Water sprites, ghost children, the grave sow, and the hell horse. And hulder, a beautiful, young woman who lured young men into the hills, from where they never returned. The hulder belonged to the underworld. Just like the Nightshades—the most mysterious and frightening of all those beings my great-gran told me about. That was what I thought anyway, as a child. Have you ever been interested in these beings from the underworld?"

Victoria shook her head.

"Many years ago, before I met your grandpa, I went out for a time with a young man who was studying them. It was very interesting. There are stories of underworld creatures all across the world and in all cultures. They differ between one part of the world and another, but originally, the legends are built on the same ancient notion that people have a life in the underworld after death. In our Norse tradition, the legends were often about people who were killed in a gruesome way. Babies born in secret, abandoned children, young women who disappeared..."

Victoria felt slightly dizzy. *The young women in the vision at the spring. The disappeared maids. Little Kirsten's grave ...*

"It's young women who have been murdered. They're the ones who are the Nightshades ..."

"That was what my great-gran told me."

"Do they really exist?"

"So I believed, in any case," her grandma said. "And most legends are founded on a certain degree of truth, so who knows?"

"Where can they be found?"

"I don't know, my dear. But, if they do really exist, I would be more interested in knowing how to keep them away. Listen, I have an idea."

"What?"

332

"Your hair looks dreadful, and I could also do with a trim. Should I not give Søren a call and see if he can fit us in this morning, and then we could go out and get lunch together?"

"But—"

"Let's do that. I'll call Søren now. I'm sure I have his home number somewhere."

She stood up and went into the next room. Victoria got her bag and pulled her notepad from it. She flicked through the pages of notes and past the list of names she had gathered of missing young women. Then, she came to the right page. The one with the word *Nightshade* in the middle, circled in red. She took a pen from her bag and added the letter S. She added two more words. Then she looked at the page.

Find the Nightshades!

I need to speak to you.
It's important.

Malou

JANUARY 10™
4:00 P.M.

Malou

"Dagny, wait!" Malou wove through the crowd of students filing out of the auditorium at the end of their lesson. She just managed to stick her nose in the door before Dagny slammed it closed.

"There's something I need to ask you about," Malou said, closing the door behind her. The noise from the students out in the hall faded to almost nothing.

"What is it, my friend?" Dagny asked, trundling over to her lectern, where she started stacking one book after another into a huge leather bag.

"The Nightshades sleep in the hall of death; the Nightshades roam in the valley of shadows," Malou said.

Dagny laid down the book she had just picked up. She looked up at Malou warily.

"I want to know what the Nightshades are. And where to find them," Malou said.

A nervous wince flitted across Dagny's face, and she started rubbing at her wrists, as if they were aching.

"Forget it, Malou. That road only leads to unhappiness and lost years," she muttered.

"I can't do that," Malou said. "I can't let myself forget about it. My best friends' lives are at stake."

Dagny's face tensed up as if she was in pain, and she kept on rubbing at her wrists. "It's best if you forget about it," she repeated. "I'm sorry, but I can't help you."

Malou had a sudden impulse. "And what if I was to tell you I know a young woman who has the same on her wrists as you do?"

Dagny stared. "That's not true!"

"It is. Her name is Kirstine and she has scars where the tree's roots twisted around her arms and legs. I've seen them. They shimmer in the dark. The same way yours do."

Dagny let go of her wrists as if she had burned herself. "That can't be right. I was the last," she whispered. "I don't believe you."

"There's an easy way to check if I'm right," Malou said. "Meet her. You can see for yourself."

"Is she a student here?" Dagny asked.

"Not anymore. And we can't meet here at school."

"Where then?"

"I can't tell you," Malou said. "But I can show you."

When Malou slipped out of the auditorium fifteen minutes later, she headed for the library but didn't make it that far before a hand grabbed her firmly by the arm.

"I got your message. You wanted to talk to me?" It was Zlavko.

She pulled out of his grasp. "Yes."

He opened the door to the Blood Magic classroom. "In you come, then."

"It's about the plan . . ." Malou said, once he had shut the door after them.

336

"I've just come from a meeting with Jens," Zlavko said. "He's looking for new bodyguards, and I recommended you. We're ready."

"It's no use," she whispered.

"What do you mean? You can't back out now!"

"I'm not backing out," Malou said. "But our plan won't work. I . . . I can't do Impero Spiritus on Jens. He's protected against that kind of magic."

"What do you mean?"

Malou took a deep breath. "Jens has a victory stone," she whispered. "It's protecting him. I've tried it myself. I borrowed one when we broke into Leah's place. She couldn't control me when I had the stone."

"What are you saying?"

"It's true," Malou said. "We need to find another way."

Zlavko buried his face in his hands. Malou held her breath. She almost wished he'd yell at her. This silence just sent cold shivers down her spine.

"I might have another plan . . . a way we can get the stone from him," she said.

"Forget it," Zlavko whispered. "A victory stone protects its owner. Jens wasn't an easy opponent in the first place." He turned away from her and looked out the window instead. There was a view over to the park's huge copper beech, its branches bare.

"But—"

"You keep away from that stone, Malou. And keep away from Jens."

"I can't. Chamomile is my friend. And she is Jens's daughter. I know about the ritual!"

337

Zlavko turned to her. She couldn't look at him. "You knew it. You knew it the whole time."

"I think I knew it before Jens even did," he said softly. "It was only a matter of time before he worked out how to become almost untouchable, and I knew he knew about the ritual." A look of bitterness crossed his face. "Because I told him about it myself."

"Why?" whispered Malou. "Why did you tell him about it?"

"I think that was why he supported me in getting this job back then. Because he thought I knew a lot about the forgotten old rituals and dark magic. And he was right about that. When I was young, I made some choices I never should have."

Malou nodded. She didn't doubt he was telling the truth.

"I got the job despite the protests of the former teacher, and I was grateful for Jens's support. He seemed kind and interested . . . *Very* interested. So, I told him about it." Zlavko closed his eyes tight for a moment. "When Leah died, I understood a lot of things. Shortly before, Jens had told me that Chamomile was his daughter, and I realized it wouldn't be long before he worked it out. His own flesh and blood is a valuable sacrifice."

"How can anyone be so sick?" Malou asked.

"Jens doesn't know how to love," Zlavko said. "And so he doesn't know about grief. He believes that dying is the worst that can happen to a person and fears it so much that he's willing to do anything at all to avoid it. But, living without the one you love is far worse than dying." Zlavko wrung his damaged hand and then rested his forehead against it. "Jens imagines that the biggest sacrifice he can make is by killing his own daughter. He doesn't understand what it really means to sacrifice yourself. The ultimate offering."

338

When he lifted his head again, Malou could see there were tears in his eyes. "You couldn't have saved Leah," she said.

"We'll never know that, will we?" He turned his back on her again. "I didn't have the courage in that moment, and I've regretted it ever since. But that's not a mistake I'll make again. And now you should go. I'd like to be alone."

"But . . . aren't we going to figure out how to stop the victory stone's powers?" Malou asked.

"*I'll* figure it out. Not you."

"What do you mean?"

"I'm assuming you contacted Chamomile when you found out about the ritual?"

"She has a right to know. So she can keep herself safe."

He shook his head.

"That was exactly why I didn't tell you," he said bitterly. "Because I knew you'd seek her out. I've used the best part of this school year to convince Jens that he can trust you. Despite who your friends were. If he finds out you've been in touch with Chamomile, it won't take him long to work out that he also cannot trust me." Finally, he turned to her. "I'm sorry, Malou. But I'm releasing you now from the promise you gave. You're free to leave the school."

She looked at him, incredulous. "But there has to be something I can do . . ." she protested.

"You can wish me luck," he whispered.

339

JANUARY 16TH
1:15 P.M.

Chamomile

Chamomile ordered coffees for them all. She would have left it at that, but then she added in a large portion of fries when the woman behind the counter just kept looking at her expectantly. There were hardly any customers, and it was a freezing cold, overcast January afternoon. A man sat at the counter reading the morning paper while he tucked into a plate of sausage and potatoes. Otherwise, there was no one. Chamomile paid and sat down at a table in the farthest corner. The steam from the kitchen had settled on the windows like mist, so they couldn't see the little harbor outside. Kirstine wiped a hole in the mist with one hand so she could see out.

After Christmas, they'd moved out of the church and into a holiday cottage not far from the harbor and this cafe where they sat now. The server brought their fries, but neither Victoria nor Kirstine ate any. Instead, they sat in silence, warming their hands on their cups.

Kirstine straightened up and dried more of the mist off the window. "Here they come now," she said. The door opened, and Malou came in. With her was a tiny, very old woman.

Chamomile stood up to let them sit on the bench.

The woman gratefully took a seat with a deep sigh.

"We're really grateful that you came," Chamomile said. "Here, the coffee is still warm. It's so cold outside."

"Ah, and fries," Dagny said, smiling. "That's something I don't often get."

"Please have them," Chamomile told her. "We can always buy more. They're actually really good."

"Did you have any problem getting here?" Victoria asked.

"No," Malou said. "Nobody saw us leave. We walked all the way down to the main road where I'd parked the car."

They sat quietly, watching Dagny, who was happily munching on the fries, as if that was what they had come here for. Chamomile gave Malou a questioning look, and Malou looked back knowingly, her eyebrows raised. Hadn't she told them that Dagny was quite unusual? Chamomile was about to say something when Dagny brushed the salt from her fingers and looked up.

"So, which one of you is the survivor?" she asked.

Chamomile looked at her in surprise. *The survivor?* She looked around at the other girls, and images formed in her head of their own accord. Malou in a hospital bed, with a huge bandage on her head. Victoria, gasping for breath and collapsing, lifeless, the first time she let herself be possessed by Trine. Kirstine screaming in pain as the fire spread around her feet at the old stone setting last year. And Chamomile herself, lying naked and unconscious in the cellars under Rosenholm, with Vitus bending over her, scratching runes into her skin. They were all survivors.

"It's you she means, Kirstine," Malou said softly. "Show her your scars."

Kirstine hesitated a moment, checking that nobody else was watching, and then she pulled up her sleeves. It had been a year since she had gotten these scars, but they were still very clear and seemed to reflect the glare of the cold, bright track lights.

"True indeed," Dagny whispered. "I needed to see it to believe it." She looked from Kirstine's wrists and forearms, which she held before her, up to her face. "You have to understand. I thought I was the only one." With trembling hands, she pushed up her sleeves to reveal the same scarring.

"Tell us about the Nightshades," Malou said.

"First, I'd like to hear your story," Dagny said, rolling her sleeves back down. "I want to hear how you got those scars. It was the tree, am I right? They gave you to the tree?"

"No . . ." Kirstine turned toward the window, where water droplets ran down, leaving dark strips through the whitish surface layer as the mist condensed. "The tree gave me the scars, but I wasn't given to the tree. It was me, who . . ." Her voice faltered, and she frowned. "It was me who killed a man. The tree took him as a gift, an offering. It pulled his body down into the earth. And in return, it gave me—"

"Terrible powers," Dagny finished her sentence.

"Far too strong," Kirstine added.

"But how did you get the scars, then?"

"We tried to get the tree to take the powers away again because I couldn't handle them. I brought it an offering, a dead hare, but the tree wouldn't accept it and attacked me."

"But you survived," Dagny nodded. "That's how it is connected. Interesting."

"What's interesting?" Malou asked.

"Are you always so impatient?" Dagny needled her. "I'll tell you my story. I've never told it to anyone before, but once you've

342

heard it, you'll hopefully understand most of it. But first, tell me you know about the Nightshades."

Victoria put her cup down and started to explain what she had told them all a few days before. "We found out that the Nightshades are young women who are dead, but in some way or other, they live on. Not as spirits, but as . . . Nightshades. Under the ground."

Dagny nodded as if Victoria were a student who'd done well. "It's correct—the Nightshades are young women who are dead, but they are not dead in any ordinary way. The women were all killed for a particular reason. A reason I discovered when I myself was a student at Rosenholm." She took a sip of her coffee, and Chamomile gave Malou a warning glance. Dagny was old, and you had to give older people time to tell their stories.

"It's almost seventy years ago," Dagny began. "Things were very different back then. We were still very few female students then, in the 1950s. It wasn't really spoken of, but girls were not considered to be as smart as boys, and we didn't even get taught the same things. The girls had to learn healing, gathering herbs, and brewing potions, whether or not they had a gift for it. Which I didn't. I did excel at rune magic. But I could just forget all about that. And the teachers were some right nasty brutes, some of them, especially to the boys. Even so, it was a good time. I had friends at school, and we used to sneak into the boys' wing at night. Then I got this really sweet boyfriend, and we were planning to get married after we finished school. But instead, something happened that changed my life forever. One night, just before our final exams, I was woken by a banging on my door. I was alone in my room because my roommate had gone home to study for the exams. I thought it might be my boyfriend, but outside the door, there was another male student. I knew him well. The whole school did, because he was one of the best students. A very promising, young blood mage who also came from an old, noble family. He said Mr. Fischer wanted to see me. Mr. Fischer taught Norse Studies in those days. There was some kind of emergency, and they needed a student with strong abilities in Earth. I felt like I was finally getting a chance to prove what I was capable of, and I went with him, happy and proud to have been asked. It had to do with a ritual out at the old tree in the woods, he said, and he gave me a cloak to wear over my nightdress.

"When we got down there, several men were standing in a circle at the foot of the tree. They were wearing masks, so I couldn't see their faces. I got scared and tried to run away, but it was too late. They threw themselves on me. Afterward, they left me to the tree. They left me for dead. The tree roots grabbed me. They burned into my skin, but the tree could feel I was still alive, and it was as if it hesitated. That lit some spark of hope in me, and I fought with powers I hadn't known I had. The tree finally let me go, and I passed out. When the sun rose, I came around, and I struggled back up to the castle, where I was admitted to the medical room.

"When I woke up again, with my arms and legs in thick bandages, Mr. Fischer was standing by my bed. He said he wanted to make sure I was okay. He apologized and said it had been some silly boys' games that had gotten out of hand. 'That's the kind of thing that happens when the boys find out a girl has loose morals,' he said."

Dagny shook her head. "Loose morals—that was the kind of awful thing they said back then about girls who went with boys," she continued. "And he had heard I had a boyfriend even though it was forbidden. But I wasn't to worry, as he had already reprimanded the boys," she said. And then he leaned over my bed and whispered: *This is never to be spoken of again, all right, missy?* Or else my poor family would suffer for it, they who had scrimped and saved all these years to be able to send me to Rosenholm. It would be a terrible shame if it was to get out, he had said. And then he left. I lay in bed for two days, crying and crying. After that, I got up, went to my last exams, and then left Rosenholm. I never even spoke to my boyfriend again."

"But what about the ones who did it?" Malou asked. "They got away with it."

"Did you know who they were?" Chamomile asked.

"That young man from the noble family, I saw him. Several of the others, I had a suspicion about who they were. But there was one more, who I was completely sure about.

"Who?"

"When Mr. Fischer leaned over me, lying there in my sick bed, I got the smell of the disgusting cigarettes he always smoked. And then I knew it. He had also been there in the woods. He was one of the masked men."

"That's so horrendous," Chamomile said. "And you never told anyone?"

"No. But I could never forget it either. I started to look up old materials and talk to elder mages. At first, of course, nobody wanted to say anything at all to a young woman from a poor background. But I was persistent. And crimes always leave some traces behind them, even when they seem impossible to find in the beginning. After many years of searching, I found descriptions of dark rituals that were carried out at Rosenholm on certain special dates. For hundreds of years, power-hungry mages had sacrificed innocent women to the tree in the woods in order to gain hidden powers.

"The disappeared maids," Victoria whispered.

"Yes, their disappearance was rarely worth wasting energy investigating," Dagny said. "They were killed—strangled or drowned—and their bodies were taken to the tree, which pulled them underground, and in return, the tree gifted the killers with terrible powers. Some got the ability to control other people's bodies or thoughts, others became as strong as animals, others became invincible." Dagny paused while Chamomile poured her more coffee. The vision from the maiden's spring rose up in her mind. All those young women who had been killed for the sake of sick men's fantasies of power and fame . . .

"After the Reform, sacrifices were, of course, forbidden," Dagny went on, "but they continued in secret. And when I found out that I was not the first to be subjected to this, I was filled with a burning desire for revenge. They should pay for what they have done. In my search for information about the rituals, I came across some descriptions of an old prophecy. You'll know yourselves about the Prophecy of the Seeress, but there are also many other predictions, most of them incompletely recorded and quite difficult to translate. Which is also true of the one known as the Nightshade Prophecy."

"Nightshade," Victoria repeated.

Chamomile nodded to herself. The note Sigsten had written. Did shades refer to Nightshades?

"It put me in mind of an old nursery rhyme. Do you know what kids say when they're doing magic tricks?" she looked at them expectantly.

"Let me see," Chamomile said, "Hocus pocus?"

"Exactly. "Hocus pocus filiocus. And do you also know where that comes from?"

Chamomile shook her head.

"It was what a priest would say in church, back in the Middle Ages, when everything was said in Latin. Or at least, it's what the ordinary churchgoers heard when they came to the service because they didn't understand anything the priest said. *Hoc est corpus filii.* This is the body of Christ. But, with time, it became a kind of magic trick catchphrase and, even later, a kids' rhyme. It's the same with the nursery rhyme about the Nightshades, who sleep in the hall of death. That has its origins in the Nightshade Prophecy."

"The kids rhyme comes from a nineteenth-century prophecy?" Malou asked, but Dagny shook her head so her gray hair swished from side to side.

"No, they first tried to translate it in the nineteenth century, but the prophecy itself is much older. The words are a mysterious mix of Old Norse words that are difficult to decipher. And the end of the prophecy has never been found."

Dagny dug into her pocket and pulled out an old notebook, worn at the corners. She flicked through it, then laid it out on the table between them. A long list of words was written in fine handwriting. Chamomile didn't immediately understand them but saw that Dagny had added the translation of each word.

Offra (to sacrifice)

Skjól (hide)

Hvila (rest/sleep)

Kona (woman)

Gamall (old)

Silfr-elk (silver-oak)

Ør (scar)

Merki (mark)

Rún (rune)

Mykr (dark)

Undirheimar (underworld)

Ungr (young)

Nattskuggi (nightshade)

Vakna (awaken)

Salr (hall)

Dauø (the dead)

Fara (walk, march, roam)

Udaud (crime, misdeed)

Hefnd (revenge)

Sleppa lauss (get free)

Lifa (live, alive, surviving)

Dagny turned to the next page in her notebook. "Based on the words I could decipher, I made my own translation, which I think comes a little closer than previous versions, though I still don't have the ending." She cleared her throat and began to read in a whisper:

"Killed in the darkness, sacrificed in secret,
the Nightshades rest in the hall of the dead.
One day, they will waken to seek their
revenge and roam out from the valley of death.
A woman with silvery scars from the oak,
marked by misdeeds but still living,
will carve the rune that opens the gateway
to the underworld.
She will set the Nightshades free."

Dagny closed the book and looked at them. "You can imagine what I thought when I understood what the prophecy was about."

"That you were the one who should set the Nightshades free," Victoria whispered.

"Precisely. And believe me, I tried. I was obsessed by the thought that I was the one who could set them free, that I was the one described in the prophecy. *A woman with silvery scars from the oak. Marked by misdeeds, but still living.* It had to be me. But no matter what I did, the gateway to the underworld would not open for me. I couldn't understand it. I felt the Nightshades were my sisters. We had suffered in the same way, our pain had been hidden and forgotten, and the perpetrators had gone free. I longed for justice. But in the end, I had to admit that it wasn't me. I wasn't the right one." She took a deep breath as if the process of telling them had left her quite exhausted.

"Then what did you do?" Chamomile asked.

"I went away. I lived abroad for many, many years. But now, in the autumn of my life, I was suddenly contacted by the vice principal of Rosenholm. It felt like a sign, and I couldn't say no. There was something I had never managed to settle. It wasn't me, but I have found the right woman. The woman with silvery scars from the oak who will set the Nightshades free. Finally."

A bright beam of light suddenly shone through the window and lit Dagny's face from side on. The headlights of a car that was parking there outside.

"Someone's coming," Kirstine said, looking out. "Four young people, they're dressed in black."

"Let me see," Malou said, putting her face up to the glass. "Shit! It's the Crows."

"H-how did they find us?" Chamomile stammered.

"I don't know, but they can't see us together!"

"Go out to the bathroom and hide, and I'll sort this out," Dagny said calmly.

"But—"

"Come on, Malou!" Chamomile said, pulling at her arm.

They stumbled through the cafe and out to the little bathroom, which was right out the back. They could just fit all of them inside, standing. Kirstine closed the door behind them and locked it. Chamomile wrinkled her nose at the smell of cleaning products mixed with stale urine, her heart thumping. There was no window; they were trapped inside.

"Do you hear something?" she whispered as softly as she could. Kirstine, who was standing with her ear to the door, shook her head.

Chamomile turned to face Malou. "Are you sure you two weren't followed here?"

"Completely sure," Malou whispered.

Victoria put a finger to her lips to signal that they should be quiet. Chamomile squeezed her hands so that her nails pressed sharply into her palms. It felt as if there wasn't enough air for all four of them. *Go away now . . . Please, just go.*

Suddenly, Kirstine shot back from the door as there was a loud knock on it.

"You can come out now. They're gone." Dagny's voice rasped from the other side.

Malou drew her knife, and Kirstine turned the lock. Dagny was standing outside, and she was alone.

"They're gone."

"What did you say to them?" Chamomile asked.

"I said I'd come here for the fries."

"Did they buy it?"

"I think so."

"Shit!" Malou groaned. "The coffee cups! There were five cups."

Dagny lifted her handbag in the air with a little smile. From it, she pulled four cups and put them on the counter. "Young people, these days," she said to the surprised woman at the register as they left the cafe and went out into the twilight.

"Will you help us?" Kirstine asked before Dagny got into the car with Malou.

"Of course," she answered, giving Kirstine's hand a squeeze. "We need to stick together, don't we? And it won't do to wait too long. It seems like those Crows you have on your heels are very keen to get to you."

"I'll be in touch soon," Malou said before pulling the door open. "Look after yourselves."

They stood watching as the car pulled away. It was only once they were back at the cottage that Chamomile's heartbeat settled to normal, but there was one question still bothering her. What on earth had brought the Crows to that little, deserted harbor out in the countryside?

We'll do it on the 22. 7 p.m. by the tree.
D will meet us there

JANUARY 21ST
10:31 P.M.

Kirstine

The wind was cold and driving icy droplets into her cheeks. Kirstine looked out over the harbor and the waves crashing wildly onto the beach. The moon and the stars lit up the sand, so it almost looked like snow.

"Would you please tell me why we're here?" Jakob looked at her, concerned, the wind blowing his hair down over his face. She could see that he was freezing. "Seriously, Kirstine, I'm really scared you're about to tell me something terrible."

Kirstine turned away. She had asked him to come out for a walk with her, but he knew her too well. He had guessed straight away that the reason she wanted to go down to the sea wasn't just to stretch her legs.

"Before I tell you, you have to promise that you won't try to stop me from doing it," she said.

"Doing what?"

"First, you have to promise. That you won't try to stop me or follow me. Otherwise, I'm not telling you."

He raised his hands in a gesture of surrender. "Okay, I promise."

"We met up with Dagny. The woman who helped Malou work out what the Nightshades really are."

"Underworldly beings," Jakob confirmed.

"Dagny knows how to find them. And how to wake them. The Nightshades want revenge for Trine. They want to get rid of Jens."

"That sounds pretty far-fetched. Do you really believe that?" Jakob asked.

"Yup," Kirstine said.

"Okay, then we have to do it. Find them and wake them."

Kirstine shook her head. "Dagny believes *I* am the one who can open the gateway to the underworld. There's an old prophecy. *A woman with silvery scars from the oak.*"

"A prophecy? A gateway to the underworld?" He looked at her, unbelieving. "Why didn't you tell me this before? Do the others know about this?"

"No, just Chamomile, Malou, and Kirstine. We didn't tell the rest of you because we're afraid you'll try and stop us from doing it."

"And is that so weird? Do you realize how dangerous that is if you really find a way into the underworld? There are things that just shouldn't be messed with!"

"We have to," she said.

"Because of the prophecy?" he asked. "Just because there is some old prediction doesn't mean that this is your responsibility, Kirstine."

She turned to look at him. Very carefully, she reached up to his face and brushed the hair away from his brow. The air crackled around them. "It's not just because of the prophecy," she said. "This is what the tree has wanted of me the whole time. That's why the roots grab at me, and the earth opens up under my feet. The tree wants to show me the way to the underworld."

He pulled back. "You're really thinking about doing it."

"Yes."

"Then I'm going with you."

"No," Kirstine said. "Remember what you promised. You mustn't try to stop me or try to follow me. This is my task."

"Kirstine . . . you mustn't do this."

"I intend to go to the underworld, but I also intend to come back," she said, her voice sounding incredibly calm.

"The underworld is not a place people come back from," Jakob said.

"There are some who do," she said. "Odin did."

"Odin is a god!" he blurted out gruffly.

"And . . . and Orpheus." Kirstine could picture the book that had lain on the floor of Sigsten Juuls office. "Orpheus comes back, right?"

"What are you talking about?" Jakob looked at her angrily. "Orpheus and Eurydice is a Greek tragedy, Kirstine. Orpheus goes down to the realm of the dead to find his loved one. He is not allowed to turn to see if she follows him, but he can't help himself. Eurydice turns into a shadow, and he loses her forever!"

His eyes glistened, but the look he gave her was harsh and uncompromising.

"That's not the way this story ends," Kirstine said. "This is not going to be a tragedy."

"I really wish I could believe in that," he said. Then he turned his back on both her and the crashing waves and headed back toward the little cottage.

JANUARY 22ND
4:13 A.M.

Victoria

The white tower stood as a proud landmark at the edge of the world. The sky stretched endlessly past the edge of the cliff. If you were to fall here, the universe would take you for its own and let your body dissolve away into atoms. Leah stood at the edge in her black dress, crying.

Victoria shouted, but she wasn't afraid, because she knew she wasn't alone. Trine was here, too. Trine had come to save her sister. But when Victoria turned toward her, it wasn't her white shadow that stood by her side. It was Jens. Victoria wanted to run, but she couldn't. She remained standing, looking into his cold blue eyes as he looked into hers, and then suddenly, they were somewhere else. A dark and cold place. She realized how scared he was. The fear lay around them both like a damp fog. All at once, everything exploded in a white light. And they woke up.

"Victoria, wake up!"

Victoria looked up in confusion into Kirstine's face. She was worried—no—scared.

"What's happened?"

"It's Beate. She can hardly breathe. Lisa can't help her here, but she says she knows of some people who can."

"What time is it?" Victoria asked, sitting up.

"It's still night. But I don't know about Chamomile . . ."

Victoria stood up from the bed she shared with Kirstine and went into the living room. In a few hours, they would be meeting Dagny out by the tree. Beate lay on the sofa. Her upper body was propped up by several cushions, and it was easy to tell by her rasping breath that she wasn't doing well.

Chamomile was sitting at her side, squeezing her hand. "It's this rotten old cottage and that damp, crappy old church," she said despairingly.

Lisa came in from outside. She had a phone in her hand and was wearing her long, dark red coat. "They're ready for us," she said. "We'll go now, Beate."

"I'm going with you," Chamomile said. She looked over at them. "I need to go."

"Of course," Victoria whispered. "Should we cancel, then?"

"No," Kirstine said, and Victoria was surprised by the conviction in her voice. "No, we'll do it today."

"Chamomile . . ." Beate whispered from the sofa. She gave a tired smile. "You stay here. I'm in good hands. Isn't that right, Lisa?" She sat up and swung her legs off the edge of the sofa. It looked as if that alone had taken a good deal of her strength.

"The best hands," Lisa said. "My old friend is the manager of an infirmary—a kind of hospital for mages," she explained. "We can trust them."

"I'll only be away for a few days," Beate said, leaning on Lisa, who put an arm around her and led her toward the door.

"But, Mom—"

"That's how it has to be, Chamomile. There's nowhere for you to stay there. They only have space for patients, and it's too far for you to go and come back." Beate's words faltered as she started to cough.

"Come on, Beate, we need to go now," Lisa said. "We'll call you, Chamomile, as soon as we get there. You don't need to worry. Your mom will soon be well again."

Victoria sensed it. Like the feeling of wearing some piece of clothing that doesn't fit properly. Lisa was not telling the truth.

"Okay," Chamomile said. "If you think . . ." She put her arm around her mother and, together with Lisa, helped her out into the car.

359

JANUARY 22ND
6:25 A.M.

Kirstine

It felt like doing the opposite of what you should do, of what you knew and of what you wanted to do. Kirstine had a sense that she was going directly into a lion's den, entirely of her own free will. There was a rumbling beneath her feet and a flickering before her eyes, and she had to focus all her strength on uttering the protective rune spells that could control the tangle of roots beginning to wake up deep below them. The scars on her arms started to glisten, and she winced at the burning pain that came with it. As a rule, the scars didn't hurt. But they were hurting now. Jakob's face appeared in her mind's eye. His look of hurt and concern. And his anger that she wouldn't let him go with her.

"Are you okay?" Chamomile looked over at her uneasily, but Kirstine didn't know how to answer.

"Let's just go," Malou said. "We can't be late."

The school was up behind them, and although it was out of sight, it felt as if they could be discovered as long as they were out in the open. Their boots squelched on the boggy ground as they walked. Kirstine felt the forest on her left side. She knew that it lay silent and dark, but for her, it seemed to be burning and sizzling in that cold January night.

"Let's wait for her here," Malou said.

They stood together in silence. Maybe most things had already been said. Eventually, a crooked figure wearing a cloak and a large hood appeared down by the meadow. She made her slow, painstaking way along first the meadow, then the marshland.

"Good morning," she greeted them when she finally reached them.

They all said a polite hello, but the old woman under the hood seemed interested only in Kirstine. "Can I see them?" she asked.

Kirstine pushed up her sleeves. The scars were glowing like embers in the dark, clearer than ever before. They were close now. Dagny examined the scars carefully, Kirstine feeling pain when she pressed her thumbs onto her lower arm.

"Mine are the same," she said. "Come on."

Kirstine couldn't help thinking about how history tended to repeat itself. The last time she had been here was with Thorbjørn and Jakob. Now, the four young women followed in Dagny's footsteps. Her hand reached for the pendants around her neck. The little plough, a symbol for Earth, her branch of magic. And the silver Valkyrie Jakob had given her. She hoped it would give her the strength to do what she had to do. She felt the tears burning at her eyes, and she blinked to hold them back. She hadn't even been able to give him a kiss, and it might be the last time she saw him.

The old woman cursed and thrashed on, casting rune spells around her to keep away the trees' flicking boughs and the thorny branches of bushes, and the more the forest seemed to want to attack them, the more determinedly she fought it back. Then, finally, they were there. They stood, somewhat disheveled, and gathered themselves at the edge of the clearing. Chamomile rubbed at her arm, where a particularly angry sprig of blackberry had scratched her so that she bled.

"The tree knows we are here," Dagny said, looking at the old oak, which pulsated in the darkness with the deep, orange glow of burning hot coals.

"Is it not a different color than usual?" Victoria whispered. "It's usually silvery, isn't it? What does that mean?"

"Maybe it's a good sign," Dagny smiled. "I never thought I would come back to this place. Not even when I said yes to the job did I ever imagine I'd come out here. But now that I'm here, it feels totally right." She shook her head, as if she was amused by her own stupidity. Then she turned to them. "If this works, and the gateway to the underworld reveals itself, I will not go with you. I'm too old for that kind of thing. The journey will be long and hard. There's no knowing what you'll meet down there or how many days it will take you to get free."

"Days?" Chamomile asked.

"They say it took Odin nine dark days to get to Hel, and he had an eight-legged horse to ride."

"But how will we find them?" Malou asked.

"Just keep going down," Dagny said. "And remember: You must not enter the dead girls' hall. It is not for the living."

Kirstine turned to the others. She had prepared what she was going to say. "You don't need to come with me. It's me the tree has marked," she said, and she wished her voice didn't sound so weak. "Ever since we found out about the Nightshades and their hall of the dead, I've been thinking that's where the tree has wanted to take me the whole time. Down under the ground. But it's only me. Not all of you. Let me do this alone."

"No way," Malou said.

362

"We've come through worse things than this," Chamomile said.

"I'm not so sure about that," Victoria said, staring at the tree, its glowing roots writhing around the forest floor like worms. "But, there's no question of us not going with you."

"Then I should tell you all what you've got to do," Dagny said. "If I've read the prophecy correctly, the tree will take you to the land of the shadows when you carve the right rune into its trunk."

"And what is the right rune?" Kirstine asked.

"You know that," Dagny said, smiling.

"No . . . No, I don't."

"Yes, you do."

"No . . . I've never . . . I don't . . ." Kirstine could feel the panic rising in her. Was that all Dagny had to offer her? "Tell me now. What rune is it!"

"I don't know it," Dagny said. "But you do."

"But I'm telling you, I don't! How do I know what the right one is?"

"If you say it's right, then it's right."

"So, it doesn't matter which rune I carve?"

"That's not what I'm saying. It's quite the opposite. Only one rune will open the portal to the shadowlands. But, fortunately, you know which one it is."

"But . . ." Kirstine flung her arms out in frustration. Then she took a deep breath and tried to ignore Dagny's little, wizened face, still smiling up at her. "Okay, give me a minute."

She closed her eyes. Soon, glowing runes began flickering in her inner eye. *Ansuz, the rune of the Gods. Kenaz, the torch rune. Naduz, the rune of need.*

Kirstine focused on what she wanted to achieve. She wanted to get access to another world. To the realm of the dead. Where Odin had also gone, riding his horse, Sleipner.

Her whole body was buzzing. Then, suddenly, one rune stood out way more clearly than all the rest. It grew before her eyes. Dagny was right. She knew which one was the right one. Kirstine opened her eyes. "I'm ready," she said. "Give me the knife."

Malou hurriedly pulled her athame from the sheath in her belt and handed it to her.

"There. And you're sure you've thought it over enough?"

Kirstine nodded and walked away from them into the clearing. The tree's roots suddenly became still, and the branches around them ceased rustling. Without hesitation, she went straight to the tree's trunk, lifted the knife, and made the first cut. Nothing happened. In some way, she had expected the tree to react, but it was completely still and quiet. Kirstine quickly carved the next three strokes into the tree's bark. An *M* gleamed at her in red. *Ehwaz The horse rune.* Connected with Odin's horse, Sleipner. The rune representing the journey between worlds, or the final journey, death. Ehwaz had to be the right symbol.

Kirstine stepped back from the tree. Nothing happened. The roots lay still, and the bare branches neither rustled nor grabbed out at her. Then she noticed how the soil was pushing up and out at the base of the tree as if a mole was clearing the excess earth from its tunnels. A strange, deep rumbling rose up from the growing molehill, and then the pile of earth collapsed into itself, leaving a hole in the middle.

"There we have it," Dagny said, stepping up to the edge of the little hole.

"That's it? The portal to the underworld?" Chamomile asked, doubtfully.

"Yes. Isn't it amazing . . ." Dagny whispered.

"It looks like a hole in the ground," Malou said.

"And that's what it is, too," Dagny said pensively. "So, hurry yourselves before the portal closes. Kirstine, you'd best jump first."

"Jump?"

"Yes, jump. Be my guest!"

Kirstine looked down into the hole. It was only three feet wide, and there was no knowing where it ended. But deep down she heard another deep rumble. "See you down there."

Then she closed her eyes and jumped.

She fell and fell. The sides of the hole scraped her hands until they bled as she tried to protect her face from flicking tree roots and loose rocks that were pulled with her in the fall. She could feel tufts of her hair being pulled out as they caught on branches and roots on the way. At one point, it felt as if she was sliding, as the hole curved and flattened out more, but shortly after, she was falling again. Then she heard a scream. Kirstine opened her eyes wide but could see nothing. Was that her own scream? No, there it was again. The heart-wrenching cry of some creature in pain.

Suddenly, she screamed, too, with pain and surprise as one of her cheeks was scraped raw by the rough sides of the hole. And then she got stuck. The hole narrowed, closing around her so she couldn't go any further. She kicked out with her feet, and she realized they were dangling in the air. There had to be a hollow chamber beneath her that she was nearly in, but the hole closed tighter and tighter around her so she couldn't get free.

"*Perthro*," she whispered. "*Perthro*." But the ground didn't stop closing in on her, pressing her chest so it was becoming hard to breathe. She wanted to scream, but no sound came out. She got soil in her mouth and eyes. "Perthro," she whispered.

It felt as if her bones were screaming in pain. A strange noise whispered around her, like the sound of the sea when it hits the shore. At once, she could see it. The sea of her childhood. The waves, breaking. The pain receded into something that was disconnected from her, and it came as a relief. She gave up fighting it.

All at once, the earth loosened its grip on her, and she fell, landing on a hard, stony surface several feet below. She was alone.

366

JANUARY 22ND
7:41 A.M.

Victoria

"Harh..."

Victoria tugged and heaved at Chamomile's arm until, finally, the earth loosened its grip on her, and she could pull her free. Chamomile took great, sobbing gulps of air, crying and coughing at the same time.

"Chamomile, are you okay? What happened?" Victoria knelt down beside her at the foot of the tree as Malou held onto her.

"We heard you screaming." Malou said.

Chamomile shook her head. "That wasn't me," she gasped, her voice sounding rough and strange. "I couldn't scream. I couldn't get any air. It was the tree... The tree screamed."

"The gateway is gone," Malou said.

"The earth closed in on me. I thought I was going to die," Chamomile sobbed. "But then, suddenly, I was up again."

Dagny looked up into the smoldering tree. "Come on, let's get you away from here."

"But, what about Kirstine?" Victoria whispered as she put her arm around Chamomile and helped her onto her feet.

"She was much farther down than I was," Chamomile cried. "If the earth closed in on her, then..."

"Kirstine was right. She is the one the tree had put its mark on. She is the one the prophecy speaks of," Dagny said. "This is her task. She'll come through it, but she still has a long way ahead of her. There's no reason to stay here and wait."

They continued through the forest, but progress was slow. Dagny seemed exhausted, and Chamomile kept having violent coughing fits. When they came to a little brook at the edge of the forest, they stopped so she could get a chance to rinse her mouth and wash her face and hands in the cold water. Dagny sat down on an overturned tree trunk to rest a while, and Victoria sat beside her.

"May I ask you something?"

"Of course," Dagny said.

"Why didn't you tell anyone about it?" Victoria asked. "About what they did to you?"

"I was ashamed," Dagny said. "Somehow or other, Mr. Fischer convinced me it was my own fault. And who was going to believe me? I'm not proud to say it, but I was also afraid. Who knows what he could have put me and my family through if I had come forward? He was a powerful man back then."

"A classic asshole," Malou said. "The ones who did that to you, they'll pay for it one day."

"You're forgetting how old I am," Dagny said. "They're all long gone now."

"What happened to Mr. Fischer?" Victoria asked.

"Not long after I left, the school got a new principal, and several of the old teachers were given early retirement, including him," Dagny told them. "The school was to be modernized, and there was talk of women's rights and equality. When I didn't find the Nightshades, and I didn't manage to get my revenge, I comforted myself with the thought that the darkest chapter in Rosenholm's history was over and that no more young women would suffer the same fate. I thought that I was the last. But I was wrong, was I not?"

Victoria nodded. "Yes. We know about one girl, in any case, who was killed at the school after your time. Trine. She was murdered in 1989, but she's not a nightshade, just an ordinary spirit. A white shadow."

"Then she wasn't offered up to the tree?" Dagny said.

"No," Victoria replied. "But her body was also never found, and she was never declared dead."

"And that is why she walks again," Dagny nodded. "Maybe her killer didn't know about the ritual and the trees' powers."

"But I'm afraid he does now," Victoria said. "He's planning another murder now, and we need to stop him before he carries out his plan."

"The Nightshades will find him," Dagny said, patting her hand. "Kirstine will set them free, and they'll find him."

Victoria looked at the old woman sitting on the tree trunk with her feet dangling back and forth. Then she looked over at Chamomile, who was still kneeling by the brook. She really hoped that Dagny was right.

"Did you never see anyone from the school again? Not even your boyfriend?" Chamomile asked, standing up. She had stopped coughing and had managed to clean the dirt off herself.

"No, never. There were times I thought of contacting him. But he got a job as a Blood Magic teacher here at the school, and at that time, I couldn't imagine having anything whatsoever to do with Rosenholm ever again. But now, here I am. And he's no longer here. I heard he died this summer. Now, it's too late."

369

Chamomile gave Victoria a look, but neither of them said anything.

"Ah, yes, life is full of missed chances and paths untrodden," Dagny said. "That's how it will always be. But sometimes I feel as if those paths I chose not to take still ended up having the most meaning in my life." She stood up very carefully. "And now I need to get back. I'll keep an eye out for Kirstine appearing down by the tree, but, as I said, it will take some time."

They parted ways with Dagny and stood, watching her go as she and her red pointed hood wobbled doggedly back over the wetland.

"Should we have told her that it's Jens?" Chamomile asked.

"That would only put her in danger as well," Malou said. "I think it's best not to."

Victoria thought about everything Dagny had said. About her shame, about the missed chances. About it being too late for her to confront her attacker. But Dagny herself was still alive. Maybe it was still possible?

"Wait a moment," Victoria said. "There's something I forgot to ask her."

She caught up with her just before she passed through the gate to the meadow.

"What now, my friend?"

"I just wanted . . . May I ask, what was the name of the young man? The one who knocked on your door that night?"

Dagny closed her eyes a moment. "In seventy years, I have never said his name. But, as I've told you my story, I'll do it. His name was Benjamin. Benjamin Brahe."

Any news?

No, no sign of her.

D says we should wait.

Oh—Jens has asked the Crows to keep a close eye on the lighthouse where Leah died. Do you know why?

No, not me. Vic do you have any idea why?

Victoria?!

FEBRUARY 1ˢᵀ
2:38 P.M.

Victoria

"I couldn't resist renting a convertible, even though it's too cold to drive with it down." Victoria's grandma checked the mirror and revved the engine. Her nails were dark red today, as was her lipstick, but she was otherwise dressed in an elegant dark blue suit with a scarf in the same color and black, suede high-heeled ankle boots.

"You're even quieter than usual," her grandma commented. "What's bothering you?"

Victoria shrugged. "There's so much right now."

For example, that her friend was trapped somewhere under the ground, left to her own fate. They hadn't heard any news of her at all. *The first will go into the darkness.* Victoria hadn't imagined that prediction would come true quite so literally. Did that mean that the rest would also quickly come true? She ran through them in her head. *The second must choose between those she loves. The third will make a sacrifice. And the fourth will pass judgment.* Which of the predictions applied to her?

"I miss driving a car," her grandma said. "You should start learning. You'll be eighteen soon."

"I know that. Thanks for driving me."

"Do you know what advice Karen Blixen gave to young women like you?"

"No," Victoria said, looking out onto the highway. Her grandma overtook a Berlingo with two boys in the back seat, and Victoria suddenly felt a lump in her throat as she thought of her brothers.

"To cut their hair and learn to drive a car. It changes your whole existence. According to her." Victoria's grandma smiled without looking up from the road. "You already have the short hair, now you just need the car."

Victoria leaned her head back. The heavy scent of her grandma's perfume was giving her a headache, and she felt a little bit car sick.

"Why don't you nap now? I'll tell you when we get there," her grandma said.

"I'm just resting my eyes a little," Victoria mumbled.

It was dark and cold around her. A damp, earthy smell clung to her nostrils, and she heard the sound of bubbling water far in the distance. Then Victoria heard a weak whisper. Out of the darkness came a chalk white horse, and upon it sat Death . . .

"Victoria?"

She gave a start when her grandma patted her on the thigh. "We're coming to the bridge," she said. "I'll need your help to find the way. I've never been there before."

Victoria straightened up in her seat. "We need to go over the first part," she mumbled as she tried to shake off the unpleasant feeling the dream left behind in her body. She could see the huge pylons rising up from the sea out to the right. "When we get to Sprogø, then we need to turn off."

"I didn't know you could do that," her grandma said.

"You can if you have permission," Victoria said. "But not otherwise."

"And this is where you were, that time . . ."

"Yes," Victoria said. She had never imagined she would come back.

Her grandma paid, and they continued over the high bridge. The frothy white peaks on the waves were bright in the sharp January sun.

"This is where you need to turn off." Victoria pointed, and her grandma put on her blinker and turned off the main road that would take them across the low bridge to Funen. They puttered slowly down toward a barrier blocking the road.

"There's a button to press here." Her grandma rolled the window down beside the contraption.

"Hello!" a scratchy voice came through the speaker system.

"It's Victoria and her grandmother. We have an appointment with Lisa," she said, and the barrier lifted. They crawled up the avenue toward some yellow-colored buildings.

"We'll just park here," her grandma said, swinging the car into the courtyard. When they got out, they heard the rushing noise of traffic on the Great Belt Bridge competing with the swoosh of the waves below. "It's lovely here," her grandma said, looking around her in the blustery wind. "Beautiful nature. How long did you stay here for?"

"One month," Victoria said.

"Yeah, a broken heart is no picnic," her grandma said. "You'll need to get a bit more thick-skinned when it comes to love."

Victoria didn't answer. It was after the thing with Louis. She had been so miserable her parents didn't know what to do with her. It was the spring before she was due to start at Rosenholm, and eventually they'd gotten in touch with the school. It was Lisa who had suggested it. The infirmary on Sprogø.

They walked up to the main building.

"Did you know they used to threaten little girls with this place when I was a child?" her grandma said, fixing her hair now that they'd come in out of the wind. "Watch yourself, or you'll be sent to Sprogø, people would say."

"Why?" asked Victoria.

"They took in young women here, who were considered 'morally corrupt,'" her grandma said, gramacing.

Victoria had heard of how the place had been some kind of institution before it became hospital for mages. "What does that mean? 'Morally corrupt'?" she asked.

"Mostly, it meant the women were sexually active but unmarried. It was only in the sixties that the place was shut down. It's not such a long time ago that you ran the risk of being locked up just for having sex! A pure witch-hunt. There was no bridge back then, so you were stuck here. Lucky for someone like me, the girls who ended up here were never from wealthy families."

They continued down a hall that opened up into a large, bright room with windows along the side, looking out over the sea. At one end of the room, Lisa was standing talking to an elderly woman dressed all in white. Victoria vaguely remembered having seen her before.

"Ah, there you are." Lisa turned to them, the corners of her eyes crinkled with laughter lines.

"Thanks for letting us come," Victoria said.

"Not at all," said Lisa, greeting her by squeezing her hands between her own. "But I must admit, I was surprised you didn't bring Chamomile with you."

"There's something I'd like to talk to you about alone," Victoria said.

"Do you want to go in and see Beate first? I've told her you're coming, but I think she might be sleeping just now."

Her grandma sat down on a moss-green sofa. "I'll wait here."

"Vibeke can bring you something to eat," Lisa said. "We've got some lovely soup for lunch."

She showed Victoria down to the ward. This wasn't where she had stayed herself; her room had been in one of the annex buildings. Still, she recognized the quiet, the bright light and the white-clad healers who quietly did their rounds of the patients.

"She's in here." Lisa put a finger to her lips and carefully opened the door. Beate was lying on the bed, her eyes closed. Her hair was spread out in a fan shape around her face. It was almost completely gray, her cheeks looked hollow, and her skin seemed yellow. She looked terribly old. Victoria tried to find her energy and felt it fluttering, weakly, like a butterfly in the wind.

"She's dying," she whispered.

"Not right now," Lisa said. "The healers have stabilized her condition. She's not having difficulty breathing anymore, but she is very weak. I think you might have some idea of why?"

Victoria lifted her eyes from Beate in the white bed and found Lisa's dark eyes staring into her own. She nodded.

"The victory stone," she whispered. "It was Beate's stone. When Jens stole it from Chamomile, at first, I was afraid that it would drain her of her energy. But the stone had never really bonded with Chamomile. In fact, it has always been Beate's stone."

Lisa nodded gravely. "Does Chamomile know?"

"No. It's as if she doesn't want to see how ill Beate is."

"And Beate doesn't want to tell her," Lisa said quietly.

"I haven't said anything because I was sure I was right to be worried. And she's got so much to deal with already." Victoria said.

"Some people say that life only serves up the challenges you are able to tackle," Lisa said.

"Do you believe that?" Victoria asked.

"No, unfortunately. We need to cope as best we can. And not all stories end well in this world, I'm afraid."

"What about this one? How does it end?"

"They can keep her free of pain and help her breathe. But the only thing that can save her is having her stone back again. As long as it is in Jens's hands, it will keep draining her of all her strength."

"Is there nothing that can be done?"

Lisa looked at her sadly. "I've spoken to Ragnhild, the director here. She is an old friend of mine. Ragnhild said that an amulet could perhaps help Beate. An amulet made especially for her. It wouldn't replace her bond to the victory stone, but it would preserve her strength and give us a little time. Ragnhild wanted to talk to the other healers, but none of them have much knowledge of amulets. It's a kind of magic that isn't really used anymore. Ancient magic."

"We can ask my grandma," Victoria said. "She's a bit of an expert on amulets. She collects them. Come on."

Victoria left the ward, but when she got to the waiting room, her grandma wasn't there. Maybe she had gone for a walk. She took out her phone to call her but discovered she had a few messages from Malou and Chamomile. She tapped the icon. Victoria froze.

"What's wrong? Has something happened?" Lisa put her hand gently on her arm.

"I . . ." Victoria's voice stuck in her throat. She cleared it. "Have you ever heard anything about some people being able to see another person's dreams?"

Lisa looked at her. "Some spirit mages are said to be able to read minds," she said. "Why not dreams as well? But I would think it would require some kind of special connection. Either a very close, loving relationship or something where the boundaries between two people have been broken down by force."

By force . . . Victoria remembered Jens's words, which she had heard inside her mind, and the feeling that he had violated her somehow. *I have the power to harm you, Victoria. Can you feel it? And not only you but everyone you care about and everyone you tell your lies to. Do you hear me?*

"We need to get hold of Malou," she said. "And it's urgent!"

378

FEBRUARY 2ND
3:00 P.M.

Malou

Malou looked at the holiday cottage. The woodwork needed a lick of paint, and the trees and shrubs on its small grounds had grown big and a bit wild. It certainly wasn't luxurious, but on the other hand, it was tucked away out of view of the main road.

"Hi, Malou, good to see you," Chamomile said, giving her a quick hug when she found her there in the little kitchen. Malou was relieved everything felt more normal between them now. But she was scared of what Chamomile would think of her once she'd revealed her reason for being there.

"I've just made tea—the last of my summer blend. Do you want some?"

Malou nodded and took a seat on a kitchen chair that wobbled a little beneath her.

"Any news?" she asked when she brought the tea over.

"Nope. I was out at the tree this morning. There's nothing to see. Dagny says we have to wait and be patient. She seems quite convinced it'll all go okay."

Chamomile nodded. "It's hard, isn't it? Just waiting."

Malou agreed, and she herself didn't share Dagny's confidence in any way but decided to let that go. There was something else she had come to convince Chamomile of, and that was going to be even harder.

She blew on her tea, looking around her. Through the living room of the stuffy house, she could see Benjamin standing, leaning over a sports bag. He lifted a T-shirt out of it and gave it a sniff before pulling off his sweater, throwing it in a corner, and then putting on the T-shirt instead.

"You all don't have much privacy here, do you?" she muttered. "Has Victoria told him?"

"No," Chamomile said. "She says she's waiting for the right time, but I think she's just dragging her heels.

"Should I tell him?" Malou asked. "I don't have any problem telling Mr. Up-Himself about his family's dark past."

"Malou!" Chamomile chided.

"Yeah, yeah, I won't go there. Victoria can have the job of dealing with the little wolf. Listen, Chamomile—"

They heard the noise of a car and looked out the kitchen window. Thorbjørn's old jalopy rolled down the little driveway, and Jakob stepped out. Shortly after, the kitchen door opened. Jakob stopped when he saw her. He was pale and thin and looked like someone who hadn't slept in a week. He raised his eyebrows in a question, but Malou just shook her head.

"He's been out looking for her again," Chamomile said. "He drives around, night and day. He says he can sense her . . ." She gave Malou a pleading look. "I'm scared he's actually starting to lose it. Not that I blame him."

"Chamomile, I need to tell you something."

"On the other hand, Lisa says my mom is doing better," Chamomile said, ignoring her comment. "But she's still tired, so they think I should wait a little before visiting her. Poor Mom."

380

Malou sought out her eyes. "Chamomile, listen to me, now. You need to move," she said softly. "You can't stay here."

"But where will we go to? We've just gotten settled here . . ."

"Yeah . . . That's just it." Malou looked at her. Her big, blue eyes stared back. This felt a bit like canceling a six-year-old's birthday party. But there was nothing else to do.

"I think the others should stay here," she said. "But you need to go somewhere else. A place only I know about. Nobody else."

"What?" Chamomile said. "Why?"

"Do you remember what Victoria told us about after Jens stopped her making her speech at her parents' place?"

"Yeah. She could see all his thoughts."

"And not only that. Victoria says the barrier between them sort of disappeared. And now she thinks she is seeing his dreams."

"But . . . how?"

"He's there, she says. He's there, when she dreams. The other night, she dreamed about the lighthouse where Leah died. The day after, Jens sent the Crows out there. And they were at the harbor. Victoria can't remember if she dreamed about the harbor, but we can't take any chances. Victoria can't know where you are. The fewer people who know it, the better. I can come and look in on you and bring food and things."

"Seriously, I am not doing that!" The big blue eyes brimmed over with tears, and Malou cursed herself. She'd have much rather had a shouting match.

"You have to," she said.

"When?" she whispered.

"Now," Malou said. "I'll help you pack, and then let's get going. We'll make a cozy little den for you in this new place. It'll all be okay."

Chamomile gave her a deathly stare, and Malou caved. "Okay," she said, "it'll be completely crappy, I know. But it's just temporary. You're strong. I know you can do this."

Chamomile looked down at her hands. "We all need to be strong. Think about Kirstine. I can also do this."

"Exactly!" Malou said. "Come on, let's get your stuff."

One hour later, they crept out while the others were making the evening meal.

"I wish I could've talked with Molly first," Chamomile said, looking back at the cottage.

"The fewer people who know, the better," Malou repeated.

"She's really been a good friend to me," Chamomile said.

"We're going this way," Malou said.

The bus didn't leave for another hour, and they decided to walk farther along the road, rather than standing still and freezing. January's darkness hung over the landscape, and it was getting frosty. They were freezing cold when they finally rested at a bus stop until one came by and picked them up.

Nobody else was on it, but still, they cozied together on one seat.

"It's almost like the old days, isn't it?" Chamomile said, and Malou had to turn her face away so Chamomile wouldn't see the tears welling in her eyes.

"It's quite a long way. You can take a nap, if you like," Malou said.

Neither of them spoke again as they continued along dark roads and through narrow, lit villages where people in thick winter coats hopped on and off in silence.

"Tell me, how it's going at school?" Chamomile said as they were finally nearing their stop.

382

"It's . . . frightening," Malou said. "A handful of students decided to leave school, but most seem to be quite convinced that the Movement is the right path."

"What about Louis?"

"I don't know . . . We don't see each other much at the moment."

"But you still love him?"

"Chamomile . . . "

"It's okay."

"I wish it wasn't like this," Malou said, meaning it. "It will never work with me and Louis."

"I'm sorry to hear that."

"Why?"

"Because I care about you, you idiot. I don't wish for you to be alone and unhappy. I mean, you wouldn't want that for me?"

Malou looked at her. She was pale, and her eyes reddened. She looked vulnerable and almost transparent. *Better alone and unhappy but alive.* "Of course not," she said, pressing the stop button. "Look, we're here. Do you remember this place?"

Chamomile looked at her, horrified. "Malou, you can't be serious."

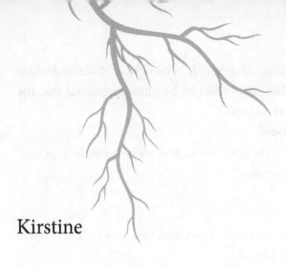

Kirstine

Kirstine felt her way along the rock face. The path she was following went downward but was no longer so steep she needed to crawl. She had rolled up her sleeves, and the scars on her arms shone with a cold, silvery glow. It was the only source of light she had and only stretched a few inches in front of her. In the beginning, she had tried using the Kenaz rune to create some light and warmth, but the rune's magic weakened her. In the underworld, there was no help at hand.

Kirstine carefully tested the ground with one foot before taking a step. Loose stones threatened to send her sliding at any time, and in some places, the path had either collapsed or was so narrow she could easily slip off the edge. Kirstine didn't know how far she would fall if she lost her footing, but by the sound of the stones that rattled down the steep slope, she knew it'd be better for her health if she didn't have to find out.

She heard a noise farther behind her on the path and turned to stare into the darkness. Maybe it was just a bat. She sometimes heard them out flying at night. Was it nighttime now? Was that why? She listened again but heard nothing more. In the general silence, even the tiniest noises startled her. A falling stone, a drop of water trickling down the lime walls, the rush of an underground stream in the distance, a bat fluttering by. The quiet was full of sounds that frightened her.

Her groping hands came to a stop when she felt water. A narrow stream of cold water ran down the rock face. Kirstine placed her mouth against the wet stone and drank. It had been a long time since she found water, but she felt neither hungry nor thirsty. There was no notion of day or night, and time had disappeared. She had no clear idea of how long she had been there. A sluggish numbness had taken over her brain, and she was surprised by how comforting it was. There was nothing to eat here, so she didn't need to think about whether she was hungry. There was no heat and no light, but she didn't feel cold. She had no map, so there was no point in wondering if she was going the right way. She just had to keep going. The only thing that actually bothered her were noises in the darkness. There was a rustling sound again.

The path began to tilt steeper downward, and the slope on her right vanished and was replaced by a solid rock wall. Now, she was inside some kind of tunnel. At first, it was nice that the steep edge was gone, and she didn't have to worry the whole time about slipping down it if the path suddenly narrowed. She could let herself walk a little faster. She couldn't maintain that pace for long, though, as the tunnel became so low she had to bend over to avoid bumping her head, and a terrible smell rose up from below. Kirstine walked but was thinking about getting down on all fours to crawl when it happened. Her left foot slipped on some loose pebbles, and she fell. She grabbed at the walls, but the tunnel descended very steeply now. She slid farther, unable to stop. She yelped as her shoulder hit a large rock sticking sharply from the wall before she tumbled further. Then she lay still. The tunnel had narrowed so much that she could touch the ceiling if she just raised her arm above her, even though she was lying down. The smell was much stronger down here, and it almost felt like she was choking on it.

Kirstine felt at the ground, which was damp and sticky, and then she heard the first of the flapping. She closed her eyes. Her rather inelegant entrance had disturbed them: the bats. The tunnel must lead into a larger cave, which was surely home to thousands of bats, who now all wanted out at the same time.

Kirstine covered her face with her arms as a huge cloud of bats flew, shrieking and hissing over her in the low tunnel. She could feel how their wings flapped against her back and how they got tangled into her hair and pulled clumps of it out as they panicked and flew on. She screamed, but her scream was swallowed up by the noise of the bats, who kept coming and coming. Finally, it grew still.

She tried to stand up, but her left foot buckled and a sharp pain shot up her leg when she tried to put her weight on it. Slowly, she crawled out of the tunnel and sat up against the rock face in the cave while she inspected her foot. Her ankle was already badly swollen. Kirstine leaned her head back and cried.

FEBRUARY 3ʳᴰ
11:35 A.M.

Victoria

Victoria watched as Benjamin paced restlessly back and forth over the creaky floor of the little cottage. "I didn't know if I should tell you or not. Maybe it was dumb to, but that's what I decided. Because I'm going to have to be away for a while—"

"Yup, it's him I'm named after," he interrupted her. "Benjamin Brahe! My dad's dad. A proud and honorable gentleman. Also, a violent criminal and psychopath. The only good thing you could say about him is that he didn't live to be very old."

"Did you know?" Victoria asked.

"No, my grandad didn't take the time to tell me about the crimes he committed in his youth, but I saw how he treated his closest family so, no, it's no great surprise to me that he was capable of that."

"I'm sorry, Benjamin."

"Can you see now what I'm up against? No matter what I do, I can't ever get free. I can renounce my inheritance—the money, the houses, the whole goddam thing—but the shame and the victims' tears, I inherit them whatever I do. Do you know that I look a lot like him? Like two peas in a pod, people say. How do you think it feels to meet people who knew my granddad and see them suddenly turn chalk white and almost faint with shock because they think I'm his ghost? I even have the man's name!"

"But Benjamin, you're not him. You're completely different. He was a blood mage, and you are Growth. You're not one and the same."

"You're wrong," he snapped. "We're also alike in that respect."

"What do you mean?"

"I mean that . . . that I'm a blood mage. Or I was. That was where my abilities lay. That was what the tree told me."

Victoria could feel his pain and his shame. He was telling the truth. "What happened?"

"I refused. I didn't want it. I made a fuss. I cried and threatened all kinds of drama. The teachers didn't know what to do. Zlavko mocked me and said I was weak. Birgit, who was principal back then, must have seen me as an exciting experiment: Is it possible to change or redirect a mage's abilities? As you know, there was another special student in that year, Vitus, who had abilities in all branches of magic. And Birgit decided that she would do the experiment. She would take care of Vitus herself, and Lisa agreed to try and see if she could help get my abilities in Growth to flourish, as she so nicely put it."

Victoria nodded. She remembered what Lisa had said about Benjamin having a difficult first year at school. That he had had a lot to struggle against.

"And it worked," she said.

"Well, Lisa took a lot of time training with me. My abilities in blood magic just got channeled elsewhere. Soon, I discovered that I could change . . ."

"You became a shapeshifter."

"Yes," Benjamin said. "They call it hybrid abilities, when you have more than one branch of magic, and as a rule, shapeshifters always do. Birgit found it all very exciting. Yeah, and you know how it turned out with Vitus."

"Yes, with Vitus. But not with you. Because you're different. You chose a different path. You are not your grandfather."

"No, but I carry his guilt with me. And that is why I can't deviate at all, Victoria. I feel like the whole time I'm walking along the edge of an abyss, and if I falter, I'll fall down into darkness."

"And you're afraid that I'm going to drag you down into the darkness?" She tried to keep her voice steady. "Benjamin, I can walk with you! I can help you not to fall!"

"Can you? And what if you were faced with choosing between us or your parents? What would you choose then? It's not only in my family that these things went on."

Victoria stood up. "What do you mean?"

"When are you going to acknowledge it? Your parents belong to dark magic—they forced you to have sex when you turned fifteen as part of some ritual. It's about time you woke up and admitted how sick they are."

"They didn't force me. I agreed to it," she said. "I could have said no."

"Could you? Why didn't you, then? Why didn't you say no?"

"I was fifteen. I was in love. You shouldn't be trying to shame me for it, Benjamin. I won't take that, not from you!"

"I'm sorry, Victoria, but this is exactly the reason we can't be together. In any case, not while you refuse to distance yourself from the things that have gone on, and still go on, in my family—as well as in yours!" He snarled at her, and suddenly she could see the animal side of him.

"Get out," she said.

He turned and stormed off. The door slammed behind him with a bang.

Victoria hugged herself tight. She suddenly felt chilled to her core, and Benjamin's words hadn't made things any better.

She took a deep breath. He had used almost the same words as her grandma that time she had read all of their fortunes. Victoria pulled the tarot cards out of her bag. The illustration on the front of the lovers was neither idyllic nor romantic. It showed a woman and a man. They were both naked and standing apart. Above them, an angel hovered, and they were separated by ominous thunderclouds. A storm was on its way. Victoria was no longer in any doubt. This was her card. *The second must choose between those she loves.*

Maybe it would soon be time for her to go home.

My grandma can't make that kind of amulet. She only collects them

Doesn't she have one we could use?

No, it has to be made especially for Beate

Maybe I know someone who can make one

And Vic? Chamomile CAN'T know about this. She needs to stay where she is, in hiding.

Okay

FEBRUARY 7ᵀᴴ
5:15 P.M.

Malou

Malou looked around Ivalo's room. She lived simply, perhaps even a little austerely. There was nothing on the walls, nothing was set out on the shelves other than a few books, and there were no vases or trinkets on the windowsill. Nothing but an armchair, a dining table, and two chairs. It struck her as the way you might live if you weren't counting on being alive especially long.

"How did you actually get the job as teacher here?" Malou asked.

"Zlavko asked me," Ivalo said. She stood in her little kitchenette making coffee.

"One or two spoons?" she asked, pointing to the jar of instant.

"Two, please," Malou answered. "Did you know Zlavko before?" For some reason, she had assumed Jens had been the one responsible for hiring the new teachers.

"Yes," Ivalo said. "I got to know him a few years back. He was living in Greenland for a time. I hadn't seen him since, but in the summer, he called me and asked if I'd like to teach at Rosenholm. And I said yes."

"Why?" Ivalo wasn't a typical teacher, and Malou was genuinely curious.

"I owed him a favor." She put one of the coffee cups on the table before Malou. "He helped me once."

"With what?"

"To get away from someone who was bothering me," Ivalo said, sitting down in the seat opposite without looking away.

Malou nodded slowly. "And now Zlavko has sent for you so you can help *him* get rid of someone?"

"Something like that," Ivalo answered.

Zlavko had hedged his bets, Malou realized. His plan that she would overpower Jens was only one of his possible strategies. Ivalo was another. "Tell me what he's planning."

"I don't know," she said. "I only know he's not ready yet."

"But what do you suspect?"

Ivalo looked at her without blinking. "I believe he is gathering strength. As you know, you blood mages can withstand a great deal. And there are ways you can make yourselves even stronger. My guess is that Zlavko is preparing himself for battle. He hasn't told me about it, and I don't ask either. I'm indebted to him, but it's not my battle. When the time is right, he'll tell me what I have to do, and I'll do it. And then we'll be done."

"And he hasn't mentioned Chamomile? The red-haired girl we saw . . . ?" Malou suddenly felt the urge to lower her gaze. They had never talked about what happened when they performed the ritual.

"No, he hasn't," Ivalo said. "But I do dream about her at night."

Malou nodded. "It's because of her that I'm here," she said. "Or her mother, actually. She used to own a victory stone, but it was stolen from her. And now—"

"Now it is sucking her inua out of her," Ivalo said. "She'll end up like an empty shell without a soul if she doesn't die first."

Malou bit down on her lip at Ivalo's harsh words. She nodded. "The healers at the hospital she's at think a special amulet could help. Until we can get her victory stone back."

"That might give her a little more time, perhaps," Ivalo said. "And now you'd like me to make an amulet for her?"

"Can you?"

"I should think so. But I'll need a lock of her hair." Ivalo stood up from the table and pulled out one of the drawers behind her. From it, she took out a white bone the same length as the flat of her hand, and she placed it on the table between them. "This is from a bowhead whale. It's a mammal that lives for a very long time. We're not sure even how long. Two hundred years, maybe more. I'll carve the amulet from bowhead whale bones, so it'll hopefully grant your friend's mother something of its inua and life force."

"Like a tupilak?" Malou had seen those before, Greenlandic figures cut from bone.

"No," Ivalo said, taking out a tool to carve the bone with. "A tupilak is an animal created through witchcraft, not a figure you can have for decoration. Those ones you're thinking of are made by the Inuit for Danish people to show what a tupilak looks like. More like a kind of souvenir."

"A tupilak is an animal, then?"

"Yes, a magical creature. Created to kill an enemy. Made from the bones of animals and people. Preferably infants."

"What? You're supposed to kill a child to make them?"

"That wasn't necessary. Life was hard; it wasn't unusual for children to die as infants back then," Ivalo said without looking up from the piece of bone she had sawed off and was now cleaning.

"And then it becomes an animal?"

394

"No. To bring the tupilak to life, you had to sing magical songs to it and allow it to drain one's strength so that it grew and became big and strong. Afterward, it could be released. But a tupilak is dangerous. Also for the creator. If it doesn't succeed in killing the enemy, it will turn back and kill its creator instead."

Malou shook her head. "That sounds so messed up."

"Now, that's as much as I can do," she said, ignoring Malou's comment. "Get me a lock of the woman's hair, and I'll finish off the amulet for her."

"Thanks," Malou said. She had a feeling that it was a little too private a matter to ask about, but she couldn't help herself. "Have you ever tried to make that kind of tupilak?"

"No," she answered. "I thought about it back then. But then I found a different solution to my problem."

Malou nodded. She had a strong feeling that solution had to do with the favor Zlavko had done for Ivalo. And which he now expected her to repay.

"I'll come over once I've got the hair," she said. Ivalo didn't look up as she let herself out.

395

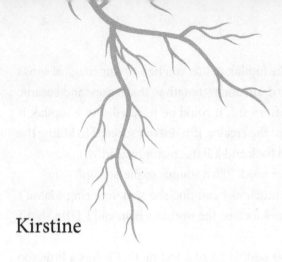

Kirstine

Mom?

She got a fright and opened her eyes. She had heard something. A whisper. Kirstine listened, her eyes wide but unseeing in the darkness. Nothing. Only stillness and the faint sound of water flowing far in the distance. A shiver ran up through her body, causing her to tremble. She was exhausted, cold, and bruised, and the last thing she ought to do was allow herself to sleep. She could sleep right into her own death.

Kirstine felt her ankle tentatively. It was still very swollen but a little less tender than before. At first, she'd hardly been able to put weight on it, but now it felt better.

She got to her feet slowly and continued down the narrow path, the one she had followed all along that took her downward. The sound of water grew clearer as the path also narrowed. She felt her way carefully along the damp rock face, finding her way forward with her feet. Even with her sleeves rolled right up, the light from her scars couldn't penetrate the deep darkness in front of her, which seemed even more immense than it had until now.

"Ouch!" Kirstine bashed her foot on a rock. No, it wasn't a rock, she realized, but a wall. That explained the impenetrable darkness.

The path simply ended here, with nothing more than a rough rock face. Kirstine felt over it with her hands. It stretched right out to the edge. She couldn't get any farther.

Kirstine could feel how tired she was. The only thing she felt like doing was sleeping. Maybe she should just do that. Lie down to sleep here, never to wake again. Suddenly, that didn't seem such a bad thing. A long, dreamless sleep with no pain.

"Maybe I've been following the wrong path the entire time," she whispered. She thought of Jakob as she gripped her little Valkyrie. She wished he were here now. He would have said something encouraging to her. Helped her to find a solution. Her eyes filled with tears. It couldn't end this way. *Damn it!*

"Argh!" she screamed out in frustration, and the scream echoed deep below. It sounded almost as if someone was answering her, and Kirstine kicked out at the air with her good foot. She knocked a stone, sending it over the edge of the path, hitting the rock face and then bouncing on. Way below her she heard a little splash. Maybe an underground stream.

She thought of the stories she knew about the underworld. Wasn't there something about a river? Yes, there was. Odin rode on Sleipner to Hel's Hall in Nilfheim to waken a dead seeress. First, though, he had to cross the Gjöll bridge over a river. Hades, the Greek realm of the dead, also had a river. Styx, it was called. Kirstine frowned. The more she thought about it, the more certain she was that she needed to get down to that water. Judging by the sound of the falling stone, the cliff was fairly sheer. But she couldn't stay here. And she wasn't even sure she had the strength to go back all the way she'd just come.

Her legs were shaking as she carefully swung them out over the edge. She felt with her feet for a hold she could press her toes into.

Only once she was standing fairly solidly did she then attempt to lift one hand from the edge. She fumbled in the dark for something to grab onto.

It was hard to say how long she clung to that steep surface. Time stopped, and there was only the next bit of rock to grip onto and the next little jutting edge to rest her foot on.

Kirstine scraped her fingertips until they bled. Her ankle ached, and both her arms and legs shook with exhaustion. The sound of the water was much clearer now, but Kirstine could also hear some other noises. Rustling, rattling noises in the dark. It didn't sound like bats. A long time had passed since she'd stumbled into them, but there could be other animals here, deeper down. She let go of the rock she had her right hand on, sought out a new spot, and took hold. Right then, her left foot slipped. She fell.

Her scream rang out all around her but stopped short as the air was knocked clear of her lungs. She lay on her back, gasping for breath. At first, it didn't even hurt. But then the pain rushed over her. It was her right leg. Kirstine sobbed in pain and despair. She felt carefully with her fingertips and felt as they got wet with warm blood. Her trousers were ripped, and a wave of nausea rose up as she felt how her shinbone stuck out through the skin. Her head spun, and everything turned to black.

Mom?
Are you coming for us now?

Malou, I'm being totally serious.
If you don't tell me where she is, then
I'm coming to force it out of you.
I'll find you at school or wherever you are.
I'll blow your cover if I have to!!!

I care about her just as much as you do

Maybe even more

Check in the old factory building.
By the empty church.
But if anyone finds out

Thanks!

FEBRUARY 10ᵀᴴ
4:12 P.M.

Chamomile

Chamomile woke up at the sound of a pigeon taking off someplace in the abandoned factory hall. The sound of the bird's wings clapping together in the air was like a gunshot. Chamomile lay still, breathing deeply into her belly until her heart stopped racing. She looked out of the old train wagon that stood lonely and deserted inside the unused plant. She actually needed to pee, but it was so cold she didn't want to crawl out of her sleeping bag. She should have lit a fire. She should have eaten something. Read a book. But she'd spent the greater part of her time in the sleeping bag, missing her mother. Or thinking about Kirstine, deep under the earth. Or about Molly, who didn't know where she was. Or Malou, who was risking her life by staying at Rosenholm. Or Victoria, whose dreams had been infiltrated by Jens.

"Chamomile, are you here?"

Chamomile sat up with a start at the sound of a voice echoing around the factory hall. Her heart was in her mouth.

"It's me. Molly."

"Molly? I'm here! Inside the train wagon!" She listened as footsteps pattered over the concrete floor between shunting trucks and pieces of clapped-out machinery.

"Whoa, is this where you're living? Chamomile, really . . . ?" Molly hopped into the wagon. She had her huge rucksack on her back, packed with a sleeping bag, sleeping mat, and the whole works.

"Are you moving in?" Chamomile asked, hugging Molly close so that she squeezed the breath right out of her.

"Yes, that's what I reckon," Molly said when Chamomile finally let her go. "Unless you'd rather stay here on your own?"

"Seriously, I'm no good at being alone. I'm just lying here feeling sorry for myself the whole time."

"Well, it's not especially lovely here," Molly said, looking around. "There has to be a better place to bed down. Have you tried the other buildings?"

Chamomile shook her head. "No, I've actually only been here," she said, feeling a little silly that she hadn't even pulled herself together to do that much.

"We can do that tomorrow," Molly said. "I brought a stove so we can boil water. Do you want a cup of tea?"

"I always want a cup of tea," Chamomile said, smiling.

Her heart ached with gratitude.

Molly rattled on about what had been happening back at the cottage as she put water on to boil, served up some muesli bars, lit Chamomile's lantern, and rolled out her sleeping mat and bag beside hers. Meanwhile, Chamomile got it together enough to go for a bathroom visit.

"How did you know where I was?" Chamomile asked when she came back, and Molly passed over her tea.

"Malou told me."

"Malou?"

"Yes. She asked if I would come and take care of you for a while."

401

"Did she? It doesn't seem like her to be so . . . well, I don't know . . ."

"Thoughtful?" Molly suggested as she wriggled into her sleeping bag.

"Yes, I guess."

"No, that's not really her style. Maybe that's why she asked me to. Because she knows you deserve a little looking after, even if she can't give you that herself."

Chamomile studied Molly's face in the flickering light of the lantern. The freckles had all but faded from her pale wintertime face, but when you knew you were there, you could still sense them.

"I like freckles," Chamomile said.

"What?" Molly said, raising her eyebrows. Then she smiled. Her green-brown eyes seemed to be sprinkled with gold.

Chamomile dropped her eyes again to look at her own hands, cupping her tea. On one wrist, she wore the bracelet Molly had made her, turquoise with a blue pearl. *Truth and healing.*

"There's something I'd like to tell you," Chamomile said, turning her mug in her hands.

"Yeah?"

"At one point, I was in love with Malou. She knows about it, but it couldn't ever come to anything. She . . . She's in love with someone else."

"Okay."

Chamomile waited, but Molly said nothing more. "Okay, that's it?" she asked.

The dimple appeared on Molly's left cheek. "Well, I'm glad you wanted to tell me, but . . . I kind of guessed that already," she said.

"Did you?"

402

Molly nodded. Now there were two dimples. "It really wasn't very hard, to be honest."

"All right. Maybe I'm just not the mysterious, secretive type," Chamomile said with a little smile.

"I don't know about that," Molly said. "I've got the feeling you have a few secrets I haven't heard about yet."

"Maybe. In any case, I'd like to just say that I don't feel like that anymore. About Malou."

"Good," Molly said.

"You think that's good?"

"Yes, I do. But you must have suspected that, too, right?"

"I wasn't sure . . . I thought you mostly dated boys. You were really into that Frédéric?"

"He's a really sweet guy," Molly said, smiling broadly now. "But I'm not into him anymore. Maybe I'm not too bothered about the whole boy-girl thing. It's more important to me that the person is nice."

Chamomile laughed and put down her cup. "Am I nice?"

"Yes," Molly said. "You're one of the nicest people I know."

She put her hand in Chamomile's lap with her palm facing upward. Chamomile slowly ran her fingers over it, tracing along the lines on her palm, and then wove her fingers in between Molly's. Her nails were short, with chipped yellow polish. Chamomile looked up. Molly's eyes were closed, and a faint smile played on her narrow lips. Chamomile felt her heart thumping. Then she leaned in toward Molly. She smelled of rosehips, cardamom, and the sea breeze. When Chamomile kissed her, she parted her lips slightly. Her tongue was warm, and Chamomile's belly was all butterflies.

FEBRUARY 14TH
8:00 P.M.

Malou

Malou stepped into the Great Gall. It was lit only by candles, which stood in two rows alongside the middle aisle, looking like a bizarre kind of runway. She walked toward the six people dressed in black who stood in a circle at the other end of the room. Elias, Louis, Amalie, Albert, Iris, Zlavko, and Jens.

"Welcome, Malou," Jens said, making space for her in the circle. "Now that we are all here, we can get started. You, who are gathered here, are my chosen ones. Malou, you are the newest member of the inner circle, and from now on, you'll be invited to these meetings, as well as acting as my bodyguard."

Malou bowed her head respectfully.

"I know that you, with your ambitions and strength of will, can achieve your goal," Jens said. "Now, I need only hear where your loyalties lie."

"My loyalty is to the Movement," Malou said, just as Zlavko had instructed her to. "I want to serve the cause of the mages."

Jens put his hand on her shoulder. She lifted her face and looked him in the eyes. This was the moment she had prepared herself for. Zlavko had said she should be as honest as possible. That she should fill her head with truth so that Jens couldn't have any suspicions at all. Malou returned Jens's intense stare. He wanted loyal and trustworthy supporters who were prepared to go all the way. And, without lying, she could say that was perfectly true of her. She was loyal. Only not to him.

Finally, he nodded at her. "*Corvi oculum corvi non eruit,*" he said, and the others repeated it. "You are now officially accepted into our circle."

Malou caught Louis's eye. He winked at her and smiled. "As you all know," Jens said, "I'm only here humbly as your inspiration and as a resource. It is you, as representatives of the students, who are the real Movement. You are the ones who are the future of magic, and it is you who must fight those who mean us harm." He took a pile of papers from a bag that stood at his feet. "Together, we have devised this manifesto, which I ask you to hand out to everyone," he said, dividing the pile among them. "I will also ask that the teachers go over this with the students in class."

Malou tried to skim the points listed, but it was difficult to read in the dim light.

"Due to the situation we find ourselves in," Jens continued, and Malou looked up again, "I must give you the disappointing news that the third-year main assignment will be canceled this year. I sympathize that it may be difficult for you to pass all of your assignments as well as carry out your duties with the Crows, and it's only to be expected that our current circumstances will mean you giving your schooling a lower level of priority. I can reassure you that all Crows will, of course, achieve their grades no matter what—you have all proven your worth by other means."

Elias gave a broad grin and nudged Louis with his elbow.

"In return, I ask that you prepare yourselves thoroughly for the rituals we will undertake this spring. The Samhain ritual was only one of the many forgotten rituals, and it is of utmost importance that these are carried out correctly. That is key if we want our project to succeed and not to be overcome by our enemies. It must not go wrong like it did the last time."

Jens let his gaze rest momentarily on Iris, whose eyes filled with tears, before he continued to look seriously around the rest of the group, taking them in, one by one. The flickering candlelight lit him from below, making angular shadows on his face, and Malou felt his pulse increasing, but she forced herself to look openly and faithfully at him the whole time in her attempt to seem like a dedicated, trustworthy disciple.

"And finally, I have an even more serious matter to inform you of," Jens said. "The threats to the school have intensified, and for that reason, we are bringing in extra classes in combat training so that students are able to defend themselves, if it should come to that. Similarly, there will be a need for increased patrols, and Zlavko, together with Elias, will have the job of recruiting more students into the Crows."

There it was again, the lie Jens tirelessly peddled to his students: that they were in danger from people who wanted to harm them. Her eyes met Zlavko's. He was standing calmly but she noticed the anger smoldering beneath the surface. She counted to ten inside her head and focused on her breath, as he had taught her to.

"It is also crucial that you find those former pupils who we suspect are playing a decisive role in our enemies' plans against us. Benjamin, Victoria, Kirstine, and Chamomile. And former teachers Thorbjørn, Lisa, and Jakob. I know these are people you previously trusted and perhaps even thought of as your friends. But we need to find them before they strike out at us. The safety of Rosenholm's students is in your hands. Thank you."

Malou clasped her hands behind her back and bowed her head forward, listening as Jens's footsteps rang out along the floor and disappeared through the double doors.

She'd done it. Now, she was part of Jens's inner circle.

MANIFESTO FOR THE MOVEMENT

- The Movement aims to secure the rights of all mages in modern society and to fight oppression and violence against mages.

- The Movement will ensure equal rights for mages of all branches and types of magic.

- The Movement demands free and equal education for those from all branches of magic.

- The Movement demands that the 1810 Reform be repealed.

- The Movement will defend the reinstatement of mages to their role as a powerful force for change in society, and campaigns for the restoration of the Committee of Magic.

- The Movement demands that the Committee of Magic alone will act as the legislative, judiciary, and executive authority for all mages.

J is pushing ahead. Recruiting.
We can't wait any longer.

I agree. We need allies.
I've thought of someone who
might help us.

FEBRUARY 16TH
2:00 P.M.

Victoria

Victoria found her father in the library. He was sitting at the big desk, looking at his computer screen. She hadn't seen him since the summer. Did he look older? A little, maybe? His silvery-gray hair was, as always, neat and trimmed, and he wore a shirt and tie even though he was working from home.

"Dad?"

He looked up when he heard her. "Victoria, it's been a long time."

She couldn't make out his expression. Was he surprised? "I thought it was about time we made peace. I miss you," she said.

"It certainly is time," her father said. "So, you've come to your senses again? Are you going back to school?"

Victoria took a deep breath. She had to be sensible here. This couldn't go wrong. "That's exactly what I wanted to talk to you about. Do you have time? Can we sit on the sofa here?"

"Of course." He took a seat on one of the deep leather sofas, and Victoria sat opposite him.

"I've decided to tell you something that will come as a big shock to you."

"That sounds dramatic."

"I should have told you before, but I was scared he would hurt you if you knew. It's Jens."

Her father nodded seriously. "Continue."

"Jens has killed a woman."

"Victoria—"

"Just hear me out. Her name was Trine. She was his girlfriend back when Jens worked as a teaching assistant at Rosenholm in the eighties. He ended up killing her. I've seen it myself."

"You saw it?"

"Yes. Trine's spirit has been following me a long while now. She showed me what happened. He strangled her."

"According to her."

"What?"

"Victoria, you know that spirits are not always to be trusted. The spirit wants you to believe that's what happened. Have you heard Jens's version of the story?"

"No." She watched her father's face closely.

He clasped his hands together and gave a sigh. "Perhaps they had a fight, perhaps she lashed out at him, perhaps she was hysterical? Perhaps she took an unlucky fall and hit her head on a rock? Can you be certain that's not how it happened?"

"Dad . . ." Victoria shook her head slowly. She had to get through to him. Not to the lawyer sitting across from her now but to her father. He had to be in there somewhere. She lifted her face and looked at him. "I haven't asked you for much before, but now I'm asking you to trust me."

"But I do trust you, Victoria," he said. She looked at him, confused, and felt him studying her face. She couldn't sense anything from him other than a tremendous sense of calm. And then she realized he hadn't been in the slightest surprised by her revelation.

411

And he hadn't dismissed it, only the circumstances of it. *He knew.*

"How long have you known?" she asked. "That Jens took his girlfriend's life?"

Her father leaned back on the sofa and crossed one leg over the other. "He came to me sometime in the autumn. He told me you hadn't started back at school, as you'd let us believe. Instead, you'd gone off to live with that disgraced Brahe boy. And he also said you might come to me, to tell me false rumors about him. Before it came to that, he wanted to explain to me what had really happened."

Victoria looked at him, unbelieving. "Jens told you this?"

"He never wanted the girl to die. It was an accident."

"How can you believe that? He's lying!"

"Perhaps. But we can't know that for certain. It was so many years ago. Should Jens and his life's work—everything he has built, everything he has done for our kind—should it all be torn down from one day to the next just because of some mistake he made in his youth?"

"A mistake—it was murder! Does Mom know about this?"

"Yes, your mother knows, and we agreed that we should support Jens in this matter." He frowned as he looked at her. "He should, of course, have behaved differently, but he panicked and hid the evidence. If we had had a Committee of Mages, that would never have happened."

Victoria shook her head. "What do you mean?"

"Jens would have felt safe going to a Committee of Mages. They would have taken care of his special situation."

She looked at him. She had known him her whole life, but she had never really understood him or managed to get through to him behind his facade. Now she could feel his sense of complete calm. A fundamental belief that he had the right to this. And the kind of satisfaction you get when you get something you've craved for a long time. She remembered Vilhelm Brahe's words about how her father had wanted, for many years, to be on the Council of Mages.

"He offered you a place on the Committee. Am I right?"

He looked at her as if he also wondered who *she* really was. "I've been thinking about you a lot, Victoria," he said slowly. "And I'm afraid I've been too absent in your upbringing. I haven't given you enough insight into how the world really works. And now, it is perhaps too late. But I'll try, nevertheless. You see, humans are predatory animals. We walk upright. We camouflage our odors with perfume. We wear suits and jackets and go to work. But we are still predatory animals. And out on the savannah, there isn't space for all the lion cubs that are born. The weakest ones must die so that the strongest can thrive. It's that simple. Eat or be eaten. And we, Victoria, we eat. We are not eaten. Do you understand?"

Victoria jumped up from the sofa and rushed out. Her heels clicked along the hall floor, and she didn't stop to close the door behind her. She just kept running.

Benjamin had been right all along. She hadn't seen it, hadn't wanted to see it. *Her own parents.* Victoria was gasping for breath, but she didn't stop running.

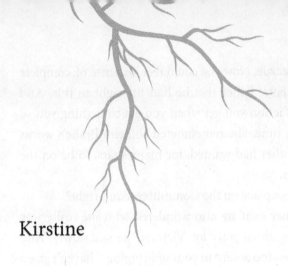

Kirstine

"Is she dead?"
 "No. She's only sleeping."
 "Should we wake her?"
 "I think she's sick. Maybe she'll die soon."
 "Are you sure it's not Mother? Maybe she came after us."
 "She's not our mother. Can't you remember what she looked like?"
 "No. Tell me about her!"
 "Not now..."

Kirstine was dreaming. Although she was awake, she was dreaming. She wasn't alone in the darkness. There was rustling and whispering around her. At one point, she was woken by somebody pulling at strands of her hair. It had to be the fever that was making her dream so vividly. Her body was shaking with the cold, but her broken leg was burning like fire. Kirstine couldn't fight to stay conscious any longer. She gave up. Unconscious, the pain was gone. She had no desire to wake up again.

FEBRUARY 23ʀᴅ
2:00 P.M.

Victoria

"What if I book a table for us somewhere?" her grandma asked, taking off her long, dark fur coat.

"No, thanks. I'd really just like to stay home," Victoria said, looking up from the book she was reading.

"But, darling, you're turning eighteen. An eighteenth birthday shouldn't be celebrated at home with your grandmother. What about your friends? Couldn't they at least come over?"

"It's not really a good time right now," Victoria said.

Her grandma looked at her worriedly. "That can't be true—"

"I'm fine, Grandma. As long as you don't tell anyone I'm living here, okay?"

She sighed. "I'll get something nice to eat at home. And Victoria? Maybe you should just do like Elizabeth Taylor always said. It's worked for me when I've been in a rough spell."

"The thing about getting a driving license?"

"No, that was Karen Blixen," she said, flicking her hair back. "Elizabeth Taylor said: 'Pour yourself a drink, put on some lipstick, and pull yourself together.'" She laughed her deep, hoarse laugh.

Victoria automatically forced a smile. "Yeah, maybe."

"Believe me, it helps. See you later!"

415

Victoria shook her head. She doubted lipstick was going to help much with her situation. *The second must choose between those she loves.* Victoria was the second one, and now it seemed like she had lost everything. Her family, her friends, her loved one.

Victoria gritted her teeth and gave her head a shake. Lipstick might be a bit silly, but her grandma was right. She needed to pull herself together. She bent back over the book she was holding in front of her. A book about ancient amulets. Something that Dagny said had given her the idea. *At first, of course, nobody wanted to tell anything to a young woman from a poor background.* But Victoria didn't come from a poor family. When she started at Rosenholm, she had kept her parents' identity secret. She had even lied and said that her parents weren't mages. Now, instead, she resolved to exploit it as much as possible. Her father didn't want to help her; she'd finally accepted that. But his name could still open doors for her.

Victoria's phone buzzed, and she found it underneath a pile of papers. It was Malou.

"Hi," Victoria said.

"Happy birthday."

"Thanks. Is there any news?"

"No, unfortunately."

"Okay . . ."

Neither said anything more. Victoria sat with the phone to her ear, listening to the fuzzy silence.

"We need to accept that she maybe hasn't made it."

Victoria closed her eyes. She didn't want to hear it, but she knew Malou was right.

"Did you have an idea of someone who could help us?"

"No," Victoria whispered. "Not in the end."

"Okay. Then I can't see any other way. We have to try and steal it."

"I know, but we need to be more prepared. I went to that library you told me about. They had a lot of material on victory stones. I'm going through it all now. Let's talk again after."

At the other end of the line, Malou sighed. "Fine. Tell me if you find anything we can use."

"Are you going to stay there?" Victoria asked.

"Yes. Jens made me a bodyguard. I'm in his inner circle now. The people closest to him. We can use that."

"Malou, be careful, okay?"

"I will. Enjoy the rest of your birthday."

Victoria said thanks and hung up. Then she returned to the book. She'd gone there yesterday, to the secret library, which held hidden information that couldn't be found elsewhere. Victoria had the idea that the library might also have the answer to where you can find a victory stone, or how you can recover one that has been stolen. The old librarian Malou told her about was no longer there, but there was a man in his fifties who had been very helpful, and Victoria had even been allowed to borrow the books and documents.

She closed the book. Its descriptions of amber amulets from the Mesolithic period didn't seem particularly useful. Instead, she opened up a tan-colored folder containing loose sheets bound together with twine. Victoria untied the knot and looked at the first page. It was handwritten and comprised several columns of notes, written as an inventory or catalog of a private book collection. The sheets were held under the label "victory stone," and that is why the man at the library had pulled them out for her. At first, she thought she'd leave this folder, but then she noticed it was Frekerik Juul—Sigsten Juuls father—who had donated some of his books to the library.

Victoria skimmed over one page after another without finding anything. It took her the best part of an hour to go through the papers. With a sigh, she gathered up the contents again and closed the folder back up. Then she froze. At the back, there was an old-fashioned library card in a little plastic wallet. The kind of card where you write the name and date of the borrower. The old library still hadn't moved to a digital system; it was completely analog. Her own name and the date stood at the bottom of the card. But the name just above hers was also familiar.

She jumped at the sound of the doorbell. Victoria stood up to go into the hall.

"Yes?"

"It's me."

The voice sounded distorted through the intercom, but nevertheless, it made her heart race immediately. "Benjamin?"

"Yes. Can I come in?"

She pressed the door release and heard the door buzz downstairs. A moment later, he was standing inside the hall. He held out a bunch of Christmas roses, with white, nodding heads.

"Happy birthday," he mumbled.

"How did you find me?" Victoria asked, taking the flowers.

"I asked around."

"Nobody knows I'm here."

He gave a wry smile. "Malou told me."

"Will you come inside?"

"Yeah, thanks."

They sat down on the floral sofa. Victoria found a vase for the flowers and placed them on the coffee table. They sat quietly, looking at them.

"You were right," she said, finally. "About my family."

418

Benjamin shook his head. "No, you were right. If it's best for you to keep hoping, who am I to interfere? It just made me so angry . . ."

She looked at him. "And what about now?"

He rubbed his forehead. "It . . . it still makes me angry. But Jakob says that's *my* problem and not yours. He says I need to deal with it myself instead of putting it onto you."

Victoria gaped at him. "You've talked to Jakob *about us*?"

"I'm worried about him. Since Kirstine disappeared . . . he's on the verge of falling apart. We were talking and, yeah . . . he gave me hell." He looked up at her, a little smile in his eyes.

"Jakob gave you hell?"

"Yes. He told me he'd gotten angry with Kirstine recently. Because she was doing something he didn't think was right. He left things badly, and maybe he's never going to see her again. And then he asked me how I'd be feeling if I had seen you for the last time." His jaw twitched, and he looked down at his hands. "Then I realized that the thing about your family maybe wasn't so important."

Victoria looked at him. It was everything she would have wanted him to say. But was it too late?

"My parents know," she whispered. "They know Jens killed Trine. He told them himself, so they knew about it already. But they're still supporting him anyway."

Benjamin sighed. "Shit . . . I'm sorry."

"That's how it is. You could see it, and I couldn't."

"You love them," Benjamin said. "That's not shameful. They're still your parents. No matter what."

"Do you still love your family?"

He frowned and ran a hand through his hair. "I don't know. Maybe, somehow? But mostly, I just feel relieved. To have severed ties with them." He looked up at her questioningly. "But I don't want to lose you . . ."

She smiled, but her heart ached. She had always felt his aura very strongly, but it was often quite fleeting. His attention was often being drawn elsewhere, so it felt particularly powerful when he was focused only on her. Like he was doing now.

"I'd be happy as well if we can be friends again," she said.

"And what about more than friends?" he asked softly. "If there's still a little chance, then I just want to say I'm ready. For anything." He took her hand and threaded his fingers through hers.

"Do you mean that?"

He nodded seriously. "One hundred percent."

She felt that her eyes were filling with tears, yet she was smiling. "Then come here," she whispered. Their kiss was frantic, as if there was a whole lot they needed to catch up on. Victoria buried her hands in his hair as he fumbled with the buttons of her shirt.

"Wait," she said, sitting up to pull it over her head instead.

"And . . . Is it okay here?" he whispered. "The sofa . . ."

"If I know my grandma like I think I do, it's probably seen quite a bit of action already," she said, pulling him to her again.

Kirstine

The cold water hit her face. She gasped for breath, but her throat felt raw and dry. The water was doing her good. She licked it from her lips.

"*Are you thirsty, Mother?*"

"*Stop calling her 'Mother.' She's not your mother.*"

Kirstine opened her eyes. There was only darkness all around her, nothing to see. But she had heard them. Two children talking.

"Who . . . who's there?" she gasped.

"*Do you want more water?*"

"Where are you?" Kirstine sat up, flailing with her arms but finding only empty space.

"*Why can't she see us?*"

"*I told you, she's sick.*"

"Who is that talking?" she shouted.

"*It's us. Me and my big brother.*"

Kirstine turned to face the voices, but it was impossible to see anything in the darkness, and the scars on her wrists were no longer illuminated. They were now merely a dull, glowing pattern. Had she lost her mind? Had she gone mad down here in the dark of the underworld? Or was she dead already? Kirstine reached up to her face and found cracked lips and her own warm breath. She touched her eyelashes with her fingertips as her eyes opened and closed. She was shivering and in pain. But she was still alive.

"*What is your name?*"

"Kirstine," she whispered.

"*I told you it's not Mother. Our mother's name was Ingrid.*"

"Where is your mother?" Kirstine asked, crawling back toward the rock face.

"*She's coming to get us.*"

"*Are you looking for your children?*"

"I don't have children," Kirstine replied.

"*Not even one of the little ones?*"

"No."

"*The little ones aren't here anyway. Not this far down.*"

"*The graveyard creature looks after them. It scares me.*" The voice was whining.

"Argh!" Kirstine jumped at the sensation of a thin hand taking her own. She pulled her hand back. "Leave me alone," she hissed.

"*Come on. We're going.*"

"*Wait. Who are you looking for if you don't have any children?*"

Kirstine pressed her back to the rock face and struggled up to stand. The pain made her dizzy, but she felt less exposed now that she was standing. She thought for a moment, then decided to tell the truth. "The Nightshades."

There was silence. Nobody spoke, and there were no rustlings or movements around her.

"Are you there?" Kirstine asked.

"*The dead girls.*"

It was the boy's voice.

"Yes. Exactly," Kirstine said. "Do you know where they are?"

422

"They're sleeping."

Now it was the girl speaking.

"I've come to wake them," Kirstine said. "Can you show me where they're sleeping?"

"If we show you, will you take us with you?"

"But what if mother comes for us? We promised we'd wait for her!"

"I don't want to be here any longer! I don't want to wait anymore."

The girl started to cry. The sound was both heartbreaking and horrifying. Water was rushing somewhere nearby, her right leg was burning, and the child's crying enveloped her.

"If you show me where the dead girls are sleeping, then I promise I'll take you with me," Kirstine said. "We'll get away from here."

"Then can we find our mother?"

It was the boy asking. She could hear everything in his voice. Doubt, mistrust, and hope.

"Yes, then we'll find your mother," Kirstine said.

She waited. Nobody spoke. Then, the boy's voice again: *"Then we are agreed."*

423

FEBRUARY 28TH
7:21 A.M.

Victoria

Victoria and Benjamin climbed into the passenger seat, and Thorbjørn started the van.

"Good morning," Victoria said.

"Good morning," Thorbjørn rumbled in reply, pulling out of the gas station where he'd picked them up. His eyes were still heavy with sleep, and he was drinking coffee from a huge thermos.

"Would you like a roll?" Victoria asked. "I baked them myself."

"Yes, thanks," Thorbjørn said, taking one with cheese that Victoria offered him. "But I'd also like to know a bit more about what it is we're doing," he said, munching noisily. "And why we're going to Thy?"

"We're looking for the same thing Jens is looking for," Victoria said. "A journal or logbook, that sort of thing. Sigsten said he'd found something in his father's journal, right?"

"That's right," Thorbjørn said through a full mouth. "He said it on the phone just before he was murdered. But we didn't find it. So we figured Jens must have taken it. But maybe he didn't?"

Victoria unwrapped another roll and handed it to Benjamin.

He thanked her with a little kiss on her neck. "I don't know," Victoria said, trying to ignore the goose bumps and the prickling sensation spreading through her whole body. "But Jens is still searching for something or other. I was looking at a record of some books Frederik Juul donated to the library. There aren't many people who'd be interested in a record like that, but apart from me, there was one other person who had taken it out the library."

"Jens?" Thorbjørn said doubtfully. "But could that not have been a long time ago?"

"No," Victoria said, "There was a date given for each patron."

"Jens took out those papers in November last year."

"After he'd killed Sigsten." Thorbjørn said.

"Exactly," Victoria said. "And that got me thinking he maybe hadn't found Frederik Juul's journal after all."

Several hours later, Thorbjørn turned into a narrow avenue of old rowan trees and parked in the courtyard. They all got out. On the main road, as well as here, there were signs showing the house was up for sale. Foreclosure. Victoria looked at the huge, dilapidated building. It had been a beautiful house once.

"It's practically in ruins," Benjamin said as they approached Sigsten's ancestral farmhouse. "Just think, an old man was living here only recently."

They approached the main entrance and pulled at the door. It was locked, so Thorbjørn led them around the back to where they found a patio door with broken windowpanes, which made it easy to stick a hand through and open up. There were footprints in the sand on the floor of the Great Hall, and Victoria noticed large, faded rectangles in several places on the walls.

"They've started clearing out the house," Thorbjørn said, nodding toward the empty walls. "Let's hope they've left the office alone."

They went up a sweeping staircase with a shabby carpet, and up on the first floor it was also apparent that paintings and furniture had been removed, as many of the rooms they could see into lay empty. Thorbjørn led them toward one of the doors. "It's in here."

Victoria gave a quick sigh of relief. The office was still bulging with stuffed bookshelves, and papers and books were strewn wildly around the floor and across the great mahogany desk.

"So, what are we looking for?" Benjamin asked.

"As Victoria said, Sigsten only mentioned a journal," Thorbjørn said.

Benjamin nodded. "Then let's start looking at notebooks and papers from Sigsten's father's era."

They searched for hours. Obviously, Frederik Juul had enjoyed taking notes and making diaries about anything and everything his whole, long life. They quickly learned to differentiate between Sigsten's own jagged handwriting and his father's sweeping signature, which he liked to sign under every little note he made as if it were some kind of official document. "If it's true you can tell things about a person from their handwriting, then I think it's fair to say that this Frederik was pretty full of himself. His signature fills about half a page," Benjamin commented.

Victoria was slowly working through what seemed to be loose pages of a diary of Frederik Juul's journey to the Faroe Islands back in the early 1900s. But the handwriting was difficult to read and the language unfamiliar. She was starting to get a thumping headache deep behind her eyes.

"Aren't you hungry?" Benjamin asked. "I am. I could happily eat another of those rolls. They were really good."

"What about you, Thorbjørn?" Victoria asked.

426

"Yeah," he said as he sat reading in an armchair by the window. "That'd be really nice."

"Then I'll go get the picnic basket."

"Thanks, honey," Benjamin said without looking up from the book he was reading.

"It's my pleasure," she said, noticing a goofy smile spreading across his face. She couldn't quite remember why, in the beginning, she'd found it annoying when Benjamin called her that.

Victoria took at deep breath in as she came out into the overgrown garden, which had a view out over the fields. They were full of small, green shoots now, which a flock of geese were pecking away at.

When she got back with their provisions, Benjamin was sitting in the exact same spot as when she left, looking at the same book.

"What are you reading?" she asked, as she unpacked some of the rolls.

"It's *Orpheus and Eurydice*," Benjamin said. "But Frederik Juul has written notes all over it."

"That book was lying at Sigsten's feet when we found him," Thorbjørn said, getting up from his spot by the window. "Kirstine found his phone underneath it."

Frederik Juul was obviously very interested in Orpheus' journey to the underworld," Benjamin said.

"Can I take a look?" Victoria asked. She flicked through the book. It was, indeed, filled with scribbles in the margins. They were in Frederik's handwriting, but the notes had clearly been scribbled in a hurry or with excitement because it didn't read like his usual writing style. The style was more clipped and defined. It was the way people write when they note down something they have to remember. And the way people write in a journal, she realized.

"Maybe Jens never found Frederik Juul's journal because it wasn't really a proper journal," she said, studying the notes closer. Some of them were linked to the text of the book, but others seemed to be about Frederik Juul's research. He had even added dates around them.

"What do you mean?" Benjamin asked.

"I think this could be what we are looking for," Victoria said. She pointed at the book and read aloud.

August 4, 2003
New breakthrough w. prophecy, nearly have the ending done.
Incredibly warm, sleep impossible.

"That must be the Nightshade Prophecy he means," Thorbjørn said.

Victoria turned to the last pages of the book. "Listen to this!"

September 23, 2003
Had a visit from J. Andersen, a teacher at Rosenholm. Very
direct and friendly. Showed great interest in victory stones,
also clearly disappointed not to find an example of one here.
Possible research partner? Shared latest version of prophecy
with him, including end, about which he was terribly excited.
Agreed to write with news of any developments.

"Jens visited Sigsten's father!" Thorbjørn said. "And Frederik Juul was most likely more easily influenced by flattery than his son. In any case, he told him the ending."

"Dagny said nobody knows the end of the prophecy," Victoria pointed out.

"But maybe Frederik had found it," Benjamin said. He took the book and studied it again.

On the final pages, there was no printed text, but Frederik Juul had used the space for his own notes instead. The writing was so cramped it was almost impossible to read. Benjamin turned to the last page. There was only half of it left. Someone had ripped the bottom half of the page out. But at the top, something was written.

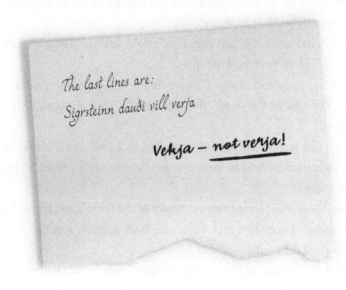

The last lines are:
Sigrsteinn dauði vill verja

Vekja — not verja!

Victoria stared at the page. Frederik had written the first two lines but not the last. That handwriting was different. *Vekja—not verja!*

"Look here," Victoria said. "What does that mean?"

Thorbjørn took the book. "It looks like Icelandic. Or perhaps Old Norse. *Sigr* means 'victory.' And *steinn* means 'stone.'"

"Victory stone," Victoria concluded. "What does the rest mean?"

"*Dauøi* means 'death,' or maybe later 'the dead,'" Thorbjørn said. "And *verja* means 'guard' or 'protect.'"

"*The victory stone will protect against the dead,*" Benjamin said. "But why does it say *vekja* underneath?"

Thorbjørn frowned. "That's in Sigsten's writing. I think that was what he was writing shortly before he died. If we had the note we found in his hand, I'm sure it would fit together. He noted down something in his father's book, and when Jens came, he ripped out the page and hid the lower half in his hand. This must be the mistake he spoke about on the phone. Frederik Juul had misunderstood the prophecy."

"But what does it mean then?" Victoria asked. "*Vekja* means 'waken,'" Thorbjørn said quietly.

"So, the prophecy doesn't mean that a victory stone protects its owner against the dead," Benjamin said. "Like Sigsten's father believed."

"And like Jens still believes," Victoria concluded. "He's afraid of the Nightshades. And he believes the victory stone protects him from them."

"But there must have been a mistake in the translation from the Old Norse," Thorbjørn said. "The prophecy actually means something quite different."

Victoria looked at him. "The victory stone will awaken the dead," she said. "You need to use a victory stone to waken the Nightshades."

Thorbjørn thumped the book, which fell to the floor. "And Kirstine doesn't have one."

PART 4
SPRING

And the hedgerow is fragrant
on Walpurgis Night,
Elves dance in the thicket, strange whispers
in the dark grove.
Silent, I kiss my bride in white,
as you sit so quiet in fine Sunday best,
while all the flowers they doze.

From the poem "Walpurgis Night," by Vilhelm Krag, 1891

Kirstine

"Come on! It's this way."

Kirstine could feel little fingers tugging at the hem of her shirt. "Wait," she groaned. "I need to rest up a second. My leg can't take anymore."

"What's wrong with your leg?"

"I fell on it."

"Does it hurt?"

"Of course, it hurts. Can't you see that it's broken?"

Kirstine leaned against the rock face. The wheeze of her breathing mingled with the sound of the stream, which bubbled past them on the right. She bent down and reached to check her bandage. She had torn the arms of her sweater into strips and wrapped the material around her leg in an attempt to hold the bone in place. At several points on the way, she'd passed out in pain, but the children had woken her, splashing cold water on her face. The bandage was still in place, but it felt stiff with the blood that had seeped through and dried out. She ought to wash the wound, but she would never get the bandage on again.

"Are you ready?"

"Not yet," Kirstine said. She was only managing to hobble a few steps along the path at a time before needing to rest again. Sometimes, the fever overwhelmed her and she fell into a restless sleep. When she woke again, she had no idea if she had slept for minutes, hours, or days, but the children were still there. They waited patiently for her every time. Kirstine could hear them bickering in the darkness. She wished she could see their faces.

"Can you actually see everything down here?" she asked.

"*Yes. Maybe you hurt your eyes too when you fell.*"

"Maybe."

"*We're nearly at the bridge. It's not far now.*"

"What's on the other side?" Kirstine asked.

"*The hall of the dead girls.*"

"Have you been there before?"

"*No. We've never crossed the bridge.*"

"*I'm scared of the water.*"

"I'll look after you. You won't fall in," Kirstine said. They continued slowly. Clinging to the wall for support, Kirstine hopped along on her good leg while eager little hands pulled at her clothes, and soft voices alternately chided her or encouraged her to keep going.

The path narrowed, and they were now walking close to the bank. The course of the water itself had also narrowed, and it no longer flowed steadily but rushed noisily by them as they walked.

"*We're here now. This is the bridge.*"

Kirstine felt her way forward. She came to the rough stones, maybe some kind of limestone, and they reached out across the rushing water. "And this goes right over to the other side?"

"*Yes.*"

"*I don't like it.*"

Kirstine looked down at herself. Her scars shone a little brighter, but still not enough to let her see anything. "We'll crawl over," she said. "If you just follow me, nothing will happen. Just give me a moment."

Kirstine took a deep breath, filling her lungs. Then she bent down to kneel on the ground. She groaned, and her head was swimming. For a moment, she feared she might faint. Then, the dizziness faded. It would work if she kept on her knees. It *had to* work.

"Are you ready?"

Kirstine crawled the first short stretch out onto the narrow limestone bridge, which seemed to have been formed by nature itself. She didn't much like the vulnerable position she was in, crawling forward on shaking knees, but she didn't dare stand up. Behind her, the girl was crying while her big brother scolded her.

"We're nearly across," Kirstine said, though she couldn't see a thing. But she could hear now from the rush of the stream that they were no longer out over the water, and she fumbled forward for the rock wall that would surely face them on the other side but was only grabbing at air. With a grunt, she got up onto her feet again. Pain shot up her broken leg, and some warm liquid trickled down it, but she didn't know if it was blood or pus from an infection.

"*Is this it?*"

"*Yes. The hall of the dead girls.*"

"Stay here. We mustn't go in there," Kirstine groaned. Even though she was speaking softly, her words echoed all around them. They stood at the entrance to a large cave or hall.

"*What now?*"

Kirstine bit her lip. "I think I need to waken them," she whispered. "But I don't know how."

"You don't know?"

"Let me think . . ." Kirstine realized she was swaying and struggling to stay conscious. "In 'Baldr's Dream,' Odin wakens the dead seeress using charms," she mumbled.

"What's that mean?"

"Enchanted songs."

"I can sing!"

"Sing the one mother always sang to get us to sleep."

"Should I?"

"Yes. Just try it," Kirstine whispered.

> *"Jesus loves me this I know*
> *For the Bible tells me so*
> *Little ones to him belong*
> *They are weak but he is strong*
>
> *Jesus loves me still today*
> *Walking with me on my way*
> *Wanting as a friend to give*
> *Light and love to all who live*
>
> *Jesus loves me! He who died*
> *Heaven's gate to open wide*
> *He will wash away my sin*
> *Let His little child come in."*

The thin voice rang out, clear and pure, filling the room. When the song ended, there was silence, and even the rush of the stream seemed fainter. Kirstine kept her eyes closed so she could listen for the slightest noise.

436

Was that a rustling? The light sound of grit scuffing down a slope? She felt the little hands reach out for her.

"Get behind me," she whispered.

She was startled by a scraping sound farther back in the cave, and she stared as best she could into the blackness.

"They're coming! They're coming!"

"Where? What can you see?"

"They're coming!"

From every direction now, she could hear stones being pushed aside and earth scraped away, invisible rustling, rummaging, and rattling. Kirstine's heart beat so fast her chest almost hurt.

"Ahhhhh!"

A whoosh, like hundreds of sighs, swept through from the cave, blowing her hair back from her face. Then came a voice, whispering: *"Who is this, who comes to disrupt us from our sleep and force us to rise again?*

She gulped. "My name is Kirstine. I'm looking for the Nightshades. I've come to waken you."

"You have found what you seek. But you cannot waken us. You can but disturb."

"I've not come to disturb you. I want to free you and take you to the surface, where you can get your revenge," Kirstine said.

"Show us the stone!"

Kirstine felt the panic rising inside her. She had no idea what to say. She heard the children whimpering behind her and could feel their little faces pushing into her from behind so they wouldn't see whatever it was that she was unable to see.

"You are not the right one. You must rest with us here, in the hall of the dead, until the right one comes."

Kirstine closed her eyes. It felt as if every drop of energy and strength had left her body, and she was nothing but an empty shell.

"No," she whispered, "No . . ."

She noticed a dry fluttering sound, which momentarily reminded her of the bats with their beating wings. But these were not bats on their way toward her now.

"Nooooo!"

"Argh!" Kirstine screamed as a hand shot out from the darkness and grabbed her wrist. It was as cold as the rocks and the water in the river, but the grip was strong. Kirstine tried to shake it off, noticing quickly how another hand had grabbed her ankle, its nails pushing into her skin. "Run!" she yelled. "Back to the bridge!"

Kirstine struck out, and her fist met with whatever it was hiding in the dark, but just as quickly, another hand grabbed her, a new body pressed into her, hissing angrily. Then new fingers with long nails came, scratching her face so that it bled and pulling at her hair. She tried to protect the children with her body, but she couldn't tell where they were in all the darkness and chaos.

"Thurisaz!" she screamed, but her rune spell had no effect on the Nightshades and their seething rage. "Get back to the bridge! I'll hold them off!" she shouted.

"It's too scary!"

"Come on!"

"We'll go together!" she yelled back, swinging out after a figure in the blackness. A searing pain made her yelp out loud when she put her broken leg down and suddenly felt the leg folding under her. Before she could understand what was happening, she landed on her back.

"NO!"

Kirstine fought to get up again, but a nightshade threw herself on her and held her down. She felt the weight of its freezing body and then its strong fingers closing around her neck. Kirstine took both hands and pulled and scratched at the cold hands to get them off. In the light of her glowing scars, she could make out the face that was leaning over her. A young woman with large, dark eyes. She looked as if she could have died only days before, except from her skin, which was dark blue.

"I'm . . . a friend," she croaked, but the nightshade only gripped harder and harder, hissing. Kirstine felt a stinging in her eyes, and she started seeing little bright stars.

"Mother!"

She opened her eyes. The nightshade was almost nose to nose with her, but suddenly, a rock hammered against its temple, and the face disappeared into the dark.

"Come on!"

A hand pulled her to her feet. The pain in her leg made her feel sick, and she heard ringing in her ears. "The bridge . . ." she groaned.

"They're blocking it! The dead girls."

"Then we jump!"

"What?"

"We jump into the water!"

"No! I don't want to!"

"Do what she says!"

"Trust me! Don't let go of my hands, do you hear me? On three."

"One, two, three."

She took their hands, and they jumped from the riverbank down into the murky water. It gathered them in an icy embrace, and Kirstine felt the air being crushed out of her lungs. The water rushed around them as their legs and arms thrashed and kicked, frothing the surface. She slipped under, lost her grip on their hands, and the water swept her onward. The current grew even stronger as the river continued to narrow. Kirstine was tossed up again toward the banks, and suddenly her head was above water. She gasped air greedily into her lungs. Where were they? She called for them, but all she could hear was the gushing of the river. She tried to battle the current and get onto the bank, but the water carried her off again. She only managed to scrape herself on sharp stones and shards of rock that defended the banks of the river like angry little soldiers. Perhaps the river's current would calm further ahead and she could find a place to crawl onto land. And maybe they'd be waiting for her there, and they'd ask what had taken her so long.

Then she felt it. The little, thin hands reached out for her in the water, and she grabbed them, clinging to them. But they weren't hands. Only dry bones that fizzled away between her fingers and disappeared in the gushing water.

They were gone. She had lost them. Kirstine screamed with grief and powerlessness. The scream rang out around her as she let herself be carried by the water, no longer fighting it. To her horror, she found she was in a tunnel. The water cut through the underground limestone, and she struggled not to panic, but the limestone walls came ever nearer and now she could reach the ceiling with her hands. And then she suddenly struck a wall.

She found herself in a cave, where the water could rise up any minute and fill the whole space. Kirstine ducked under the water and fell forward with her hands. There was a small opening farther down, nothing more than a crack, but the water was streaming out again on the other side. She tried to measure the gap with her hands. Maybe she could squeeze through, but then what was waiting on the other side? An even narrower tunnel? Kirstine brought her head up again for air. She'd never manage to fight the rushing current, which was pressing her up against the limestone wall and causing the water to rise, bit by bit. Kirstine tried to take as many breaths as she could, deep into her lungs. Then, she ducked under.

The sound of rushing water ceased. Kirstine found the opening. First, she stuck an arm through. Getting her head through was also fine, but her shoulders got stuck. She wriggled her body, the stones tearing at her skin, but then one shoulder was through and the next was even easier. She used her arms to push as her broad hips held fast, but the current helped her, pushing her through, and then suddenly she was free.

It grew still. No current, no rushing water, no jagged rocks. Only the black, ice-cold water around her. Kirstine felt herself slowly drift into unconsciousness. Any moment now, she could fall asleep, and then she would be there in the dark water forever.

You can't give up, Kirstine.

It was Jakob's voice. He was calling her. *Kirstine, come back. Don't give up.* She started to kick with her one good leg. Slowly, she moved upward, and now it was as if she could sense a light glow above her, the darkness yielding a little. Red dots were dancing before her eyes, and she felt dizzy, but she kept on kicking. *Don't think, just focus and kick and kick.* In her mind, she conjured up Dagaz, the daylight rune, which took her up and up, and above her, the water became ever brighter.

MARCH 5TH
10:11 A.M.

Chamomile

Chamomile crossed the yard between the empty redbrick buildings, taking care not to trip on the railway tracks, which ran right inside the grounds of the abandoned factory. Despite the rundown air of the place, the red buildings actually looked nice, with their tall, arched, iron windows, many with panes missing. She had googled it and found out the old sugar factory was established in 1912 and had once been the largest of its kind in the country. On the grounds of the factory, besides production halls and warehouses, workers' accommodation had also been built. The best residence was, of course, the manager's, but there were also homes for ordinary workers and dormitories for the seasonal workers drafted in at peak times. The dormitories looked the worst for wear. The windowpanes were smashed, graffiti covered the walls, and one door had been broken open and now stood banging in the cold wind, giving her a fright as she passed. Chamomile stopped and glanced quickly around her before hurrying on.

The huge silos at the back of the factory had been used to preserve sugar, and they stood in sharp contrast to the beauiful factory buildings. They had been built in a different era when

442

functionality was the only thing that mattered. Chamomile squinted up at them briefly. She liked it when people made things about more than just making a profit. It was the kind of thing that would have gotten Malou calling her sentimental or nostalgic. But Chamomile just liked old, beautiful things. Even if that meant they were a bit impractical.

She was freezing, so she jogged the last stretch to the entrance of the main building, where she locked herself in. A wide stair took her farther up until she stood at the door of the big corner office. A sign still on the door showed this was the manager's office. She gave the signal knock and heard the lock slide open.

"In you come!" Molly opened and closed the door quickly again behind her. "Whoa, it's cold out there, right? It sounds like the wind's picking up."

"It's bloody freezing," Chamomile admitted, setting down the water can. The manager's plush office was complete with dark mahogany furniture, a plush green carpet, and metal filing cabinets. Yet it was as if some force of nature had invaded the room and had begun—slowly but surely, to turn it into something pretty homey. Now it had scarves, dried flowers, and cushions scattered all over. In the middle, they'd made a bed with sleeping mats and duvets from the secondhand place, and they'd even found a large, flowery throw to cover it. They had a petrol stove in the corner, and on the window ledge was a collection of vases, a pile of round stones, several crystals, and three egg cartons, in which marigolds and sunflowers were germinating. Despite everything, they'd managed to create a cozy little pocket in the midst of all of the dreadful things going on. And as long as Chamomile could stop herself from thinking about everything that might go wrong, they were doing okay. Yeah, better than that, in fact. As strange as it sounded, Chamomile couldn't remember a time when she had ever felt so happy as she did when she was with Molly.

"I'll just make a flask of tea, and then we can get going, okay?" said Molly, tipping some water into a little pot.

"I still don't understand how you could just take your parents' car, and they're not angry?" Chamomile asked.

Molly looked up at her. "It's actually my car. I got it from my parents when I turned eighteen."

"They gave you a car? A brand-new car?"

"Yes. But I hadn't used it before because I was so angry with them."

"That puts the silver ring I got from my mom kind of into the shade," Chamomile muttered. "Why didn't you say anything?"

"You're not the only one who keeps secrets about their family," Molly said, winking at her as she flung tea bags into the simmering water. "Mine are stinking rich. Richer than Victoria's—but don't tell anyone that. It doesn't fit with my image." She smiled, but Chamomile could see the hurt somewhere behind it.

"I'll just have to try and live with it," Chamomile said. "The fact that I've fallen for a pampered rich kid."

Molly laughed. "At least my parents don't go around in matching anoraks like Jakob's," she said.

"Yeah, poor him." Chamomile smiled.

Molly poured the tea into the flask and stood up. "Shall we go?"

Chamomile nodded. "I'm really looking forward to seeing her."

"It's you two!" Lisa looked at them, astonished, as they walked into the large, bright room at the hospital.

"Yeah," Chamomile said, going up to greet Lisa. "I know we should have called first, but there's always some reason or other that we shouldn't come. I just need to see my mom. I really miss her." She looked around. The bright, spring sunshine streamed in through the big windows looking out to the sea. A vase of fresh tulips and a bowl of fruit sat on the table. Patients were sitting on the soft green sofas, reading or talking quietly with one another, while the healers in white uniforms went calmly around, greeting them politely. It was a nice place to be, and the knot in Chamomile's stomach loosened a little.

"Your mom is in her room," Lisa said, giving them both a hug. Her dark eyes lingered on Chamomile a little. "Beate has been very ill. She's doing better, but she may look a bit different. You should prepare yourself for that."

Chamomile nodded. "Okay. I can't wait to see her again."

"Follow me."

"Should I go with you, or . . . ?" Molly asked.

"Of course you should come." Chamomile smiled. "She'll be so happy to hear about us."

They carried on down a hallway. A large figure came walking toward them. He wore a light linen shirt, and his feet were bare in a pair of backless sandals.

"Thorbjørn, is that you?" Chamomile smiled, giving the big man a hug before she even got to thinking that they weren't really on hugging terms.

"Good to see you," Molly said. "You look like a hippie. It suits you."

"Uh . . . um . . ." Thorbjørn spluttered.

"They're here to see Beate," Lisa said.

Thorbjørn glanced from Chamomile to Molly and back to Lisa. "I think she's sleeping right now," he said. "I was in there a little while ago, but she wasn't awake."

Lisa nodded over to one of the doors. "That's her room."

Chamomile opened the door. The white curtains were pulled so the light was less bright. A single picture hung on the wall. In the middle of the room was a bed, and in the corner, an old woman sat sleeping in an armchair. Her long white hair hung loose over her shoulders.

"Beate, Chamomile's here to visit," Lisa said softly.

"What . . . ?" Chamomile looked from the woman in the chair to Lisa. It was as if the ground had disappeared from under her feet. "But . . ."

"Chamomile . . ." the woman in the chair whispered.

"Mom? What's happened to you?" Chamomile ran to her and threw herself down to her knees by the armchair. She threw both arms around the thin body and buried her face, sobbing, into her mother's shirt. "What's going on around here?"

"Hey," Beate comforted her, stroking her hair. "I'm sick, Milly, but I'm doing better. Ivalo helped me. And they're taking really good care of me here."

"But you said you had asthma . . ." Chamomile let go of her mother and turned to Lisa. "You've all been lying to me!" she yelled. "You said she was doing okay. Tell me what's wrong!"

Lisa looked down at the floor. There was silence, except for the weak sound of her mother's labored breathing. Chamomile turned to her mom. "Why won't anybody tell me what's wrong with you?"

"It's my stone," her mother whispered. "I had it for so long. It had become a part of me, and we're still connected. When Jens stole it, it started to drain my strength."

"But . . . you have to put a stop to this!" Chamomile said, looking at Lisa. Why was she just standing there staring, stupidly? Why wasn't she doing something?

446

"We can't," she replied softly.

"What do you mean?"

"Chamomile—"

One of the healers appeared at the door, having heard Chamomile's shout as it rang loudly through the quiet hallways.

"Your mom is still weak. She needs quiet," Lisa said. "Come on, we can talk about this somewhere else."

"No, I'm staying here."

"Chamomile . . ."

Her mother's breathing suddenly worsened, and her chest heaved and sank as if she was fighting to get air. The healer crossed the room to help her mother into her bed.

"What's happening?"

"It's okay, Milly. I just get tired so quickly at the moment," she rasped.

"But, Mom—"

"Come on." Lisa took her by the shoulder and led her out, down the hall and into the lounge area.

It was as if Chamomile was trapped in a nightmare. All that time, she had thought her mother was getting better; in fact, she had been lying here at death's door. Why hadn't Chamomile come before this? Why hadn't they called her?

"I thought she was doing well. You all told me she was doing well!" Chamomile said when they were back in the lounge area.

"Beate didn't want us to say anything. And she *is* doing well," said Lisa. "She's not in any pain."

"She's *dying*!"

"All of us are going to die at some point in time."

Chamomile pushed Lisa away. "This is my mom you're talking about! She's still young. She can't die!"

The subdued conversations around the lounge area fell silent with her outburst. Lisa and Thorbjørn stared at her as if they had no idea what to say. Chamomile felt like screaming at them. At that moment, the door to the lounge opened, and Malou, Victoria, and Benjamin came storming in.

"Chamomile!" Malou halted. "What are you doing here?"

The sight of her filled Chamomile with an overpowering rage, which boiled up and burst forth. "Did you know about this?" she yelled.

"What do you mean?"

"Answer me! Did you all know?"

"Chamomile . . ." Malou went toward her.

"Don't touch me! I'll never forgive you all for this! You knew she was dying, and you didn't tell me anything!"

"It was for your own sake. I didn't want—" Malou began.

"What? What didn't you want?"

"Anything to happen to you, damn it! For you to do anything dumb."

Chamomile shook her head. "Come on, Molly. We're going."

"Where are you going?" Malou asked.

"I'll find him. It's me he wants anyway! I'll find him and get him to give me the stone back."

"Just listen!" Malou grabbed hold of her by the sweater and pressed her up against the wall. "Jakob has found Kirstine. He's on the way with her now. She's alive!"

"Kirstine?" Chamomile looked around. A buzz of activity had started in the big room. Lisa and Thorbjørn were deep in conversation with Victoria and Benjamin while healers ran back and forth at speed as if they were suddenly very busy.

"Stay here," Malou said. "We've got a plan. I promise you. Jens

448

has made me a bodyguard. We're going to get your mom's stone back. But not today." She let go of Chamomile and stepped back.

Chamomile stood as if she was frozen, tears blurring her vision. She shook her head. "No."

"Chamomile . . ." Molly opened her arms and enfolded her in an embrace. Chamomile sobbed as Molly quietly rocked her back and forth. Her mom was not just ill; she was dying. The realization was like being in a freefall, and Chamomile couldn't stop her tears.

"They're here!" Benjamin shouted, and Chamomile looked up.

Two healers opened the doors. In came Jakob, white as a sheet, and in his arms, he was carrying a lifeless young woman.

"Help me," he pleaded.

MARCH 10TH
10:01 A.M.

Kirstine

Kirstine felt her eyelids flickering, and how it seemed to take all her strength just to open them. She tried, but as the light blazed in her eyes, she shut them again immediately.

"Kirstine?"

She smiled behind her closed eyes. She wasn't in pain anymore. There was no cold water. Just light and Jakob's voice.

"Should I close the blinds?"

She heard his steps crossing the floor. The blinds being lowered. Something about that sound felt very real. This was reality, she realized.

"Can you hear what I'm saying?"

She blinked and nodded slowly. "Where are we?" she whispered.

"In a hospital. You're safe here."

"How—"

"I found you lying on the shore of a lake, some distance from Rosenholm. Do you remember?"

She shook her head carefully, and the movement made her dizzy. "I got carried off by the water," she whispered.

"I should go tell Lisa you're awake."

450

"No, wait a bit." She opened her eyes a moment. She had difficulty focusing on his face, but slowly, it became clear. "I couldn't," she whispered. "I didn't have the stone."

"I know," Jakob said. "We found the end of the prophecy. It's the stone that has to waken them."

"And I let the children down." Kirstine cried. She wished he could hold her. Or take her hand, at least.

"What children?" he asked gently.

"They helped me. They saved my life, but I let them down. They disappeared into the water. I'd promised them I'd take them with me."

"From where? I don't understand, Kirstine . . ."

"I met them down there."

"In the underworld?"

"Yes. They were waiting for their mother. She was supposed to go and fetch them. I promised them I'd take them away from there with me so they could find her."

"Myling," Jakob whispered. "That must be what you met."

"What?"

"That's what they're called. Children who were cast out. In the olden days. Left in the forest to die."

"Why?"

"Sometimes because they were born outside of marriage, or maybe they were sick or disabled. Or maybe their parents just couldn't look after them anymore. People were poor, starving, or maybe had more children than they could feed."

"That's dreadful," Kirstine whispered. "I promised them."

"Kirstine, they weren't real children. They've been dead for hundreds of years. You couldn't save them."

"I know that," she said. But she cried anyway. She cried for the dead children and the murdered young women. And she cried for the fiasco she'd just been through and all the loneliness and pain she had suffered. And all the while, Jakob stayed sitting there by her side. Finally, she had no more tears left, and she felt empty inside.

"Sleep a little, sweetheart," Jakob whispered, and she let the drowsiness roll over her and sank back down into the dark.

MARCH 12ᵀᴴ
2:30 P.M.

Victoria

Victoria sat in a chair by Kirstine's bed, looking at Frederik Juul's old edition of *Orpheus and Eurydice*. She was trying to understand his tiny scribbles, but there was still a lot that she couldn't decipher. Kirstine stirred in her sleep, and Victoria folded the book shut and laid it on her bedside table. The duvet had slid off, and she stood up to pick it up. Kirstine had a brace on the lower part of her right leg. The bone was broken when Jakob found her, but Lisa thought it would still heal and grow together again. Victoria looked at the serious expression on Kirstine's face, her sandy-colored hair, which still lay in long, matted clumps over the pillow. As soon as she'd gotten better, Victoria would ask her if she could brush out her hair for her. Her eyes flickered now, and seconds later, one eye opened.

"Good morning, sleeping beauty," Victoria said, smiling at her.

Kirstine sighed and let out a kind of cooing noise as she stretched. "Good morning," she mumbled.

"Do you want to sit up a little?" Victoria asked and helped her raise the head of the bed. "How are you doing?"

"Good, I think," Kirstine said. She wriggled her toes a little and grimaced.

"It's going to heal," Victoria said, nodding down toward the leg. "Are you hungry?"

"Yes. And thirsty."

Victoria smiled. "Good. I'll go get you something."

When she came back, carrying a tray with butter rolls and a big glass of soda, she found Kirstine looking at the book. The low sun shone in through the window, and her lips were moving as she slowly sounded out the text.

"Here you are." Victoria put the tray on her little table.

Kirstine lay the book in her lap and drank the soda greedily down. "Where are the others?" she asked.

"Chamomile and Molly have gone back to . . . well, I don't actually know where it is. Chamomile wanted to stay here with her mom, but it's best that as few people as possible know about her hiding place. There are too many of us here."

"How's Beate doing?" Kirstine asked, biting into a roll.

"Not so great, I'm afraid," Victoria said. "Thorbjørn stays with her a lot. He's taking good care of her. That's at least a comfort to Chamomile when she can't be here herself."

"And Malou?"

"She's still at Rosenholm."

"You're planning on stealing the stone," Kirstine said.

"How do you know that?" Victoria asked.

"We tried with the banewort. We tried to waken the Nightshades. It didn't work. Now, we have to go straight for the stone. It's the only solution," she said.

"My grandma says there's always more than one solution," Victoria said, leaving out the fact that her grandma mostly claimed this when she was struggling with a crossword puzzle and then started to make up her own words.

454

"Are you living with her now?" Kirstine asked. "Your grandma?"

"I've been here a lot of the time," Victoria said. "But, yeah, I live there now. Benjamin's coming to get me in an hour to take me back to Copenhagen." For some reason, she couldn't help but smile.

"Victoria . . ." Kirstine said, looking at her, questioningly. "Are you back together?"

Victoria nodded. "Since my birthday. It's so weird. In the middle of all this terrible stuff, I feel—yeah, almost happy. It sounds kind of wrong."

"It's brilliant. Imagine that—you had a birthday while I was away. So much has happened. And Chamomile and Molly are together?"

"Yeah. It's great, isn't it? Love blossoming even in such difficult circumstances." Victoria stopped when she saw Kirstine's face. "Sorry! That was a dumb thing to say when you and Jakob can't . . ."

Kirstine gave a smile. "It's okay. I'm just happy for you," she said, putting her glass down on the table. "And now you have to tell me what the plan is."

Victoria avoided her eyes. Kirstine was still weak, and their plan wasn't even a proper plan, more of a terribly risky and desperate last resort. She sighed. "Okay . . ."

June 27, 2003

Made an incredible find, a document written by a monk from Vitskøl Monastery in 1162. Seems to contain the prophecy and Valdemar the Great's interpretation of it, written in Old Norse, but fairly tattered and hard to read. Still, it would seem it could be possible to deduce the end of the prophecy from this document! Eureka!

MARCH 19TH
3:54 A.M.

Malou

Malou's hand trembled as she leaned over the old door handle. She fumbled with the lock. She'd last picked a lock a long time ago, maybe in the eighth grade. This door wasn't kept locked before, but safety was paramount all over the school now. Her master keys, which opened all the classrooms and the Library, didn't open this one. She studied the ancient keyhole. Normally, they were easy to force. It only needed a key of roughly the same type, but she didn't have one. She stuck a screwdriver into the keyhole and turned it slowly, but nothing happened. The person behind her stirred, and Malou had to turn her focus on her so she wouldn't start making too much noise. This would have been best done with three people so she could have one person keeping watch.

Malou checked the time. Since becoming one of Jens's bodyguards herself, she knew the schedule. Right now and during the next three hours, only one guard was posted outside the door to Jens's private apartments. She took a deep breath to calm her nerves. *Come on, you can do this!* She turned the screwdriver again. The lock gave a little click, and she felt some resistance. She pushed the screwdriver in a touch farther and grasped the door handle. The door to the big office opened up.

It was dark in the principal's office. So far, so good. She had noticed it that time Jens held the party in here. The office door lock was basic and old, and from the office, there was direct access to his private quarters. A small clock struck with a crisp, ringing sound, which gave her a start. At the same time, the figure started moving in small, jerky twitches as if she'd been given a shock, and Malou had to force herself to concentrate. This could not go wrong because of her lack of focus. Soon, the young woman stood calmly again, her dark eyes wide open. Malou tried to ignore the rushing feeling it gave her inside. She was only doing it because there was no other possible way, she reminded herself, and not because it felt more thrilling than anything else she'd tried.

"Find the stone," she whispered. *"Find the stone and go out the same way you came in."* The young woman turned straight toward the open door and went slowly, but without hesitation, into the office. Malou resisted the urge to wait there and watch her. She must not, under any circumstances, be found here. Silently, she closed the door and slipped away as fast as she could.

She went back quickly but not to her own room. She needed an alibi. Louis was sleeping deeply as usual and didn't even move as she crawled in under the covers. That was good. If it all went wrong, he would be able to say that she had been sleeping there the whole time. *Find the stone. Find it and come to me.* Malou closed her eyes, but not to sleep. She searched for that exhilarating feeling from before, but she felt only a weak buzzing.

She had never tried this before. She didn't know if it could be done at such a distance. *Find the stone.*

The minutes passed by. Soon, it was half an hour since they'd been standing outside the door. That ought to be enough. Malou

458

clasped her hands under the covers. *Come back. Find your way back to me now.*

She repeated it to herself over and over, but the buzzing sensation only grew weaker and weaker. *Come back!*

Maybe she was just walking slowly, or maybe she was having trouble finding the way. Maybe Malou should have let her go back to her own room instead. There were so many possible reasons for her not being there yet. Malou checked the time on her phone. Another minute had passed, and her body was screaming at her to get up and go out into the hall and start searching, but she lay where she was. If the girl really had been discovered, Malou had to keep well away.

An insistent knocking on the door made her snap her eyes wide open. Could it be her?

"What . . ." Louis muttered, lifting his head sleepily from the pillow.

"It's nothing. Go back to sleep," Malou whispered and went over to open the door a crack.

"Yes?"

"Come with me!"

"Why . . . ?"

"*Come on!*"

"Who is it?" Louis asked.

"It's just Zlavko," Malou whispered. "I don't know what he wants, but I better go."

"But—"

She closed the door without hearing what Louis had to say. Zlavko stood out in the hall. He didn't look like someone who'd just been wrested from his beauty sleep, but he certainly was not his usual well-groomed self. His skinny, black trousers were dirty, his T-shirt looked old and ratty, his hair was unkempt, and the dark circles under his eyes were prominent in his thin face.

"What do you want?" Malou asked.

"Not here," he hissed, grabbing her arm. "Come on!" He pulled her down toward the teachers' wing. Malou tried to pull her arm away, but he only tightened his grip. She winced at the cloying, sweaty smell hanging over him.

"What is this?" he hissed, having almost flung her into his apartment and closed the door behind them.

"This? This is a complete disgrace," Malou said, looking around her. Zlavko's normally orderly room was a dirty mess, with bottles and—as she noticed to her horror—bloody rags heaped in a corner.

"Drop it, Malou," he sneered. "Are you going to explain this?" He pointed. In the middle of his little living room, a young woman was lying out on the low sofa.

"That looks like Asta," she answered. "Has something happened to her? Shouldn't you have gotten hold of Ingrid instead?"

"Ingrid doesn't know anything about blood magic. I doubt she has ever seen a person under the influence of Impero Spiritus. But I have."

"I've no idea what you mean," Malou said.

"We both know you're the only person who could have put Asta into that state. Tell me now why I found her lying in convulsions outside the principal's office."

"She was lying outside?" Malou asked. Every cell in her body cried out for her to go and check Asta's pockets.

"You sent her in there to get the stone, didn't you?" he whispered.

"And what if I did?"

460

"You stupid little fool! Do you imagine he lays it on his bed-side table so any old idiot can wander in and take it?" His voice trembled with malice. "How did you imagine Asta was going to find it without waking him? You haven't even got any idea where it is!"

"Around his neck," Malou whispered. "I think he wears it around his neck. Haven't you seen how he always reaches for the collar of his shirt? I thought he maybe takes it off to sleep. He stole it from Chamomile while she was sleeping—why can't we just do the same?"

"Because Jens isn't just some dumbass schoolgirl like Chamomile. He knows what that stone is worth to him. And besides, he has his spirits, who no doubt helped him steal the stone and will stop anyone who tries to take it from him. It cannot be done in this way!"

"So, she didn't find it?"

He snorted. "No. And what do you think he would have done to her if he had found her in his bedroom?"

Malou shrugged. "He's got no reason to suspect her of anything. She's too stupid to have any agenda. That's why I chose her. Jens would just have yelled at her a bit and sent her away."

"But you don't know that, do you? On the other hand, you do know what he's capable of. And you were willing to let one of your colleagues risk their life to carry out your stupid plan."

"Was that not also what you were planning with me?" she hissed again. "Putting my life at risk so you didn't have to?"

"That's *not* the same!" He turned away from her. "When I saw that you didn't have a chance against Jens anyway, I dropped the plan right away. Yes, there was a risk, but there was also a high chance of it succeeding if Jens hadn't had the stone. What you were up to, that was destined to fail. But you were lucky. Jens wasn't there."

"What's happening with her?" Malou asked.

"I've given her something calming to get her to sleep, to stop the convulsions. I imagine she'll be more or less herself again in the morning. I—"

A loud bang on the door made them both jump. Zlavko stared at her wildly.

"It's too early," he whispered. "I'm not ready."

There was another knock.

"Zlavko?"

Malou closed her eyes. It was Jens.

"Hide!" Zlavko whispered, but Malou stood frozen to the spot. Jens tried the door. It was locked.

"I'm coming!" Zlavko shouted, grabbing her by the arm and pulling her over to the bedroom door. "Hide in there. And Malou? Stay here. No matter what. Do not try to do anything stupid." His dark eyes bored into hers, and pain shot up her arm. "Okay?"

"Okay."

He closed the door behind him, and Malou squeezed under the low bed. Her heart was thumping so loud it would be hard to hear what they were talking about. She held her breath.

"I'm sorry to disturb you at this time," Jens said. His voice was friendly and calm, as ever. "I've just returned to school, and there's something I'd like to talk to you about, and I'm afraid it can't wait because . . . Tell me, who is that?"

"That's Asta," Zlavko said. His voice was also calm and didn't reveal any of his nerves or anger. "She was having difficulty sleeping, and I helped her with a little glass of something. I think I

462

misjudged the quantity a little, though, because she fell asleep immediately after drinking it."

"Ah . . ." Jens said. "Did she come looking for you in the middle of the night?"

"I've helped her before," Zlavko said casually. "But what was it you came to talk about?"

"It's lovely to hear that you're helping the students," Jens said, ignoring Zlavko's questions. "At all times of the day," he continued. "Do you perhaps have several students hidden around here? There may be others suffering from insomnia?"

Zlavko laughed as if Jens had said something funny. "No, there's only Asta and me here."

"So, I can have a look in your bedroom?" Jens asked.

"Of course, I've nothing to hide," Zlavko answered.

Malou was startled as Jens opened the door, and light flooded in. She pressed herself down into the floor as if that would make any difference if Jens came into the room and looked under the bed. But he didn't. She could see his black shoes and black trousers at the open door.

"That's fine," Jens said with that warm voice. "It's just that I can't understand why you're lying to me, Zlavko?"

"What do you mean?"

"Do you know who Jakobsen is? He is my most trusted helper. He lived here in the castle fifty years ago. An old caretaker. Jakobsen keeps an eye on things for me when I'm not around. I'd asked him to keep watch over my apartment while I ran an errand. Jakobsen tells me that Asta was lying outside my office. And that you came by. Almost as if you had some reason or other to be there. Almost as if you expected to find her."

"Ah," Zlavko said, laughing softly. "You see right through me.

The truth is, I had an arrangement with this young woman this evening. Life here in the school can be lonely, and Asta has been a good . . . friend to me."

"No," Jens said.

"No?"

"I was very good at chess in my younger days. Have I ever told you that?" Jens's feet disappeared from Malou's view as if he was strolling a little around the room. "My greatest strength was that I was good at predicting what my opponent could get out of their moves. But I find you difficult to understand, Zlavko. What would you get out of that?"

"I don't know what you mean. I've had a long night."

"Yes, I understand that. But, you see, Jakobsen told me that Asta was having some kind of fit when you found her. And that before then, she'd been inside my office. And my apartment. Jakobsen thought she was in some kind of trance. And the strangest part was that the whole time, she was mumbling: *Find the stone. Find the stone . . .*"

"I don't understand that," Zlavko said. "I've no idea why she would have been in your office."

"Let's drop the formalities here, dearest Zlavko," Jens said. "We both know how this ends, and I have one more thing to take care of right now. But tell me, for the sake of old friends: Why?"

"For Leah," Zlavko whispered.

"What?"

Suddenly, Zlavko had a knife in his hand; he must have had it tucked in his waistband. Malou followed the movement with her eyes. Jens was caught off-guard, but he neither took a step back nor lifted his hands to defend himself, and the knife was aimed directly at his heart. But just before it hit its target, everything

464

exploded in a roaring, splitting light, and Zlavko screamed with pain and collapsed to the floor.

Malou closed her eyes. When she opened them again, she saw the knife laying on the floor at Jens's feet. He bent over calmly and picked it up. Zlavko was on his knees before him, gasping for air in short, shallow breaths. Malou wanted to scream at him to get away, but instead, she pushed her clamped fist into her mouth and forced herself to lie still.

"And what about your lovely protegé, who you've defended so relentlessly? Is she also a little traitor?" Jens said casually.

"She . . . knows . . . nothing," Zlavko groaned.

"You're lying," Jens insisted, gripping tighter on the knife. He hesitated for a moment, then he pulled back on the knife, and with a very deliberate movement, he stabbed Zlavko in the stomach three times in quick succession. *"For Leah,"* he said, snorting. "I've never heard anything so stupid." Then he threw the knife to the side, turned, and left the room.

Malou was rooted to the spot. She couldn't take her eyes off Zlavko. He turned his face slowly toward her. Blood trickled from his mouth.

"Get away from here," he whispered. Then he collapsed forward onto the floor.

Everything went black before Malou's eyes. Her legs were shaking, but she managed to crawl out from under the bed and stumbled to the window. Zlavko's apartment was on the second floor. But blood mages heal easily. Malou opened the window, swung her legs over the edge, and jumped.

MARCH 19TH
6:30 A.M.

Chamomile

"Molly?" Chamomile did the secret knock again, but when nobody answered, she tried the door. It wasn't locked. "Hey, you forgot to shut the bolt."

Chamomile elbowed the door open. In one hand, she carried the watering can, and in the other, she had a little bunch of the first dandelions to have grown up through a crack in the asphalt. "Molly, did you fall asleep again?"

Chamomile took the heavy watering can over to the corner and put it down by the sink, where the manager of the sugar factory had probably bathed in the olden days. Normally, they didn't get up too early, but neither of them had been able to sleep. They were waiting for a reply from Malou. Had she managed to do it? Or had she been discovered?

Chamomile straightened up. In the middle of the room, there was an overturned chair. The flowers dropped from her hand.

"Molly, is something wrong?"

She was lying on the bed. Her dark hair covered her face. Chamomile went slowly closer. "Molly?" she whispered.

"She's not going to wake up."

She jumped. It was as if she could see it all, all at once. How he had forced his way into the room where Molly had tried to fight him off. How he had overpowered her and laid her on the bed so it would look like she was just napping.

She turned slowly around. Jens stood over by the door. She had walked right past him.

"What have you done to her?"

"Let's not talk about that right now," he said as if she were a disruptive student who was interrupting his class. "Let's talk about us two, instead."

"Keep away from me!"

"Relax, there's no need to be so melodramatic," he said, fixing her with a stare. "We'll take it a step at a time. You've been good enough to help me on several occasions. You've even saved my life. Now, you can get the chance to do it once more."

Chamomile sank to the floor by the side of the bed. Her hands fumbled over the green rug on the floor.

"Is this what you're looking for?" He held up her phone.

"No," she whispered.

"They're not coming to help you. So, take it nice and easy. We're going to leave here now, and—Argh!" Jens lifted his hands up to his face as Chamomile threw the little kettle from the spirit stove at him.

She had put the last of the water on to heat up before going out to fetch more. She didn't wait to see if he had been hit by the boiling water but just stormed out the door.

"It's no use running away!" he yelled after her.

Chamomile raced down the stairs, but suddenly she felt a push in her back. She tripped, flew through the air, and landed with a thump on the cold, marble floor of the hall.

"Stop her!" shouted Jens, who was coming over the first step already himself, and Chamomile struggled to her feet and ran out the main door. She fled in panic, like a rabbit getting chased down by a bird of prey, but again, it was as if some invisible force knocked her flying. She tumbled down to the ground, scraping her hands and knees so that they bled.

"Leave me alone!" she screamed at the invisible strangers.

"There's no use," said Jens, who had also gotten to the yard edged by red buildings. "There are far too many of us."

"To hell with you and your rotten spirits!" Chamomile spat and started running again. This time, she ran in zigzags to try to fool Jens's invisible minions, but to no avail. Again and again, she was cast to the ground while Jens calmly came nearer and nearer. She was crying with rage and frustration, but once again, she got to her feet.

"Help!" she screamed. It echoed around the buildings, and she set off running again. But this time, she didn't run toward the car park and the town. Instead, she ran farther into the factory grounds. As she took hold of the bottom rung of the ladder, she heard him shout.

"No, Chamomile! Do you want to kill yourself? You'll never get down from there!"

"I'd rather that," she whispered as she started to crawl upward. She was only useful to him alive. If she died, he wouldn't have killed him herself, and all his sick plans would be ruined.

"Wait!" he screamed, and she knew that he was talking to his spirits now, ordering them to hold back so they didn't risk pushing her off. Chamomile concentrated on looking at the next rung and nowhere else. The wind pulled at her hair and her clothes. The external ladder on the silo was rusty and felt very precarious when she stepped on it.

468

"Help!" she yelled again, inwardly hoping that this impulse of hers to climb up the silo could buy her some valuable time. Maybe somebody would hear, maybe they'd come. And if not, then she could take the only way out.

The silos were very high. They could be seen miles away. It would be over quickly. Chamomile felt tears blurring her eyes, but she carried on, higher and higher. The clouds scudded across the sky. She brought her gaze back down. Looking up actually made her dizzier. The rusted rungs flaked a little under her touch. It had been many years since the factory had been in use. Nobody had thought of maintaining the old ladder out on the tall silos. Who would ever use them again?

Her knees started to shake. The world seemed so far away now, and she had stopped screaming for help. Suddenly, she realized there were no more rungs. She was at the top of the ladder. With a strange sound somewhere between a snarl and a groan, she swung one leg over the little railing at the top of the silo and let herself drop on the other side. She landed on her back and lay flat. A flock of gulls circled high above her, screeching. She felt, more than she heard, vibrations in the frail ladder. He was coming up. Chamomile got up and moved slowly, as far from the ladder as she could. The thought of what Jens could do if he had the power he longed for; it was more than she could bear. He'd be unstoppable. It could not happen. She mustn't let it happen.

She reached the railing on the other side. From here, she could see for miles. Right out to the sea. What would it feel like? Like floating? Would there be a little breath of peace, of freedom, on the way down, or would there only be fear? She swung her legs over the railing, one after the other, keeping her eyes on the horizon and the pale morning sun, which bathed her cheeks. Soon, the trees would be blossoming, and the light would return for real. She would have liked to experience this spring. And summer. There were so many things she'd have liked to experience, but that wasn't how it was going to be. At least she had experienced loving and being loved. Not everyone is able to say that. *I'm so sorry, Molly* . . .

Chamomile closed her eyes. She could hear nothing but the screeching of the gulls through the noise of the wind, although he must have reached the top. Time had run out. It had to be now. She held the railing behind her with both hands. All she had to do was let go and lean slightly forward. She didn't even have to jump. But she didn't let go.

I can't. She sensed, at that same moment, how the wind came into stillness around her while invisible creatures surrounded her body. Jens's spirits were holding her in place, not that they even had to, and the recognition of that made her start to cry. When it came to the crunch, she didn't have the nerve.

She felt him grab her shoulders. From the outside, it could surely have looked like a father who wanted to save his daughter from falling. Chamomile wanted to scream, but she had no control over her own voice. It only came out in a soft whimper.

"Hush. Sleep now," he whispered in her ear.

470

Dear All,

I know you are probably worried about me, but you do not need to be. I'm well and am safe with friends.

I've realized that I made a mistake. I've been working against the very thing that, in the end, will come to save all of us. And I regret leading you astray and creating division among us mages. But it's not too late. Not for me—and not for you. Join us! Let's stand together. Rosenholm's door is open to all those who support the cause of mages and want a bright future together.

Best wishes,
Chamomile

MARCH 19™
11:03 A.M.

Malou

Her feet were strangely pale and numb. Malou focused on generating heat. She felt the warm blood near her heart flowing through her veins right down into her toes until the jagged pain made her grimace. She had no shoes or jacket on, and the thin T-shirt and pajama bottoms had gone cold and damp in the drizzly rain. She continued along the road. She had long ago lost her sense of time and also had no idea where she was. Malou gripped her phone in her pocket, but it had run out of power and the screen was smashed.

She heard the sound of a car drawing nearer and jumped into the ditch for safety's sake. It could have been Jens, having discovered that Malou, rather than Zlavko, had forced Asta into his rooms. That it was she who had tried to steal the stone. Not him. The car slowed and pulled onto the side.

"Malou?"

The voice was soft and didn't seem to belong at all to the large man behind it. Malou looked up from the ditch. Thorbjørn got out and opened the passenger door for her. "Hurry up," he said.

Malou jumped in. Thorbjørn slammed the door and, seconds later, started the engine. She looked around. The van was full of tools, but there were also sports bags full of clothes. Thorbjørn's van was like some kind of mover's van. She recognized a bag full of Kirstine's clothes and also a pair of old sneakers, maybe Benjamin's, and she pulled them on as they drove.

Then she could hear that the road surface changed. They were driving on a gravel path now, and their speed had slowed. Soon, the van slowed to a stop. Malou pushed the door from the inside, but it would only open once Thorbjørn had unlocked it from the outside.

"What's happened?" she asked. "Is it Chamomile?"

"Come on." He turned his back on her and strode off into the trees surrounding the little car park they'd stopped in. They were somewhere in a forest. Thorbjørn vanished between the trees, and Malou did her best to keep up with him. She had hurt her leg when she jumped out the window, but it wasn't too bad. Malou fought with everything she had to keep her hopes up. But she also knew fine well: If Chamomile had been okay, then Thorbjørn would have said so.

Thorbjørn turned off the path and continued through the trees, and then they came into view. They were sitting on the forest floor like wounded soldiers waiting for reinforcement. Victoria was in floods of tears in Benjamin's arms, and if that wasn't enough to give Malou the answer she was searching for, she only needed to look at Kirstine's stricken face and Jakob's dark expression.

"Damn it!" she screamed. "Who let it slip? Who was it? Who spilled where she was?"

"Malou," Thorbjørn said softly.

"Nobody said anything."

"Someone must have told him! Was it you? Answer me!"

Molly looked up at her with red and puffy eyes. Malou hadn't even noticed her getting close, but already she stood with both fists clasped on Molly's sweater, shaking her back and forth.

"Malou, let her go!" Victoria screamed. "It wasn't Molly!"

"We were the only ones who knew where she was," Malou snarled, still not letting go of Molly's sweater despite Victoria tugging to tear her off. "Did he persuade you? Or force it out of you?"

"It wasn't me!" Molly screamed as if it was only just dawning on her what Malou was talking about. "I love her. Why would I do that?"

"That's ENOUGH!" Thorbjørn's voice boomed throught the forest, and Malou felt her feet lifting from the ground as he grabbed her and walked a few feet away before dropping her heavily to the ground. Malou lay on the forest floor, trying to steady her breathing again.

"It wasn't Molly," Victoria repeated. "None of us have said a thing."

"Then how? How did he find her?"

"Maybe he was following you or overheard you talking about it," Jakob suggested quietly.

"Did you write it down anywhere?" Benjamin asked.

"No, of course not," Malou said.

"Not even on your phone?"

She felt a chill in her stomach.

"You texted me where I could find her," Molly whispered. "I deleted the message as soon as I'd read it."

"What about you? Did you delete it?" Thorbjørn asked.

"But . . ." Malou shook her head. "My phone is always on me. Nobody has a chance to look at it. There's a password."

474

"Face it, Malou," Benjamin said. "One of Jens's little spies has looked in your messages. It was you who led Jens to Chamomile's hiding place."

Malou became cold all over. Zlavko's words echoed in her head. *It's the only weak point in my plan: that you'll let something slip.*

"No." She hid her face in her hands. He was right. She knew it.

"You need to stop all this. If we spend our time arguing, then . . ." Victoria stopped there; she didn't need to say anymore.

"We'll find her," Thorbjørn said. "We'll find her before it's too late. We need to try and understand how Jens thinks."

"He's thinking about killing her!" Jakob said, getting to his feet. "What are we waiting for?"

"We need to act cleverly," Thorbjørn said. "Jens will be expecting us to come."

He handed Malou a letter. The handwriting looked like Chamomile's, but it was otherwise obvious that it came from Jens. "He's trying to lure us into a trap," she said.

"But we're not planning on walking into it," Thorbjørn said.

"Why not?" Benjamin said, getting up beside Jakob. "I'm ready to fight. Why don't we just go up to the main door and break it down?"

"If we go to Rosenholm now like a bunch of hotheads, it'll end badly," Thorbjørn said. "We're not as strong as you think. Jens has the victory stone. Besides, he's trained up a troop of little soldiers and may well have called in reinforcements from outside," he continued. "Malou, can we trust that Zlavko will fight against Jens when the time comes?"

"Zlavko's dead," she whispered. "Jens killed him last night. He must have gone to the factory just after."

"Are you sure?" Victoria asked.

"I saw it." *It's my fault. He didn't need to die.*

"I'm sorry about that," Jakob said. "His life was full of pain."

"So was his death," Malou muttered. To her surprise, she found she was crying.

"Let's all hope that he finally finds the peace he never found in life," Thorbjørn said mournfully.

"Now we have no ally inside the school walls," Benjamin concluded.

Malou dried her eyes. "We still have friends at Rosenholm," she said. "Or maybe not friends, but something even better. People who have debts to pay. Give me a few hours, and I can find out where she is."

Malou stood up and left without waiting for an answer.

Chamomile

At first, there was just darkness. Then the pain came. A fuzzy, aching pain that grew sharper, more stabbing. After that, she noticed the cold. And thirst. But none of these, the pain, cold, or thirst, were the worst. The worst moment was when she finally came around completely, and everything came flooding back to her. Molly, lying lifeless on the bed. Jens, standing waiting for her. The gulls, who had been the only witnesses.

Chamomile fumbled forward in the blackness. Her hands didn't get far before they met damp stone walls. The ceiling was so low she couldn't stand. He had thrown her into a hole. But where? Chamomile strained to breathe. It suddenly felt like there wasn't enough oxygen. Was she to die in this hole? She screamed. But the stones around her absorbed the sound of her voice. Nobody would hear her. Nobody would come.

Pay off your debt.

I owe nothing now. He's dead

But promises must be kept.
Even to the dead.

Sorry but there's nothing
more for me to do here

That's not true. You said it yourself.
It's your fate, too.

The red-headed girl?

Yes.

Then tell me what I have to do

MARCH 19ᵀᴴ
4:00 P.M.

Malou

She ran in the mornings. Louis ran in the afternoons. He was not especially ambitious with his training, so there was no guarantee he would pass by. Malou sat at the forest edge and waited. But she wasn't left waiting long. She heard footsteps approaching on the gravel path. Was it just her imagination that she could hear it was him? Just by the sound of his footsteps? Or was it her instinct, her subconscious, maybe, that could sense his presence in a way she didn't understand herself?

She stepped out onto the path just before Louis passed her, and he nearly ran into her.

"Malou!"

She swung her fist into his face, hitting him full on the mouth and splitting his lip. He stepped groggily back a few paces, and one kick to his groin had him on the ground. He didn't fight back; he just protected himself against the blows that were now raining down on him. She hit him until she was out of breath. Then she stood up and kicked him in the kidneys. He sobbed, face down on the gravel. Then he lifted his head.

"Malou!" he gurgled through a mouthful of blood, which dripped onto the path.

"You looked at my phone," she hissed. "You went to Jens, and you ratted out where she was. You betrayed me!"

"You don't understand," he snuffled, clasping his mouth to try and stop the blood. "That's not how it was."

"So, tell me how it was," she snarled.

"Chamomile is Jens's daughter," Louis whispered. "He told me himself. They've brainwashed her into thinking she can't trust her own father. Jens just wants to talk to her so she can see that they're lying, Malou."

"So, Jens just wants to have some quality time with his daughter. Really? That's how it is?" asked Malou. "Then, where is she now? Why has she disappeared from the surface of the earth shortly after you squeaked to Jens?"

Louis's eyes flashed. "She disappeared?"

"You're a total idiot. Jens has taken Chamomile somewhere. If anything happens to her, I'm going to kill you. You know that?"

"He won't do anything to her. She's his daughter! Malou, listen to me!"

"I'd love to listen to you." She stood with her hands on her hips as he sat up. "I'd love to hear. Was Jens happy when you sold me out to him? Was it worth it, Louis? Was it hard for you? Or are you just a very good little actor?"

"I didn't tell Jens how I knew about it," he said gruffly. "I didn't even mention your name. Malou! I would never do anything that would hurt you. You have to believe that. I did it to help Jens. To help the Movement. Us. You and me."

"There is no us," Malou said. "There never has been. And now you're going to tell me where he has hidden Chamomile."

"I don't know," he sobbed. "I don't know where she is. I can ask Zlavko . . ."

"Zlavko's dead," she said. "He's been working against Jens the whole time, but Jens found out. He killed him last night."

"No," Louis whispered. "That can't be right."

Malou looked at him. Deep down, she knew that Jens would never involve Louis in his plans. Not directly, in any case. But maybe indirectly. Jens had made himself dependent on the Crows for protection.

"What are your instructions for today?" she asked.

He looked at her. There was no resistance in him. No hope that he could save this situation. Jens had flattered him into talking. She had beaten it out of him, but the result was just as depressing. She despised spineless people.

"Answer," she said quietly.

"Guard duty on all entrances around the clock. Nobody enters or leaves except the Crows. Patrols of all the halls, extra watch on Jens's apartments. And a bunch of new people have arrived from outside the school. They're on guard as well, but I don't know where."

"He's scared we'll come after her," Malou said. "She's at Rosenholm. Anything else?"

He shook his head. "Not that I know of."

"Are you sure? There hasn't been notice of a particular date when something special will be happening?"

"Yeah, but what—"

"What's the date?"

"Jens has invited people to join an ancient ritual for Ostara. It's on March twenty-first."

"That's it," Malou said. "That's when he wants to do it. We don't have any more time."

"What is it he wants to do?" Louis asked.

481

"I'll tell you," Malou said. "He wants to kill Chamomile. After that, he'll take her out into the forest and present her body to the old oak tree. And as thanks, the tree will give him powers that you couldn't imagine in your worst nightmares. That's what he wants to do, Louis. And if he succeeds, it will be your fault. Because you told him where she was."

"No, that's not true. That's not how this ends. I saw it, how you would save me . . . It was in my vision."

"Believe me," Malou said. "I've no inclination to save you. Goodbye, Louis."

She turned on her heels and left without a backward glance.

She's at Rosenholm
The ritual will take place the day after tomorrow, at sunrise.
Ostera.

Chamomile

Chamomile lay curled in a ball to keep warm. She might have slept a little. Her throat was dry and raw. She had screamed until she lost her voice. Then, there had been silence. But now, a noise had woken her from dozing. There was a scraping sound somewhere. Chamomile sat up and crawled toward the sound. She felt her way across the walls and found a rough and uneven surface. A wooden hatch. Chamomile banged on it with her fists.

"I'm here!" she croaked.

The scratching noise continued, and then there was a faint whine. It was an animal. It was trying to get in, but Chamomile wasn't afraid. It sounded like a dog begging for food. A forlorn sound, which instinctively aroused sympathy in the listener.

"I'm here!" Chamomile coaxed it again. "Come on."

The animal answered with a short yap, but the scratching noise stopped. She heard no more.

"Come back!" she whispered.

Chamomile felt at the hatch. It was made of thick wood, and there was no handle on the inside. She fumbled along the sides of the hole, looking for loose rocks. Maybe she could find a sharp stone she could scrape a hole through the hatch with. She found only gravel and pebbles. There was a bigger stone at the far end, but it was round. Chamomile picked it up and threw it at the wall. It bounced back and hit her on the leg but stayed in one piece. Chamomile picked it up to try again, but she stopped short at a new sound. A scratching, not hollow and clear as before, but further away. She felt her way over to where the noise was loudest. She had no doubt it was the sound of little paws digging. Soon, she could hear the whining noise again. Chamomile started to dig earth and grit away from between the larger stones that formed the walls. She dug her fingers in and tried to loosen the stones until her fingertips were moist with blood, and the whole time, she kept calling, "Come on, I'm here." "Come on, little one."

Now, she could suddenly hear the animal snuffling. It must have made an opening. Chamomile was afraid it wouldn't fit through the narrow gap, and the large stones of the wall were immovable. She put her hand as far as she could into the hole she had dug herself, and suddenly, she felt claws on little paws and then a wet nose. And fur. "Come on, you're nearly there!" she urged.

The animal whined and squeaked, but Chamomile kept on encouraging and calling it, and finally, it managed to squeeze through the hole. Chamomile cried and laughed in turn as the animal jumped up at her and snuffled its nose into her hair. It was a fox, she guessed, although she couldn't actually see it. But she felt its soft fur, bushy tail, and pointed snout. The fox let her stroke its fur and feel its soft ears, and it licked the tears from her face. And much later, when she curled up to sleep, it lay close beside her to keep her warm.

MARCH 20TH
6:25 A.M.

Kirstine

The sun rose as they drove up through Jutland. It started to look more and more like home. Kirstine turned off the highway and continued down an empty country road. Thorbjørn's rattling old van grumbled on sluggishly, and she opened the window a crack to let in some fresh air. Her leg ached, but she didn't have the heart to waken him.

Jakob slept with his head against the window. It reminded her of their very first meeting. They had taken the same bus to Rosenholm, and Jakob had fallen asleep with his head on her shoulder. Did she know then, already, that she had fallen in love? Maybe. Kirstine remembered, in any case, how she'd decided, from then on, to be *the new Kirstine*. She smiled bitterly to herself. They say you should be careful what you wish for because it might just happen. All she wished for now was to find her way back to herself.

It was a beautiful, cold, spring morning. She rolled the window down as she turned into the little road to the churchyard. Jakob woke up—the sound of the wheels on the rough gravel most likely disturbed him.

"Are we there?" he asked, drowsily. "How long have I been sleeping?"

"We lost you somewhere back on Funen."

"Hey, why didn't you wake me so we could switch?"

"I like driving," Kirstine said, swinging the car into a parking space and cutting the engine.

"You like being in the driving seat, you mean?" he said, giving her a wink.

They sat for a while without moving.

"I can't quite work out . . ." Kirstine muttered, but her voice petered out mid-sentence.

"If we're losing our minds?" Jakob asked. "Yes. You just don't do something like this. It's—"

"Unforgivable?"

"Maybe. It's not something normal people do, in any case."

"But, we're not exactly normal," said Jakob. "We never have been, and we never will be. And imagine if this actually works."

Kirstine nodded and opened the door. The church car park was empty. She would rather have done this at night, under cover of darkness, but there was no time. Tomorrow was Ostera, and Jens would perform the ritual at sunset.

She zipped her jacket right up to her neck. The skies were clear, and there must have been frost in the night. Jakob opened the glove compartment and took something out. She recognized his scarf. The same one she'd borrowed from him that very first day they met and which she had never returned.

"I saw it hanging on a peg at the cottage. I grabbed it just before we left." He held it out to her.

"But it's yours," she said.

"No, it's yours now. You've earned the right to keep it. That's how it works."

Kirstine took it and wrapped it around her neck. It still had his smell. For some reason, that old scarf meant more to her than the piece of jewelry he'd given her for her birthday.

They went in through the gate. Kirstine had a crutch for support and limped slightly with the brace on her leg. The graves were still covered in sprigs of spruce, but in several places, snowdrops and the first hyacinths were pushing up between them. Fresh flowers lay at one of the graves.

"Here it is," Kirstine said.

"Little Kirsten and Prince Buris," Jakob read. "Couldn't you try to explain how you got this whole idea?"

"It was Frederik Juul's book. Victoria left it for me. The one about Orpheus and Eurydice."

"Oh. The one Sigsten called his journal?"

"Yeah, but it wasn't only a journal. I took some time to read it while I was in hospital. It seems that Frederik Juul was interested in the myth of Orpheus and the underworld because he hoped he could connect that myth to the story of the Nightshades," Kirstine told him. "He must have given up on that at some point. His final notes are about the prophecy, in particular, its ending, but also about King Nidung's victory stone, which Frederik Juul was convinced could be found in Thy. And when we were sitting back there in the woods, it came to me. Sigsten did write it to us, after all. On his note. It was there the whole time."

"I'm not following you," he said.

"Sigsten told us when Thorbjørn and I went to see him. His father had searched for a victory stone belonging to a king called Nidung. Victory stones are often passed down from one generation to the next, right? What if that stone was also passed down? What if it was owned, hundreds of years later, by another king called Valdemar the Great?

488

"And Valdemar was . . ."

"Little Kirsten's brother," Kirstine said. "It was Valdemar who killed his own sister. *Sleep, my sister, beneath this stone.* That's what he wrote on her tombstone. Later, he snuck into the churchyard and chiseled another word onto the stone."

"Sigsten," Jakob said. "Victory stone."

"I really hope this is the right thing to do," she whispered. And then she leaned forward and took hold of the long, flat stone lying on the ground, and Jakob did the same. The stone was heavy, but Kirstine felt her scars gleam. Her powers buzzed under her skin, and it didn't take them long to shove it aside. They had to do it in two separate pieces, as it had broken at some point in the hundreds of years it had lain there.

Are you okay?" Jakob asked.

She nodded. "Let's get this over with," she said, and Jakob bashed the spade into the hard-packed, sandy ground.

It took them several hours to get down to the grave itself, and Kirstine was starting to believe there was nothing at all under the heavy stone and that they'd gotten it all wrong. That they'd disturbed the grave on account of some crazy idea she'd concocted on the back of the mad notions of a long-dead, brain-addled gold digger. But then, the earth started to change. It became more crumbly, and they realized what they were digging now were the remains of a coffin. Kirstine examined the earth to be sure.

"This is wood. Oak, maybe. It's all decayed, but it is wood," she said to Jakob, who stood digging. "Be careful. You could hit bones."

"I'll do my best," Jakob said, out of breath. "But I'm not sure an archaeologist would be too happy with this. I think there's something here."

489

Kirstine stuck her head over the grave's edge. Jakob was on his knees down in the hole. He was shirtless, despite the cold, and had laid the spade to one side while he carefully shifted earth with his hands.

"Do you see that?" He sat up, and Kirstine looked down into the hole.

She could just make out the contours of a skull. "Let me do it," she said.

Jakob stood up and helped her down into the grave. Then he placed his hands on the grave edge and pulled himself up. Carefully, she lifted the bones from the sandy earth. The skeleton was surprisingly intact. And there it lay, on the breastbone. The victory stone. Kirstine had no doubt. It was smooth, oval, and so black it was almost blue.

She took it in her hand. The skull looked up at her with its empty eye sockets. Kirsten, Little Kirsten, killed by her own brother because she was pregnant by the man she loved. Kirstine imagined how the king, her brother, had gotten scared as he stood by his sister's body. Perhaps he knew the old children's rhyme about the Nightshades—the army of dead girls who came roaming through the night to seek their revenge. Perhaps that was when King Valdemar decided to lay the stone in his sister's coffin. The victory stone, which would protect against the Nightshades, as the old prophecy told. The king may have hoped the victory stone could keep his sister in her grave so she could never waken and seek him out. *Sleep, my sister, beneath this stone.* It didn't mean the gravestone; it meant the victory stone. But Valdemar hadn't understood the ancient prophecy. If Sigsten was right, the victory stone had never held that power. Instead, it was exactly the one thing needed for the Nightshades to get what they sought. *Revenge.*

There was only one night left to wait. Then it would happen. His daughter would join the ranks of nameless women who had served the greatest cause. He loved her. This was his way of immortalizing her. He sings to her so she doesn't feel lonely in the dark.

Your boyfriend's name was Sigsten.
He didn't die of old age.
He was murdered.
By the same man who
killed Trine.

We need your help.

MARCH 20ᵀᴴ
11:25 P.M.

Kirstine

The tree was bare of any leaves and smoldered like molten iron in the night. Kirstine was no longer afraid of it, and it was as if the tree knew that. It couldn't touch her, there was no rustling or sizzling around her, and she wasn't watching the forest floor for roots bursting up through the soil. The dark blue stone lay in her hand, pulsating with heat like a live coal. Even the pain in her broken leg was nearly gone.

"What now?" Jakob whispered, looking up to the crown of the tree.

"Now, we wait," Kirstine said. She felt oddly calm. The fog and darkness felt dense, and the forest was silent. There was no birdsong, animal noises, or wind tearing at the branches. Only the fog, the darkness, and the quiet, sizzling sound of the tree. What happened next would decide everything. But she couldn't do it alone. She needed to wait and have faith that it would happen.

"Do you believe what the prophecy says?"

"Yes," Kirstine said. "The victory stone will waken the dead ones."

"Maybe this will be the end," Jakob whispered.

"Yes. Maybe."

"Come on, let's sit here." He sat on the gnarly roots of the tree, leaning up against the trunk, and Kirstine thought she heard a deep rumbling from inside it, like a sign of permission for them to be there. She sat beside him. Close enough to feel the warmth of his body, close enough to catch the faint smell of wood smoke and forest that he often carried and that she liked so much.

"Do you remember how I once said I regretted it?" He didn't turn his face toward her but looked out between the trees.

"Yes."

"Actually, it's been the best thing to ever happen to me. *You* are the best thing that's ever happened."

"No matter how things go?" Kirstine whispered.

"Yes. I love you, Kirstine."

She closed her eyes and smiled. "I love you, too."

She felt him shift and could sense him moving a little closer. She turned her face to his, eyes still closed.

"Kirstine," he whispered.

Then she felt his mouth on hers. It was a slow and intense kiss, a whole life's dreams and hopes in one. Maybe this would be all they would get.

"Be careful," she whispered. "Nothing's happening to me."

Kirstine realized he was right. There was no painful current between them when she touched him. Her powers no longer felt like a simmering ball of fire, ready to flare up any moment because of her feelings for him. She was fully in control.

"It's the stone," he whispered hoarsely, touching her hand that held the victory stone. He showed her his unharmed fingers. "Look."

He was right.

494

"Stay here." She stood up and placed the stone in the pouch she was wearing around her neck. After that, she took off her clothes piece by piece until she stood naked before him. The scars on her arms and legs glowed the same deep color as the tree. The sonorous rumbling vibrated through her body, and she was no longer sure if it came from herself or from the tree. It beat faster and in time with her pulse.

"Kirstine . . ." He reached out to take her hand.

"First, you have to promise me one thing," she said. "That you'll let me do what I'm destined to do. That you won't try to stop me."

"Not again, Kirstine . . ."

"Yeah, I'm afraid so."

"You're asking a lot of this love-struck soul," he said. "The last time, I was sure I'd lost you. I don't know if I can handle it again."

"You can. Promise me."

His eyes welled up, but his voice was steady. "I promise you."

"Good," she whispered. Then she took his hand and let him pull her down into his arms.

Chamomile

The flashlight blinded her, and strong hands reached out to grab her ankles. Chamomile screamed and kicked out. She dug her nails into the pressed earth of the floor, but it didn't make a difference. They were too strong, and she felt herself being pulled out of the little hatch and onto the floor.

A heavy body lay over her, pressing her down into the ground. Chamomile blinked into the flashlight's beam. Then it went dark again, as a hood was pulled over her head. Chamomile wanted to scream, but she couldn't get any air. She felt a rope being tied around her wrists, and then she was pulled up to her feet. She sobbed as her legs gave way. Strong hands grabbed her by the upper arms and marched her off.

MARCH 21ˢᵀ
1:55 A.M.

Malou

Malou checked her phone again. They couldn't wait any longer. Sunrise was at 6:18 a.m., and they had to find Chamomile before that. She lifted her head in a signal to Thorbjørn. They had stretched it for as long as they could. They could certainly have made good use of Kirstine in the event of a fight. Jakob too. Now, they would have to make do with the little troop they had, hiding at the edges of Rosenholm's big park. Malou was far from certain they would be enough if they were discovered.

The dampness from the dewy grass had soaked through her pants and top, and she had goose bumps. She noted absently how wet and cold she'd gotten from crawling over the big lawn on the grounds. Dressed in black, they were almost impossible to see in the moonless night, but Thorbjørn wasn't taking any chances. They must not be discovered at this point. The longer they could hold off from getting into an open fight, the better their chances were.

Rosenholm loomed over them a little farther off, and the little gang halted their peculiar, worming progress on a signal from Thorbjørn. A few of the windows were lit up, and Thorbjørn didn't want to get too close, where the light from the castle might reveal them and where students, teachers, or lookouts could spot them.

They changed their course and pushed across the last stretch of the open lawn, coming around to the side of the castle. Here, they were more sheltered among the large rhododendron shrubs and could allow themselves to run forward, crouched low.

Malou glanced up at the castle. From this side, there was only one window with a light on. The sight of Rosenholm normally gave her a feeling of calm and security. Perhaps even a feeling of belonging. But now, the building just seemed like a bad omen. This was no longer her home, and it came to her then that she didn't have a place where she felt at home.

They ran silently along beside the path to avoid crunching on the gravel. Malou ran right behind Thorbjørn, his huge silhouette almost masked by the dark night, but he came to such an abrupt halt that she nearly crashed into him. He ducked down behind the big shrubs, and the rest of their little troop hurriedly followed suit. Malou looked out through the foliage. A flashlight beam was sweeping around on the other side of the moat. A guard. Malou couldn't make out who was holding the flashlight; she could only hear steps and see the light hopping randomly around. The guard was alone and coming from behind the castle toward the front while they were headed in the opposite direction. The footsteps passed them quickly, and the person on the other side of the moat thankfully didn't think to direct the beam out into the park. Malou also felt pretty sure it wouldn't have made a great difference, given they were all well-hidden by the tall shrubs. Louis hadn't lied. The number of guards had increased. Malou had never known the Crows to patrol the outside of the castle before.

They waited until the footsteps had stopped. In an ideal world, they'd have had time to observe the guard and see if he did his round once every hour or just this once. Or if he, in the worst case, circled the castle constantly all night, making it almost impossible for them to cross the moat without being caught. But they had no time for that.

They carried on as fast as they could without making noise. They were soon around the back of the castle. There were only lower bushes and small trees here; the wilder part of the park, known as the boys's park, now left behind them. Thorbjørn allowed himself a pause to check no other guards were stationed here, but Malou knew he'd be thinking the same as her. If they hesitated for too long, they risked the first guard returning and finding them before they'd reached their goal. Malou tried to ignore the unease growing in her belly. Thorbjørn was the one leading, but this plan had been hers. And the whole thing depended on one person who she wasn't even totally sure she could count on. *I can get us in. We just need to get to the back of the castle; then I can get us in.* She had made it sound very convincing. But now she was frozen by doubt. If they managed to cross the moat unseen, sneak up to the castle, and find the back entrance in the dark, would there be somebody on the other side to let them in? Or would the whole thing fail before they even got inside?

Thorbjørn clearly didn't dare wait any longer, and he gave a gentle sound that was remarkably like a night owl. The signal. Slowly, and careful not to make any noise, they moved out from the scattered bushes and down toward the moat. The grass was wet, and Malou lay on her stomach and let herself glide carefully down into the cold, dark water. The moat was not wide, but the icy water made it a grueling swim nevertheless. Malou suppressed a gasp on feeling something cold and slimy touching her hand. It would be one of the big carp sometimes visible in the moat under careful inspection. Still, she got an unpleasant flashback to the vision she'd had, filled with black, cold water. She was almost afraid she would suddenly feel the Sea Mother's long red hair wrapping itself around her wrists and pulling her down underwater.

Malou was gasping for breath when she reached the opposite bank. The edges were steep and the wet grass slippery, but she heaved herself up quickly and fell onto her back. The others were still in the water, as far as she could tell from the little muted sounds of arm strokes. There was no sign of the guard with the flashlight, so she let herself lie for a moment. Unlike the water, the air felt almost humid despite her soaking wet clothes. The castle windows were dark, apart from one where the curtains were closed, but enough light shone out for her to make out the door they were heading for. She ran her eyes farther along the castle wall. In a small crevice opposite her, only a few feet away, she spotted a shape she didn't remember seeing before. At first, she thought it was a black stone sculpture. Then she realized it was a young man whose face was black because he wore a mask to cover his ruined face. *Elias.*

"Hi, Malou. Nice of you to come by. You are exactly the person I was waiting for." He stood up and pulled a knife from his belt. Malou got to her feet. "It's always nice to feel missed," she said in a snarky tone as her eyes flicked from side to side.

Was there more than just Elias keeping watch along the castle wall? Would they come rushing as soon as they found out what was going on? The door they needed to get to was only about 30 feet away, but it might as well be 30 miles if they were discovered now. Malou turned her focus back onto Elias. She had to stop him before it went that far. She searched for the feel of his pulse and found it, but it was too late. With a furious roar, he lunged at her. Malou averted his attack and avoided his knife, which jabbed out after her like an invisible snake in the darkness. She got in a punch, which hit him on the arm with the knife. It hurt—she was sure of it—but it wasn't enough to disarm him.

"Go to hell," he snarled, but Malou was no longer listening to him. She searched after the roaring in his veins, and she found it. Straight away, a warm wave of calm and well-being filled her. Control. A half-choked gurgle told her that Elias was trying to call for help, but it was impossible. His own blood had turned against him. It pressed in his throat; it forced his muscles to stop moving his body. If she held that pressure, he would be dead in only a few minutes. He sank to his knees.

"Malou! They're coming!" Thorbjørn's voice hissed in the darkness, followed by the sound of footsteps running on gravel and voices barking orders. Elias's roar must have alerted the guard with the flashlight, who was on the way now with backup.

Malou struck Elias on the temple with her elbow, and he fell to the grass. Then she ran.

"Hey!"

The shout bounced back off the castle walls. They'd been seen.

They raced off, Malou having no idea if they had even all gotten out of the water. The flashlight beam danced around between their feet. He was right behind them, but Malou kept running. They had to get to the door. Or they'd never get into the castle.

"Keep going!" Thorbjørn yelled gruffly, and Malou saw he had stopped. There was an angry roar, and she knew Thorbjørn was fighting the guards.

She put the last few feet behind her and almost crashed into the old wooden door at the back of the castle.

"Nightshade!" she hissed breathlessly. "Nightshade!"

Malou held her breath. She sensed other bodies reaching the door and standing behind her in the darkness, and she heard the scream of pain as one of the guards fell victim to Thorbjørn's rune spells. *Is she there?*

A rattling at the door made her heart race. Malou pulled her knife and held it aloft in front of her as the door slowly opened. "You can put that away again, my friend," said a gravely, older voice. "And hurry in, for the love of Freya. Inside, all of you!" Dagny stepped aside and herded them all through the door and into the low hallway.

Malou stepped over a lifeless form on the ground. Someone had been keeping watch at the back door, too. Dagny had apparently dealt with that herself. Last of all, Thorbjørn almost fell through the door.

"I dealt with those guards," he panted. "But there'll be more coming soon. Hurry!"

"Good luck," Dagny croaked, taking the door handle.

"What are you going to do?" Malou asked her, puzzled.

"I'm going out to do my job properly. Finish it," Dagny said, winking at her. Then she disappeared out the door, diligently closing it behind her.

"Come on!" Thorbjørn said. "We don't have much time before the whole castle is after us."

Malou stood for a second, looking at the closed door that Dagny had vanished through. Then she turned and followed the others.

MARCH 21ˢᵀ
2:39 A.M.

Kirstine

Kirstine stood alone. Jakob had kept his promise. He had headed for the castle, though his tearful expression had been almost too much for her to bear. At one point, she feared she wasn't strong enough after all. That she wouldn't be able to let him leave. But where she was going, he couldn't follow. Tears wet her cheeks. This was the price of loving another person, and she couldn't stop feeling amazed that people put themselves through that. No matter what, it would always end with you losing what you loved. Even if both she and Jakob lived beyond this night, nothing lasted forever. Only eternal sleep.

A quiver rustled through the tree's boughs, and Kirstine caught a glimpse of a figure emerging from the darkness. She'd come. She'd been hidden so far by the fog, but now it released her so that Kirstine could make out a little woman walking slowly and unevenly but without hesitation toward the glowing tree. Dagny's eyes were fixed on the roots, bumps, and moss on the forest floor, and she only looked up once she'd gotten right up to her.

"So, we meet again," the old woman said, lowering her hood. She had to tip her head right back to make eye contact with

Kirstine, who felt like she was almost bending over as she would greet a small child as she took Dagny's outstretched hands in hers.

"You came," Kirstine said.

"Of course," Dagny said as she dropped her hands and rolled up her sleeves so Kirstine could see her scars, which also glowed as if they were alight. "Tell me then, how do we get down to the hall of the dead?"

"You knew?"

"Not before now. But as I walked toward the tree, I realized I must have misunderstood the prophecy all these years," Dagny said. "At one time, I believed I was the right one myself. I had the scars. When I met you, I became convinced that you were the one who could wake the Nightshades. And you almost succeeded. But the prophecy doesn't speak of one woman, but rather two. That's how it makes sense. You can't do it alone, can you?"

"No." Kirstine shook her head. "You're right. It needs two women."

"A young one and an old one," Dagny said. "I'm ready. I've been ready for an age. But you need to lead and show me the way. I'm afraid I may actually be too old now for this kind of adventure."

Kirstine turned to face the trunk of the tree. Behind her lay the forest and, on the other side, Rosenholm. Where Jakob was. Where the people she held most dear were in the midst of an attempt to break into a place where their enemies might end up killing them. Everything she loved could be taken from her in the course of this night. And before her lay an insurmountable challenge.

"Do you know the meaning of the name Dagny?" asked the old woman beside her.

"No," Kirstine said.

"It means, quite simply, 'new day.'" I always think of that when the night is at its darkest. A new day will come. And light will displace the dark.

Kirstine nodded. She pushed away all her thoughts and worries. There was no use thinking about the long, dark journey under the earth that lay before them, or the things she had faced down there in the depths, or the pain of her broken leg, which had been so severe she still dreamed about it at night. There was no use thinking about how she would have a weak, elderly woman in tow and how they had so little time, she almost felt it was already too late. There was only one path, and she had to take it, no matter how hopeless it might appear.

Kirstine turned to the tree and placed her palm on its pulsating trunk. She was answered by a deep rumble down below the ground, and the tree, far from being cold and dead, felt warm and pulsed as if it was breathing. She felt the same as if she had laid her hand on some large prehistoric creature, an animal long thought extinct but which now stood here in the forest, breathing deeply. Kirstine noticed her own breathing become calmer. When she lifted her hand again, the bark gleamed yellow like a flame where she had touched it. She didn't have a knife with her, but instead placed her finger on the bark and drew the rune she knew would let them into the underworld. *Ehwaz.*

A glowing *M* appeared in the trunk, and the deep rumbling grew stronger.

The earth began to tremble under their feet, and the sound swelled like a thunderstorm that suddenly gathers overhead. Alarmed, Kirstine took a step back from the tree and just managed to reach for Dagny and pull her back before the ground started to collapse. A hole opened up by their feet, this time much bigger than the last, and still growing. Tree roots wound themselves around one another at the edges of the hole. They sizzled like hot iron submerged in water. Then it became still again, and the roots lay unmoving along the edge of the great hole. Kirstine peered into it. Uneven steps led down into the darkness.

"A staircase," Kirstine muttered. "It wasn't like that last time."

"How convenient," Dagny said. "I'm not sure I could have managed the jump. But I've got the feeling the tree hasn't just created this portal for my sake. Something has changed since last time, am I right?"

"Yes," Kirstine said. "We found the last part of the prophecy. And we have also found the thing the prophecy mentions." She pulled out the leather purse she wore around her neck. "A victory stone. According to the prophecy, a victory stone will waken the Nightshades."

"A victory stone," Dagny whispered. "Of course. After you, my dear friend." Dagny gestured her forward as if she was inviting her in for coffee and not down a pitch-black hole.

Kirstine held out her arm. "Let's go together."

And the two of them stepped down the first step and slowly allowed themselves to be swallowed up by the earth.

506

Killed in the darkness, sacrificed in secret,
the Nightshades rest in the hall of the dead.
One day, they will waken to seek their revenge
and roam out from the valley of death.
Two women with silvery scars from the oak,
marked by misdeeds but still living,
will carve the rune that opens the gateway
to the underworld.
They will set the Nightshades free.
The victory stone will waken the dead.

MARCH 21ˢᵀ
3:00 A.M.

Victoria

They set off running, making no sound other than faint footsteps on the castle floor. Thorbjørn loomed ahead of them. Now and then, they heard shouts, but they were still some way off. Victoria guessed they must be coming from guards outside the castle who had discovered their colleagues knocked out by Thorbjørn's runes.

They were headed for the castle cellars, but to get down there, they would need to pass the busiest areas of the castle, including the Great Hall. With so many guards outside, Victoria thought it unlikely that Jens would have left the Great Hall unguarded. As they neared its doors, Thorbjørn slowed down and signaled to tuck themselves along the wall. Then, he stopped altogether and gave a nod to Benjamin, who took a quick glance around the corner before pulling his head back again.

"Two guards," he whispered. "Men, mid twenties."

"No others?" Thorbjørn whispered.

"No."

"We *have* to get past," Thorbjørn whispered. "I'll handle them. Hopefully, without making too much noise. If not, then be ready to fight, everyone." Without waiting for an answer, Thorbjørn turned his back on them and left their hiding place.

Thurisaz!

Thorbjørn's voice was deep and firm, though not loud, but his incantation hurled across the room toward its target with a loud whooshing sound, such was its power. Victoria held her breath, but she heard neither the moans of the men it felled nor the angry shouts of guards ready to fight. Instead, the castle echoed with the sound of a terrible, chilling scream.

"What was that?" Victoria gasped.

"I don't know," Benjamin said. "Stay here!" He sprang from their hiding place. Victoria looked around her. The others were running, and she followed. She wasn't going to stand here on her own while the others fought, and that scream, still ringing around them, would have everyone flocking to the castle in no time.

Just as Benjamin had described, two men stood outside the great double doors to the hall. She recognized them as the sons of one of her father's friends. But huddled between their feet sat a little girl with wide, white eyes, rocking back and forth. She was the one who had screamed.

"Iris!" Malou yelled.

Victoria realized the girl was a former classmate, a young woman, who now confusingly seemed more like a child curled up on the floor. More than that, she was the reason Thorbjørn's rune spell had failed. In front of the three of them, and also in front of the door to the hall, a great white veil rose up.

"She summoned a spirit shield," Victoria said. "We can't get to them!"

"Well, look who's turned up," said one of the men, whose name was August. "We meet again, then, Malou. This time, though, I don't think you're going to get out of that dance."

Malou answered by spitting on the floor, to which August smiled. "I'm so glad I came tonight."

"Iris, ask your spirits to pull back so we can get by," Lisa said pleasantly, as if she was asking her to close a classroom window at the start of a lesson.

"Save us your fake-friendly crap, Lisa," said the other man. Unlike his brother, he was tall and slim and spoke in an affected manner, which Victoria had always found repulsive whenever he had deigned to speak to her. "Iris is on our side. Like every other person with a brain."

"The rest of Jens's thugs will be here soon," Thorbjørn growled. "We need to get rid of these guys. Victoria, can you break the shield down? Or weaken it enough for us to push through?"

Victoria nodded. She could try, in any case. She closed her eyes, took a deep breath in, and opened her mind to the spirit world. When she opened them again, her eyes were white like Iris's, and she could clearly see the spirits the other girl had called upon. There were so many of them. It was no wonder Thorbjørn's spell had rebounded. Most of them were blurry and hard to distinguish. *The white shadows.* But there were also others Victoria recognized from her years at Rosenholm. An older man with a big white tongue who constantly licked his lips. A tall, bony-looking man she had once seen out in the woods. Some were unsettled, others aggressive. Impatient or troubled. What they had in common, though, was that Iris had summoned them. This wasn't their fight.

Trine, we need you now. It will all be settled tonight. We need you.

It felt like a cry for help, even though she knew the others hadn't heard a sound.

Be gone!

For a moment, Victoria thought it was the spirits talking to her, but then she realized it was Iris.

Be gone from here!

Victoria felt the power radiating from Iris's frail form. Her energy was wild and violent but also vulnerable, and Victoria imagined it was taking all her strength and focus to hold the wall of spirits up.

Trine, I summon you!

Victoria sensed the familiar presence by her side. A human soul is like a face. Each has its own features, distinct from all the other souls in the world. And she knew that Trine would come, even before she saw her. Luminous white, but visible to all. A young girl with a serious, determined expression.

I'm ready. I have waited for this so long.

Victoria nodded and saw that Trine was holding her hand out toward her. Victoria took it and found, to her surprise, that Trine's spirit had a physical form. Victoria could feel Trine's hand in hers, and the feeling of connection with the young woman, across time and death and pain, was overwhelming. When she looked up, she saw they were both crying.

"Hurry, they're coming!" Benjamin's voice sounded distant, and she was aware of shouting and the thudding of running footsteps behind them. Victoria did not turn toward the sounds to see how many were coming now. Instead, hand in hand with Trine, she approached the spirits who were either hissing curses at them or pleading for their mercy.

I release you now from your ties. You are free. Leave this place.

Yet another scream rose from Iris's throat. It grew stronger and stronger until it seemed it might burst Victoria's eardrums. The spirits screamed with her, and the whole castle reverberated with that dreadful sound. Victoria and Trine kept advancing.

When they reached the spirit wall, Victoria hesitated, but Trine pulled her further without pausing into the screen of raging souls, who gathered closer and closer around Iris with their unearthly, heart-wrenching screams.

It's over. Let them go.

These were Trine's words, speaking directly now to Iris. They were surrounded by white shadows that prevented Victoria from seeing. The eerie screaming went on and on and lay around them like a wall of sound, and she felt as if her senses were being rendered powerless.

Then, suddenly, it fell quiet. The spirits had allowed them to pass, and the screaming stopped. Iris sat by their feet as if frozen, her large white eyes staring out into the distance, her body shaking as if it was in spasm.

Sleep.

Trine reached her free hand out and touched Iris on the forehead. The young woman's eyes closed, the spasms in her body stopped, and she sank to the floor.

The wall of spirits was down.

MARCH 21ˢᵀ
3:21 A.M.

Malou

"They're coming!"

Malou whipped around at the sound of Lisa's voice. The spirit wall had fallen, but it was too late. The Crows were already upon them. Amalie was in the lead, and Malou heard Benjamin roar as he threw himself at her. But Malou knew how well-trained she was in combat, and the tall, dark-haired girl deftly evaded him, instead making a long, bloody slash on Benjamin's arm with her athame.

"That one's for Iris!" Amalie screamed at him.

Molly tumbled onto the floor beside Malou after a hit to her face but quickly got back up on her feet again.

"Malou! The door!" Thorbjørn's voice boomed as he struck out at one of the opposition who crashed to the floor without a sound.

Malou turned to the Great Hall doors and started to run. She screamed with rage when she saw how the men at the door laughed while easily deflecting Lisa's attempts to force her way in.

Malou concentrated on the taller of them, and when she was almost right up at him, she jumped. With all her weight, she hit his knee, which gave a dry sound like a branch snapping as his leg folded under him. Malou rolled aside as Lisa furiously threw herself on him.

Malou quickly got back on her feet, but August was quicker. A shooting pain ran through her head as his fist met her temple. The blow made her dizzy. She hit out at him but missed, and her legs suddenly felt like jelly. She gave her head a shake and spat.

August looked at her with a mixture of amusement and admiration. "It's such a shame you and I never came to be," he said.

Malou wasted no energy on talking. She had trouble focusing her eyes, and the sound of many punches being thrown around her rang in her ears alongside the pain. She lunged at him but didn't hit with anything like the same strength, and it certainly wasn't enough to wipe the stupid grin from his face. Behind her, she heard a scream but couldn't tell if it was a friend or foe. She blinked again. She was still woozy, and every movement brought dancing spots to her vision. He spotted her weakness and got in another punch. Malou managed to dodge so it landed on her chest rather than her face. August was strong, and it almost knocked the breath right out of her. She gasped for air.

She needed to put him out of the game. *Focus!*

Malou picked out his heartbeat from all of the others. It was like catching a single fish from a shoal, one she wasn't going to let go again. It was almost as if she could see the blood coursing around in his body and heart, which hammered with adrenaline and bloodlust.

"Shall we finish this?" he asked. "I must admit, I thought you'd last a bit longer, Malou."

He still hadn't noticed how far in she'd gotten. But, as he made to step toward her, smiling, to grab her by the throat, his foot wouldn't lift from the floor. His face froze, and now she was the one who was smiling.

"Now, you're not going to start crying, are you?" she said, kicking him in the groin with all her strength.

August collapsed with a half-swallowed roar of pain, which Malou answered with one more kick, this time aiming the toe of her boot directly at his mouth, which burst in a rush of blood and loose teeth.

Then she fell.

It happened slowly so she had time to see all the details. The floor, coming nearer. A shoe, stepping into her range of vision. A face. *Amalie.*

The tall girl stood over her. Malou hadn't heard her approach and hadn't felt the blow. She was paralyzed, and her hearing was gone. Amalie's lips were moving, but Malou couldn't hear a thing. She could only see her raising her knife and bringing it to her throat.

"I thought you were one of us." It sounded like Amalie was speaking to her underwater. *"Corvus oculum corvi non eruit.* A Crow never attacks one of their own. Did you forget that? You goddamned traitor!"

Amalie's eyes were wide, her pupils dilated. Until suddenly, they were gone.

Malou blinked, the sounds around her returned, and a hand reached down.

"Can you stand?"

"Jakob? You're here?" Malou took his hand and let him pull her up. She was still reeling but no longer had spots in her vision when she moved her head from side to side.

"Come on, Malou!"

She turned toward the great double doors. They were locked, but Jakob soon sprung them open with a powerful rune spell.

"In here!" he yelled. It rang inside her head.

Malou turned her head and took in the scene behind her. Molly was pulling Lisa away from the tall man and forcing her through the doors. Benjamin bled from a slash above one eye. He was half-carrying, half-dragging a young boy Malou didn't recognize.

"Help me carry her, Malou."

She looked down. By her feet, Victoria sat beside Iris. She was unconscious, and Victoria stuck her hands under her armpits to pull her into the hall. "Hurry up—there'll be more of them coming any moment!"

"What are you doing, Victoria? Leave her there!"

"But she'll die!" Victoria moved steadily off with the unconscious girl, as Malou stood.

"Come on!" Benjamin grabbed her arm firmly and pulled her with him and finally, Thorbjørn came lurching in the doors with a student over each shoulder.

Jakob barricaded the door by first drawing a rune with his finger across the door and afterward pushing several wooden benches in front of it. "That'll hold them out for a little while," he said, but it didn't sound as if there was anyone on the other side of the door. The last Crows who were still standing must have run off to get back up.

Thorbjørn carefully put the wounded students onto the ground. Molly found the switch and turned on the light. There were three, not counting Iris. A girl and two boys. And they were all dressed in black and had a silver feather pinned to their chest.

"Why are they in here?" Malou asked. "They're Crows."

"Look at them," Thorbjørn mumbled. "They're just children."

Lisa placed her hands on them, one after the other. "They're alive. But they need care."

Malou looked at their faces. Thorbjørn was right. She remembered them from the combat training sessions she'd led. "They're first-years," she said. "They shouldn't even be in the Crows."

"Cannon fodder," Thorbjørn said, bitterly.

"We can't leave them here alone," said Lisa.

"We can hardly take them with us!" Malou said. "And why is Iris here? She's a third-year, and she's old enough to know what she's gotten into."

"We can't leave her to die," Victoria said. "We can't leave any students behind to die. Not if it's possible to save them."

"And what about Chamomile? Are we not saving her anymore?"

"We'll split up," Lisa said. "I'll stay here." She sat down beside the unconscious students and placed her healing hands on the nearest boy. A huge bruise was swelling by his eye.

"What are we waiting for?" Malou asked. "Let's get down to the cellars."

"I'll stay as well," Victoria said. "Soon, they'll be back, and somebody needs to guard the door."

"Victoria, you can't do that alone," Benjamin reached out to her, but she pulled back.

"I'm not alone." She nodded over toward the entrance. "I'm never alone."

A white shadow stood with her back to them and both hands raised to the door. "Trine and I will keep them out," she said. "Go, now! You can't waste the extra time we can buy you. Promise me you'll find her."

Benjamin nodded. "I promise."

"Victoria's right. We've no time. Come on!" Thorbjørn started running, and Malou turned to follow him. Last, Benjamin left the Great Hall through the kitchen, letting the door shut behind him.

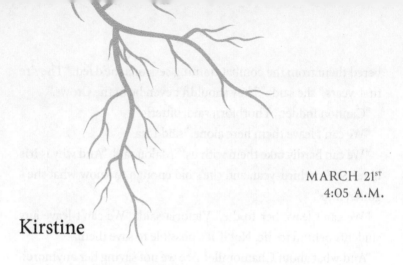

MARCH 21ˢᵀ
4:05 A.M.

Kirstine

They moved forward under the ground. It was like a completely different place. Everything had changed, and Kirstine recognized none of it. Where before she had fumbled on hands and feet along narrow paths and through tight passages, now they were walking on an even path on a gentle descent. Glowing tree roots lit their way so they didn't have to stumble through the dark, and there were no rustling noises or whispering children's voices. At certain points the path turned into broad stairways of roughly carved steps. Farther below them, the river flowed by, but the path was so wide, they didn't need to worry about falling in. Nevertheless, the walk was hard for Dagny. The old woman leaned on Kirstine for support and walked increasingly slowly. Kirstine felt a mixture of impatience and sympathy battling inside her. The clock was ticking, and every minute down here meant it was more likely they'd be too late.

At last, the path ended at a steep, sandstone staircase, which must lead directly down to the river. They could hear it gurgling by, someplace below.

"How far is it to the water, my young friend?" Dagny said, casually, though Kirstine could hear the exhaustion in her voice and the wheezing sound from her lungs, which didn't have the strength to breathe properly so deep under the ground.

Kirstine peered over the edge. "It's still a good way."

"Maybe . . ." Dagny took her hand and gave it a squeeze. "You might need to carry me. I can piggyback."

She nodded and crouched down to let Dagny climb up. Kirstine proceeded slowly. Strangely, she couldn't feel anything from her leg. The victory stone's powers must take away all pain and vulnerability. Dagny's fingers pressed into her shoulders. She was surprised at how strong a grip the old woman had. On the other hand, she weighed little more than a full rucksack. They began their descent. The steps here were narrower, but the glowing roots helped her not take a wrong step and offered her something to grip if she lost her balance. The noise of the rushing water grew louder as they got farther down, and soon she could see the river gushing by so fast that little white whirlpools formed along the banks. She couldn't help but shiver as she pushed the memory of that cold water from her mind.

Finally, they reached the end of the steps, and Kirstine continued along the path with Dagny on her back. And then they were there. The bridge crossing the river. The hall where the dead rested. She could sense it through the darkness. The last time it had taken her many days to get this far. Did this mean there was an even better chance that they could manage in time?

"We're at the bridge," Kirstine said softly.

"Put me down, my friend. I want to go the last stretch myself." Kirstine bent over so Dagny could clamber down from her back. They edged out onto the bridge, the water rushing fast under them and tree roots glistening above like a starry sky. The sound of the water receded as they reached the opposite bank. The huge hall lay ahead of them. There were no bright tree roots here, only darkness and quiet.

"How did you wake them the last time?" Dagny asked.

"It was . . . a song," Kirstine whispered.

"Ah, of course. Like Odin did when he wakened the seeress, right? Then just sing, my friend. My voice isn't what it used to be."

This was it. They wouldn't have any other tries. And she could only think of one song. Kirstine cleared her throat and let her voice lift to fill the whole hall:

> *"I dreamed a dream this night*
> *Of silk and finest furs*
> *In a dress so smooth and light*
> *In twilight's fine sun rays—*
> *now, the clear morning awakes."*

As soon as the song ended, the Nightshades began to waken around them, but even the sounds of this were different than before. There was no scratching or scraping and no sound of people crawling. Instead, it sounded like an army moving in synchronized response to orders from above. Kirstine could visualize them, standing at attention in the darkness. *An army of dead girls.*

She loosened the pouch at her neck, took out the victory stone, and held it out before her. It was no longer lusterless but gleamed with a dark blue light. And then the Nightshades spoke.

"The victory stone will waken the dead."

They spoke as one, and the sound of their voices flooded over them like an ice-cold wave.

A blood sacrifice will set them free.

Kirstine looked at Dagny. "A blood sacrifice?"

520

The old woman nodded. "Ancient magic has its price. That's how it has always been."

"Okay," Kirstine said, revealing her forearms. Her scars gleamed brighter than ever before. With one finger, she drew an X on her arm. *Gebo*—the gift rune. The symbol for human willingness to sacrifice. Her finger left a quivering track on her skin, where soon little drops of blood bubbled through, slowly forming a cross. Kirstine stretched her arm forward in the darkness, hoping the Nightshades would accept her offering, but before she could say a thing, she felt a hand on her arm.

"*Uruz,*" Dagny whispered, and the rune immediately healed the superficial wound so the blood stopped flowing. "That's not enough. Blood is life, and it is life that's needed. This is my fate, the fate I've searched for for so long. To waken the Nightshades from their sleep. To avenge all those young women who were killed. I belong here, together with the others. My sisters. In the hall of the dead girls, I shall rest."

"No . . ." Kirstine whispered as Dagny's words sunk in.

Dagny turned to her and smiled. "Soon, I'll go into the hall. Don't look so horrified. I have hankered after death for a long time now. I've asked myself why I kept on waking up every morning, and now I know. I had to fulfill my task first. Now, I am at the end of the journey. But your journey has just begun. You mustn't follow me."

"This can't be right," Kirstine protested. "That can't be what it has to mean—"

"But it's exactly right. And it's exactly how it should be. Nobody can escape their own destiny. Not me. And not you. As soon as I enter the hall, the Nightshades will follow you. Lead them into battle so that justice can be fully served, Kirstine. That is *your* fate."

Dagny squeezed her hands for a moment. Then she dropped them and slowly started to walk away. A humming noise arose from the blue-black shadows, who could vaguely be made out standing in rows by the entrance to the huge hall. It sounded like a tribute, a farewell hymn to the old woman walking one step after another into the dark. Kirstine's eyes filled with tears. Dagny turned and lifted her hand in a wave. Then she took her last step and let herself be swallowed by the darkness. The nightshade's humming faded away.

"Goodbye, Dagny," Kirstine whispered. Then she turned and started walking. She was followed by the sound of bare feet on the stones.

MARCH 21ST
4:37 A.M.

Malou

"It's empty—there's nobody here."

"Look again. That can't be right!" Malou cried, even though she knew it was the truth. If Chamomile had been here, she would have sensed her pulse somewhere. She knew it so well. But the dark cellars under Rosenholm were empty. Had they come too late?

"Malou, over here," Benjamin called. He was kneeling in a corner in front of a hatch. They were in a part of the cellars that had previously been kitchens. These cold rooms had been used to store foodstuffs, and Malou guessed this hatch might open to a storage larder for potatoes.

"This... This is where she's been?" Malou crouched down beside Benjamin despite the fact what she most wanted to do was to turn away. The small, dark hole gave her a sickening feeling of claustrophobia. *A living nightmare.*

Benjamin showed her an empty water bottle. "This was lying inside. He made sure she survived."

"He's going to pay," Malou whispered. "He is going to pay for this!" She got up. "She's not here. She's not in the cellar. They've moved her."

The others stopped their search of farther rooms and corners.

"Where to now?" Jakob asked, and she realized they were all looking at her for an answer.

She racked her brain, but nothing came to her. Chamomile must still be somewhere in the castle, or else Jens wouldn't be going to such trouble to defend it, calling in extra guards. "I don't know. Maybe his own apartments? He held a party there earlier this year."

"We can take the back stairs up to the second floor," Jakob said.

"Come on!" Malou set off at a run. In normal circumstances, these stairs were rarely used. They were very narrow and dark, and their original use was for maids to get around the castle without disturbing the students or teachers. Malou pulled at the dilapidated door and flung it wide open. Then, she stopped dead. On the other side was a dark-haired girl with big, wide eyes. She had been standing alone in the dark. She was shivering with cold, or perhaps it was fear.

"Asta?"

"I've sent for the others," she said. "They'll be here soon. They're all coming."

Malou could sense that others stood behind her. "Asta, where have they taken Chamomile?"

Her eyes flickered, and Malou had the sense that Asta didn't know what she was talking about.

"I won't tell you anything!" she said, doggedly, pushing her chin out like a child disobeying their parents.

"Where's Jens?" Malou asked, instead. "Where are his guests?"

"I've no idea."

This time, you're lying.

Malou listened to her pulse. It wasn't hard to find; it was like

524

the pulse of a rabbit caught in a trap. She let herself be filled with that rush of warmth that came over her when she took control of another person. She had done it with Asta before. She had tasted her blood, and that made it even easier. There was no resistance; she flowed into her the way water soaks into a piece of cloth. Malou made Asta's blood freeze her body, but she left her throat and vocal cords free so she could still speak. Asta's eyes widened in fear.

"I know you're lying. I can feel it. Tell me where Jens is, and I'll leave you alone," she whispered.

"Go to hell, Malou" she hissed.

Malou shook her head. "Try again," she said, letting the blood press on the lungs. "I know you don't want to die here."

"Malou, what are you doing?" Thorbjørn said, but she didn't respond. They had no time.

"The library," Asta whispered. "They're guarding the library."

"Thank you," Malou said, releasing her grip on Asta's body. Asta immediately collapsed, and Malou stepped over her to continue up the stairs.

The steps were narrow and worn, and she almost slipped several times. Malou looked back. Benjamin was right behind her. For some reason, she remembered the time she'd met him in the hall behind the Library. The spot where all the old photos of former students hung.

"Can we come around by the back entrance to the library?" she asked.

Benjamin hesitated. "It's a little detour, but yeah, we can."

"You show me the way."

Benjamin led them through dark hallways and another set of stairs. He stopped them by a door Malou vaguely recognized.

"Great thinking, Malou," Thorbjørn whispered once they were gathered in the stairwell. "This door leads us into a corridor with a back door into the library. If we're lucky, most guards will be at the main door, but I don't think we can avoid fighting anymore. You're all adults, and you can decide for yourselves," Thorbjørn said, looking truly sorry that he couldn't just be teaching them lessons and sending them to bed early. "But you should each think about it carefully. It's not only Crows Jens has gathered around him, and there's no guarantee we'll all survive this."

"If you're finished with your little speech, Thorbjørn, then let us pass," Malou said. "If anyone has second thoughts, the way out is that way."

"I'm ready!" Molly whispered.

"What's our plan?" Jakob asked.

"We run down the hall and into the library," Malou said. "And if anyone tries to stop us, we fight our way through."

Chamomile

She lay on the floor. The room was warm, but she couldn't see anything. The hood's fabric clung to her face, and she struggled to breathe. Her hands were bound behind her back, but she stretched them as far as she could to see if she could feel warm fur with her fingertips. For some reason, it mattered to her where the fox had ended up. It had been her only friend in the gloom, and if this was to be the end, she only wished to not be alone.

"Where are you?" she sobbed.

She heard footsteps around her, as if several people were closing in on her. A low chanting began. Chamomile gasped for air. It felt as if she were choking.

The chanting sound around her was interrupted by a yell, which sounded as if it came from some place further off.

"They're at the back entrance!"

She recognized Louis's voice. And then, her father's.

"Send the Crows out that way instead! Hans, you go with them!"

Running feet passed her.

"We carry on!" Jens ordered. "Keep going!"

The chanting got louder, almost as if those standing around her were trying to drown out the sounds of fighting from the other side of the door. Chamomile tried to hear what was happening, but it was impossible to tell one voice from another. Instead, she heard something else. *A soft whine.*

MARCH 21ST
5:01 A.M.

Malou

Thorbjørn was right. The Crows had been posted at the library's main door, but they weren't the biggest challenge. Far greater powers were ready to defend Jens.

"Watch out!"

Malou ducked a rune spell that crashed into the wall behind her, smashing one of the old photographs into a shower of glass fragments. Malou nodded thanks to Benjamin for his warning. He returned her nod but switched his attention back to the tall, bald woman, who Malou remembered seeing at Jens's party and who was casting devastating runes to the left and right, the air around her fizzing. To her right, Molly was throwing a punch at a second-year student's face, and farther up by the library door, Jakob exchanged blows with a tall, gray-haired man. Malou recognized him, too, but couldn't quite place who he was. He wore a supercilious expression and was deflecting Jakob's attacks almost effortlessly as if it slightly bored him. In his right hand, he held a long staff, which he suddenly swung at Jakob the way a snake pounces. It struck him on the chin with a crackling, static sound, and Jakob fell to the floor.

Malou swept the legs from under a blonde girl she faintly

recognized as one of Asta's friends and continued toward the door. The tall, gray-haired man swung his staff at Thorbjørn, but he was just out of reach.

"Well, well, Hans," Thorbjørn thundered, as he shook off a young man trying to jump at him. "Have you become too sophisticated for a fist fight?"

Malou could see what Thorbjørn was trying to do: hold the man farther from the door. But he wasn't that easy to fool.

They were well prepared. Before the double doors to the library stood five first-year students, shoulder to shoulder, wide-eyed with fear. Their silver crow feathers glinted on their chests. *A human shield.* It was despicable yet effective. If they tried to force the door open, they risked taking the students out in the process. Malou had to get them away from there.

Thorbjørn was embroiled in close combat with the tall man, whose staff showered them both with sparks every time it hit its target. Malou took the chance to get closer. She grabbed Jakob and pulled him to his feet.

"Are you okay?"

Blood trickled from the corner of his mouth, but he nodded. "We need to get the students away from the door!" she insisted.

They ducked the flying sparks and small electrical flashes shooting from the man's staff and from the rune spells Thorbjørn cast wildly in return.

"Move!" Malou screamed, grabbing the nearest student, a handsome, dark-haired boy who stood stiffly by the door, facing all the chaos unfolding in the hall. A dark patch spread over the front of his pants.

"Get away!" she yelled, grabbing him to pull him aside, when she noticed a sharp pain in her side. She stopped, shocked, and looked down at herself. A short dagger stuck from her waist. Malou looked at a blond boy standing to the side. He smiled at her proudly, as if he expected to be praised for his good work. She punched him in exactly the right spot on the chin to knock him out like a light. With a scream, she pulled the knife free. *Shit.* It was bleeding like crazy.

"Thorbjørn!"

Jakob's scream caused her to turn. Thorbjørn had sunk to his knees. He held both arms up to protect himself as the gray-haired man delivered blow after blow on him mercilessly. The staff scored long, bloody gashes into his bare forearms, giving off a stench of burnt flesh.

"No!"

Malou didn't manage to react. Molly appeared from nowhere and threw herself at the man. She clung tight to his arm so that he had to let go of the staff with one hand as he tried, irritated, to shake her off.

"Thurisaz!"

Jakob's rune spell was so powerful she got a whiff of her hair sizzling as it whooshed by her. But it didn't hit its target. A windowpane behind the man shattered, and he hissed as he cast Molly to the floor and pointed his staff at her. A bolt of electricity flashed from the staff, scoring a deep gash into her throat. A thick stream of blood gushed out.

No. No, no, no . . .

MARCH 21ST
5:16 A.M.

Kirstine

The day was dawning, and the haze would soon lift. Kirstine limped across the boggy meadow, the victory stone in her hand feeling warm in the cold morning. She didn't look back, but she knew that behind her, in the first light of day, the blue bodies marched.

MARCH 21ˢᵀ
5:20 A.M.

Victoria

Lisa made her way quietly between the more seriously wounded students. They lay on the floor on rugs, scarves, jackets, and whatever else they could find.

In a corner of the hall, another group of students had settled. These were uninjured in combat but who sought refuge here when they were woken by the noise. Sara and Sofie sat close together, and Anne had her arm around a girl from first-year who was crying for her mom. Victoria passed a young man dressed in black, pressing his silver feather in his hand. He sat alone, and the other students threw suspicious glances his way. As she passed him, he lifted his head. When their eyes met, a shiver ran through him, and his whole face pulled into a weird grimace.

Victoria looked over to a fair-haired woman who sat rocking back and forth. Ingrid. The school's doctor and healer, looking in no state to help anyone, not even herself. A sudden banging on the door made Ingrid start, but she didn't look up.

"Victoria! Let us in!"

It was Benjamin. Victoria ran to the door, where Trine stepped aside for her to open up. Benjamin came in carrying Molly. Blood poured from a large wound in her throat.

"Lisa!" he screamed. "Quickly!"

Lisa ran toward them. Benjamin lay Molly down on the floor to let her come around, and Lisa placed her hands on the wound, which quickly stopped the bleeding. Still, Molly's pale face and blood-soaked clothes made Victoria fear the worst.

"What happened?"

Benjamin looked at her. He shook his head. "Victoria," he whispered.

She put her arms around him. "This isn't going to end well, is it?"

He pulled her close to him. "No matter what, I love you," he whispered. Then he let her go and went over to one of the large windows facing the castle's little courtyard. She could see from his shoulders that he was crying.

"She's lost a lot of blood," Lisa confirmed.

"Is there anything I can do?" Victoria asked. She sensed Molly was fighting for her life. Her energy flickered, like a flame at the point of going out.

"They're coming." Benjamin turned away from the window. He had a hunted look in his eyes.

"What's happening?" Victoria asked.

"Stay here!" he said. "Promise me you'll stay here!" He turned away from her and started running.

"Benjamin!" she called after him, but he was gone. The door slammed behind him. She edged over to Albert, who was still sitting rubbing the silver feather in his hand.

"Albert!"

His whole body trembled, but he didn't look up at her. Victoria leaned over him. "You need to protect the door if the Crows come. I know you can do it. Call on the good spirits."

Finally, he met her eyes.

"It's not too late to do the right thing," she said, in a low voice. "This is your chance."

He nodded. The muscles in his jaw twitched. Then, after blinking once, his brown eyes rolled away and turned to white.

Victoria straightened up and ran to the door. Lisa was so busy trying to save Molly's life that she didn't even look up as she passed.

She ran down the dark corridors. Through the windows, she could see the sky outside was beginning to get light, and Trine was by her side. She found her way to the stairs, which led her up to the hall behind the library. As soon as she reached the top step, she could hear the sounds of the struggle up there. She sped up, and when she reached the landing before the door, she stopped. A figure sat slumped on the floor, head bent down.

"Jakob?"

"You mustn't go in there!" he groaned, but she ignored him and opened the door.

What she saw made her insides turn to ice. Injured people lay all around the floor of the broad hallway. A bald woman lay with a large wound to her throat, and Victoria couldn't tell if she was already dead. In the middle of the passage, two figures faced one another. One was in the form of a wolf. The other was a tall, imposing man with silver-gray hair.

Her father.

Chamomile

Chamomile could sense they were close around her now. The chanting sound went on and on and mixed with the screams from outside. Every time someone screamed, a shiver ran through her, and she sobbed. They were so near. Just out there on the other side of the door, and yet still so far away. They would die out there in the hallway, while she was to die in here.

A violent crash made the door shake.

"Continue!" Jens ordered, his voice sounding maniacal. "Louis, remove her hood. That's enough now. The sun will soon be up."

Chamomile felt a shaking hand fumble with the hood they had pulled over her head. The fabric lifted from her face. She took deep breaths of air into her lungs and squinted her eyes in the bright light of the room. A pale face stared back at her in horror.

"Help me," Chamomile whispered, but Louis stood as if frozen. Jens grabbed his shirt and pulled him away, as if he were a scrap of trash.

Chamomile looked around the faces that were watching her.

She was looking for one she recognized.

536

"Help me!" she screamed, but the pale faces looked away to avoid her eyes.

"The knife. No, wait. I—" Jens rolled up his sleeves.

Chamomile screamed and tore at the ropes binding her hands at her back.

"Shush," he said. "Stay still." He put his hands on her throat. At first, softly. Then he pressed harder. Chamomile struggled for air, the sounds around her faded, and she felt a dark fog spreading before her eyes.

At that moment, Louis landed his fist into Jens's temple, and a white flash almost blinded her. Jens let go of her neck and looked up, confused. The punch ought to have knocked him out, but Jens seemed only surprised. Louis looked at his hand in disbelief. Then he started to scream with pain as he pulled it in to himself.

"Louis?" Jens said, in disbelief. Then he turned to the figures behind him. "Take him!"

Two other men approached Louis. Unlike Jens, they weren't protected by the victory stone's power, and Chamomile saw how Louis jumped and kicked one on the chest, then elegantly spun in the air and hit the other.

She was startled, then, to feel a warm tongue on her wrist and sharp teeth gnawing at the rope on her wrists.

"Ignore them!" Jens screamed. "We continue with the ritual!"

He turned to her and raised his hands again, up toward her throat. "Argh!" he screamed as a white animal streaked out at him, biting and scratching at his face. He flung the arctic fox to the ground. "Where did that come from?"

The fox doubled up on the floor beside Chamomile and growled. Then it suddenly arched its back like a cat. The fur split all the way down its spine, and from the fox's white pelt, a naked woman emerged. Her long black hair hung loose, and she sprang forward at the nearest figure and head-butted him. He reached up to his forehead, where blood was beginning to run, and he sank to his knees.

"Get her!" Jens screamed.

538

MARCH 21ˢᵗ
5:41 A.M.

Kirstine

The Nightshades walked slowly but without hesitation. The guards fled when they saw them approaching, and they entered the main door and went through the Great Hall and up the wide stairs without meeting any resistance. It was as if the Nightshades themselves knew where they needed to go, and she no longer led them but walked among them, as if she were one of them. Several of the blue-black bodies were twisted with deformities. Feet that faced the wrong way, knees and elbows pointing in the wrong direction. One had a broken neck, and the head hung to the shadow's side. But they pushed onward with ease. Their many bare feet made little sound on the cold floors and stairs of the castle, but a deep sound did come from them all, almost as if they were singing a song Kirstine didn't understand. It was eerie sounding, but she didn't fear them. She was not the one who should feel afraid.

It was only on reaching the stairs up to the library that they came across anyone. Two of the Crows were keeping watch at the door. She recognized Amalie, who held out a knife before her in trembling hands. A stocky, thickset man yelled at them. His mouth was a bloody wound, and as he spoke, Kirstine could see that some of his teeth had been knocked out. "Get away from here!"

"We need to pass," Kirstine said.

"Get them away!" Amalie screamed.

"I can't do that," Kirstine answered. "They won't leave until they've had their revenge."

Amalie hesitated a moment. Then the knife slid from her shaking hands and landed on the floor with a clatter. She turned and fled through the door and up the stairs. But the man stayed put.

"Get out!" He bent down to pick up the knife, but they were already on him. Kirstine looked away. She had no desire to see it. He screamed.

Say her name!

The hissing order came from one single voice. He screamed again. And again.

"Therese," he sobbed, finally. Then there was silence.

540

MARCH 21ˢᵀ
5:58 A.M.

Victoria

The struggle in the hallway raged back and forth. The wolf snapped, and the staff sparked. Along the walls, the wounded from both sides huddled together. Victoria screamed.

Her father looked up for a moment. It was just enough that he lost his balance. He stepped back but tripped on the leg of someone lying unconscious behind him. He fell. The wolf leaped on him.

"Let him go, Benjamin!" Victoria screamed, hurling herself at them. She grabbed and tugged at the fur, but the wolf gripped her father's arm and pulled at him to get him toward the stairs.

With a crash, the door to the stairwell opened, and an icy wind blew through the hallway. Victoria let go of the wolf's hide, and the wolf released her father's arm. All eyes turned to the open door.

A naked woman stepped in. Her skin was blue-black, her feet faced backward, and her hair had an indeterminate mossy-green color and hung down her back in matted tangles. Her eyes were open and black. She walked slowly forward, like tidewater that cannot be stopped. And behind her, others followed.

More blue-black women, calmly walking on, humming a strange melody. And in the midst of them all, Kirstine limped along.

"The Nightshades," Victoria whispered. "She found them!"

"And now it's too late," Benjamin said behind her. He was himself again, the wolf gone, and fleetingly, she registered that he was naked. "I tried to get him away from here. You shouldn't have to see this." He stood and lifted her up.

"What do you mean?" She wriggled in his arms. "Let me go!"

Her father stood up.

"What is this madness?" he shouted.

The Nightshades pushed slowly up and around him. "Get away from me!"

"Victoria, you mustn't watch," Benjamin pleaded, his voice cracking.

Say her name!

542

MARCH 21ST
6:05 A.M.

Malou

Malou sat, frozen, watching as the Nightshades threw themselves on Victoria's father, only stopping once his screams had long fallen away. Then the shadowy women righted themselves again and set off down the hallway. Malou held her breath as they passed, but they didn't touch her. The icy wind again threw the door open, and the dead girls continued into the library.

"Are you okay?" Kirstine asked.

Malou gradually got to her feet. She groaned with pain and noticed how the blood had started to pour again from the wound in her side. At the other end of the hall, Benjamin sat with his arms around Victoria, who sobbed into his chest, her face hidden. There was nothing they could do. Her father was dead.

The cool morning air drifted in through the broken window. The sun was not yet up. It wasn't yet too late.

"Chamomile..." Malou whispered, turning to the library door, but Kirstine placed her hand on her arm.

"Wait—"

At that moment, a man's scream suddenly rang out from inside the library. Then another, and another. The screams grew louder, and it was hard to tell how many voices they were hearing. Malou clapped her hands over her ears, but it didn't help. At last, it fell silent.

"Come on," Kirstine said, and they carefully passed through the doors and in between the tall shelves of the library. Here and there, shelves had been overturned, tipping their store of old, leather-bound books onto the floor. Malou could make out some bodies lying lifeless in the dark corners, but she felt no need to look any closer. A fire was roaring in the hearth, and sparks flickered up the chimney.

The Nightshades stood around the fireplace in a half-circle, and on the rug before the fire lay Ivalo. Her chest was rising and falling, but Malou could sense only a very weak pulse from her. Louis sat by her side; his head drooped toward the floor. He was bleeding from a great wound on his temple, which had colored his white hair red, and he was nursing one hand in at his chest. It was black and charred and looked like a burnt branch.

"They need help," Kirstine whispered, turning around. "Benjamin!" she yelled urgently. "Get Lisa. Now!"

"Louis . . ." Malou knelt beside him. "What happened? Where's Chamomile?"

"He took her with him," he gasped. "He fled . . . with her."

"Which way?"

With his good hand, he pointed toward one bookshelf. The books had been shoved aside and the shelves knocked out, revealing a little door and a stairway leading up.

"I tried to stop him. I tried . . ." His voice broke off.

"We'll find her," Malou said. "And Lisa's on her way. She'll know what to do." She took his face in her hands. "Just hold on," she whispered.

544

He lifted up his good hand and placed it over hers. "You . . . saved me. Just like I said you would. Just like my vision."

"Louis . . ."

"Yes, Malou. You got me to do the right thing," he whispered. "Can you forgive me?" His glistening gray eyes filled with tears, but he didn't take his eyes off her.

"Yes," she whispered, "I forgive you, Louis."

He smiled, the tears streaming down his cheeks and mixing with the blood running from his head. "I was wrong," he said, hoarsely. "I thought I was doing the right thing. But all of it was wrong. I promise you, when this is all over, I'll make it all right again. *We* can make things right again, Malou. Together."

She looked at him. *It worked out for some people. Why not for them?*

"We'll do it together," she whispered. "It'll all be all right again."

He lifted her hand up to his cracked lips and gave it a tender kiss, and she could see it in his eyes. He didn't need to say anything. He loved her.

Benjamin came running with Lisa behind him. She bent over Louis straight away and put her hands on his head wound. He closed his eyes, gratefully.

"Come on, Malou. We need to find Chamomile," Kirstine said. "Lisa will help Louis now."

Malou got up. She didn't want to leave him, but she knew Kirstine was right. They had to hurry if they were going to find Chamomile alive. They turned and ran to the little staircase.

"Wait . . ." Victoria came striding after them. Her large brown eyes were wide, and she was physically shaking, like she might collapse any moment. But she gave them a steely look. "Wait for me."

All three of them went through the door and continued up, with the Nightshades behind them. Their throaty song filled the narrow stairwell. Malou realized where they were headed. The old drying loft. The place where the Crows had held their parties, where she had kissed Louis for the first time. Where the maids had their rooms in the olden days. The forgotten maids. The ones nobody missed if they suddenly disappeared. They were here for their sake as well. For all the dead girls.

The drying loft was quiet. The morning light pushed in through the loose roof tile. In the middle of the room was a round cylinder, which she thought at first to be made of white material. Then she realized the white wall was flickering and fluctuating, and she knew that behind this mystical wall, Jens was there with Chamomile.

Malou started to run. "Jens!" she shouted. "Don't you touch her!"

"Watch out!" Kirstine grabbed her arm and held her back.

Hesitantly, Malou reached her hand out toward the white wall, which crackled and sparked in her direction. She got a huge shock, and a jolt of pain ran up her arm.

Kirstine muttered various runes, but every time, the wall retorted with a shower of sparks, scattering electrically around them. "We can't get through," she whispered.

Malou remembered the white light around Jens like snow that time at the Yule celebration when she had tried to get into his blood. She remembered the explosion when Zlavko tried to stab him with a knife. She pictured Louis's charred hand before her.

"He's in there!" Malou screamed to the Nightshades. They had to overpower Jens. Dagny had said so herself. But the Nightshades stood quietly around the white cylinder. *They can't get him. They can't go through the white light.*

"No!" Malou screamed. "This can't be happening!" They were so close, and they had been through so much. And now they were going to lose her anyway. Chamomile would die.

No, Malou was not going to let it happen. "There has to be something we can do. There must be a way in!" She looked from Kirstine, desperately flinging runes at the white light, to Victoria, who stood frozen, staring with those dark eyes, as if she saw something Malou couldn't see. A thought came to her. That's how it was. Victoria could see things the others couldn't. She grabbed Victoria's arm. "Find his secret!" she yelled.

Victoria looked at her, alarmed.

"You need to see into Jens's secrets!" Malou yelled, shaking her. "Tell me how we can get through the wall of light!"

And then, it seemed she understood. Victoria blinked, and her eyes turned white.

MARCH 21ST
6:12 A.M.

Victoria

Malou was right. Victoria recalled how Jens had seen her thoughts and her secrets. And how he had consequently invaded her dreams. But she had also seen *his* dreams. Dark, clammy nightmares of rustling noises and whispering voices in the dark. And she understood. Jens could see into her secrets, but she could also see into his.

Victoria directed her gaze onto the white wall Jens had conjured up. It wasn't a spirit shield; she would have recognized that. And it was not the victory stone either, protecting him now. What was his secret? What kind of magic was this?

She closed her eyes. She had no need for her vision or any of her other ordinary senses. She had to use her abilities to feel other people's feelings and read their thoughts.

Once she let it happen, it wasn't difficult. Jens had created a connection between them, which he had forgotten to close off again. Now she opened it up wide—she had nothing left to hide. But he did.

Ranks of black-clad young people marching somewhere under a blazing sun. They gathered in front of a huge stage, and on the stage, there he was. Jens. He smiled and looked over the gathered crowd as they celebrated and shouted slogans. Victoria felt their fervor; it was infectious. It felt fantastic to have a cause. No, not a cause. The truth. To know the truth. But it wasn't the truth; it was only lies, betrayal, and the pursuit of power. This was Jens's plan for the future, and Victoria shifted her attention, as this wasn't what she needed to see.

The scene changed. An old man sat in a chair. He was writhing in pain. Victoria held her hands out toward him, but they weren't her hands—they were broad and strong, with thick, short fingers and closely clipped nails. She was looking through Jens's eyes. This was his memory, and these were his hands, inflicting pain on a man without touching him. A white light left the man's body, the way the sun breaks through a cloud, just as a vile dark color spread across his chest, forming an X. It was Gebo—the gift rune, which marked the man as Jens's offering. Victoria felt how her lips were moving while a voice that was not hers muttered a formulae she had never heard before. Finally, the man collapsed, and Victoria saw how the hands closed around the white light while her lips formed the final words of the ritual that would turn a death into dark magic. Into a shield, which—together with the victory stone's powers—would protect Jens. And she felt his feeling of triumph, which she also knew wouldn't last. It wasn't enough. It was never enough. He is scared . . . Remember that. Victoria remembered what Trine had said to her one summer night long ago, and she knew it was true. Jens was always afraid.

Suddenly, the scene changed again. Now, it was Jens's fear she saw, and this time, the images ran in and out of one another. Many only appeared fleetingly, dark mud and wet bones, whispering voices in the gloom, sleeping bodies in a huge hall, blue figures in the dawn light. And then she was back. Back at the steep bank with the blooming violets.

The wind whistled in the poplar trees, and Jens walked with Trine in his arms. Victoria had seen this in a vision. Back then, she couldn't see his face, but now she could. She wasn't frightened. The sight of Jens carrying the lifeless young woman filled her instead with pure contempt. He was afraid; he was a coward. He would do anything at all to protect himself, but he could never imagine that somebody would put their own life in danger for the sake of another person. Suddenly, the vision disappeared, and Victoria stared again into the white, blinding light. In front of her, a strange symbol was taking shape, in the form of a T. It stood out more and more, and now Victoria could see it. It was not a T. It was a cross in the shape of a T, but from it, a man was hanging upside down. The Hanged Man.

Victoria opened her eyes.

"What did you see?" Malou asked.

"The third will make a sacrifice," she whispered.

The first will go into the darkness.
The second must choose between those she loves.
The third will make a sacrifice.
And the fourth will pass judgment.

MARCH 21ˢᵀ
6:16 A.M.

Malou

Of course. Malou pulled her knife from her belt and handed it to Victoria, then turned to face the wall. It wasn't difficult. Tough and painful, maybe, but not difficult. It was just a case of putting one foot in front of the other and keeping on going. Malou stepped toward the wall of light, and with that, it enveloped her. Everything around her was gone.

There was only light. Malou kept on walking forward. One step at a time. It felt like an endless march through white light. Like white snow. Like the hope of living in a white day forever.

Various memories rose up in her, coming and going, and she watched them with a tender curiosity. She was six years old. She woke up in the night and called for her mother, but the apartment was empty. She was alone. She was walking through Rosenholm; she had just started at the school and didn't want to be a blood mage, didn't want to be someone who sacrificed themselves for others. She was standing alone in the rain on Christmas Eve, looking in people's windows; she felt Chamomile laying a duvet over her and calling her her little hamster. She saw Kirstine carrying Victoria in her arms; she saw Leah standing at the cliff edge. She felt Louis's lips touch her forehead; she saw him smile and say her name. She heard Zlavko talking about love and loss. About making the ultimate sacrifice.

She saw it all, loneliness and vulnerability and pain and joy, and she saw that the thing that had meaning, the thing that was left now—it was love. And she stepped out of the light.

Jens looked up, horrified. She could see it in his eyes. He hadn't imagined anyone would do that. That anyone would make the ultimate sacrifice to save another life. Jens believed that dying was the worst thing that could happen to a person. But he was wrong. *The worst thing is to betray the ones you love.*

He let go of Chamomile. Her blue eyes looked into Malou's.

"You came," she whispered.

Malou smiled. *Of course, I came.*

MARCH 21ˢᵀ
6:16 A.M.

Kirstine

"Malou!"

It all happened so fast. The white wall swallowed her up in a blinding flash, and Kirstine felt her insides turn to ice. But a moment later, Malou became visible again. The wall of white light had turned into a thick gray mist. Malou had broken its magic, and now she stood in front of Jens. Chamomile was on her knees at his feet. She was crying and shaking all over, but she was alive.

"*Thurisaz!*" Kirstine screamed. The rune spell hit Jens in the chest and unsteadied him so he wobbled a few steps backward, but he wasn't knocked out. The white light's magic no longer protected him, but he still had the victory stone, and it would protect its owner in battle.

"For nothing!" Jens screamed. "All of this has been for nothing. How many young people have you forced to their deaths? And what for? Nothing! This cannot be stopped. I've got too many people on my side. My followers will never let you stop this now."

The Nightshades hissed angrily at the sound of his words, and they slowly pushed closer until they had formed a circle around them.

"They can't touch me—don't you know that?" Jens's eyes flashed at the blue-black figures.

"Is it the victory stone you're thinking of?" Kirstine asked. "Then I'm sorry to have to disappoint you. Frederik Juul got the prophecy wrong. A victory stone does not protect against the Nightshades, but the owner of one can waken them from their sleep. And, as you can see, I've already done that." She held her victory stone up to him, it was still glowing blue. "*Vekja*. Not *verja*."

"You're bluffing!" Jens yelled, fumbling for the leather pouch he wore on his neck. "Nobody can touch me. I'm untouchable."

"Maybe for us. But not them. *Thurisaz!*"

The rune knocked Jens back another step, and the Nightshades' hoarse song grew louder as they threw themselves toward him. Jens screamed and fought to get free of their strong fingers and thin bodies and sharp nails, but there was nothing he could do. The nightshades fell on him and pinned him to the floor.

"Chamomile!" Victoria ran to her and helped her up to stand. "Are you okay?"

"Yeah, I am now," she whispered.

Kirstine turned around. "Come on. Let's finish this," she said.

MARCH 21ˢᵗ
6:18 A.M.

Chamomile

Chamomile's legs shook beneath her. The blue bodies of the Nightshades lay over Jens so only his head and torso were free. He screamed for help. He pleaded with her; he yelled threats at them. Chamomile leaned over him. With shaking hands, she tried to open the pouch at his neck, but she couldn't.

"Here," Victoria said, passing her Malou's knife.

Chamomile sliced the leather cord to wrestle the pouch free. She held the dull black stone in the palm of her hand. The little flecks of crystal inside it sparkled, as if they recognized her.

"No, no, Chamomile," Jens whispered. "You mustn't do this." She looked at him. His skin was gray, his eyes dull. The victory stone's powers were no longer his.

"*Thank you.*"

Chamomile looked up. The figure of a white woman stood before her. "Trine," she whispered.

The woman nodded and reached out her hand with the palm turned up. Chamomile looked at the stone in her hand, and then she understood. It was the knife she wanted. *Leah's athame.* She nodded. Then she reached out and placed it in Trine's hand.

"I'm your father," Jens sobbed. "You can't!"

Chamomile turned to him. "Say her name!" she commanded.

"No! You can't do this!"

The Nightshades hissed with rage and dug their long yellow nails and teeth into his arms and legs, and Jens screamed in pain.

"SAY HER NAME!"

"Trine . . . Her name is Trine," he moaned.

Chamomile nodded to the white figure beside her, and Trine bent over him and thrust the knife into his chest, piercing his heart.

MARCH 21ST
6:25 A.M.

Kirstine

The Nightshades fell silent. Everything was silence. Then she heard a muffled groan. Kirstine turned around. Malou stood, clasping her chest. Slowly, she bowed her head to look down at herself. Then she turned her palms toward them. They were red.

"Malou!"

It was as if time stood still. She watched as Malou's legs buckled under her, her head fell back, her eyes rolled in her head, and slowly, incredibly slowly, she collapsed onto the floor.

Chamomile and Victoria ran over to her. Chamomile lifted her black top, which was soaked through with blood. But there was no wound on her chest. It was as if the blood was pushing out through her skin. Chamomile placed her hands on her, reeling off healing formulae, while Victoria desperately tried to stop the bleeding that just went on and on.

Kirstine stood. Outside, the sun had come up, and a new day was beginning. But not for everyone. Not for Malou.

The Nightshades gathered around the lifeless body, lying in a pool of blood. They lifted their arms to the sky, like trees in a forest. Kirstine realized they were screaming. Their screams got shriller until the sound was too high to be heard by the human ear. Instead, she noticed a rumbling noise. It felt like the old floorboards of the drying loft were vibrating under her. Something like roots shot out from the Nightshades' feet. Black roots, which bored in between the floorboards and slowly split them apart or tore them to shreds. She watched as the floor began to creak, ominously, and one large board split right along its length, sending splinters flying. She wasn't afraid. It was as if it had nothing to do with her.

"*We need to get her out of here,*" said a white figure beside her.

"Yes," Kirstine said, going over to the others.

Victoria yelled something to her, and Chamomile grabbed her hand. She was crying. Kirstine could see their mouths moving but heard nothing of what they were saying. Instead, she bent over and lifted Malou in her arms. Her mouth still bore the hint of a smile.

They pulled at her and shouted at her, but Kirstine stood a little longer, looking at Malou. Then she started walking. There was only one thing that meant anything now. Getting her out of here. Nothing else mattered.

Black roots slithered down the steps between their feet, threatening to pull their legs from under them or burst out through the old stone walls, and they made the smooth layer of white plaster shatter like a mirror and splinter off in great flakes. Chamomile and Victoria kept pulling at her, sobbing and screaming, but Kirstine was still unable to hear their cries. She heard only the deep rumbling and the Nightshades' roots breaking through the castle walls. Stones and debris fell in a shower from the ceiling, exploding on the floor, while confused and frightened students crowded toward the exit.

The black roots multiplied and moved faster and faster. They grabbed at the castle's stones and crushed them, smashing ceilings down and splitting floors and stairs. A deep rumbling sound was followed by a huge crash as the stairwell collapsed on itself higher up. Kirstine felt shards of glass biting into her cheek when a window-pane shattered to her right, but she carried on walking with the lifeless girl in her embrace.

At the end of the stairs, they could see the doors to the great hall standing wide open, and Lisa and Benjamin came running out, carrying an unconscious student between them. A figure stumbled after them. Kirstine stopped.

"No."

Louis's lips formed the word over and again. He limped slowly toward her. Behind him, the black roots broke through, causing the whole of the great hall's ceiling to fall in with an ear-splitting crash. A cloud of dust and debris pushed out through the open doors, and everything around them disappeared. Kirstine lost her bearings and no longer knew where the others were.

"No . . ."

Louis was crying. He reached out toward her, and Kirstine passed the body of the young woman into his arms. Sobbing, he took Malou's lifeless body and pulled her into him, sinking to the floor at Kirstine's feet.

It went silent. It was only the two of them, her and Louis. And Malou, who had closed her beautiful blue eyes for the last time. Kirstine stood like a statue, covered in white dust. It didn't seem important to find the way out anymore. Instead, she looked down. The floor was alive with black roots, boring down between the old, worn flagstones of the hall. The earth shook beneath her. Huge cracks opened around her feet, and with a sound like a thunderclap, a blue-black female figure burst from above and vanished down through a crack in the floor.

560

She closed her eyes. *This is where it all ends.*

Then she felt a hand in hers.

"The castle is collapsing!" Jakob screamed. His voice got through to her. She saw him.

"Kirstine! Come on!"

"Malou," she said. "We need to bring her with us."

He looked down. "Oh no," He shook his head, as if he couldn't believe his eyes.

Yet another nightshade disappeared with a crash down through the floor nearby to them. Jakob squeezed her hand. "You take Malou, and I'll help Louis!"

He lifted Malou into her arms and then carried Louis, who pressed his face into his chest, sobbing.

"Kirstine! Come on!"

Jakob chided her, and she felt her feet move of their own accord. He led her to the door onto the courtyard, and they were welcomed by the now rising sun as they stepped outdoors. Kirstine held Malou close. Their footsteps rang hollowly on the little wooden bridge over the moat, and it was only once they were a stretch into the park that they stopped.

Students stood in small groups all over the park. Some were crying; others seemed frozen in shock and had their eyes fixed on the castle. Kirstine knelt down and lay Malou on the grass, Louis collapsing on the other side of her ruined body.

"*No, no, no.*"

Malou's expression was peaceful. Kirstine brushed a lock of her hair back from her cheek. There was a layer of dust over her fine features and curved eyelashes, and she looked like a child who had fallen asleep after a hard day's play.

"Malou!"

Chamomile and Victoria came running. Chamomile threw herself on Malou and held her in her arms. She screamed. She kept on screaming, and the sound mingled with Louis's heart-wrenching sobs as Rosenholm collapsed behind them in an inferno of dust and rubble.

APRIL 30TH
7:00 P.M.

Kirstine

The forest's edge looked bright and green. The evening was light, and the air was cool. A blackbird was singing someplace high in the tall poplars while the sun sank farther toward the horizon. Besides the birdsong, there was nothing but the sound of the gurgling stream. Kirstine looked at Victoria and Chamomile, who were walking with her in the dusk. It was Walpurgis Night. The night that marked the beginning of summer. The night they would say goodbye to two young women who hadn't deserved to die but who now would be laid to rest together.

They reached the steep bank where the violets grew; the ruins of the once proud castle now somewhere behind them.

"Is it here?" Kirstine whispered, and Victoria nodded.

They kneeled down in the grass. Kirstine cut the turf with a knife and laid it aside. Then, they began to dig. They dug with their hands; it felt only the right thing to do. The soil was loose, but it still took a long time. The sun set as they kneeled there by the hole, scraping the earth aside.

It was already dark when they found the first bones, glinting white in the black earth. Kirstine lifted them from the hole and laid them carefully on the damp grass. Then, they continued in silence. At last, Victoria gently lifted the skull from the earth before laying it along with the rest of Trine's skeleton.

They stood up, and together, they carried the bones into the forest. Mournful sounds came from between the trees, and the singing grew ever stronger. It was the students who sang. They lined the path, holding candles aloft, and they stepped in to follow behind them when they passed. Night had fallen, and the moon was high in the sky, lighting their way. The others were waiting beside the tree. Lisa stood alone, but her dark eyes smiled as they came out into the clearing. Thorbjørn had an arm around Beate, supporting her as she silently wept. Her hair was pulled into a braid that shone white in the moonlight, but her eyes were alert and full of life, as they had been before. Ivalo had offered Molly an arm to hold onto. Benjamin stood together with Jakob. When he saw her, he looked up at her with tears in his eyes. And in the darkness behind them stood Louis.

Victoria lay the skull by the foot of the tree, and Chamomile and Kirstine carefully placed the rest of the bones beside it. Benjamin stepped forward and passed Chamomile a charred clay pot. It was Malou's urn.

Around them, the singing grew louder, a wordless melody full of sorrow. Lisa's voice rose above all of them, and Kirstine sang too. She let go and let all the pain pour out, and her tears flowed. Then there was silence.

Sobs shook Chamomile's body as she painstakingly lowered the pot down into the hole dug out between two of the tree's great roots. Then she straightened up again.

"Goodbye, Malou," she said quietly, her voice trembling with emotion, but she fought bravely to get the words out. "For me, you were like a star in the summer night. Beautiful, but difficult to reach. You suffered so much, but you were so brave. Your life was far too short, and it was far too hard, my dear friend. Never again will you feel pain or fear. Never again. Rest in peace, Malou."

Chamomile leaned over and took a handful of earth from the forest floor. Slowly, she let it sprinkle through her fingers and down into the hole, then she stepped back and let Victoria do the same, then Kirstine. She whispered her goodbye as she let the earth fall into the little hole at the foot of the tree, and when she stepped back, another figure came forward. *Louis.*

He had a bold red scar on the side of his face, and where his right hand used to be, he now had only a stump hidden behind thick bandages. His face was contorted with pain as he gathered a handful of earth and cast it into the hole. Kirstine, standing as close as she was, could make out what he whispered: "I love you, Malou. You saved me. You saved all of us."

Tears streamed down his face as he stepped back. After him came Benjamin, and so it continued with those gathered until the hole in the forest floor was no more. Kirstine imagined how the tree roots would now embrace the little pot and protect it against all that was evil in the world. She looked upward to the treetop. The straight beech trees surrounding the ancient oak were lush with new green leaves, but the oak tree itself was bare. *It's dying.*

Chamomile stepped forward again. "Malou Nielsen," she said. "May you rest in the hall of dead girls. Forever." The tears fell down her cheeks, and her voice quivered. She nodded to Victoria and gave in to her grief, letting herself fall sobbing into Molly's arms. Victoria stepped up to the tree while Kirstine knelt down by the pile of Trine's bones. She looked up to the treetop.

"Rose Katrine Severinsen," Victoria said. "Trine . . . May you rest in peace in the hall of dead girls. Forever."

Kirstine bowed her head. "Take her," she whispered. "And take my powers with her."

There was a rustling all around them. Slowly, the tree roots began to move. Not quickly and not snaking as they had seen before, but hesitantly and laboriously, as if it were a struggle for the tree to push its roots through the forest floor. Kirstine waited. The roots felt carefully for the bones. Slowly, they clasped them, and the earth opened up for them. And they searched farther and found her. Kirstine closed her eyes and felt the roots snaking around her ankles and wrists but without burning her skin. They searched further up, on her stomach and chest, and they lay themselves across her face. It felt as if they were also inside her as if they were encircling her heart and lungs and brain and arteries. And when they pulled back again, she knew something had changed.

Are you sure? Jakob had asked her. *Now you have your own victory stone. You can control the powers.*

I'm sure, she had replied. *I'm just longing to be my normal self.*

Kirstine heard a startled outburst from the students, and she opened her eyes. The bones were gone, and the roots were, too. But where they had been lying, now stood two white figures in the night: Two young women holding hands. Trine and Malou.

The white Malou turned toward her, and Kirstine remembered the first time she had seen her. That time, all she had seen was Malou's tough exterior. All her brash steeliness, which had sometimes scared her and kept her from getting any closer. But now, she could see it all. The courage, love, and strength of will. But also the pain, vulnerability, and fear, which Kristine recognized all too well from herself. In actual fact, they'd had a lot in common. They were both afraid of being rejected and judged. Afraid that nobody would put up with them, with all their flaws and failings. They had both believed that becoming something really mattered. Becoming something other than who they were.

At that moment, she heard Malou's voice in her head. *You know it already, Kirstine. Now, you just have to live it.*

Kirstine nodded. *I promise.*

Malou smiled at her one last time before looking farther on. At Victoria. At Chamomile. At Louis. His inconsolable sobbing again brought tears to Kirstine's eyes.

Finally, Malou turned to the tree. She was alone. Trine had vanished, and Malou was also fainter now, just a whispy white shadow. And slowly, she dissolved before their eyes and was gone. It was over.

Kirstine got up. She felt suddenly weak but then sensed Jakob's arms around her and leaned into him, burying her face in his neck. No painful jolts ran through her. Only the feeling of his body against hers.

"Look!" Benjamin whispered, pointing to the tree.

A name had appeared on the bark, and now the letters glowed from the old tree's trunk. *Astrid.* The name shone for a moment, then it faded and was replaced by another. *Ingeborg.*

The names kept on changing. *Gudrun. Kathrine.* Jakob hugged Kirstine close. They were both crying. Chamomile held Molly's hand. Benjamin and Victoria stood facing the tree.

Trine

Dagny

Malou

The last name remained for the longest time, but it, too, finally disappeared. There was a deep sigh, which sounded like it came from the earth under them. Kirstine knew it was the tree taking its last breath. Its time was at an end. It would accept no further offerings, and it would never gift its powers to another person ever again. It would be left standing here in the forest, and slowly, its branches would rot and break off. One day, a storm would destroy its previously proud trunk, and the rest would be left to the mushrooms and the beetles. And, like the dead girls, it would become part of the earth itself, and a new era would begin. *Their era.*

They stood awhile in silence. Gradually, the students began to leave the clearing. Benjamin and Victoria went, hand in hand. After came Molly, her arm around Chamomile, and after them Thorbjørn and Beate and Lisa, who gave a nod as she passed, and finally Ivalo too disappeared into the trees.

Louis stepped out from the shadows and knelt in front of the tree, where he stayed, face toward the ground, his fingers buried in the earth, quietly weeping.

"Should we . . . ?" Jakob whispered.

"No, leave him be," Kirstine said. "Let him say goodbye in peace."

They turned and started walking out to the forest's edge. Jakob still had his arm around her. He breathed in the smell of her hair. "What happens now?" he whispered.

"Now?" Kirstine said. "Now, I want to go home."

"To Thy?"

"Yes. I promised someone something."

"So did I," he said. "But I don't think I can do it without you."

"Do you want to come?" Kirstine asked, turning to face him and look him in the eyes. "Will you come with me?"

He smiled through his tears. "There's nothing I'd like better."

EPILOGUE

7 years later

Chamomile

Chamomile stretched her legs out in front of her on the rug and wriggled her toes. "Do you think they'll ever be normal again?" she asked.

"Hmm," Molly said, lowering her hands, which held the wreath she was in the middle of making using bright yellow dandelions. She tilted her head to one side and squinted her eyes a little as she examined Chamomile's swollen feet. "No, I'm sorry, but you're never going to squeeze those sausage toes into a pair of shoes again. Maybe you could borrow your mom's Crocs?"

"Ha-ha," Chamomile said. "Aren't you supposed to say I look beautiful anyway, or something like that?"

"What do you mean? I love sausage toes." Molly winked at her and placed the dandelion wreath on her head. "You do look beautiful."

Chamomile smiled and turned to look across the grass. Four figures were approaching through the park. "There they are," she said.

"Come on, I'll give you a hand." Molly stood and held out both hands to pull Chamomile to her feet. Her belly was so heavy now; there was no hiding what she was carrying inside.

"Hey, mind my ribs, you," Chamomile moaned, placing her hand on her bump and the little feet stretching her belly outward.

"Is the shrimp kicking?"

"Trying to bust out, more like," Chamomile said, taking Molly's hand in hers.

"Are you nervous?" she asked.

Chamomile shrugged without taking her eyes from the little family approaching. The tall woman waved when she saw them.

"A little, maybe," Chamomile admitted, waving back. "It's been so long now since we've seen each other."

"The boys have gotten so big," Molly said.

Chamomile nodded, looking at the two strawberry-blond boys running back and forth around their parents. How old were they now? Three and five, maybe? Kirstine and Jakob walked hand in hand; her long hair was loose. She looked just like herself, but at the same time, something was different. Something Chamomile couldn't quite place. Perhaps it was just the time that had gone by. Kirstine had become a grown woman, just as she had herself.

"Look, Eskild!" the oldest boy yelled, and they ran ahead. But before reaching Chamomile and Molly, something else caught their attention, and they changed direction. They raced full pelt across the grass and disappeared behind the huge rhododendrons, which bloomed with white-and-pink flowers.

"Boys!" Jakob called. "Not too far!" He had a beard and a receding hairline, but he was still as thin and lanky as ever.

"Hi!" Chamomile said when they finally reached them. She felt her eyes well with tears when Kirstine hugged her. "It's the hormones," she said, shaking her head at Jakob's concerned look.

"It's good to see you both," he said. He had gotten laughter lines. It suited him.

"Congratulations," Kirstine said. "It's so great for you both." She squeezed Molly's hand. "When are you due, Chamomile?"

"In two weeks," she said. "But I'm hoping it comes sooner. Or else, I'm afraid I might explode."

"Maybe that's how it feels, but you look fantastic," Kirstine said.

"You're lying, but thanks," Chamomile replied.

"It's so strange to be here again," Kirstine said.

"Strangely good? Or strangely bad?" Chamomile asked.

"Strangely good, I think."

"I'm really happy to see it all, anyway," Jakob said. "But first, I better check that the boys aren't setting fire to something." He gave a nervous smile and went over to the bushes their sons had run to. Chamomile wasn't quite sure if he was joking or not, but Kirstine seemed incredibly calm despite her children having vanished.

"Here comes Victoria now," Molly said, nodding toward the avenue of old chestnuts.

They all watched as she came, smiling, toward them. Her dark hair was longer than she usually wore it, reaching almost to her shoulders. Her arms were tanned against her simple white full-length cotton dress. She was more beautiful than ever.

"She's on her own?" Molly said. "Is she not with Benjamin anymore?"

"It's probably a bit complicated," Kirstine said.

"I think there will always be *them*," Chamomile said, "but just not in the traditional sense."

"You mean not like us?" whispered Molly, squeezing her hand.

Chamomile smiled. "No, not like us."

"That reminds me, I should have fitted the car seat," Molly muttered.

"Chamomile!" Victoria jogged the last stretch and opened her arms wide to embrace them all. Chamomile gave up holding the tears back.

"I've missed you all so much," Victoria said. "Chamomile, you look amazing. And, Kirstine! Where are the boys?"

"They ran off," Kirstine said, "but they tend to pop up again. You'll hear them before you see them!"

"What shall we do first?" Chamomile asked once she'd dried her eyes. "Go up to see the school? Lisa's looking forward to seeing you all, and Mom, of course, can't wait. She would have been down here with a welcome party if I hadn't put a stop to it."

"Then we should hurry," Victoria said, linking her arm under Chamomile's.

"And whatever you do, remember to make a fuss of Thorbjørn's new grand hall," Chamomile said. "He built it himself, with the help of his Viking friends. If you think Thorbjørn is awkward . . ."

The sun was sitting low in the sky by the time they finished eating all the food Beate had prepared. Chamomile breathed the evening air deep into her lungs and happily looked over the school buildings spread across the large park grounds. The golden light made them seem like they almost glowed. The first houses had been built with rough larch wood, with huge windows facing onto the park. The new grand hall was made of oak and looked like an ancient king's hall from the Viking age. Behind the houses lay the ruins of the old castle. Most of it was gone, but a team of students had taken on the task of converting parts of the ruin into teaching spaces. A wooden framework was rising from the old foundations.

"It's lovely," Victoria said. "You've made it really beautiful."

Chamomile smiled. She knew what Victoria meant. Rosenholm Castle had also been beautiful, with its white towers and red roof tiles, but in a different way. More grandiose and imposing. The new school buildings were accessible to everyone. They were honest and open.

They stood a little longer without talking while they waited for the last person they were missing. Finally, from the hall came a tall man with white hair and a nasty scar on one side of his face. His right arm went only to his elbow.

Louis nodded to them amicably. "I'm sorry, I had an anxious student with a question about an assignment."

"It's no problem," Chamomile said.

Lisa had been the principal of Rosenholm for the last seven years, and one of the first things she had done was appoint Louis to Zlavko's old position. Since then, he had worked tirelessly at rebuilding the school.

"Shall we do it?" Kirstine asked, taking Jakob by the hand. They had left the boys with Chamomile's mother, who seemed excited at the chance to practice in her role as soon-to-be grandma.

"Yes, let's do it," Chamomile said. "It's down by the great blood beech. I like to think that Malou, as the talented blood mage she was, would be quite tickled by that."

They went down through the park. The dew had not yet settled, and the grass felt pleasantly cool under Chamomile's bare feet. The great blood beech sat regally on the wide expanse of lawn, and its leaves, glowing red in the evening sun, formed a dome above them as they gathered around the stone erected at the base of the trunk. Chamomile read the inscription, which Louis had carved into the stone himself.

IN MEMORY OF MALOU NIELSEN

Beneath that, in smaller letters:

ERECTED BY MALOU NIELSEN'S MEMORIAL FOUNDATION
FOR DISADVANTAGED YOUNG PEOPLE

Chamomile lifted the flower wreath carefully from her hair. The dandelions had closed their yellow heads, but she laid it on the stone anyway. The tears ran down her cheeks and fell to the ground and onto the wilted flowers.

"It's a beautiful stone," Kirstine said, her arms around Jakob. "You did a great job."

Victoria stepped forward and put a hand on Chamomile's shoulder. She rested her other hand on the stone as if she were touching an old friend. "Malou would have liked it," she said, and Chamomile could hear from her voice that she was also crying.

"Thorbjørn told me the memorial foundation helps a lot of students," Jakob said. "Not only with money, but with advice, guidance, therapy, and that kind of thing."

"That's right," Louis replied, "Even though I don't quite understand how. We didn't exactly collect all that much money."

"Ah, I think I can explain that one," Victoria said. "If you promise not to tell anyone. Benjamin's father died a few years ago, but Benjamin didn't want the inheritance. So, he gave it to the foundation instead."

"What a lovely gesture," Molly said.

They stood a while in silence before going their separate ways. Louis went back to the school. Kirstine and Jakob were heading to Jutland, and Victoria to Copenhagen. Chamomile and Molly stayed longer under the beech after saying goodbye to all the others. The sun had sunk behind the tall trees, and dew was settling on the ground. Chamomile gave a little stretch and leaned into Molly.

"Do you think it'll be just as long before we see them again?"

"Maybe," Molly said, putting her arm around Chamomile's back and her hand on her belly. "But with some people, you don't need to see each other often to know you're there for each other. You'll always have a special connection."

Chamomile nodded. The wind caught the branches of the tree, and around them, the birdsong gradually faded away as the darkness settled in. Molly was right. They would always have each other.

Chamomile, Victoria, Kirstine. And Malou. Forever.